ISAAC ASIMOV'S
ROBOT CITY™

ISAAC ASIMOV'S
ROBOT CITY

BOOK 2: SUSPICION
MIKE MCQUAY

A Byron Preiss Visual Publications, Inc. Book

ACE BOOKS, NEW YORK

This book is an Ace original edition, and has never been
previously published.

ISAAC ASIMOV'S ROBOT CITY
BOOK 2: SUSPICION

An Ace Book/published by arrangement with
Byron Preiss Visual Publications, Inc.

PRINTING HISTORY
Ace edition/September 1987

ISBN: 0-441-73126-0

Ace Books are published by The Berkley Publishing Group,
200 Madison Avenue, New York, New York 10016.
The name "Ace" and the "A" logo are trademarks belonging to
Charter Communications, Inc.
PRINTED IN THE UNITED STATES OF AMERICA

10 9 8 7 6 5 4 3 2 1

For Brian Shelton and the "bruised banana"

CONTENTS

THE LAWS OF HUMANICS
ISAAC ASIMOV

I am pleased by the way in which the Robot City books pick up the various themes and references in my robot stories and carry on with them.

For instance, my first three robot novels were, essentially, murder mysteries, with Elijah Baley as the detective. Of these first three, the second novel, *The Naked Sun,* was a locked-room mystery, in the sense that the murdered person was found with no weapon on the site and yet no weapon could have been removed either.

I managed to produce a satisfactory solution but I did not do that sort of thing again, and I am delighted that Mike McQuay has tried his hand at it here.

The fourth robot novel, *Robots and Empire,* was not primarily a murder mystery. Elijah Baley had died a natural death at a good, old age, the book veered toward the Foundation universe so that it was clear that both my notable series, the Robot series and the Foundation series, were going to be fused into a broader whole. (No, I didn't do this for some arbitrary reason. The necessities arising out of writing sequels in the 1980s to tales originally written in the 1940s and 1950s forced my hand.)

In *Robots and Empire,* my robot character, Giskard, of whom I was very fond, began to concern himself with "the Laws of Humanics," which, I indicated, might eventually serve as the basis for the science of psychohistory, which plays such a large role in the Foundation series.

Strictly speaking, the Laws of Humanics should be a description, in concise form, of how human beings actually behave. No such description exists, of course. Even psychologists, who study the matter scientifically (at least, I hope they do) cannot present any "laws" but can only make lengthy and diffuse descriptions of what people seem to do. And none of them are prescriptive. When a psychologist says that people respond in this way to a stimulus of that sort, he merely means that some do at some times. Others may do it at other times, or may not do it at all.

If we have to wait for actual laws prescribing human behavior in order to establish psychohistory (and surely we must) then I suppose we will have to wait a long time.

Well, then, what are we going to do about the Laws of Humanics? I suppose what we can do is to start in a very small way, and then later slowly build it up, if we can.

Thus, in *Robots and Empire*, it is a robot, Giskard, who raises the question of the Laws of Humanics. Being a robot, he must view everything from the standpoint of the Three Laws of Robotics—these robotic laws being truly prescriptive, since robots are forced to obey them and cannot disobey them.

The Three Laws of Robotics are:

1—A robot may not injure a human being, or, through inaction, allow a human being to come to harm.

2—A robot must obey the orders given it by human beings except where such orders would conflict with the First Law.

3—A robot must protect its own existence as long as such protection does not conflict with the First or Second Law.

Well, then, it seems to me that a robot could not help but think that human beings ought to behave in such a way as to make it easier for robots to obey those laws.

In fact, it seems to me that ethical human beings should be as anxious to make life easier for robots as the robots themselves would. I took up this matter in my story "The Bicentennial Man," which was published in 1976. In it, I had a human character say in part:

"If a man has the right to give a robot any order that does not involve harm to a human being, he should have the decency never to give a robot any order that involves harm to a robot, unless human safety absolutely requires it. With great power goes great responsibility, and if the robots have Three Laws to protect men, is it too much to ask that men have a law or two to protect robots?"

For instance, the First Law is in two parts. The first part, "A robot may not injure a human being," is absolute and nothing need be done about that. The second part, "or, through inaction, allow a human being to come to harm," leaves things open a bit. A human being might be about to come to harm because of some event involving an inanimate object. A heavy weight might be likely to fall upon him, or he may slip and be about to fall into a lake, or any one of uncountable other misadventures of the sort may be involved. Here the robot simply must try to rescue the human being; pull him from under, steady him on his feet and so on. Or a human being might be threatened by some form of life other than human—a lion, for instance—and the robot must come to his defense.

But what if harm to a human being is threatened by the action of another human being? There a robot must decide what to do. Can he save one human being without harming the other? Or if there must be harm, what course of action must he pursue to make it minimal?

It would be a lot easier for the robot, if human beings were as concerned about the welfare of human beings, as robots are expected to be. And, indeed, any reasonable human code of ethics would instruct human beings to care for each other and to do no harm to each other. Which is, after all, the mandate that humans gave robots. Therefore the First Law of Humanics from the robots' standpoint is:

1—A human being may not injure another human being, or, through inaction, allow a human being to come to harm.

If this law is carried through, the robot will be left guarding the human being from misadventures with inanimate objects and with non-human life, something which poses no ethical dilemmas for it. Of course, the robot must still guard against harm done a human being *unwittingly* by another human being. It must also stand ready to come to the aid of a threatened human being, if another human being on the scene simply cannot get to the scene of action quickly enough. But then, even a robot may *unwittingly* harm a human being, and even a robot may not be fast enough to get to the scene of action in time or skilled enough to take the necessary action. Nothing is perfect.

That brings us to the Second Law of Robotics, which compels a robot to obey all orders given it by human beings except where such orders would conflict with the First Law. This means that human beings can give robots any order without limitation as long as it does not involve harm to a human being.

But then a human being might order a robot to do something impossible, or give it an order that might involve a robot in a dilemma that would do damage to its brain. Thus, in my short story "Liar!," published in 1940, I had a human being deliberately put a robot into a dilemma where its brain burnt out and ceased to function.

We might even imagine that as a robot becomes more intelligent and self-aware, its brain might become sensitive enough to undergo harm if it were forced to do something needlessly embarrassing or undignified. Consequently, the Second Law of Humanics would be:

2—*A human being must give orders to a robot that preserve robotic existence, unless such orders cause harm or discomfort to human beings*.

The Third Law of Robotics is designed to protect the robot, but from the robotic view it can be seen that it does not go far enough. The robot must sacrifice its existence if the First or Second Law makes that necessary. Where the First Law is concerned, there can be no argument. A robot must give up its existence if that is the only way it can avoid doing harm to a human being or can prevent harm from coming to a human being. If we admit the innate superiority of any human being to any robot (which is something I am a little reluctant to admit, actually), then this is inevitable.

On the other hand, must a robot give up its existence merely in obedience to an order that might be trivial, or even malicious? In "The Bicentennial Man," I have some hoodlums deliberately order a robot to take itself apart for the fun of watching that happen. The Third Law of Humanics must therefore be:

3—A human being must not harm a robot, or, through inaction, allow a robot to come to harm, unless such harm is needed to keep a human being from harm or to allow a vital order to be carried out.

Of course, we cannot enforce these laws as we can the Robotic Laws. We cannot design human brains as we design robot brains. It is, however, a beginning, and I honestly think that if we are to have power over intelligent robots, we must feel a corresponding responsibility for them, as the human character in my story "The Bicentennial Man" said.

Certainly in Robot City, these are the sorts of rules that robots might suggest for the only human beings on the planet, as you may soon learn.

It was sunset in the city of robots, and it was snowing paper.

The sun was a yellow one and the atmosphere, mostly nitrogen/oxygen blue, was flush with the veins of iron oxides that traced through it, making the whole twilight sky glow bright orange like a forest fire.

The one who called himself Derec marveled at the sunset from the back of the huge earthmover as it slowly made its way through the city streets, crowds of robots lining the avenue to watch him and his companions make this tour of the city. The tiny shards of paper floated down from the upper stories of the crystal-like buildings, thrown (for reasons that escaped Derec) by the robots that crowded the windows to watch him.

Derec took it all in, sure that it must have significance or the robots wouldn't do it. And that was the only thing he was sure of—for Derec was a person without memory, without notion of who he was. Worse still, he had come to this impossible world, unpopulated by humans, by means that still astounded him; and he had no idea, *no idea,* of where in the universe he was.

He was young, the cape of manhood still new on his shoulders, and he only knew that by observing himself in a mirror. Even his name—Derec—wasn't really his. It was a borrowed name, a convenient thing to call himself because not having a name was like not existing. And he desperately wanted to exist, to know who, to know *what* he was.

And why.

Beside him sat a young woman called Katherine Burgess, who had said she'd known him, briefly, when he'd had a name. But he wasn't sure of her, of her truth or her motivations. She had told him his real name was David and that he'd crewed on a Settler ship, but neither the name nor the classification seemed to fit as well as the identity he'd already been building for himself; so he continued to call himself by his chosen name, Derec, until he had solid proof of his other existence.

Flanking the humans on either side were two robots of advanced sophistication (Derec knew that, but didn't know how he knew it). One was named Euler, the other Rydberg, and they couldn't, or wouldn't, tell him any more than he already knew—nothing. The robots wanted information from him, however. They wanted to know why he was a murderer.

The First Law of Robotics made it impossible for robots to harm human beings, so when the only other human inhabitant of Robot City turned up dead, Derec and Katherine were the only suspects. Derec's brief past had not included killing, but convincing Euler and Rydberg of that was not an easy task. They were being held, but treated with respect—innocent, perhaps, until proven guilty.

Both robots had shiny silver heads molded roughly to human equivalent. Both had glowing photocells where eyes would be. But where Euler had a round mesh screen in place of a human mouth, Rydberg had a small loudspeaker mounted atop his dome.

"Do you enjoy this, Friend Derec?" Euler asked him, indicating the falling paper and the seemingly endless stream of robots that lined the route of their drive.

Derec had no idea of what he was supposed to enjoy about this demonstration, but he didn't want to offend his hosts, who were being very polite despite their accusations. "It's really . . . very nice," he replied, brushing a piece of paper off his lips.

"Nice?" Katherine said from beside him, angry. "Nice?"

She ran fingers through her long black hair. "I'll be a week getting all this junk out of my hair."

"Surely it won't take you that length of time," Rydberg said, the speaker on his head crackling. "Perhaps there's something I don't understand, but it seems from a cursory examination that it shouldn't take you any longer than . . ."

"All right," Katherine said. "All right."

". . . one or two hours. Unless of course you're speaking microscopically, in which case . . ."

"Please," she said. "No more. I was mistaken about the time."

"Our studies of human culture," Euler told Derec, "indicate that the parade is indigenous to all human civilizations. We very much want to make you feel at home here, our differences notwithstanding."

Derec looked out on both sides of the huge, open-air, V-shaped mover. The robots lining the streets stood quite still, their variegated bodies giving no hint of curiosity, though Derec felt it quite possible that he and Katherine were the first humans many of them had ever seen. Knowing nothing, Derec knew nothing of parades, but it seemed to be a friendly enough ritual, except for the paper, and it made him feel good that they should want him to feel at home.

"Is it not customary to wave?" Euler asked.

"What?" Derec replied.

"To wave your arm to the crowd," Euler explained. "Is it no customary?"

"Of course," Derec said, and waved on both sides of the machine that clanked steadily down the wide street, the robots returning the gesture with more nonreadable silence.

"Don't you feel like a proper fool?" Katherine asked, scrunching up her nose at his antics.

"They're just trying to be hospitable," Derec replied. "With the trouble we're in here, I don't think it hurts to return a friendly gesture."

"Is there some problem, Friend Katherine?" Euler asked.

"Only with her mouth," Derec replied.

Rydberg leaned forward to stare intently at Katherine's face. "Is there something we can do?"

"Yeah," the girl answered. "Get me something to eat. I'm starving."

Rydberg swiveled his head toward Euler. "Another untruth," he said. "This is very discouraging."

"What do you mean?" Derec asked.

"Our hypotheses concerning the philosophical nature of humanics," Rydberg said, "must have their foundation in truth among species. Twice Katherine has said things that aren't true . . ."

"I *am* starving!" Katherine complained.

". . . and how can any postulate be universally self-evident if the postulators do not adhere to the same truths? Perhaps this is the mark of a murderer."

"Now wait a minute," Derec said. "All humans make . . . creative use of the language. It's no proof of anything."

Rydberg examined Katherine's face closely. Then he pressed a pincer to her bare arm, the place turning white for a second before resuming its natural color. "You say you are starving, but your color is good, your pulse rate strong and even, and you have no signs of physical deterioration. I must conclude, reluctantly, that you are not starving."

"We are hungry, though," Derec said. "Please take us where we might eat."

Katherine fixed him with a sidelong glance. "And do it quickly."

"Of course," Euler said. "You will find that we are fully equipped to deal with any human emergency here. This is to be the perfect human world."

"But there are no humans here," Derec said.

"No."

"Are you expecting any?"

"We have no expectations."

"Oh."

Euler directed the spider-like robot guiding the mover, and the machine turned dutifully at the next corner, taking them down a double-width street that was bisected by a large aqueduct, whose waters had turned dark under the ever-deepening twilight.

Derec sat back and stole a glance at Katherine, but she was busily pulling bits of paper from her hair and didn't notice him. He had a million questions, but they seemed better left for later. As it was, he had conflicting emotions to analyze and react to within himself.

He was a nonperson whose life had begun scant weeks before, when he'd awakened without past or memory to find himself in a life-support pod, stranded upon an asteriod that was being mined by robots. They had been searching for something, something he had accidentally stumbled upon— the Key to Perihelion, at least one of the seven Keys to Perihelion. It had seemed of incredible import to the robots on the asteroid. Unfortunately, he had had no idea of what the Keys to Perihelion were or what to do with them.

After that was the bad time. The asteroid was destroyed by Aranimas, an alien space raider, who captured Derec and tortured him for information about the Key, information that Derec could not supply. There he had met Katherine, just before the destruction of Aranimas's vessel and their dubious salvation at the hands of the Spacers' robots.

The Spacers also wanted the Key, though their means of attaining it seemed slightly more civilized and bureaucratic than Aranimas's. Katherine and Derec were polite prisoners of bureaucracy for a time on Rockliffe Station, their personalities clashing until they were forced to form an alliance with Wolruf, another alien from Aranimas's ship, to escape their gentle captivity with the Key.

They found that if they pressed the corners of the silver slab and thought themselves away from the Spacer station, they were whisked bodily to a dark gray void that they assumed to be Perihelion. Pressing the corners again, another thought brought them to Robot City. And then their thinking took them no farther, stranding them in a world populated by nothing but robots.

And that was it, the sum total of Derec's conscious life. He had reached several conclusions, though, scant as his reserve of information was: First, he had an innate knowledge of robots and their workings, though he had no idea from where his knowledge emanated; next, Katherine knew more about him than she was willing to tell; finally, he couldn't escape the feeling that he was here for a purpose, that this was all some elaborate test designed especially for him.

But why? Why?

It was worlds that were being turned here, physical and spatial laws that were being forced upside down—all for him? Nothing made sense.

And then there was the Key, the object that everyone wanted, the object that was safely hidden by the person who couldn't control it. The robots here didn't know he had it. Were they looking for it, too? He'd have to find out. The Key seemed to be the one strain that held everything else together.

Keeping that in mind, he determined to move slowly, to try always to get more in the way of information than he gave. He'd been at a disadvantage for the entire length of his memory. From this point, he wanted to keep the upper hand as far as possible.

But there was, of course, the murder.

Derec stood on the balcony of the apartment given to him and Katherine by the robots, looking out over the night city. A stiff, cold wind had come up, the starfield totally obscured by dark, angry clouds that seemed to boil up out of nowhere. Lightning flashed in the distance, electrons seeking partner protons on the surface. It was a beautiful sight, and frightening. Derec watched the distant buildings light to near daytime before plunging once more into darkness.

"There," he said, pointing to a distant tower. "It wasn't there a centad ago."

Katherine walked up beside him, leaning against the balcony rail. "Where was it?" she asked, mocking.

"It wasn't anywhere," he replied, turning to take her by the shoulders. "It didn't exist."

"That's impossible," she replied, then turned and walked back into the large, airy apartment that sat at the top of another tower like the one Derec said had sprung from nowhere. "I wish they'd get here with our food."

"They're probably fixing us something extra special," Derec said, joining her in the living room. "And impossible seems to be the way of our lives right now, doesn't it? I'm telling you, Katherine, that along with everything else that doesn't make sense, this ... city is growing, changing right before our eyes."

"How can that be?" she asked, and looked around uneasily. "I mean ... cities are built, aren't they? They don't just grow."

Derec stared a circle around the room. It was hexagonal, like standing on the inside of a crystal, with no visible line of demarcation for the ceilings and floor. The furniture seemed to flow from the walls, as the table seemed to flow upward from the floor. Light concentrated from the ceiling and lit the room comfortably, but it seemed the ceiling itself that was alight, with no external apparatus to make it happen.

"Look around you," Derec said. "Everything's connected to everything else, and connected seamlessly. And it all seems to be made from the same material." He walked to a sofa that flowed out of the wall and sat on the cushion that formed its base. "Comfortable," he said, "but I think it's made from the same material as the harder stuff—some kind of steel and plastic alloy—just in different measure."

Katherine had walked to the table and was staring at it. "If you look closely," she said, "you can see a pattern to the material."

Derec stood and walked up beside her, leaning down on

the table to get a close look. The pattern was faint, but readable. The table was made up of a collection of trapezoidal shapes, interwoven and repeated over and over.

"Interesting," Derec said.

"How so?"

"Is the shape familiar to you?"

She narrowed her brows in concentration for a moment, then looked at him with wide eyes. "The same shape as the Key," she said.

He nodded.

Katherine left him standing there and hurried back out to the balcony.

"It's almost like individual pieces stuck together," he called to her. "I wonder how they connect . . ."

"It's gone!" she shrieked, and Derec hurried onto the balcony. "Your tower from before, it's gone!"

"No it's not," he said, pointing farther to the east.

"It's moved?"

He shook his head. "I don't think so." He pointed to the huge, pyramidal structure that dominated the landscape to the west. It was at the top of that place where they were first brought by the Key. "That's the only building I think doesn't change. And we couldn't see it from the balcony a moment ago."

"You mean, *we've* changed?"

"Something like that."

She put a hand to her head. "I didn't see . . . feel, I . . ."

"It's kind of like watching clouds," he said. "If you stare at them from moment to moment, they seem to be solid and stationary, but once you turn away and then look back, they've changed. It's almost like some sort of evolutionary growth . . ."

"In a building?"

"If you stay out there much longer, you will probably get wet," came a voice from behind them. They turned to see Euler's glowing eyes staring at them in the darkness.

"We've gotten wet before," Katherine returned, looking

past Euler to the food being set out on their table. "Ah, a last meal for the condemned."

"The rain here is particularly cool," the robot said, and watched as Katherine shoved past him and ran into the dining area, "perhaps uncomfortably cool for the human body temperature."

Thunder rumbled loudly in the distance, a brilliant shaft of lightning striking the top of the towering pyramid. Derec turned from the spectacle and moved toward the doorway, Euler stepping aside to let him pass.

He walked to the table, sitting across from Katherine, who was already piling food from a large golden bowl onto her plate, also gold-colored. The food seemed to be of a uniform, paste-like consistency, its color drifting somewhere between blue and gray. Golden cups filled with water sat beside the plates.

"Are these utensils made of gold?" Derec asked, clanging a spoon melodiously against his plate.

"Correct," Rydberg said. "It's a relatively useless soft metal that is a by-product of our mining operations. Its one major virtue besides its use as a conductor is the fact that it doesn't tarnish, making it ideal for human eating utensils. We made these things for David's visit."

Derec watched the serving spoon slip from Katherine's grasp to clang loudly against her plate. And for just a second her face turned white.

"That's what you told me *my* name was," Derec said, finding the coincidence a little too close for his comfort.

She fixed him with unfocused eyes, then shrugged, looking normal again. "It's a common enough name on Spacer worlds," she said, returning her attention to her plate.

She picked up the spoon and went back to the job at hand. Derec looked up at the robots who stood beside the table and the small servo Type-I:5 robot waiting patiently near the door for the return of the utensils.

"Would you care to sit with us while we eat?" Derec asked, and felt Katherine kick him under the table.

"Delighted," Euler said without hesitation, and the two robots sat at table attentively, apparently enjoying in their way the human familiarity.

Derec took the serving spoon and began filling his own plate. "I take it that David was the other human who came here?" he asked.

"That is correct," Rydberg said.

"Then he came in a ship?" Derec pressed.

"No," Euler said. "He simply walked into the city one day."

"From where?"

"I don't know."

"Aaaahhh!" Katherine yelled, spitting out food and grabbing for the glass of water, drinking furiously. The robots swiveled their heads to watch, then exchanged glances. "Are you trying to feed us or kill us?" she demanded.

"Our programming would never allow us to kill you," Rydberg said. "That would be quite impossible."

Derec tentatively dipped his spoon into the porridge-like mixture, taking a small bite. Not sour, not sweet, it simply had a strange, *alien* taste accompanied by a slight noxious odor, one he was also uncomfortable with.

"This stuff stinks!" Katherine said loudly, the robots looking at her, then turning expectantly toward Derec.

"She's right," Derec replied. "What is this?"

"A perfect, nontoxic mixture of local plant matter, high in protein and balanced carbohydrates," Rydberg said. "It's good for you."

"The other human ate this?" Derec asked.

"Quite enthusiastically," Euler said.

"No wonder he's dead," Katherine muttered. "This is simply unacceptable. You're going to have to find us something else, something that tastes good."

Derec took another bite, this time holding his nose. Disassociating the smell from the food helped some, but not too much. The gruel left an unpleasant aftertaste. How could the other man have eaten it and not complained? Less made sense all the time.

"How long before you can get us something else?" Derec asked.

"Tomorrow?" Rydberg suggested. "Although they were proud of this in food services. Finding something of equal nutritional value will be difficult."

"Forget nutritional value to a degree," Derec said. "Study other human foods and see how well those can be duplicated exactly with the know-how you have here." He looked at Katherine. "We should probably try and choke some of this down to keep our strength."

She nodded grimly. "I'd already figured that," she said, and looked at Rydberg. "Bring me lots of water."

The robot hurried to comply, fetching a gold pitcher from the servo-cart and refilling her cup.

"When did he die, this David?" Derec asked, holding his nose and taking another bite.

"Seven days ago," Rydberg said, sitting again and carefully positioning the pitcher within everyone's easy reach on the table.

"Well, that rules us out as suspects then," Derec said happily. "We didn't arrive here until last night."

"You'll have to excuse me," Rydberg said politely, "but Katherine has already exhibited a penchant for speaking less than honestly—"

"What's that supposed to mean?" Katherine said angrily.

"No disrespect intended," Rydberg said. "It is simply the case that your veracity must be in question in light of our conversations of this afternoon. At this point, we don't know if we can trust anything either of you says."

"We don't even know where this place is," Derec said.

"Then how did you get here?" Euler asked, swiveling his head to stare directly at Derec.

"I . . ." Derec began, then stopped himself. He wasn't ready to admit any knowledge of the Key. It was their only weapon, their only potential salvation; he couldn't give it over so early in the game. "I don't know."

Rydberg stared for several seconds before saying, "To believe you means that you either materialized out of the ether or were somehow brought here totally without your knowledge or consent."

Derec responded by taking the conversation away from the robot's control. "You say this David also seemed to appear out of nowhere. Did you ever question him about his origins?"

"Yes," Euler said simply.

"And you know nothing about his background," Derec said, trying to keep his mind off the food by concentrating on the investigation. Across from him, Katherine was swallowing her food whole and washing it down with large gulps of water. "How was he dressed?"

"He was naked," Euler said. "And he stayed naked."

The two humans shared a look. Nudity was common and casual on many Spacer worlds, but the climate here would hardly recommend it. "When can we see the body?" Derec asked.

"That's not possible," Euler told her.

"Why?"

"I cannot tell you why."

"Cannot or will not?" Derec asked, exasperated.

"Cannot and will not," Euler replied.

"Then how do you expect us to investigate the cause of death?" Kate asked.

"If either or both of you are the murderers," Euler said, "you already know the cause of death."

"You've already decided our guilt," Derec said, pointing. "That's not fair or just."

"There are no other possibilities," Rydberg said.

"When the possible has been exhausted," Derec replied, "it is time to examine the impossible. We are innocent, and you can't prove that we aren't. It only follows that the death was caused by something else."

"Humans can murder," Euler said, as thunder crashed loudly outside. "Humans can lie. You are the only humans here, and murder has been done."

"We came out of nowhere," Derec returned. "So did David. Others could also have come out of nowhere, others you haven't discovered yet. Why, had we committed a murder, would we stay around for you to catch?"

The robots looked at one another again. "You raise logical questions that must be answered," Euler said. "We certainly sanction your investigation."

"How can we investigate without full access?"

"With all the other resources at your command," Rydberg said, then stood. "Are you finished eating?"

"For now," Derec said. "We'll want real food tomorrow, though."

"We will do our best," Euler said, and he, also, stood. "Until then, you will stay here."

"I thought I might go out," Derec said.

"The rains will come. It's too dangerous. For your own safety, you will stay here tonight. We have found that we cannot be certain if what you tell us is correct, so we're leaving a robot at the door to make certain you stay in."

"You don't know that we've done anything wrong. You can't treat us like prisoners," Katherine said.

"And we shall not," Rydberg said, moving toward the door; the servo whirred up to the table, its metal talons pulling the bowls and plates into its innards.

"There are many things we need to talk with you about," Derec said.

"Tomorrow will be the time," Euler said. "We will have a long interview at a prescribed time, where many issues will be discussed. Until then, we cannot fit it into our schedule. We are currently quite busy." The robots turned to go.

"A couple of questions first," Derec said, hurrying to put himself between the door and the robots. "You say we aren't prisoners, yet you have locked us up. How long do we have to stay in this place?"

"Until it is safe," Rydberg said.

"Then if you do let us out," Derec persisted, "how can you be sure we won't try to escape?"

"We will have to keep a very close watch on you," Euler replied.

With that, the robot firmly, but gently, pushed Derec aside and moved out the door, the servo following quickly behind. Derec tried to follow them out, but a squared-off utility robot blocked his path, its body streaked with random bands of different colored paints like the colors on an artist's pallet.

"Stand aside," Derec told the machine.

"It is dangerous for you outside. I am to keep you inside where it is safe, and have no more conversation with you lest you try and deceive me."

"Me?" Derec said. "Deceive?"

The robot pushed the door stud and the unit slid closed. Derec turned to Katherine. "What do you make of it?"

She moved to sit on the sofa, then stretched out, looking tired. "We're being held prisoner by a bunch of robots with no one in charge," she said, sighing deeply. "The dead man was an exhibitionist who could, apparently, eat anything. They want us to prove our innocence, but refuse to let us see the body or investigate." She sat up abruptly, eyes narrowing. "Derec, we've got to get out of here."

"They won't do anything to us without proof of our guilt," Derec replied. "It's not in their nature. We'll stay around and get this straightened out. Then they'll be happy to send us on our way. Besides, this place has got me really curious. How does it work . . . *why* does it work?"

She lay down again, staring at the ceiling. "I'm not so sure they'd really let us leave," she said, voice distant. "I think we've stumbled into something completely crazy. A robot world without humans could take any sort of bizarre turn."

"But not a . . . what did you say . . . completely crazy turn," he replied. "They can't be crazy; there's no logic to crazy. Besides, what makes you think we've stumbled into anything? We were brought here, plain and simple, for a reason that hasn't been made clear yet. Maybe a little time here will help us ferret it out."

"You ferret it out," she said. "I'm tired."

"Well, I'm not." He moved to the balcony, feeling the stiff wind on his face as the light show continued to rage outside. "I'm going out tonight and do a little poking around."

She was up from the couch, moving toward him. "They said it was dangerous," she said quietly, a hand going to his forearm. "Go out tomorrow."

"Under their watchful eye?" he said, then shook his head. "We need to get around on our own, and this is the time. Besides, a little rain can't hurt me."

"Stay," she said. "I'm afraid."

"You?" He laughed. "Afraid?"

She pulled her hand away. "All right," she said. "Go out and get yourself killed. I'm tired of looking out for you anyway."

"You're angry."

"And you're an idiot." She turned from him and stared out across the magnificent city, realizing that its beauty was for them alone to appreciate. There was something unutterably sad about that. "How will you get past the door guard?"

"We'll take his advice and deceive him," Derec said.

"We?"

"Will you help me?"

She turned and walked back into the apartment. "Anything to get you out of my hair," she said over her shoulder.

Derec's plan was simple enough, but it was one he could use only once. The robots learned quickly enough of human duplicity, arming themselves with the knowledge as a protection. But just this once, it might work.

He crouched beside the sofa, knotting into a tight ball. Just as soon as he was well out of sight of the door, Kate took a deep breath and tried to open it—locked.

She shrugged once in Derec's direction, then began screaming in terror. A second later the door slid open, the utility robot blocking the entry.

"What's wrong?"

"It's Derec!" she cried, pointing. "He fell from the balcony!"

Without hesitation, the robot rolled into the room, ready to check her story for lies and deceit. He quickly moved toward the balcony, leaning way over the edge to get a look into the night.

Derec jumped up from behind the couch and hurried quietly out the door and into the elevator that took him all the way to the ground and his first positive step in uncovering the mystery of Robot City. He was free, but what that meant here he could only guess.

Derec exited onto the wide street, hurrying across it to the shadows of buildings a half a block away. From there he took a few minutes to turn back and study the surroundings he had just left behind, trying to memorize the positions and shapes of the buildings near his tower. If his feelings were correct and the city was evolving outward, finding his way back could be a difficult, if not impossible, task. He didn't worry too much about it, though. He felt completely safe in this world of robots and figured that if he got lost, he'd simply turn himself in to the nearest robot of decent sophistication and be sent back.

That dwelt upon, he turned his attention completely to exploring the new world that an unseen fate had guided him to. In his current pristine state of innocence and awareness, it was difficult for Derec not to see the hand of destiny in his wanderings. It was as if his amnesia was an emotional and intellectual purging of sorts, set in motion to prepare him for a journey of which Robot City could be only a part. Since that was the only feeling or need he had to work with, he plunged himself into it with relish, enthusiasm, and as much good humor as he could muster. Katherine would never understand his feelings in this matter, but then Katherine had a life to go back to and memories to sustain her. For Derec, this was it, his whole world, and he wanted to know as much about it as he possibly could.

The city stretched all around him like some magnificent clockwork. The shapes of the buildings, from towering spires to squat storage warehouses, were all precise and multifaceted, like growing crystals. And the shapes seemed to be designed as much for aesthetic pleasure as pragmatic necessity. This concept formed the core of a theory within Derec's mind, and one that he would want to explore in greater detail when he had time for reflection. For nothing exists in a vacuum. Robots were not motivated independently by unreasoning emotion. They had to have reasons for their actions, and by what Derec had seen, their actions were all directed absolutely, despite Rydberg's claims of autonomy.

The cold winds sliced through him like a knife through water, and the sky rumbled and quaked, yet all around him he watched a furious activity that kept the mechanism of Robot City moving to its own internal rhythm and purpose. Hundreds of robots filled the streets around him, all moving and directed. All ignored his presence.

Streets were cleaned, even as spray painting was conducted on dull-sheened buildings, the sprayers held close to the target in the stiff wind—which probably explained the bands of paint on the utility robot that guarded the humans. Converted mining cars sped by, filled with broken equipment and scrap metal, their beamed headlights illuminating the streets before them like roving mechanical fireflies. Once he took to the shadows as a whole squad of drones, accompanied by a supervisor robot he hadn't seen before, drove past in an open-bed equipment mover and passed his position without a look before disappearing around a distant corner. He thought about following them, but decided that he would continue exploring slowly at first, getting a feel for his world and its parameters.

The questions in his mind seemed endless, and their answers only led to more questions. Who began Robot City, and why did the robots not know of their own origin? Why this place, this particular planet? Why a city of human proportions for a world of the nonhuman? Euler had called Robot City the perfect place for humans—why? The murder, to Derec, was nothing but a small nuisance with large complications. What really interested him was the motivation behind the city itself.

The lousy food raised a great many further questions in his mind. Spacer robots were designed solely as mechanical helpmates to human masters. Spacer robots *knew* how human beings reacted to food. The robots here had basic human knowledge and the Laws of Robotics as their core, yet remained ignorant of specific, conditioned reactions to humans. It was almost as if their design had geared them toward an equal human partnership, rather than a master/-servant relationship, and they were feeling out their relationship with the animal called *human*. It was a dizzying concept to Derec, one that he'd also have to think out in greater detail.

And, finally, the dead man. Where did he fit into the picture . . . and why? Derec's mind, being a blank slate, soaked up everything around him like a sponge, unhampered by the intrusion of past thoughts and feelings that muddied observation. His eye for detail missed nothing, especially the reaction of Katherine to hearing Euler say the man's name—David.

What could it mean? He had literally stumbled upon Katherine, yet she seemed an indispensable part of the puzzle. What role did she play? Again, destiny seemed to rule the day—a place for everything, everything in its place. He was a blind man with a jigsaw puzzle, feeling his way through, groping sightlessly for the connections. He liked the girl, couldn't help it, and felt a strong physical attraction for her that he wouldn't even try to wish away; yet he couldn't shake the feeling that she was deeply involved in covering up his real identity and purpose. And again, his eternal question—why?

He continued moving down the street. Though the buildings were beautiful, they were nondescript, without markings of any kind. He recognized warehouses because parts were being moved in and out of them, but everything else seemed devoid of purpose. If he could find an official building, he could try to hook up to a terminal and make his own inquiries. The pyramid where he and Katherine had materialized, the place the robots called the Compass Tower, had seemed solid to him. Even though it appeared to be the point upon which all else hinged, he wasn't ready to go back to it yet.

The robots on the street ignored him as he moved through their midst. There seemed to be a sense of urgency to them that he couldn't understand. He stopped a utility robot like the one he had snuck past at the apartment, except this one had huge scoops for hands.

"Can you talk?" he asked.

"Yes, most assuredly," the robot answered.

"I need to find the administration building."

"I don't believe we have one here."

"Where would I find the closest computer terminal?"

"I regret that I cannot say."

Derec sighed. The runaround. Again. "Why can't you say?"

"If I told you that, you'd know everything."

"Know everything about what?"

"About the thing that I cannot talk about. If you'd like, you can stay here and I'll report to a supervisor and have him come out and find you."

"No, thanks," Derec replied, and the robot turned to walk away. "Hey, what's your hurry?"

"The rain," the utility said, pointing toward the sky. "The rain is coming. You had better get to shelter." The robot turned and hurried off, his box-like body weaving from side to side as he rolled along.

"What about the rain!?" Derec yelled, but his words were lost in a sudden gust of wind.

He watched the figure of the robot for a moment, realizing that the street he had come down looked different than it had a moment before. The whole block, street and all, had seemed to shift positions, bowing out to curve what had once been straight. A tall, tetrahedral structure, which he had used as a reference point, had disappeared completely. Ten minutes on the street and he was totally lost.

He pressed on, the wind colder now, more intense. If this was such a perfect world for humans, then why did the weather seem so bad?

He reached an unmarked corner and found himself on the street he had ridden down earlier, during the parade. It was extra wide, a large aqueduct bisecting it.

He moved to the edge of the aqueduct and stared down at the dark, rushing waters that filled it no more than a quarter full. Where had the waters come from? Where were they going? Had Robot City been built here for the water, or was the water somehow a consequence of the building?

The water rushed past, dark and inscrutable, much like the problem of Derec's past and, perhaps, his future. Yet he could know about the water. He could trace it to its source; he could follow it to its destination. He could *know*. The thought heartened him, for he could do the same with his life. Accepting that destiny and not chance had brought him to this impossible place, it then followed that the sources of that destiny could be traced through the city itself.

If he pursued it properly, he could trace the origins of the city and, hence, find his own origins. It seemed eminently logical, for he couldn't escape the concept that he and Robot City were inextricably linked, physically, emotionally, and, perhaps, metaphysically.

If his searching came to naught, at least he'd be keeping himself, keeping his blank mind, occupied. He'd begin with the water—trace it through source and destination, find out the why of it. He'd work on the robots, finding out what they knew, what they didn't know, what they'd be willing to tell him, and what he could find out from them unwillingly. And there was Katherine. He'd have to treat her like a friendly adversary and use whatever limited wiles he had at his disposal to find out her place in all this.

The water plopped below him, as if a large stone had been tossed in. He looked around but saw nothing save the gently glowing buildings and the distant robots hurrying about their secret business.

The water plopped again, farther down the aqueduct, then again, near the last place. He turned to stare in that direction when his shoulder was splashed by a drop of icy water.

A drop hardly described it. What hit him was more like a glassful. His jumpsuit sleeve was soaked, his shoulder cold. Water splashed on the street beside him, a drop bigger than a clenched fist, leaving a wet ring.

Derec had about a second to appreciate what was happening, for his mind to begin to realize what a major storm could mean, when the deluge struck.

With a force that nearly doubled him over, the rain fell upon Derec in opaque sheets that immediately cut off his field of vision. He was cold, freezing; the rain lashing him unmercifully, its sound a hollow roar in his ears.

He used his arms to cover and protect his head as the freezing downpour numbed his shoulders and back. He had to get to shelter quickly, but he had already lost his bearings in the curtian of water that surrounded him three-sixty.

He tentatively put out a foot, hoping he was moving in the direction of the buildings across from the aqueduct. Were he to move in the wrong direction, he'd fall into the aqueduct and be lost in its flowing waters.

Movement was slow as he felt his way, still doubled over, toward the buildings and safety. It seemed as if he should have reached them three times over—they couldn't have been more than ten meters distant—yet he hadn't gotten there yet. Could he have gotten turned the wrong way and simply be moving down the center of the street?

Keeping his balance was getting more difficult. Water on the street was up to his ankles, moving rapidly against his direction. He lost his footing and went to his knee, but managed to rise again. His clothes were now soaked through, and hung like icicles from his body. Every step was a labor.

"The perfect world," he muttered, a thin smile stretching his lips despite his predicament.

Just as he was about to give up on his present direction and pick another one at random, the hulk of a building began to define itself in his vision. A few more treacherous steps and he was suddenly out of the rain, standing beneath a short awning that overhung the building front.

He used a hand to wipe the water from his face, then hugged himself, shivering, against the damp cold, taking stock of his position. The overhang protected the building front only for about a meter, and it extended for perhaps three meters in either direction from where he stood.

Beyond the awning, he could see nothing. The roaring water was impenetrable. The building front was no better. It was totally blank, no doors or windows. Yet, oddly enough, when he touched it, it felt warm, resisting the chill of the air. He was stuck in a world one meter wide by five meters long. The ground water had risen from his ankles to his calves, its current always pulling at him.

He stood there for several minutes, cold, teeth chattering, cursing the fate that would bring him to this hellhole. His numbness and melancholy soon, inevitably, turned to anger.

"Damn you!" he screamed, to whom, to what, he didn't know. "Why me?"

In frustration, he turned to the wall behind him. Hands balled into fists, he pounded viciously at the wall and—his hands sank right into it!

"Aaaahh!"

He screamed in surprise, instinctively jumping backward.

The water cascading from the awning caught him on the face, and as he tried to duck away from it, the ground current took him down.

He went under, then came up gasping for breath. But his control was gone and he was caught in the current. It pulled him back across the street; even the street itself seemed tilted at an angle toward the aqueduct. At this point, trying to regain his footing was out of the question. Keeping his head above water was the only priority. Staying alive was everything.

He felt himself go over the lip of the aqueduct and plunge into its raging waters. He bobbed down, at no point touching bottom, then rose again, totally numb and choking as the swift current carried him away, pulling at him, sucking him ever down.

He had wanted to see the terminal point of the waters. He would now see it quickly—if he could stay alive long enough.

Katherine stood with Euler by the opening to the balcony, staring out at a completely opaque wall of water that made her think that Robot City didn't really exist at all, but was simply an image conjured by an overactive brain exposed to too much cosmic radiation. The rain came down in never-ending torrents, rain such as she'd never seen or even thought could exist. It frightened her, a fright that almost overcame her anger at their predicament. Almost.

"Why did he go out?" Euler asked.

"I've already told you," she replied, turning away from the incredible downpour and moving back into the apartment. "He wanted to see the city."

"But we told him it was dangerous."

Katherine sat on the couch, folding her arms across her chest. A black hole could swallow Derec *and* his robots for all she cared. "He either didn't believe you or didn't care," she said. "Why are you standing here asking me the same thing over and over when you could be out there looking for him?"

Rydberg came in from the bedroom, where he had apparently been searching in case Katherine had been lying. "Everything that can be done is being done," he said. "We appreciate your concern. Ours is every bit as great as yours."

"I'm not concerned," she said. "I couldn't care less."

The robots exchanged glances. "You don't care about the possible loss of a human life?" Euler asked.

Katherine jumped up from the couch. "You mean he could possibly be . . . be . . . ?"

"Dead?" Rydberg helped. "Of course. We warned you that it was dangerous."

For the fiftieth time since Derec's leaving, she hurried back to the balcony doorway and stared into the blank wall of water. He'd been gone for several hours, far longer than he should have been. If anything had happened to him—

"Why did he go out?" Euler asked from beside her.

"Again!" she said loudly. "That same question. Why do you keep asking me that?"

"Because we don't understand," Rydberg said, moving up to join them. "You must know that robots don't lie."

"Yes," she replied.

"Then, when we said it was dangerous, why did he risk his life?" Euler asked.

"To begin with, his definition of danger might be different from yours," she said. "But beyond that, he wanted to know about this crazy city of yours more than he was afraid of the danger."

"You mean," Euler said, "that he could have purposely risked his life just for the sake of curiosity?"

"Something like that."

"Astounding."

"Let me ask you a question," she said, poking Euler in his chest sensors with an index finger. "If you want people to live here so much, why did you pick a place with such dangerous weather?"

Rydberg seemed to hesitate, as if he were weighing the answer he was about to give by some sort of internal scale. "The weather here is not naturally like this," he said at last.

"Naturally," she repeated, zeroing in on the key word. "Does this mean that something has affected the weather adversely?"

"Yes," Euler said.

"What?" she asked.

"We cannot tell you that," Rydberg said, and walked over to peer beneath the couch.

"Will it stop soon?" Kate asked.

"Probably within the next hour," Euler said. "At which time we can conduct an extensive search for Friend Derec."

A thought struck Katherine. She wanted to suppress it, but couldn't. "Is this how the other man . . . David, died?"

"He may have caused the rains," Euler said. "but he didn't die from them."

"I don't understand."

"It is quite late for humans," Rydberg said, moving toward the door. "You must sleep now or risk damaging your health."

With that, the two supervisor robots moved silently into the hallway, the door sliding shut behind them.

Katherine was alone, except for the robot standing guard in the hallway outside. She moved to the couch and curled into a tight ball. "Oh, David," she cried into the sleeve of her jumper. "Why did this have to happen?"

Derec rode the aqueduct like a log in a sluice, his body numb, his senses and his fate out of control. The waters raged in his ears as his entire existence turned on the simple act of trying to keep his head above water. Nothing else mattered; life had reduced itself to its essence. There was no fear, no time for it, and any yearnings to have his life pass before his eyes went unsatisfied, since he had no life to reflect upon. There was only the water and the numbing cold—and the ubiquitous companionship of Death.

His ride could have lasted a minute or an eternity—he was beyond calculating time—but when he felt himself freefalling in midair, his brain snapped to the new reality and questioned.

He was falling, surrounded by a hot, moist wind. A bare glow of light seemed to envelope him, but before he had a chance to appreciate it, he splashed into hot water.

He had gulped down water with his quickly sucked breath, and when he bobbed to the surface like a cork, he was choking and coughing, his head pounding with a heart-beat throb. He panicked, then forced himself into control when he realized the water he was in wasn't flowing, but pooling.

As he treaded water, he found himself grateful to his former life for giving him the lifesaving advantage of swimming lessons. He leaned back and floated on his back, small currents pulling him this way and that. His body ached horribly from the battering he had taken in the aqueduct; every bit

27

of strength had drained from him.

There was a ceiling of some sort above him, tiny lights making it dimly visible. The roar of waterfalls filled the hollow cavern completely, and he turned his head to the side to get a glimpse of his surroundings.

He was a hundred meters from the edge of a large square pool that stretched perhaps a thousand meters across. Red lights set at regular intervals bathed the entire area in an eerie glow. In the middle of each side of the pool were aqueduct runoffs, four in all, their cascades shimmering like fading pulsars in the red haze. These four runoffs provided the incredible noise that churned inside his head, all of it echoing within the confined space.

Where was he? A collection point of some kind, perhaps a reservoir. Any city needed a water supply. This was probably connected to a water treatment plant meant to sustain the human population that didn't live there. This only strengthened Derec's earlier speculation that this was not a city simply meant for robots. What was going on here was serious colonization.

Another realization occurred to him, too. The reservoir had saved his life. He had been showing the beginning signs of hypothermia during his wild ride down the aqueduct, but the hot water of the reservoir was thawing him out.

Why hot water? The water was definitely warmer than human body temperature, perhaps as much as fifteen degrees, and incredibly hot winds were raging through the chamber, competing with the charging runoff waters in loudness. In fact, the soothing heat and the rest were already beginning to lull his senses, and he realized that if he wasn't careful, he could end up at the other end of the physical spectrum with hyperthermia. Whether hypo or hyper, though, the results were still the same. He was going to have to get out of the water or risk overburdening his heart.

Still on his back, he churned his legs lightly while propelling himself with his arms. There seemed to be robotic movement at the far end of the reservoir, but he didn't have the strength to swim that far. Having no idea of which way to go, he simply moved toward the closest shoreline. The process was time-consuming, though, for the runoffs created their own currents.

He swam with leisure, but determination, taking the time to check out his body. He had taken a beating in his wild ride down the aqueduct, but besides general bruises, nothing major seemed to be wrong.

As he neared the edge of the pool, he could see that the runoff streams had slowed considerably, leading him to speculate that the rain had stopped outside. Fuzzy light was also beginning to seep in around the dark edges of the covered pool, and he realized that day had broken.

He finally reached the edge of the pool, its surface made from the same material as the rest of the city. Metal ladders were set at regular intervals around the edge, and he floated to the nearest one to begin his climb out.

The water was barely three meters from the top of the pool, and fortunately so, because as soon as Derec began his climb he knew he wasn't doing well. His body, so light in the water, felt like it weighed a ton. The combination of emotional stress, the ordeal of the aqueduct, and the over-heated water of the pool had all had an effect on his body. He dragged himself slowly up the ladder, then rolled, gasping, onto the edge of the pool and lay there.

He closed his eyes, just for a minute, and he was gone. He didn't know how long he had slept, but when he awoke, it was with a start. A loud rumble assailed his hearing. He sat up quickly, darting his head around, and saw a large vehicle moving around the pool toward him, its engine noises amplified to a roar in the cavern-like surroundings.

Standing was a problem, since Derec still felt weak. But he got up on shaky legs and moved toward the areas of light beyond the reservoir. While he was still out and on the loose, he wanted to see as much as he could. For, this time, the robots wouldn't be so quick to let him out of their sight.

As he moved toward the light, he passed open caverns

that were filled with conduits for moving water. The huge pipes were twisted like knotted rope and seemed to be moving, writhing, like a snake pit—almost as if they were alive. He was taken over these areas by railed walkways that simply extended from the edges of the pit at his approach, growing—like crystals—before his eyes.

After the pits, he passed several squat buildings where he surmised the actual water treatment was performed. Drone robots moved in and out of the facilities rapidly, mostly moving machinery in both directions. Derec briefly considered going into one of the structures to search for a terminal, but the still-approaching vehicle made him change his mind.

"HUMAN!" came a loudspeakered voice. "YOU WILL HALT YOUR PROGRESS WHERE YOU ARE. IT IS UN-LAWFUL FOR YOU TO PROCEED."

He turned to the sound. It was coming from the robot-controlled vehicle that was rapidly closing the distance on him. It was time to move!

He ran past the buildings toward glowing walls of light just beyond.

"HUMAN!" the loudspeaker called again.

He raced to the wall, his legs heavy. The entire wall seemed lit and wrapped a circle around the reservoir area. It was translucent, like a shower curtain, and he realized that it was simply so thin that outside light passed right through. He pushed on it, but it felt solid. He pushed harder, and it gave under his hand, just like the wall last night.

Just then, he saw a drone approach the wall twenty meters distant and move right through it. He hurried there, with the robots in the vehicle closing rapidly on him. He stood at the spot, seeing no entry, but when he raised his hands to push against it, the wall irised open and he stepped through into the daylight.

It was morning, bright and calm, with no sign of the deluge that had taken place the previous night. The sun was still low in the sky, but Robot City was alive and active.

He was in the very heart of it here, the hub upon which

the wheel of the city turned. He could see the aqueduct that had brought him cutting through the city like a spoke, and he could see other aqueducts, other spokes, slicing through the wheel of the city. And he began to think of the areas between the spokes as quadrants.

Robots in large numbers hurried quickly through the streets, always going somewhere, always busy with predetermined tasks. Many of them were disappearing into the treatment plant.

He moved a small distance from his exit point, then looked back at the reservoir, shocked to find a forest there! Then he realized that the forest had been planted above the reservoir, the land area serving double duty. But why a forest? Not for robots, certainly.

Out of the corner of his eye; he noticed the large, wheeled vehicle that had been tracking him within the reservoir moving through the exit point to the outside. He looked back at the city, then up at the forest. He would find escape in its random chaos.

Angling himself away from his pursuers, he ran back toward the huge reservoir building, preparing to climb one of the struts that helped support the outside edge of the forest. But as soon as he reached the place and put his hands on the arched strut, it seemed to melt away, changing into a gently sloping stairway.

He hurried up the stairs without a question and entered the forest. The ground was moist and spongy, muddying his already-soaked shoes. The trees were small, in many cases smaller than the underbrush that grew thick around them. A haze seemed to fill the entire forest, and the farther he plunged into it, the hazier it became.

Derec was no expert in vegetation, but he assumed the trees were all offspring, many generations removed, of trees that had once grown on Earth. Spacers, though hating to mention any connection to the planet of their ancestry, nevertheless made it a point to bring Earth vegetation and animal life to whatever planet they colonized. Where he'd gotten such information, he had no idea; the small glimpses of his own mind were maddening in their incompleteness.

He wandered the forest, pushing through the haze and the dense undergrowth, feeling jittery in untamed surroundings. And he knew that these were also the feelings of a Spacer pushing through his mind. He didn't much like the forest; he longed for the order of the city. But for a human being, this had its place. Untamed but finite, aesthetically pleasing without being uncontrollable. This place existed for the aesthetics—for human aesthetics.

His foot hit something hard and uncompromising, and he tripped, going hard to soft ground, getting mud all over himself. He turned to the object that had caused his fall and found a small section of pipe sticking out of the ground. A fog-like haze was pumping from the pipe, the same haze that filled the entire area, and Derec began to see a master plan at work here.

He stood, then ducked when he saw a shadow moving through the haze not five meters from him. It was one of the robots. He listened and could hear them thrashing through the brush all around. They were slowly cordoning off the entire area, boxing him in.

He took a deep breath, then scrunched up into a ball and lay on the ground, listening as they moved near him. The forest was built over the reservoir so that condensing water could feed up to the trees from beneath and nourish the roots directly. Further, the haze was probably carbon dioxide vapor feeding the forest to promote health and growth. Where did the CO_2 come from? Perhaps a bleed-off from their industrial processes, which could also explain the heat in the reservoir area. The set-up was sophisticated and civilized, a city built around its ecological needs. Was it all of robot design?

A metal foot clanked down just an arm's reach away from his position. He stifled the urge to rise up for a breath of normal air. Within seconds, the robot moved on.

As he heard the search party sweep past, he jumped to his

feet and charged back in the direction he had come. The robots were much faster and stronger than he was, so he was going to have to make things happen quickly at this point.

He reached the edge of the forest in minutes, and rushed to the place where he had climbed up. The strut was already solid again, the steps nowhere to be seen. He looked over the edge of the forest. It was ten meters to the ground; jumping was out of the question.

"You, Derec!" came a robot voice behind. "Stop now! Stop!"

He sat on the ground and dangled his legs over the edge of the strut. Steps miraculously formed again. He ran down just as several robots reached the edge of the forest, calling for him to stop.

Amidst the confusion near the water treatment facility, he saw a large flatbed vehicle, filled with what looked like broken computers, ready to pull out. He took the last steps in leaps and charged the machine, the robots behind already reaching the bottom of the stairs.

The truck pulled out before he reached it, but with a burst of speed, he caught it and jumped into the back. A small, round drone the size of his head squeaked at him from among the broken computers.

Katherine stood at the wash basin, watching the lukewarm water flow from the tap, and wondered how plumbing could possibly be accomplished in a city that didn't stand still. She splashed her face with water, then stared into the small mirror that was inset above the basin. Her eyes were puffy and dark, showing the results of no sleep, but her face remained calm, remarkably calm considering the terror that had been flashing through her for most of the long night.

He was gone, perhaps dead, and she was alone on this crazy world. Though David/Derec, whatever he wanted to call himself, had never looked on this place as anything but an adventure, to her it had been nothing but a prison. A first priority for anyone marooned in a Spacer port would be access to radio communications to inform search parties and anxious waiters; yet the robots seemed reluctant—no, evasive—when it came to the topic of communications. That frightened her more than anything else that was going on.

"Did you sleep well?"

She jumped to the sound, turning quickly to see Rydberg standing in the doorway, a light static issuing from his loudspeaker.

"I didn't invite you in here!" she said in anger and frustration. "Get out! Now!"

The robot turned without a word and moved from the door, Katherine following him out into a small hallway.

"What do you want?" she asked. "Has there been any . . . news about Derec?"

Rydberg turned back to her. "I did not mean to intrude upon your privacy," he said. "Please accept my apologies. I've brought you food."

"I'm not hungry."

Rydberg just stared at her.

"Has there been any word about Derec?" she asked again, softly this time.

"Yes," the robot replied. "He was seen not three decads ago, but ran away when another of our supervisors called to him."

She clapped her hands together loudly. "So, he's alive!"

"Apparently so. Why would he run away? Is this a sign of guilt?"

"It's a sign that he wants to check out this crazy place without a gaggle of robots hanging all over him." She moved past him toward the living room. "Now, where's that food? I'm so hungry I could eat a . . ." She stopped herself, then looked at the robot. "I'm hungry."

"But you just said . . ."

"Forget what I just said. Correction!" She caught herself before the robot could explain its memory. "I mean never mind. Where's the food?"

He led her back down the hall to the living room, where the food sat at the same table she had eaten at the night before. Strangely enough, the room was different, squatter, wider than it had been the previous night, the table closer to the wall.

She moved quickly to the table. There was a variety of what appeared to be fruits and cooked vegetables there. She sat down and tentatively ate a small piece of greenish fruit. It was delicious. Rydberg stood nearby as she greedily sampled everything on the table, all of it good. She didn't invite the robot to sit with her as Derec had done. The machines were servants and needed to be treated as such. She'd never understand his insistence on treating them as anything other than the machines they were.

"When do we get to make outside radio contact?" she asked once the initial hunger pangs had died down.

"We will all meet later and discuss those questions."

"Are you going to put us on trial," she asked, "for the murder of this other human? We are entitled to a trial, you know."

"Derec has told us that he will try to solve this mystery," Rydberg said.

Katherine stopped eating and stared at him. "And what if he doesn't? What if we don't *ever* discover what really happened? You have no right to hold us here as it is. We can't go on indefinitely like this."

"If he cannot find out the truth of the matter," Rydberg said, "then we will assume our original supposition to be correct."

"I don't believe you," she said. "You have no right to determine my guilt or innocence without proper evidence. I'm not Derec, and I hold no romantic visions of a robot-controlled world. You cannot be allowed to have any power over the way I live my life. If you want to hold me for murder, you must put me on trial and prove it. If you put me on trial, I must be allowed to defend myself. I therefore demand immediate access to a radio so that I may provide myself with proper defense representation. I want a certified legal rep, and I want one now!"

"We will discuss the situation later today," the robot said, "after Friend Derec has been returned to us. Meanwhile, your food is getting cold and will lose its appeal."

"It already has," Katherine returned, pushing the plate away from herself. She didn't like the way this was turning. The radio seemed to get more and more distant to her, and with it, any hopes of ever leaving this place. Her arguments to Rydberg were based solely on laws and customs common to Auroran society. But all law, all freedom, was merely a rationalization away where a robot civilization was concerned.

The final result to her was quite simple: the machines were in charge and they could do anything they wanted.

Derec knew nothing with which to compare the size of Robot City, but as he drove its breadth, he couldn't help but feel its vastness.

As the parts truck moved quickly through the city streets, the round drone bounced from one machine to another, squeaking loudly, its silver body lighting up in dozens of places, then winking out again as it performed automatic (but definitely sub-robotic) pre-troubleshooting functions on the broken machinery. Finally, it came to rest on Derec's lap, all of its lights blinking madly, its squeaks turning into a high-pitched whine.

"So, where are we going?" he asked the troubleshooter while idly stroking its dome.

The machine whirred and bounced, but never answered. All at once, its whine turned to a loud, siren-like wail.

"Stop it!" Derec ordered, turning to the front of the truck to make sure he wasn't attracting attention. He bent double over the thing, trying to muffle its sound without success.

"You're going to have to stop," he told the thing. "I can't just . . ."

It sent a jolt of electricity through its body, shocking Derec, moving him off.

"All right," he said, pointing a shaking finger at the silver ball. "I don't have to take that from you."

The thing started bouncing up and down, higher and higher. Derec looked both ways over the truck back, then calmly brought up a foot and shoved the thing right off the truck, where it hit the street angrily, its wail louder as it bounced around like a rubber ball.

Within a few blocks, the vehicle slowed its pace, then got in line behind several other trucks, all filled with equipment. Derec got on his knees and looked over the piles of computers.

The trucks were pulled up to a gate, where a whole line of robots were moving up to the truck back, each taking a single piece of equipment and returning with it to a blockhouse that wasn't much larger than a single doorway. Beside the blockhouse was the most amazing thing Derec had ever seen in his short memory.

A huge, gray machine rumbled softly, yet with undeniable strength and power. From it issued what could only be described as a ribbon of city. In five-meter-square slabs, the city appeared to be simply extruding from underground through the medium of the gray machine.

It pushed itself along, the slabs gradually forming and reforming as they moved, following some incredible pre-programming that actually let them *build* themselves. And as the slabs formed walls and floors and corners and stories and windows, they spun off in every direction in a slow, graceful dance that pushed against the already existing buildings, the mechanism that triggered the entire magnificent clockwork of Robot City.

It was as if the entire city were one mammoth, living organism always growing outward, always changing and replicating like the cells in a body, moving in imprinted patterns toward a complete, fully formed being.

It was a plan of monumental scale, an atmosphere of total,

logical control for a given end. As he watched a skyscraper literally build itself from the ground up, each story pushing up the story above it and self-welding according to some unseen plan, he experienced the grandeur of an idea so vast that his limited knowledge was humbled by its power. This civilization was the product of a mind that refused to believe in limited options, a mind that accepted that what the imagination could conceive, the hands could make.

To such a mind, anything was possible. Even, perhaps, Perihelion.

The truck lurched, nearly knocking him from his knees. It had pulled up to the gate. The line of robots was now reaching into *his* bed for their equipment.

If all the action was happening below ground, that's where Derec wanted to be. Hurrying out of the truck, he grabbed a small terminal that looked as if it had been shorted out by water, and took his place behind a robot heading toward that doorway into the ground.

He reached the doorway, cradling the computer like a baby. Warm air greeted him as he stepped through into barely lit darkness. He was confronted by a short flight of stairs leading down, and followed the robot that walked down before him.

The stairs terminated in a large holding area, brightly lit, frenetic with activity. Automated carts carried robots and mining equipment at breakneck pace. The cars zipped around one another in seemingly rehearsed fashion, their movements perfected over time, since it seemed impossible to Derec that they could move so quickly without hitting one another.

On the far wall sat a bank of elevators, perhaps twenty in all, some of them remarkably large. The robots that moved down the stairs headed toward these elevators, apparently going from here to a lower level where repair or scrap work was being done.

Having no idea of where to go, Derec chose an elevator at random and moved toward it with his burden. A large elevator nearby slid open, and a group of minerbots, covered with mud and soot, moved out bearing the non-operating carcass of one of their own above their shoulders.

Derec reached the elevator. It had no formal controls, but opened for him as soon as he stepped near.

A voice boomed behind him. "Nothing awaits you below, but death!"

He turned to see a huge supervisor robot, twice the size of a man, glaring down at him with red photocells. The robot's body was burnished a bright, shimmering black.

"I've come to inspect your operation," Derec said, feigning authority. He turned back to the elevator and began to step in.

The robot's arm flashed out, his mammoth pincers clanging loudly around Derec's forearm, squeezing tightly but not painfully.

"You are caught," the machine said, and Derec's computer crashed loudly at his feet.

CHAPTER 4
THE COMPASS TOWER

As the door to the apartment slid open, Derec tucked under the arm of the big robot, watched Katherine's facial expression change from horror, to relief, to unbridled amusement — all in the space of three seconds.

"Let me guess," she said, putting a finger to her lips, "you're a ditty bag."

"Cute," Derec returned as the robot set him gently on the ground. He looked up at the huge, black machine. "Thanks for the ride, Avernus."

"My pleasure, Friend Derec," the robot replied, bending slightly so that the hallway could accommodate his height. "But I must ask you to stay away from the underground. It is no place for a human."

"I appreciate your concern," Derec said noncommittally. He walked into the apartment, then turned back to Avernus. "Will we see you at the meeting?"

"Most assuredly," he returned. "All of us look forward to it with great expectation."

"You can go now," Katherine told Avernus coldly, the robot nodding slightly and moving off, the utility robot guard sliding quickly to fill the door space with his squat body.

Katherine punched the door stud, the panel sliding closed. "You missed breakfast *and* lunch," she said, moving to sit listlessly on the couch.

"Avernus got me something before he brought me back,"

Derec said. "He got my wounds cleaned up, and even let me sleep for a while." Finally, he couldn't ignore her mood any longer. "What's wrong?"

"You," she said, "this place . . . everything. I don't know which way is up anymore. Did you find out anything?"

Derec spotted the CRT screen set up on the table and walked to stand before it. "It's a place designed for humans," he said, "and the building is going on at a furious pace, as if they're in some kind of hurry to get finished. I think the buildings may be . . . I don't know, alive, I guess is the best way to put it." He pointed to the screen. "Where did this come from?"

"Rydberg brought it," she answered, "But it only receives. What do you mean, the city's alive?"

"Watch this," Derec said, and ran full speed across the room, banging into the far wall. The wall gave with him, caving inward, then gently pushed itself back to a solid position.

"I laid awake all night worrying about you, while you were discovering the walls are made of rubber?" she asked loudly.

He turned to her, smiling. "Did you *really* worry about me?"

"No," she replied. "What else?"

He walked over and sat on the couch with her, his tones hushed. "I saw the city building itself, literally extruding itself from the ground. I tried to go down there, but Avernus caught me. I think he's in charge down there. The only thing I can figure is that there are immense mining operations underway below ground and that the buildings are positronic, some kind of cellular robots that make up a complete whole. It's fascinating!"

Katherine was unimpressed. "Did you find a way out of here?"

He shook his head. "Not yet," he answered, "but I don't really think that's going to be a problem."

"That's because you're so eaten up with your robot friends you *can't* think of anything else!" She suddenly jerked her head toward the wall. "If the walls are robots, I wonder if they can hear us now?"

Just then the screen on the table came to life, Rydberg's face filling it. "So, you are back, Derec," he said. "Good. Prepare yourselves. An honor guard is coming right now to bring you to your preliminary trial."

"Trial?" Derec said.

"Uh oh," Katherine said, putting a hand to her mouth. "That may be my fault. I all but dared them to put us on trial."

"But we haven't had a chance to investigate yet."

She shrugged. "I was trying to find if we could have access to outside communications." She snapped her fingers. "Maybe this means we're going to get it."

"Yeah . . . maybe," Derec said, but he was skeptical. Robot City was too precious a gem to be hanging out in the ether for anyone to pluck. At this point, he wasn't even sure if he *wanted* to communicate with the outside.

He looked at the screen. It had already gone blank. "Whatever the reason," he said, "I believe we're going to get some answers at this point."

"Let's hope they're answers we can live with," she sighed. "I don't want to spend the rest of my life here."

Within minutes, the utility robot was knocking on the door. Derec hurried to open it. Euler greeted him, accompanied by a supervisor robot he'd not seen before. This one was the robot most closely molded to a human that Derec had seen, with chiseled, though blank, mannequin-like features.

"Friend Derec," Euler said, "Friend Katherine Burgess, may I present Arion, who will be in attendance at our meeting."

"Pleased to meet you," Derec said.

"Rydberg called it a trial," Katherine said.

"This is a great moment for us here," Arion said. "I trust that your stay so far has been satisfactory. I am doing my best with what little time I have to try and prepare some entertainment for you. We know that humans enjoy mind diversions."

"We'd appreciate anything you could do," Derec said.

"Sure," Katherine said. "How about conjuring up a radio for us to call the outside for help?"

"Oh, that's quite impossible," Arion said.

"That's what I thought," Katherine answered.

"I have a present for each of you," Euler said, extending his right arm. "Then we must be off to the meeting."

Derec moved to the robot. His pincers held two large watches, dangling on gold chains. "You may know the time here now," Euler said. "It is of importance to humans, and so, to us. We will do more to make you feel comfortable in this regard."

Derec took the watches, giving one of them to Katherine. They had square faces encased in gold. On both of them, the LCD faces read 3:35. "They run on a twenty-four hour day," said Euler. "We thought it would be more comfortable for you if we adjusted the length of our hour than if you had to adjust to a twenty-and-one-half hour day. Our hours, decads, and centads are approximately eighty-five percent of standard." Derec walked out onto the veranda and looked into the sky. The sun had already passed its apex and was slowly crawling toward the eventual shadows of evening.

"Right on the money," he said, returning to the apartment.

"You doubted it?" Arion asked, looking at Euler.

"Do you understand now?" Euler said to him.

"Interesting," Arion said, cocking his head in an almost human fashion.

"We must go," Euler said and hurried out of the apartment, the others following.

They rode the elevator to street level and boarded a multi-car tram that had no apparent driver. It started off immediately when they were seated. Euler turned to Derec, who sat, with Katherine, behind him and Arion. "You put yourself in extreme danger last night," the robot said. "Why?"

"I've a better question," Derec returned. "If this is such a perfect human world, why was it so dangerous?"

"Spacer worlds conquered weather problems eons ago," Katherine interjected. "For you to have them in such an advanced culture makes no sense."

Arion turned to her and bowed his head. "Thank you for calling our culture advanced."

"The weather," Euler said, "is quite honestly part of our overall problem right now. It is under our control, but also not under our control. Unfortunately, for security reasons, we cannot discuss it in detail."

"Great," Katherine said. "Everybody can do something about the weather, but nobody talks about it."

"To answer your original question," Derec told Euler, as he watched them move in a direct line toward the tower where they had initially materialized, "I have no memory and no past. My curiosity, my search for answers about myself, leads me to do things not necessarily in my best interest."

"Amnesia?" Euler asked. "Or something else?"

Derec looked at him in surprise. "What else?"

The robot answered his question with another question, an old one. "How, then, did you come to our planet?"

Derec realized that the robot was playing word games with him that tied directly to the word games Derec had initiated the night before. He decided to keep playing. "What did the dead man, David, say when you asked him that question?"

"He said he didn't know," Euler replied, and turned back around in his seat. Over his shoulder, he said, "He claimed he'd had amnesia."

The tram came to a halt beside the mammoth pyramid that dominated the landscape of Robot City, the place the inhabitants called the Compass Tower. Katherine put a hand on Derec's arm, squeezing, and he knew she had the same fear that he'd felt. Here, about halfway up the tower, was where they had hidden the Key to Perihelion that had brought them to the city. Had the robots found it? Were they confronting them with the evidence, or, worse yet, taking it away?

But Euler said nothing of the Key. Instead, he simply climbed from the tram and led them directly to the base of the tower, a tower that Derec had surmised was solid.

He'd never been more wrong.

At the robot's approach, an entire block of the solid matter that formed the base simply melted away, leaving a gently sloping runway leading into the structure, another example of Derec's theory about the intelligence of the building materials themselves.

They moved into the pyramid through a short, dark hallway that emptied into a maze of criss-crossing aisles and stairs that, in turn, led off in all directions within the structure.

"Try and memorize our path," Derec whispered to Katherine. "Just in case."

"In case of what?" she asked. "In case you haven't figured it out, we're not going anywhere."

"This is the most important building in our city," Euler said, as he took them up a series of stairs and escalators that zig-zagged at every landing and culminated in a long, well-lit hallway. "This is where decisions are made, where . . . understanding takes place."

They walked the hall, Arion hurrying ahead and disappearing down some stairs. The surrounding walls glowed lightly, with connecting hallways intersecting every ten feet.

They followed Arion's path, changing direction several times before finding themselves standing in a large, well-lit room whose four walls angled in toward a ceiling, fifteen meters above, that poured in sunshine like a skylight.

The floor of the room was tiled in the form of a large

compass, its four points forming the cornerstones of Robot City. In the center of the compass, under the direct rays of the sun, stood six robots in a circle, arms outstretched, their pincers grasping those of their neighbors on either side with space left for one more—Euler.

"This is the place where we seek perfection," Euler said, and joined the circle, closing it.

"It's almost religious," Derec whispered to Katherine.

"Yeah," she replied. "It give me the creeps."

Derec looked around the room. There were no chairs or tables, nothing upon which a human being could rest. The walls were inset with CRTs jammed side to side around the entire perimeter. Each screen showed its own view of Robot City. Many showed excavation sites, the large movers pushing and leveling soil. Other pictures were of the extrusion plant he had visited, and he was led to conjecture that there might be more than one. There were pictures of the reservoir he had splashed into, and strange, underground pictures taken through the eyes of roving cambots that showed mining tunnels, kilometer after kilometer of deserted tunnel. And finally, many of the screens simply showed the pink-tinged blue of the sky.

"You have come to this place," Euler said loudly, "to help us in our search for correctness, for perfection, for completeness. We are the keys—human and robot—to the synergy of spirit. Synnoetics is our goal. I will introduce the rest of us and we will begin."

"Synnoetics?" Katherine whispered.

"Man and machine," Derec replied, "the whole greater than the sum of the parts."

"It *is* religious!" she rasped. "And how did you know that?"

Derec shrugged. "This all feels so . . . comfortable to me."

"You know Rydberg," Euler said, "and Avernus and Arion." The robots nodded as their names were called. "The rest of us . . . Waldeyer . . ."

"Good day," said a squat, roundish robot with wheels.

"Dante . . ."

"I welcome you," Dante said, his telescopic eyes sticking out several inches from his dome.

"And Wohler."

A magnificent golden machine bowed formally without removing his pincers from his neighbors'. "We are honored," Wohler said.

"We will answer what questions we can from you," Euler said, "and hope that you will do the same."

"If, as you say," Derec told them, "we are all looking for truth and perfection, then our meeting will be fruitful. I would like to begin by asking you why there are certain areas of life here that you will not discuss with us."

Rydberg spoke. "We are in a standby security mode that renders certain information classified by our programming."

"Did our arrival prompt the institution of the security mode?" Katherine asked.

"No," Euler said. "It was in effect when you arrived. If, in fact, you arrived when you said you did. We must ask you again how you came to be here."

Derec decided to try a little truth. It couldn't hurt as long as no mention was made of the Key. Perhaps a dose of the truth might get them to open up about the Key's existence. "We materialized out of thin air atop this very building."

"And where were you before that?" Wohler, the gold one, asked.

Derec walked slowly around the circle, studying his questioners. "A Spacer way station named Rockliffe near Nexon, right on the edge of the Settlement Worlds quarantine zone."

Arion, the mannequin, asked, "What means, then, did you use to get from one place to the other?"

"No means," Derec said. "We were simply transported here."

There was silence for a moment. "This does not coordinate with any information extant in memory," Avernus said, his large dome following Derec's progress around the circle.

"You've found no ship that could have brought us," Derec

said, "and I'm sure you've searched."

"That is correct," Euler said, "and our radar picked up no activity that could have been construed to be a vessel in our atmosphere."

"I can't explain it beyond that," Derec said. "Now, you answer a question for me. Where did you come from?"

"Who are you addressing?" Euler asked.

"All of you," Derec said.

Avernus answered. "All of them except for me were constructed here, on Robot City," he said. "I was . . . awakened here, but believe I was constructed elsewhere."

"Where?"

"I do not know," the large robot replied. "My first i/o memories are of this place. Nothing in my pre-programming suggested anything of an origin."

"Are you trying to say," Katherine broke in, "that all of you know nothing but the company of other robots? That your entire existence is here?"

"Correct," Rydberg said. "Our master programming is well aware of human beings and their societies, but no formal relationship exists between our species."

"Then how did you come to build this place?" Derec asked. "How then, did it become important to you to make a world for humans?"

"We are incomplete without human beings," Waldeyer said, his squat dome swiveling to Derec and then Katherine. "The very laws that govern our existence revolve around human interaction. We exist to serve independent thought, the higher realms of creativity that we are incapable of alone. We discovered this very quickly, without being told. Alone, we simply exist to no end, no purpose. Even artificial intelligence must have a reason to utilize itself. This world is the first utilization of that intelligence. We've been building it for humans, in order to make the perfect atmosphere in which human creativity can flourish to the greater completeness of us all. Without this world we are nothing.

With it, we are vital contributing factors to the ongoing evolution of the universe."

"Why would that matter to you?" Katherine asked.

"I have a theory about that," Dante said, his elongated eyes glowing bright yellow. "We are the product, the child if you will, of higher realms of creative thought. It seems impossible that the drives of that creative thought *wouldn't* permeate every aspect of our programming. We want for nothing. We desire nothing. Yet, the incompleteness of our inactivity makes us . . . feel, for lack of a better word, useless and extraneous. Given the total freedom of our own world, we were driven to function in service."

Derec suddenly felt a terrible sadness well up in him for these unhappy creatures of man's intelligence. "You've done all this, even though you never knew if any people would come here?"

"That is correct," Euler said. "Then David came, and we thought that all would be right. Then came his death, then the calamities, then you . . . suspects to murder. We never meant for anything to be this way."

"When you say calamities," Derec said, "are you speaking of the problems with the storms?"

"Yes," Rydberg said. "The rains threaten our civilization itself, and it's all our own fault. We are breaking apart from the inside out, with nothing to be done about it."

"I don't understand," Derec said.

"We don't expect you to, nor can we tell you why it must be this way," Euler said.

Derec thought about the hot air pumping through the reservoir. "Is the city's rapid growth rate normal?" he asked.

"No," Euler said. "It coincides with David's death."

"Is it because of David's death?"

"We do not know the answer to that," Euler said.

"Wait a moment," Katherine said, walking away from the circle to sit on the floor, her back up against the north wall. "I want to talk to you about our connection with all this . . .

and why Rydberg called this a preliminary trial."

"You were the one who first mentioned the concept of a trial," the robot replied, leaning out of the circle to stare at her. "I only used that term to make you feel comfortable."

"Okay," she said. "I'll play. You say this is a civilization of robots that have never had human interaction, yet obviously someone gave you your initial programming and ability to perform the work on this city."

"Someone . . . yes," Euler said.

"Someone who's in charge," she said.

"No," Euler said. "We are now in group communication with our master programming unit, but it simply provides us with information from which logical decisions are made. Our overall philosophy is service; our means are logical. Other than that, our society has no direction."

"Then why put us on trial at all?" she asked.

"Respect for human life is our First Law," Rydberg said. "When we envisioned our perfect human/robot world, we saw a world in which all shared respect for the First Law. We envisioned a system of humanics that would guide human behavior, just as the Laws of Robotics guide our behavior. Of course, we have been working entirely from theory, but we have made a preliminary list of three laws that would provide the basis for an understanding of humans."

"Cute," Katherine said. "Now they want us to follow the Laws of Robotics."

Derec interrupted her complaint. "Wait. Let's see what they've come up with."

"Thank you, Friend Derec. Our provisional First Law of Humanics is: A human being may not injure another human being, or, through inaction, allow a human being to come to harm."

"Admirable," conceded Derec, "even if it isn't always obeyed. What is your Second Law?"

Rydberg's hesitation before answering gave Derec the

clear impression that the robot wanted to ask a question of its own, but his took precedence under the Second Law of Robotics.

"The Second Law of Humanics is: A human being must give only reasonable orders to a robot and require nothing of it that would needlessly put it into the kind of dilemma that might cause it harm or discomfort."

"Still admirable, but still too altruistic to be always obeyed. And the third?"

"The Third Law of Humanics is: A human being must not harm a robot, or, through inaction, allow a robot to come to harm, unless such harm is needed to keep a human being from harm or to allow a vital order to be carried out."

"Not only is your experience with humans limited, so is your programming," Derec said, shaking his head. "These 'laws' might describe a utopian society of humans and robots, but they certainly don't describe the way humans really behave."

"We have become aware of that," said Rydberg. "Obviously, we are going to have to reconsider our conclusions. Since your arrival we have been subjected to human lies and deceit, concepts beyond our limited understanding."

"But the First Law must stand!" Avernus said loudly, his red photocells glowing brightly. "Human or robot, all are subject to respect for life."

"We certainly aren't arguing that point," Derec said.

"No!" Katherine said, standing angrily and walking back to the circle. "What we're talking about is the lack of respect with which *we're* being treated here!"

"Kath . . ." Derec began.

"Shut up," Katherine said. "I've been listening to you having wonderful little philosophical conversations with your robot buddies, and I'm getting a little tired of it. Listen, folks. First thing, I demand that you give us access to communications with the outside and that you let us leave. You have no authority to hold us here."

"This is our world," Euler said. "We mean no offense, but all societies are governed by laws, and we fear you have broken our greatest law."

"And what if we have?" she asked. "What happens then?"

"Well," Euler said. "We would do nothing more than keep you from the society of other humans who you could harm."

"Great. So, how do you prove we did anything in order to hold us?"

"Process of elimination," Waldeyer said. "Friend Derec has previously suggested some other possible avenues of explanation, but we feel it is incumbent upon both of you to explore them—not because we are trying to make it difficult for you, but because we respect your creative intelligence more than we respect our own deductive intelligence in an area like this."

Derec watched as Katherine ran hands through her long black hair and took several deep breaths as she tried to get herself together and in a position to work with this. "All right," she said, more calmly. "You said before that you won't let us see the body."

"No," Euler said. "We said that we *can't* let you see the body."

"Why?"

There was silence. Finally Rydberg spoke. "We don't know where it is," he said. "The city began replicating too quickly and we lost it."

"Lost it?" Derec said.

Derec knew it was impossible for a robot to be or look embarrassed, but that was exactly the feeling he was getting from the entire group.

"We really have no idea of where it is," Euler said.

Derec saw an opening and quickly took it. "In order to do this investigation and prove that we're innocent of any First Law transgressions, we *must* have freedom of movement around your city."

"We exist to protect your lives," Euler said. "You've been caught in the rains; you know how dangerous they are. We can't let you out under those conditions."

"Is there advance warning of the rain?" he asked.

"Yes," Rydberg said. "The clouds build in the late afternoon, and the rain comes at night."

"Suppose we promise to not go out when the conditions are unfavorable?" Derec asked.

Wohler, the golden robot, said, "What are human promises worth?"

Katherine pushed her way beneath the hands of the robots to stand in the center of the circle. "What are our lives worth without freedom?"

"Freedom," Wohler echoed.

A dark cloud passed above the skylight, plunging the room into a gray, melancholy halflight, illumination provided by a score of CRT screens, many of them now showing pictures of madly roiling clouds.

The circle broke immediately, the robots, agitated, hurrying toward the door.

"Come," Euler said, motioning to the humans. "The rains are approaching. We must get you back to shelter. There is so much to do."

"What about my suggestion?" Derec called loudly to them.

"Hurry," Euler called, waving his arm as Derec and Katherine walked toward him. "We will think about it and let you know tomorrow."

"And if we can investigate and prove our innocence," Katherine said, "will you then let us contact the outside?"

Euler stood still and fixed her with his photocells. "Let me put it this way," he said. "If you don't prove your innocence, you'll *never* be allowed to contact the outside."

CHAPTER 5
A WITNESS

Derec sat before the CRT screen on the apartment table and watched the "entertainment" that Arion was providing him in the form, at this moment, of sentences and their grammatic diagrams. Before that it had been a compendium of various failed angle trisection theorems, and before that, an incredibly long list of the powers of ten and the various words that had been invented to describe the astronomical numbers those powers represented. It was an insomniac's nightmare.

It was a dark, gray morning, the air heavy with the chill of the night and the rain that had pounded Robot City for many hours. The sky was slate as the remnants of the night's devastation drifted slowly away on the wings of the morning.

He felt like a caged animal, his nerves jangling madly with the notion that he couldn't leave the apartment if he wanted to. They had been dropped off in the early evening after the meeting at the Compass Tower and hadn't seen a supervisor robot since. The CRT had no keyboard and only received whatever data they chose to show him from moment to moment. At this particular time, they apparently felt the need to amuse him; but the time filler of the viewscreen only increased his frustration.

He hadn't slept well. The apartment only had one bed and Katherine was using it. Derec slept on the couch. It had been too short for him, and that didn't make sleeping any easier.

But that wasn't the real reason he'd been awake.

It was the rain.

He couldn't get out of his head the fact that the reservoir had been nearly filled when he'd been flung into it the night before. How, then, could it possibly hold the immense amounts of water that continued to pour into it with each successive rainfall? He'd worried over that point: the more rain, the greater the worry. The fact that the supervisors hadn't contacted him since before the storm seemed ominous. All of their efforts seemed to revolve around the weather problems.

How did the weather tie in with the rapid growth rate of the city? Were the two linked?

"You're up early," came Katherine's voice behind him.

He turned to see her, face soft from sleep, framed by the diffused light. She looked good, a night's sleep bringing out her natural beauty. She was wrapped in the pale green cover from her bed. He wondered idly what she was wearing beneath it, then turned unconsciously to his awakening, after the explosion in Aranimas's ship, in the medical wing of the Rockliffe Station to find her naked on the bed beside. Embarrassed, he pushed that thought aside, but its residue left another thought from that time, something he had completely forgotten about.

"Can I ask you a question?" he said.

Her face darkened and he watched her tighten up. "What is it?" she asked.

"When we were at Rockliffe, Dr. Galen mentioned you had a chronic condition," he said. "Later, when he began to talk about it, you shut him up."

She walked up to look at the screen, refusing to meet his gaze. "You're mistaken," she said. "I'm fine . . . the picture of health."

She turned slightly from him, and there seemed to be a small catch in her voice. When she turned back, her face was set firm, quite unlike the vulnerable morning creature he'd seen a moment ago. "What's happening on the screen?" she asked.

He looked. A pleasant, always changing pattern of computer generated images was juicing through the CRT, accompanied by a random melody bleeped out of the machine's tiny speaker.

"You make it very hard for me to believe you," he said, ignoring the screen. "Why, when we need total honesty and trust between us, do I feel that you're holding back vital information from me?"

"You're just paranoid," she said, and he could tell he was going to get nothing from her. "And if you don't change the subject quickly, I'm going to find myself getting angry, and that's no way to start the day."

He reluctantly agreed. "I'm worried about the rains," he said. "They were worse last night than the night before."

She sat at the table with him. "Well, if this place is getting ready to have major problems, I hope we're out of here before they happen. We've got to get something going with the murder investigation."

"Do you know what makes rain?" he asked, ignoring the issue of the murder.

"What has that got to do with our investigation?" she asked, on edge.

"Nothing," he said. "I'm just wondering about these rains, I . . ."

"Don't say it," she replied holding up a hand. "You're worried about your robot friends. Well, let me tell you something, your friends are in the process of keeping us locked up for the rest of our lives . . ."

"Not locked up, surely," he interrupted.

"This is serious!" she said, angry now. "We have a very good chance of being kept prisoner here for life. You know, once they make a decision like that, I see no reason that they would ever change it. Don't you understand the gravity of the situation?"

He looked at her calmly, placing a hand over hers on the

table. She drew it away, and he felt his own anger rise, then rapidly subside. "I understand the problem," he explained, "but I fear the problem with the city is more pressing, more . . . immediate."

"But it's not *our* problem. The murder is."

"Indulge me," he said. "Let's talk about weather for just a minute."

She sighed, shaking her head. "Let's see what I remember," she said. "Molecules respond to heat, separating, moving more quickly. Water molecules are no exception. On a hot day, they rise into the atmosphere and cling to dust particles in the air. When they rise into the cooler atmosphere, they turn into clouds. When the clouds get too heavy, too full of water, they return to the ground in the form of rain."

"Okay," he said. "And wind is simply the interplay of heat and cold in the atmosphere."

She shrugged. "The cold, heavier air pushes down and forces the warm air to move—wind."

"I think I'm beginning to see a connection," he said, excited. "Look. Robot City is building at a furious pace, sending a great deal of dust into the atmosphere." He thought about the reservoir. "Meanwhile, they are somehow liberating a great deal of water from the mining processes that are needed to build the city. Along with the mining processes comes a tremendous amount of kinetic energy, heat, which they are venting into the atmosphere near the water, forcing the heated molecules to rise as water vapor and cling to the dust particles that are thick in the atmosphere right now. At night, the temperature cools down a great deal . . ."

"That could be an uncompensated ozone layer," she said.

He pointed to her. "Ozone. That's what seals in our atmosphere. As goes the ozone layer, so go our temperature inversions. So, it cools at night, the rain clouds forming, the cool air bringing on the big winds, and the rain falls."

"So," Katherine said, "if they slowed down the building pace, it could slow down the weather."

"It seems logical to me," he replied.

"So why don't they do it?"

"That's the mystery, isn't it?"

The door slid open and Wohler, the golden robot, moved into the room, flanked on either side by smaller robots.

"Good morning," Wohler said. "I trust your sleep-time was beneficial."

"You're going to have to learn to knock before you come barging in here," Katherine said. "Now go out and do it again."

Derec watched the robot dutifully march outside the door and slide it closed. He knew that Katherine was simply venting frustration. On Spacer worlds, robots were considered simply part of the furniture and their presence was not thought about in terms of privacy.

There was a gentle tapping on the door, the nature of the material muffling the sound somewhat.

"Come in," Katherine said with satisfaction, and the door slid open, the robots reentering.

"Is this the preferred method of treatment in future?" Wohler asked.

"It is," she replied.

"Very well," the robot said, then noticed Derec's sleeping covers on the sofa. "Should these be returned to the bedroom?"

"You only provided us with one bed," Derec replied. "I slept out here."

Wohler moved farther into the room, coming up near the table. "Did we err? Was the sleeping space too small . . ."

"Katherine and I would simply like . . . separate places to sleep," Derec said.

"Privacy?" Wohler asked. "As with the knocking on the door?"

"Yes," Katherine said, and he could tell she was unwilling to delve into the social aspects of human sleeping arrangements, so he left it alone, too.

"On-line time is a matter of priorities right now," the robot said, "but we will see if we can arrange something for you that is more private."

"Thanks," Derec said. "And if it takes another day to arrange it, that's all right with me. It's Katherine's turn to sleep on the couch tonight."

"What?" she said loudly. Derec grinned broadly at her. She wasn't amused.

He quickly changed the subject. "What brings you here this morning, Wohler?" he asked. "Have you reached a decision about our requests of yesterday?"

"Yes," the robot replied. "And it is our sincerest wish that the decision be one that all of us can accept. First, in addressing the issue of your investigation and freedom of movement. We conferred at as great a length as time would permit under the present circumstances, and decided that, despite your flaws, you *are* human, and that fact in and of itself demands that we give you the benefit of the doubt in this situation. Many of our number were concerned about your veracity, or lack of it, but I reminded them that a great *human* philosopher once said, 'Isn't it better to have men being ungrateful than to miss a chance to do good?' And so my fellows voted to do good in this regard."

"Excellent," Derec said.

"But . . ." Katherine helped.

"Indeed," Wohler returned. "It is my place to philosophize in any given situation, and I need remind you now that one must always be prepared to take bad along with good."

"Just get on with it," Katherine said.

Wohler nodded. "On the matter of your safety, and your . . . unpredictability, it was decided that each of you would have a robot companion to . . . help you in your investigations."

"You mean to guard us," Katherine said.

"Merely a matter of semantics," Wohler countered, and Derec could tell that the robot had been geared for diplomacy. "Actually, in this case, I believe you may find these robots more useful as assistants than as protection. In fact, one of them was present during the death of David and the subsequent confusion."

Katherine perked up. "Really? Which one?"

The robot to Wohler's left came forward. Its body was tubular, its dome a series of bristling sensors and photocells. Without arms, it seemed useless in almost any sense.

"What are you called?" Katherine asked the machine.

The machine's tones were clipped and precise. "I am Event Recorder B-23, Model 13 Alpha 4."

"I'll call you Eve, if that's all right," Katherine said, standing and wrapping her blanket a little tighter around herself. She looked at Derec. "I want this one."

"Fine," Derec said, then to the other, "come here."

The robot moved up close to him. "You'll answer to Rec."

"Rec," the robot repeated.

"We call these robots witnesses," Wohler said. "Their only function is to witness events precisely for later reporting."

"That's why they have no arms," Derec said.

"Correct," Wohler replied. "They are unequipped to do anything but witness. Once involvement begins on any level, the witness function falters in any creature. These robots only witness and report. They will know the how of almost everything, but never the why. They will answer all of your questions to the best of their ability, but again, they are unable to make any second-level connections by putting events together to form reasons."

"I'm going to go get dressed," Katherine said, the happiest Derec had seen her in days. She hurried out of the room, disappearing down the hall to the bedroom.

"Where will we be denied access?" Derec asked. "Or is the entire planet open to us?"

"Alas, no," Wohler said. "You will be denied access to certain parts of the city and certain operations. Your witness, however, will tell you when you've stepped into dangerous water, as it were."

"What are the chances of me getting around a terminal,"

Derec asked, "and talking to the central core?"

"The central core has sealed itself off because of our present state of emergency," Wohler said. "It will not accept input from any sources save the supervisors, and we are unable to help you in this regard."

"How do the day-to-day operations survive?" he asked.

"Essential information can be gathered through any terminal," the robot answered. "But input is limited."

"You don't mind if I try?"

"That is between you and the central core. We all have our jobs to do. All that we insist upon is that you honor your commitment to come back here when the rains approach. We must put your safety above all else. Having failed in this regard with your predecessor, we perhaps err on the side of caution. But all privileges will be denied should this directive be overlooked or ignored."

"I understand," Derec replied, "and will respect your wishes."

"Your words, unfortunately, mean very little right now," the robot said, turning to the door, his head swiveling back to Derec. "By your deeds we will judge you in future. As an Earth philosopher once said, 'The quality of a life is determined by its activities.' Now, I must go."

With that, Wohler moved quickly through the opening and departed hurriedly down the elevator. The activity bothered Derec; it said to him that things were not going well in Robot City. He had intended to ask Wohler about the effects of last night's rain, but then decided a first-hand look might be better and determined that Rec would take him where he wanted to go.

"There," Katherine said, coming down the hall to bustle around the room. She wore a blue one-piece that the dinner servo-robot had brought with it the night before. "Finally, we can start moving in a positive direction. Where do you want to start?"

"I thought I'd go down to the reservoir," he replied, "and see how much rain fell last night."

She stopped walking and stared, unbelieving, at him. "Don't you realize that every moment is precious right now? We need to find that body and see what happened. It could be . . . decomposing or something at this very minute."

"I've got to see if there was any damage," he said. "I'll try and join you later."

"Never mind," she said angrily, and walked quickly to the door. "Satisfy your stupid urges. I don't *want* you with me. You'll just get in the way anyhow. Come on, Eve. We've got a *corpus delecti* to find."

She walked out of the apartment without a backward glance and was gone, Derec frowning after her. He couldn't help the way his feelings ran on this. He felt that so much of his own life, his own reasons for being, hinged upon the future of Robot City that its troubles seemed to be his own.

"I want to go to the reservoir," he told Rec. "Can you take me there?"

"Yes, Friend Derec," the robot answered, and they left together.

When they arrived at street level, Derec was disappointed to find that the supervisors hadn't left any transportation for him to use. A great deal of time would be wasted walking from place to place. Perhaps he could talk to Euler about it later, though he feared that the reasons had much to do with keeping him from going very far from home.

"Do you want to go the most direct route?" the witness asked him.

"Yes, of course," Derec said as they set out walking. "Let me ask you a question. Is the rain a result of the work being done on the city?"

"For the most part," Rec answered through a speaker located on Derec's side of his dome. "It is also the rainy season here."

"If they slowed down the building, would it slow down the rain?"

"I do not know."

Derec was going about this wrong, asking the wrong

questions of a witness. "How does the city make rain?" he asked.

The robot began talking, recalling information in an encyclopedic fashion. "Olivine is mined below ground and crushed in vacuum, releasing carbon, hydrogen, oxygen, and nitrogen, from which water vapor, carbon dioxide, methane gas, and traces of other chemicals are liberated. Iron ore is also being mined for building materials, along with petroleum products for plastics . . ."

"Plastics?" Derec asked.

"Plastics are used as alloys in making the material from which the city is constructed. Do you wish me to go on with my previous line of witnessing?"

"Let me tell you," Derec said, "and you tell me if I'm right. Water vapor, along with the heat energy from the mining process, is pumped into the air, heat also being pumped into the reservoir. The CO_2 is bled into the forest to help growth. The reason that the weather is so rainy now is that the city is growing too fast, giving off too much heat, dust, and water."

"I do not know why the weather is *so* rainy right now," Rec said. "I do not even understand what *so* rainy means. The other statements you made are juxtapositional with statements I heard Supervisor Avernus make, which I assume to be correct."

"Fine," Derec said. "Is there a problem with the ozone layer?"

"Problem?" the robot asked.

Derec rephrased. "Is any work being done on the ozone layer?"

"I do not know," Rec said, "although I did hear Supervisor Avernus say on one occasion that the 'ozone layer needs to be increased photochemically to ten parts per million.'"

"Good," Derec said. "Very good."

"You are pleased with my witnessing?" Rec asked.

"Yes," Derec replied. "Will the supervisors be asking you to witness later what we've discussed?"

"That is my function, Friend Derec."

They walked for nearly an hour by Derec's watch, the city still subtly changing around them. It sometimes took a while to get information out of the witness, but if questions were phrased properly, Derec found Rec an endless source of information, and he wondered how Katherine was faring with her witness.

Derec knew they were nearing the reservoir long before they arrived there. A long stream of robots was moving toward and away from the site, followed by large vehicles bearing slabs of city building material.

They walked into an area sonorous with activity, echoes raising the pitch enough that Derec covered his ears against the din. Within the confines of the reservoir area, his worst fears were realized. The water had reached the top of the pool and was splashing over slightly in various areas.

For their part, the robots were doing their best to stop it. Large machines, obviously converted from mining work, had been modified to lift huge slabs of the building material to the top of the pool, where utility robots with laser torches were welding the higher sections together, trying for more room, bathing the area in various sections in showers of yellow sparks.

It was a massive job, the reservoir covering many acres, as the robots worked frantically to finish before the next rain. And to Derec's mind, this could be no more than a stopgap measure, for unless the rain was halted, it would overflow even the extra section in a day or two.

"What happens if the water overflows?" he asked Rec.

"I am unable to speculate on such matters, Friend Derec," the robot said. "It is not overflowing. When it does, I will witness."

"Right," Derec said, and moved forward, closing on the workers.

"Do not get too close," Rec called. "It is dangerous for you."

Derec ignored him and moved closer, recognizing Euler,

who was helping with the movement of a slab. He was directing a large, heavy-based machine with a telescoping arm that held a six-by-six-meter slab in magnetic grips. He was holding his pincers at the approximate distance the arm had yet to travel so that it would be flush with the edge of the pool and the slab next to it. Utility robots physically guided the slabs to the ground and held them so the welders could set to work immediately.

"Euler!" Derec called, the robot jerking to the sound of his name.

"It is too dangerous for you here!" Euler called back, waving him away. "We have no safety controls over this area!"

"I'll only stay a centad," Derec said, moving up close to him. He could look past the end of the last slab and see the dark waters churning the top of the pool. In the distance, all around the reservoir, he could see the same operation being repeated by other crews.

"What are you doing here?" Euler asked him.

"I had to see for myself," Derec answered. "I knew the levels were rising. Why don't you stop the building pace and let these waters recede?"

"I can't tell you why," Euler said.

"But what happens when this overflows?"

"We lose the treatment plant," Euler said, holding his pincers up to signify to the arm to stop moving the slab. Then he motioned toward the ground, the arm bringing the slab down very slowly. "We lose much of our mining operations. We lose a great many miners. We will have failed."

"Then stop the building!"

"We can't!"

Just then, a utility robot working the slab was bumped slightly by the moving metal and lost its footing on the wet floor. Soundlessly and without drama, it slipped from the edge of the pool and fell into the dark waters, disappearing immediately.

Everything stopped.

Euler pushed past Derec to hurry to the water's edge, where he stood, head down, watching. The rest of the crew did the same, lining up quietly beside the water. Derec moved to join Euler.

"I'm sorry," he said.

Euler slowly turned his head to look at the boy, not saying anything for a long time. "I should have paid more attention," he said.

"How deep is the water?" Derec asked.

"Very deep," Euler replied. "I was talking with you and didn't give the job my complete attention."

"Can it be saved?"

"Had there been more time," Euler said, "the job would have been studied for safety and feasibility and this wouldn't have happened. Had I known better, I wouldn't have allowed you to come so close. A robot is lost, and the supervisor is to blame."

"There was nothing you could have done," Derec said.

"A robot is dead today," Euler told him. "I will not answer any more of your questions right now."

"If the city keeps moving," Katherine asked, "how can you take me to the location of the murder?"

"Triangulation," Eve, the witness, said. "Using the Compass Tower as one point and the exact position of the sun at a given time as another point, my sensors are able to triangulate the position where I first witnessed the body. The time is the only real factor at this point. We must gauge the sun in exactly 13.24 decads to get the position right."

They were walking through the city, Katherine feeling a mixture of fear and exuberance at her first solo trip outside. They were walking high up, above many of the buildings, bridges between structures seemingly growing for her to walk across, then melting away after her passage. Eve apparently needed the height in order to take the precise measurements.

Katherine was angry at Derec for his lack of interest in their predicament, but she knew him well enough to know how stubborn he could be. She, in fact, knew him far better than he knew himself, and that was maddening. They were caught in a web of intrigue that existed on a massive level, and as long as she was trapped there, she had to play the situation with as much control as she could muster. And that included not telling Derec any more about his life than he could figure out for himself. Her own existence was at stake, and until she could escape the maze that had locked up their activities, she desperately feared saying anything more.

She *had* to get away from Robot City. The pain had increased since her arrival here, and, for the first time in her life, death was a topic she found herself dwelling upon.

And her only crime was love.

She felt the tears begin to well up and fought them back with an iron will. They wouldn't help her here. Nothing would, except her own tenacity and intelligence.

"Tell me about your involvement in David's death," she asked Eve, who was busy calibrating against the sun.

"In approximately two decads," the robot said, "it will have happened exactly nine days ago. We go down from here."

Eve moved directly to the corner of the six-story structure they were standing upon, and railed stairs formed for them to walk down. As they descended, the robot continued talking.

"I was called upon to witness the attempts to free Friend David from an enclosed room."

"An enclosed room?" Katherine said. "I've never heard about this. How could he get trapped like that in this place?"

"The room grew around him." Eve said. They reached street level and the robot headed west, away from the Compass Tower. "It sealed him in and wouldn't let him leave."

"Why?"

"I do not know."

"Does anyone know?"

"I do not know."

"All right," Katherine said, watching a team of robots carry what looked to be gymnasium equipment into one of the buildings. "Just report what you saw."

"Gladly. I was called upon to witness the attempt to free Friend David from the sealed room. When I arrived, Supervisor Dante was already on the scene . . ." The robot stopped moving and for several seconds stared up into the sun. "Precisely here." Eve pointed to a section of the street. "Friend David was caught inside the structure and we could hear him shouting to be let out."

"Who?"

"Myself, Supervisor Dante, a utility robot with a torch, and another household utility robot who first discovered Friend David's problem."

"What happened then?"

"Then Supervisor Dante asked Utility Robot #237-5 if the laser torch was safe to use in such close proximity to a human being, and Utility Robot #237-5 assured him that it was. At that point, Supervisor Dante tried to reason with the room to release Friend David, and failing that, he requested that the room be cut into with the torch."

"And that request was complied with?"

"Yes. Supervisor Dante, in fact, asked Utility Robot #237-5 to complete the project quickly."

"Why?"

"I do not know."

Katherine thought about the nature of the witness and asked another question. "Were there any other events that coincided with this event?"

"Yes," Eve said. "Food Services complained that Friend David could not be served lunch on time and inquired if that would be dangerous to his health; several of the supervisors were meeting in the Compass Tower to discuss ways in which Friend David might have come to the city without their knowledge; and the city itself was put on general security alert."

"Does a general security alert alter the way in which functions are performed?" she asked.

"Yes. We were all called to other emergency duties, and were here only because of the danger to Friend David and the need to release him."

"Which you did."

"Not me," Eve said. "I only witnessed. But Friend David was freed from the enclosed room."

"Did you notice anything odd at that point?"

"Odd? Friend Katherine, I can only. . ."

"I know," she interrupted, a touch frustrated. "You only witness. Then tell me exactly what happened."

"Supervisor Dante asked Friend David to return to his apartment because a security alert had been called. Friend David said that he was not ready to return to his apartment, that he had business to do. Then he complained of a headache. Then he started laughing and walked away. Utility Robot #237-5 then asked Supervisor Dante if Friend David should be apprehended, and Supervisor Dante said he had weighed the priorities and had decided that the security alert took precedence and ordered us to proceed to our emergency duties, which, in my case, involved witnessing something that I am not at liberty to discuss with you."

"Then what?" Katherine asked, anxious.

"Then I performed the security duty that I had been assigned."

"No, no," Katherine said. "What happened then in regard to David?"

"Approximately nine decads later, I was again called upon." Eve began moving quickly down the street, Katherine right behind, having to run to keep up. "I am taking you to the approximate place of the second incident," the robot called from a speaker set in the back of its dome. "I was called here, along with Supervisor Euler this time, by Utility Robot #716-14, who had discovered several waste control robots trying to take the body of Friend David away."

Eve moved quickly around a corner, then stopped abruptly, Katherine nearly running into the robot.

"Here," Eve said, "is the approximate place where the body was alleged to have fallen."

"Alleged?"

"It was no longer here upon my arrival."

"What story did the utility robot tell?"

"Utility Robot #716-14 said that he sent the waste control robots away, then examined Friend David for signs of life without success. During the course of the examination another room began to grow around the body and enclose it, at which point Utility Robot #716-14 removed himself before becoming trapped, and put in an emergency call to us. We returned to the scene together, but the body was gone. That is the last time anyone has seen Friend David."

"Were there signs of violence on the body?"

"Utility Robot #716-14 reported that the body appeared perfectly normal except for a small cut on the left foot. Since I can only report hearsay in this regard, I am unable to render this as an accurate examination."

Katherine leaned against the wall of a one-story parts depot, the wall giving slightly under her pressure. It seemed more than coincidence that David's plight in the sealed room and the alert conditions of the city happened concurrently—but how were they connected?

"Do you feel, then, that the body moved simply because the city moved it?" she asked.

"I cannot speculate on such a theory," the witness said, "but I heard Supervisor Euler make a pronouncement similar to yours—hearsay again."

"Given the growth rate of the city," Katherine said, "calculate how far and in what direction the body of David could have traveled if, indeed, the movement of the city took him from this place."

"Approximately ten and one-half blocks," Eve said without hesitation, "in *any* direction. The city works according to a plan that is not known to me."

"Ten and a half blocks," Katherine said low. "Well, it'll sure give me something to do to fill in the time." She looked at Eve's bristling dome. "Let's take a walk."

"That is your decision," the robot replied, as Katherine picked a direction at random and began walking, looking for what, she didn't know.

ACCESS DENIED was written in bold letters across the CRT, and it was a phrase Derec had run into over a dozen times in as many minutes.

He stood at a small counter set beside a large, open window. Through the billowing clouds of iron-red dust floating into the sky, he could see the long line of earthmovers inching their way along the rocky ground, the teeth of their heavy front diggers easily chewing up the ground to a depth of 70 centimeters, then laying out the mulch in a flat, even plain behind, holes filling, rises falling, the ground absolutely uniform behind. A series of heavy rollers completed the unique vehicles, packing the ground hard for the slab base of the city to push its way into that section as it was completed.

After leaving the reservoir and its tragedy behind, he had asked Rec to take him to the edge of the city. He had wanted to see for himself the creation of the cloud dust and also to try and find access to a terminal far out of the reach of the supervisors. The robot had been hesitant at first, but after Derec had assured him that he'd go no farther than city's edge, Rec had readily agreed.

But now that he was here, Derec resented the time it had taken to come this far out. The terminal had been a complete bust. He'd found himself able to access any amount of information when it came to this part of the city operation: troubleshooting info, repair info, time references, equipment specs, personnel delineation, and SOPs of all kinds; but beyond that, access was impossible.

He had tried various methods of obtaining passwords, but it seemed he was stymied before he got started. He came away with the impression that once the city was on alert, terminals became place-oriented, only able to pick up specific data as it related to their possible function in a given location. He found this difficult to believe, for if the robots were in total charge of access and passwords it belied the nature of their "perfect human world." It struck him that access would have to be humanly possible for very basic philosophical reasons.

But not here; not at this terminal.

So, where did that leave him? The rains still came, with or without his presence; the central core was still denied to him, and with it any answers it might possess; he was still a prisoner (a fact he *did* take seriously, despite Katherine's feelings); and he still knew nothing about his origins or reasons for being in Robot City.

That thought returned him to the basics. When he had visited the Compass Tower, Avernus had been pointed out as the first supervisor robot, the one that had initiated the construction of the other supervisors. Derec had been successful in determining the origin and destination of the water; now he would work on the origin of the city itself. The only place to start was with Avernus and the underground. The mining was needed to produce the raw materials to build the city. Everything else sprang from that foundation. He would go to the source—to Avernus.

He shut down the useless terminal and walked out of the otherwise bare room to find Rec intently studying the rising dust clouds, taking readings. It was his obsession.

"I want to go into the mines and speak with Avernus," he told the robot. "Is that acceptable?"

"I will take you to the mines, Friend Derec," Rec answered, "but from that point on, the decision will belong to Avernus."

"Fair enough," Derec said, and prepared for another long walk. Then he spotted one of the trams parked near the excavation and walked toward it. "Let's ride this time."

"We were not given this machine," Rec said. "It is not ours to take."

"Were you told *not* to let me take the machine?" Derec countered.

"No, but . . ."

"Then let's go."

Derec jumped in the front, but saw no controls with which to drive it. He knew that this was probably the means by which the robots working the movers got here, but the witness was unable to make that speculation and consequently folded up. "How does it work?"

"You speak your destination into the microphone," Rec said.

"The underground," Derec said, then shrugged at Rec.

Within seconds, the car lurched forward and moved speedily away from the digs.

They traveled quickly, moving through an entire section full of nothing but robot production facilities that were running full tilt, furiously trying to keep up with the record-setting building pace. As the number of buildings increased, so, too, did the number of robots to service those buildings and the people who didn't live in them. They passed vehicle after vehicle jammed full of new, functionally designed robots who stared all around, seeing their world for the first time.

They also passed other small forests and what seemed to be large sections of hydroponic greenhouses, for when large-scale food production became a reality. Then they whizzed past a large, open area that seemed to serve no function.

"What's that?" Derec asked.

"Nothing," Rec answered.

"I don't mean now," Derec said. "What's it going to be?"

"I do not often deal in potential," the robot replied, several red lights on his dome blinking madly, "but I recall Supervisor Euler once referring to this place as a future spaceport."

Derec was a bit taken aback. Robot City was absolutely unable to deal with incoming or outgoing ships in any form. It led him down another avenue.

"If the spaceport hasn't been constructed yet," he said, "where do you keep your hyperwave transmitters?"

He asked the question casually, knowing full well that Rec would undoubtedly tell him the information was classified; but he was totally unprepared for the answer he received.

"I do not know what a hyperwave transmitter is," the robot replied.

"A device designed for communication over long distances in space," Derec said. "Perhaps you call it something else."

"I have witnessed nothing designed to communicate beyond our atmosphere," Rec answered.

"You don't send and receive information from off-planet?"

"I know of no such instance," Rec replied. "We are self-contained here."

The tram jerked to a stop, jerking Derec's thoughts along with it. Somehow, it had never occurred to him that they really were trapped on this planet. The Key and its proper use suddenly became of paramount importance to him.

"We have arrived, Friend Derec," Rec said.

"So we have," Derec replied, getting slowly out of the car. What was going on here? Who created this place? And why? It was a pristine civilization removed from contact with anything beyond itself, yet its Spacer roots were obvious. Could David, the dead man, have been the creator?

He walked past the lines of robots carrying their damaged equipment, past the huge extruder and its never-ending ribbon of city, and stood at the entrance to the underground. He turned to see Rec standing beside him.

"Find Avernus," he said. "Tell him I want to speak with him. I don't want to break protocol by going somewhere off-limits to humans."

"Yes, Friend Derec," the robot answered and moved aside to commune with its net of radio communications.

Derec sat on the ground beside the doorway and watched the robots walking back and forth past him. He was beginning to feel like a useless appendage with nothing to do. He felt guilty even ordering the robots around; they had more important things to do.

He glanced at his watch. It was two in the afternoon, and soon they'd be approaching another night of rain, another useless night of speculation as the water level rose higher and higher. "We will have failed," Euler had said, and in that sentence the robot had spoken volumes. Like Derec, the supervisor knew that Robot City was a test, a test designed for all of then. If Euler and the others were unable to solve the problem of the rain, they would have failed in their attempt to build a workable world. He also knew that the salvation of this world would take a creative form of thought that most people felt robots incapable of. Perhaps that's where Derec fit in. Synnoetics, they had called it, the whole greater than the sum of the parts. For that to take place, Derec would have to begin by convincing the robots they had to confide in him despite their security measures.

"I'm extremely busy, Friend Derec," the voice said loudly. "What do you want of me?"

Derec looked up to see Avernus's massive form bending to fit in the door space.

"We need to speak of saving this place," Derec said. "We need to approach one another as equals, and not adversaries."

"You may have done murder, Derec," Avernus said. "I am not the equal of that."

"Neither is Euler," Derec replied, "but his inattention caused a robot to die today."

"You were also present."

Derec looked at the ground. "Y-yes," he said. "I had no right to bring that up."

"Tell me what you want of me."

"Answers," Derec said. "Understanding. I want to help with the city . . . the rains. I want someone to know and appreciate that."

The robot looked at him for a long moment, then motioned him inside. They walked down the stairs together and into the holding area, Rec following behind at a respectable distance. Avernus then took him aside, away from the activity, and made a seat for him by piling up a number of broken machines of various kinds.

Derec climbed atop the junk pile and sat, Avernus standing nearby. "We are in an emergency situation, and my programming limits my communication with you."

"I understand that," Derec replied. "I also know that many situations require judgment calls that you must sift through your logic circuits. I ask only that you think synnoetically."

"If you ask that of me," the robot said, "I must tell you something. The concept of death holds more weight with me than with the others. My logic circuits are different because of my work."

"I don't understand."

"The robot's stock-in-trade is efficiency," Avernus answered, "and in jobs requiring labor, cost efficiency. But in the mines cost efficiency isn't necessarily cost efficient."

"Now I'm really confused."

"The most cost-effective way to approach mine work may be the most dangerous way to approach it, but the most dangerous way to approach it may result in the loss of a great many workers because of the nature of the mines. So, the most effective way to work the mines may not be the most cost-efficient in the long run. Consequently, I am programmed to have a respect for life—even robotic life—that far and away exceeds what one could consider normal. The lives of my workers are of prime importance to me beyond any concept of efficiency."

"What has that got to do with me?" Derec asked.

"If you have killed, Derec, you will be anathema to me. The fact that you are accused and could be capable of such an action is almost more than I can bear. I voted against your freedom when we met on this issue."

"I swear to you that I am innocent," Derec said.

"Humans lie," the robot answered. "Now, do you still wish me to be the one to 'appreciate' your position?"

"Yes," Derec answered firmly. "I ask only that I be given the opportunity to show you that I have the best interests of Robot City at heart. I am innocent, and the truth will free me."

"Well said. What do you want to know?"

"You are the first supervisor," Derec said. "What are your first recollections?"

"I was awakened by a utility robot we call l-l," Avernus said, his red photocells fixed on Derec. "l-l had already awakened fifty other utility machines. I awakened with a full knowledge of who and what I was: a semi-autonomous robot whose function was to supervise the mines for city building, and to supervise the building of other supervisors to fulfill various tasks."

"Were you programmed to serve humans?"

"No," Avernus said quickly. "We were programmed with human information, both within us and within the core unit, which was also operational when I was awakened. Our decision to service was one we arrived at independently."

"Could that be the reason that the robots here have been less than enthusiastic about Katherine and me?" Derec asked. "Not knowing human reality, you accepted an ideal that was impossible for us to live up to."

"That is, perhaps, true," Avernus agreed.

"How long ago did your awakening take place?"

"A year ago, give or take."

"And did you see any human beings, or have knowledge of any, at that time?"

"No. Our first action was the construction of the Compass Tower. After that, we began our philosophical deliberations as to our purpose in the universe."

"How about l-l? Did he have any contact with humans?"

"It never occurred to us to ask," Avernus said.

"Where is l-l now?" Derec asked, feeling himself working toward something.

"In the tunnels," Avernus said, gesturing toward the elevators. "l-l works the mines."

Derec jumped off the makeshift seat. "Take me there," he said.

"Security..." the robot began.

"I'm a human being," Derec said. "This world was designed for me and my kind. I'm sorry, Avernus, but if you exist to serve, it's time you started to act like it. If you respect your own philosophies, you must accept the fact that your security measures were not designed to keep you secure from human beings. If they were, there is something desperately wrong with your basic philosophy."

"It is dangerous in the mines," Avernus replied.

"You can protect me."

The robot stood looking between Derec and the elevator doors. "I must deny you the central core," he said at length. "I must deny you knowledge of our emergency measures. But you are a human being, and this is your world to share with us. I will take you to 1-1 and protect you. If, at some point, protecting you means sending you back to the surface, I will do that."

"Fair enough," Derec said, looking at his watch. "We must go."

They moved toward the elevators, Rec joining them within the large car. In deference to the supervisor, the other robots let them have the car to themselves. Avernus pushed a stud in the wall and the door closed. The car started downward.

It went down a long way.

"The trick to movement in the mines is deliberation," Avernus said, as the car shuddered to a stop.

"Deliberation," Derec repeated.

The door slid open to delirious activity. Thousands of utility robots moved through a huge cavern that stretched as far as Derec could see in either direction. A continuous line of train cars rolled past on movable tracks, delivering raw ore to the giant smelters that refined it to more workable stages where it was heated and alloyed with other materials. The ceiling was thirty-five meters high and cut from the raw earth. Clean rooms filled the space at regular intervals.

"Iron!" Avernus said, stretching his arms wide. "The foundation upon which the ferrous metals are based, from which the modern world is made possible. We mine it in huge quantities, using it in its raw state to make our equipment, and alloyed with special plastics to form our city. There!"

He pointed to a machine through which layers of iron were belt-feeding, together with imprinted patterns of micro-circuits. The congealed mass issued from the top of the machine and proceeded through the ceiling in a continuous ribbon, the building material that Derec had seen extruded on the surface.

"That is the stuff of Robot City," Avernus said. "Iron and plastic alloy, cut with large amounts of carbon, and using carbon monoxide as a reducing agent. The 'skin' is then imprinted with millions of micro-circuits per square meter. In centimeter, independent sections, the 'skin' is alive with robotic intelligence, geared to human needs and protection. The whole is pre-programmed to build and behave in a pre-scribed fashion, and to react to human needs as they arise."

"That's why the walls give when I push on them," Derec said, moving gingerly out of the elevator and staying close to Avernus.

"Exactly. Now remember, deliberation. Stay close."

Avernus moved out into the middle of the furious activity, machines and robots and train cars rushing quickly all around them. As Avernus stepped into the path of on-rushing vehicles, Derec froze, wanting to pull back. But the expected accidents never took place, the robots and their machines gauging all the actions around them and reacting perfectly to them.

That's when the concept of deliberation became clear to Derec. Movement needed to be deliberate, with constant forward momentum. All judgment was based on the idea that movement would be steady and could be avoided once gauged. It was the erratic movement that was dangerous— the abrupt stop, the jump back; down here, such movements would be fatal.

Once he understood the concept, it became easier to walk

into the path of on-rushing vehicles. And as they moved through the center of the great hall, Derec began to feel more comfortable.

"Let me ask you a question," he said to the big robot. "Did you invent the 'skin' of Robot City?"

"No," Avernus replied. "Its program was already within the central core."

"So its activities are all pre-programmed?"

"Correct. All we did was use it once we decided to be of service to humanity."

They reached an edge of the hall, dozens of smaller tunnels branching off from it.

"We ride now," Avernus said, climbing into a cart that was far too small for his immense bulk. Derec and Rec climbed in with him, and Avernus started off right away, taking them down a barely lit tunnel.

"This one looks deserted," Derec said, and they hurried along at a fast clip.

"It was, until two days ago," Avernus said. "It is now, perhaps, going to save us."

"How?"

"You will see."

They rode for several more minutes through the dark, going deeper into the earth. Then Derec heard activity ahead.

"We are approaching," Avernus said.

"Approaching what?" Derec asked.

Avernus turned a corner and they were suddenly confronted by a widening of the tunnel, several hundred robots working furiously within an ever-growing space, scooping out dirt into any available container or skid, anything that would move earth. They then would take the earth and move quickly with it down adjoining tunnels, refilling that which had been excavated sometime previously. Like an ant farm, they moved in graceful cooperation and determination, and standing atop a cart, looming above them, was Rydberg, silently pointing as he transmitted his orders by radio to the toiling robots.

Avernus turned and looked at Derec. "Somewhere in there," he said, "you will find l-l."

Katherine's first thought had been that it was a monument, but then she realized there were no monuments on Robot City. It was set on a narrow pedestal about one hundred feet in the air. Located in the middle of a block, the city had simply built itself around the object in a semicircle, leaving it set apart from all other structures by a gap of fifty feet. She had spent several hours walking the changing topography of Robot City without success, but she stopped the moment she came upon this place. If she wanted to compare the workings of the living city to a human body, this room atop the pedestal was like a wound, sealing itself off with scar tissue to protect it from the vital workings of the rest of the body.

It was no more than a room. Katherine stood at ground level staring up at the thing. A box, perhaps five meters square, totally enclosed. The robots took the workings of their city for granted and simply accepted this anomaly. To the creative eye, it stuck out like a solar eclipse on a bright afternoon.

Katherine continued to stare up at it because she didn't want to lose it. Even now, the city continued to move, to grow before her eyes, and as the buildings turned in their slow waltz of life, she turned with them, always keeping the room within her vision. Eve, meanwhile, was trying to round up a supervisor who could effect a means of getting inside the structure and checking it out.

During the course of this excursion, Katherine had begun

to develop a grudging respect for the workings of the city. Obviously, things were not going well right now, but in the long run such a system could be quite beneficial to the humans and robots who inhabited it. The safety factor alone made the system worthwhile. Derec's harrowing ride down through the aqueduct resulted in nothing more than fatigue and a few bruises, all because the system itself was trying to protect him. To Katherine's mind, such a journey on Aurora would have caused Derec's death. She smiled at the thought of a Derec-proof city.

She'd also had time, while waiting for Eve to reach a supervisor, to notice the changes taking place around her. She felt as if she were visiting a resort at the tail end of the off season, all the seasonal workers arriving and getting the place shipshape for the influx of visitors. Clocks were being installed in various parts of the city, and street signs were beginning to go up. The largest change taking place, however, was the increased production and distribution of chairs. Robots had no need for sitting or reclining, and chairs were at a premium; but as they tried to make their city as welcome as possible for humans, they worked diligently to do things just right, despite the fact that the city's emergency measures were forcing many of them into extra duty. She wondered if she'd be this gracious if it were her city. The thought humbled her a bit.

Despite the differences, despite the bind the robots had put them in, they really were trying to make this world as perfect as they could for the travelers, travelers whom they suspected of murder. She had never before considered just how symbiotic the binding of humans to robots really was and, at least for the robots, how essential. She hoped that they would, eventually, have their civilization, complete with humans to order them around stupidly. She found herself smiling again. Her mother had a phrase that could apply to the robots' longing for human companionship—a glutton for punishment.

She heard a noise behind her and turned, expecting to see

a supervisor arriving. Instead she saw two utility robots moving toward her, carrying between them what looked for all the world like a park bench. Without a word, they moved right up to her and placed the bench just behind. She sat, and they hurried off.

She sat for barely a decad before Arion came clanking around a corner, along with a utility robot with a bulky laser torch strapped on his back. It took her back for a second, a seeming replay of the scene Eve had described to her when David had first become trapped in the sealed room.

"Good afternoon, Friend Katherine," Arion said as he moved up to her. "I see you are taking advantage of one of our chairs to rest your body. Very good."

"What's that on your wrist," Katherine asked, "a watch?"

The supervisor held up his arm, displaying the timepiece. "A show of solidarity," he said.

"You're in charge of human-creative functions on Robot City, aren't you?" she asked.

"Human-creative is a redundant term," Arion replied. "Creativity is the human stock-in-trade. I hope you've found satisfactory the entertainments I've provided for you."

"We'll talk about that later," she answered.

"Of course."

"I thank you for coming so promptly," Katherine said.

"This is a priority matter," the robot said, gazing up at the sealed room. "You believe this to be the location of the body?"

"I'm certain of it."

"Very good. Let's take a closer look."

Katherine stood and walked to the base of the tower with Arion. The pedestal was approximately the size of a large tree trunk, just large enough that she could almost reach around it if she tired. Arion reached out and touched the smooth, blue skin, and magically a spiral staircase with railing jutted from the surface and wound around the exterior of the tower.

"After you," the robot said politely.

Katherine started up, the design of the staircase keeping her from any sense of vertigo. As she climbed, she could feel that the air was cooling down, the presage to another night of destructive rain. Behind her, Arion, the utility robot, and the witness followed dutifully, and she realized that she was in the lead because it was the natural position for her in regard to this inquiry. This was her notion, her case—the robots at this point were merely her willing cohorts. Finally, she could give orders again and have them carried out!

She reached the top quickly. The flat disc of the pedestal top curled up and inward all around to make it impossible for her to fall off. That left the room itself. Uncolored, it was a natural gray-red and perfectly square. She walked completely around it looking for entry, but her first assessment had been correct: it was locked up tight.

"What do you propose at this point?" Arion asked her, as he followed her around the perimeter of the room.

"We're going to have to get inside," she said, "and see what there is to see. I suppose there's no other way to get in except by using the torch?"

"Normally, this situation would never arise," Arion told her. "There are no other buildings in the city that behave like this. There is no reason to seal up a room."

"You mean you don't know why or how the rooms have sealed themselves up?"

"The city program was given to us intact through the central core, and only the central core contains the program information. Other than through observation, we don't know exactly how the city operates."

Katherine was taken aback. "So, the city is actually a highly advanced autonomous robot in its own right, operating outside of your control."

"Your statement is basically inaccurate, but containing the germ of truth," Arion said. "To begin with, it is not highly advanced, at least not in the same sense that a . . . supervisor robot, for example, is highly advanced."

"Do I detect a shade of rivalry here?" she asked.

"Certainly not," Arion said. "We are not capable of such feelings as competitiveness. I was simply stating a known fact. Furthermore, the city's autonomy is tied directly to the central core. Although it does, in fact, operate outside of supervisor control."

"Can you affect the city program, then?"

"Not directly," Arion said, running his pincers up and down the contours of the building as if checking for openings. "The central core controls the city program, and the supervisors do not make policy by direct programming."

"I think I'm beginning to truly understand," Katherine said, motioning for the robot with the torch to come closer. "The data contained in the central core is the well from which your entire city springs. All of your activities here are merely an extension of the programming contained therein, for good or ill."

"We are robots, Friend Katherine," Arion said. "It could not be otherwise. Robots are not forces of change, but merely extensions of extant thought. That is why we so desperately need the companionship of humans."

"Cut here," Katherine said pointing to the wall, and the utility robot waited until she had backed away to a safer distance before charging the power packs and moving close with the nozzle-like hose that was the business end of the laser torch. She turned to Arion. "Does cutting through the wall like this break contact with the main program?"

"No," the robot answered as the torch came on with a whine, its beam invisible as a small section of the wall glowed bright red, smoking slightly. "The synapses simply reroute themselves and make connection elsewhere."

There was a sound of suction as the torch broke through to the other side of the wall, a sound that any Spacer knew well, the rushing of air into a vacuum. The room had sealed totally and airlessly. The torch moved more quickly now, cutting a circular hole just large enough for a human being to get through without working at it.

The edges tore jaggedly, the walls that seemed so fluid under program fighting tenaciously to hold together otherwise. Despite Arion's claims, Katherine was still impressed with the city-robot.

The welder was halfway done, pulling down the jagged slab of city as he cut. Katherine had to fight down the urge to run up and peer through the opening already made, but her fear of the torch ultimately won out over her impatience.

"Are you capable of doing autopsies here?" she asked Arion as an afterthought.

"The medical programming is in existence, and at this very moment several medically trained robots are being turned out of our production facilities, along with diagnostic tables and a number of machines. Synthesized drugs and instruments are coming at a slower rate. So much of the city is geared toward building right now, and these considerations never became a problem for us until David's death."

"Done," the utility robot said, the cut section falling to clang on the base disc.

"Witness!" Arion called, as Katherine hurried to the place and climbed through the hole.

The naked body lay, face down, in the middle of the floor. Katherine walked boldly toward it, then stopped, a hand going to her chest. She had been so intent upon fulfilling her mission that she had failed to consider that it was death— real death—she'd be dealing with. It horrified her. She began shaking, her heart rate increasing.

"Is something wrong?" Eve asked from the cut-out.

"N-no," she replied, her eyes glued to the body, unable either to move forward or pull back.

"If there's a problem," she heard Arion say, "come out now. Don't jeopardize yourself."

Come on, old girl. Get yourself together. "I'm fine," she said. *You've got to do this. Don't stop now.*

She took a deep breath, then another, and continued her walk to the body. Bending, she touched it gingerly. The surface was cool, the muscles tight.

"Is everything all right?" Arion asked.

"Yes," she said. *Won't they leave me alone?*

There was no sign of decomposition, and she realized that it was because the room had been airless. At least that was something.

She examined the body from the back, her heart rate still up, her breath coming fast. Looking at the foot, she could see a small cut on the left instep and realized immediately what had caused it. Something stupid. Something she had done herself before. A misstep, perhaps a broken fall, and the bare feet came together, a too-long toenail on the other foot scraping the instep. It was nothing. There was some dried blood on the side and bottom of the foot, but that was it. She was going to have to roll the body over.

She moved to the side of the body, reaching out to try and turn it over, finding her hands shaking wildly. *Will this be me soon—fifty kilos of dead meat?* She tried to push the body onto its back, but there was no strength in her arms.

"Could you help me with this?" she called over her shoulder. Arion came through the cut-out to bend down beside her. She looked up at the nearly human-looking machine. "I want to roll it over."

"Surely," Arion said, reaching out with his pincers to push gently against the side of the body. It rolled over easily, dead eyes staring straight at Katherine.

She heard herself screaming from far away as the shock of recognition hit her. It was Derec! Derec!

The room began spinning as she felt it in her stomach and in her head. Then she felt the floor reach up and pull her down; everything else was lost in the numbing bliss of unconsciousness.

"Don't try to leave without me to lead you!" Avernus called to Derec as the boy waded into the churning sea of robots. "You could become hopelessly lost in these tunnels."

"Don't worry!" Derec called back, thinking more about the danger of the main chamber than the labyrinthine caves.

He moved slowly through the throng, walking toward Rydberg. It was damp, musty in there, plus a bit claustrophobic, but Derec was so fascinated by the spectacle of the eleventh-hour plans that he never allowed his mind to dwell on the all-too-human problems of the location.

Rydberg saw him approaching, and turned to stare as Derec closed on him. He climbed atop the cart and joined the supervisor.

"What are you doing here?" Rydberg asked, the words crackling through the speaker atop his dome. "It is too dangerous underground for you."

"I talked Avernus into bringing me down and protecting me," Derec replied. "What's going on here?"

"We're trying to tunnel up to the reservoir," Rydberg said. "We are trying to work out a way to drain off some of the reservoir into the deserted tunnels below to keep it from flooding."

Derec felt an electric charge run through him. "That's wonderful!" he yelled. "You've made a third-level connection—a creative leap!"

"It was only logical. Since the water was going to come into the mines anyway, it only made sense that we should try to direct it to parts of the mines that would cause the least amount of damage. Unfortunately, our estimates show such a move could only hold off the inevitable for a day or two longer. It may all be in vain."

"Why are you digging by hand?" Derec asked. "Where are the machines?"

"They are tied up in the mining process," Rydberg said. "The current rate of city-building must take precedence over all other activities." The robot turned his dome to watch the excavations.

Derec put his hands on the robot's arm. "But the city-building is what's killing you!"

"It must be done."

"Why?"

"I cannot answer that."

Derec looked all around him, at the frantic rush of momentum, at a civilization trying to survive. No, they weren't human, but it didn't mean their lives weren't worthwhile. What was the gauge? There was intelligence, and a concerted effort toward perfection of spirit. There was more worth, more human value here in the mines than in anything he had seen in his brief glimpse of humanity. And then it struck him, the reason for all of this and the reason for the state of emergency and security.

"It's defensive, isn't it?" he said. "The city-building is a way for the city to defend itself against alien invasion?"

Rydberg just stared at him.

He grabbed the robot's arm again, tighter. "That *is* it, isn't it?"

"I cannot answer that question."

"Then tell me I am wrong!"

"I cannot answer that question."

"I knew it," he said, convinced now. "And if it coincided with David's appearance in the city, then it is somehow tied to him. For once, Katherine's in the right place.

"This whole thing is a central core program," Derec said, "and obviously the program is in error. There must be some way you can circumvent it."

"Robots do not make programs, Derec," Rydberg said.

"Then let me into it!"

"I cannot," Rydberg replied, then added softly. "I'm sorry."

Derec just stared at him, wanting to argue him into compliance, and fearing that the argument would simply present the robot with a contradiction so vast it would freeze his mental facilities and lock him up beyond hope. He didn't know where to go from here. He'd had a tantalizing glimpse of the problem, yet, like a holographic image, it still eluded his grasp.

"You still have not told me why you came down into the mines," Rydberg said. "Humans have such a poor sense of personal danger that I fail to see how your species has survived to this point. If you cannot present me a compelling reason for your presence, I fear I must send you away now."

"If humans have a poor sense of personal danger," Derec said, angry at Robot City's inability even to try to save itself, "then it has been justly inherited in *your* programming. I've come down to visit l-l on a matter not of your concern. Would you please point him out to me?"

"Our first citizen?" Rydberg said, and Derec could tell the robot wanted to say more. Instead, he turned up his volume. "WILL ROBOT l-l PLEASE COME FORWARD."

Within a minute, a small, rather innocuous utility robot with large, powerful looking pincer grips moved up to the cart. "I am here, Supervisor Rydberg," the robot said.

"Friend Derec wishes to speak with you on a personal matter," the supervisor said. "Do as he asks, but do not take an excessive amount of time."

Derec jumped off the cart. "I hear you were the first robot awakened on this planet," he said.

"That is correct," the robot said.

"Come with me," Derec said. "Let's get out of the confusion."

They moved through the rapidly widening chamber to the place where Avernus had first dropped him. "I am searching through the origins of Robot City," Derec said, "and that search has led me to you. You were the first."

"Yes. Logical. I was the first."

"I want you to tell me exactly what your first visual input was and what followed subsequently."

"My first visual input was of a human arm connecting my power supply," the robot said. "Then the human turned and walked away from me."

"Did you see the human face?"

"No."

"What happened then?"

"The human walked a distance from me, then disappeared behind some machinery meant to help in our early mining. I was to wait for one hour, then turn on the other inoperative robots in the area. Then we were to begin work, which we did."

"Of what did that original work consist?"

"There were fifty utility, plus Supervisor Avernus. Twenty-five of us built the Compass Tower from materials left for us, while Supervisor Avernus and the other twenty-five began the design and construction of the underground facilities and commenced the mining operations."

Derec was puzzled. "Avernus didn't supervise the construction of the Compass Tower?"

"No. It was meant as a separate entity from the rest of the city. It was fully planned, fully materialized. There was no need for Supervisor Avernus to take an interest in it."

Derec heard an engine noise and saw lights, far in the tunnel distance, gradually closing on his position. "What do you mean when you say it was 'meant as a separate entity'?" Derec asked.

"The Compass Tower is unique in several respects, Friend Derec," 1-1 said. "It is not part of the overall city plan in any respect; it has the off limits homing platform atop it; and it contains a fully furnished, human administration office."

"What!" Derec said loudly, as he watched the mine tram rushing closer toward him in the tunnel. "An office for whom?"

"I do not know. Perhaps the person who awakened me."

"You've never spoken of this with the supervisors?"

"No one has ever inquired before now."

"Why did you call it the administration office?"

"The construction plans are locked within my data banks," 1-1 answered. "That is what it was called on the plans."

The tram car screeched to a halt right beside Darren, the huge bulk of Avernus stuffed in its front seat. "We must go," the supervisor said.

"Just a minute," Derec said. "Why did you call it a homing platform?"

"We must go now," Avernus said.

"It was designed as a landing point of some kind," l-l said. "Nothing is ever allowed on its surface, or within twenty meters of its airspace."

Avernus took hold of Derec's arm and gently, but firmly, turned him face to face. "We must go," Avernus said. "Something has happened to Friend Katherine."

Derec reeled as if he'd been hit. "What? What happened? Is she all right?"

"She is unconscious," Avernus said. "Beyond that, we do not know."

Derec hurried into the apartment to buzzing activity. Arion was there, and Euler, plus Eve and several utility robots. There was also a rather frail-looking machine with multiple appendages that Derec surmised to be a med-bot.

The living room seemed different, much squatter, but he really wasn't paying attention.

"Friend Derec . . ." Euler began, hurrying to intercept Derec as he crossed the living room floor.

"Where is she?" he asked, still moving.

"The bedroom," Euler said. "She has regained consciousness and is resting. I do not think you should try and see her just yet."

"Nonsense," Derec said, hurrying past him. "I've *got* to see her."

"But you don't underst . . ."

"Later," Derec said, moving down the hallway. There were now two bedroom doors. He opened one to an empty room, then turned to the other, pushing the stud. It slid open. Katherine was sitting up in bed, her face drained of all color, her eyes red.

"Are you all right?" he asked.

Her eyes focused on him, then grew wide in horror.

"Noooo!" she screamed, hands going to her straining face.

Derec ran to her and took her by the shoulders. She kept screaming, loudly, hysterically, her body vibrating madly on the bed.

"You're dead!" she yelled. "Dead! Dead!"

"No!" he yelled. "I'm here. It's all right. It's all . . ."

Euler was pulling him away from her, robots filling the room. "What are you doing?" he yelled. "Let go, I . . ."

"You must leave now," Euler said, lifting him bodily in the air and carrying him, Katherine's screams still filling the apartment.

"Katherine!" he called to her as Euler carried him out the door. "Katherine!"

Euler carried him all the way to the living room, then simply held him there, the med-bot slipping into her bedroom and sliding the door closed, muffling the screams somewhat.

"Put me down!" Derec yelled. "Would you put me down?"

"You must not go in there," Euler said. "It is dangerous for Katherine if you go in there."

He felt the anger draining out of him. "What's going on?" he asked sheepishly. "What's happened to her?"

"She's suffered some sort of emotional trauma," the supervisor said. "May I put you down?"

"Believe me," Derec said, "at this point, I don't want to go back in."

Euler set him gently on the floor. Derec rubbed his arms to get the circulation back into them.

"I am sorry if I caused you any discomfort," Euler said. "Truly."

"It's all right," Derec replied. "Tell me what happened."

Thunder crashed loudly outside, both Derec and Euler turning to look at the building thunderheads through the open patio door. They were in for another bad one. From the bedroom, the sounds of screaming had died to occasional whimpers.

"Katherine found the body of David," Euler said, "and had a utility robot cut into the sealed room that contained it." The robot swiveled its head to take in the rest of the room. "Perhaps it is better to have Arion witness the story. He was present for it." He motioned for the human-like machine to join the discussion.

"Friend Derec," Arion said as he moved up close. "I had no idea that seeing the body would have this kind of effect on Friend Katherine. I would never have allowed her to come close to it had I known."

"I understand," Derec said. "Just tell me what happened."

"She was examining the deceased," Arion said, "when she called me in to help her roll the body over. I, of course, complied. She screamed when she saw the face, then lapsed into a state of unconsciousness."

"She's been disconsolate ever since," Euler said. "Most peculiar. She persisted in the belief that the dead man was you."

"Why would she do that?" he asked, moving to sit at the table. Arion's CRT was busily finding the cube roots of ten-digit numbers.

"I don't know," Euler said. "Perhaps because the body looked like yours."

Derec sat up straight, staring hard. "You mean . . . just like me?"

The robots looked at one another. "Perfectly," Arion said.

"Doesn't that strike you as odd?" Derec said, dumb-founded, still not believing the information.

"No," Euler said.

"I don't understand," Derec said. "When you first saw me, didn't you take note of the similarity of our appearances?"

"Yes," Euler said, "but it didn't mean anything to us."

"Why not?"

Arion spoke up. "Why should it? We've only seen three human beings. Robots certainly can look exactly alike, why not humans? We knew you and Katherine were different, but that didn't mean that you and David couldn't be the same. Besides, we *knew* that David was dead; so, consequently, we *knew* that you couldn't be David. Simple."

The med-bot came gliding down the hall, moving quickly

up to Derec. "She's calm now," the robot said. "She's lightly sedated with her own pituitary endorphins, and wants to see you."

Derec stood, uneasy after the last time. "It'll be all right?" he asked the med-bot.

"I believe she understands the situation now," the med-bot responded in a gentle, fatherly voice.

"I'd like to see her alone," he told the others.

Euler nodded. "We'll wait out here."

He moved down the hall, unsure of his feelings. It had hurt him to see her in such pain, hurt him emotionally. She could get on his nerves so badly, yet seemed such an integral part of him.

He knocked lightly on her door, then opened it. She sat up in bed, her face still sad. She held her arms out to him. "Oh, Derec . . ."

He hurried to the bed, sitting next to her, holding her. She began to sob gently into his shoulder. "I was so afraid," she said. "I thought . . . thought . . ."

"I know," he said, stroking her hair. "Arion told me. I'm so sorry."

"I don't know what I'd do without you," she said, then pulled away from him. "Oh, Derec. I know we've walls between us . . . but please believe me, I have no idea what this place is and what's going on here."

"I believe you," he said, reaching up to wipe tears from her eyes. He smiled. "Don't worry about that now. How are you doing?"

"Better," she said. "The med-bot stuck me a couple of times, but it really helped. All I've got is a headache."

Thunder rolled again outside. "Good," he said. "It looks like we're locked in for the night anyway. What do you say we send the robots away, get some dinner sent up, and compare notes. I've got a lot to tell you."

"Me, too," she said. "It sounds good."

* * *

They had a vegetable soup for dinner that was the best thing Derec had eaten for quite some time. The rains pounded frenetically outside, but Derec didn't worry so much since he figured the precautions taken by Euler and Rydberg would, at least, get them through the night. And the best he could do now was to live day to day. Even Arion's entertainment was beginning to diversify. The CRT was exhibiting an animated game of tennis played by computer-generated stick figures on a slippery surface. It was actually quite amusing.

After the servo had cleared the dishes away and left, they made themselves comfortable on the couch and recounted the details of the day. Derec, for reasons he wasn't quite sure of, left out the fact that there were no hyperwave transmission stations on the planet. Counting on Katherine's experiences to help him, he listened alertly to her account of the discovery of the body.

"The fact that he looked just like you," she asked when she'd finished, "what does it mean?"

"To begin with," he said, "it finally knocks the idea of our trip to Robot City being an accident right out the air lock. We were brought here; why, I don't know. The dead man is either the one who brought us or was brought himself. We'll have to continue to ferret that out. What interests me more is the fact that the city-robot works independently. I believe that the city is somehow replicating itself as a defensive measure. If it operates independently, the supervisors may not be *able* to stop it."

"What does that mean?"

He looked at her. "It means that I've got to."

"That brings us back to our same old argument," she said, darkening a bit. "The city or the murder investigation."

"Not necessarily," he said, standing. "This should make you happy." He walked back to the patio door and idly watched the downpour, feeling now that it could, eventually, be beaten. He turned back to her. "I believe that David and the city alert and replication are inexorably linked."

She jumped up, excited, and ran to him, throwing her arms around him. "You're going to help me solve the murder, aren't you?"

"Yes," he laughed, returning the embrace. "Tomorrow we go back to the body and pick up where you left off." He moved away from her and intertwined his fingers. "It's all like this, all connected. If we can put a few of the pieces together, I'll bet the rest fall into place. Whatever, or whoever, killed David, is the reason for the alert."

"First thing in the morning, we'll have Eve take us back there."

"Not first thing," he said. "First thing, I've set up a brief meeting with the supervisors at the Compass Tower."

"Why?"

"Two reasons. First, I want to ask them some questions about their underground operations; and second, I want to be able to poke around the building for a bit."

"Looking for the office?"

He nodded. "l-l said it was fully furnished. I bet we'll find answers there."

Her face got suddenly serious. "I hope you find the kind of answers you're looking for," she said.

A table had been set up in the meeting room. It was long and narrow and included seats for nine. Derec sat at the head of the table, with Katherine at his right. The supervisors took up the rest of the seats, still holding hands, with the two at the end of the line holding hands over the tabletop.

"Why do human beings lie, Friend Derec?" Supervisor Dante asked, his elongated, magnifying eyes staring all the way down the table. "The most difficulty we've had with you is your penchant for lies and exaggeration. It is what keeps us from trusting you completely."

Derec licked dry lips and watched them all expectantly watching him. He knew he'd have to get beyond this hurdle if he were to work with them in solving the city's problems.

"Robots receive their input in two ways," he said, hoping his explanation would be adequate. He'd gotten up early to think it out and prepare it. "Through direct programming, and through input garnered through the sensors that is then tested in analog against existing programming. Your sensors record events accurately, with mathematic precision, and classify them through the scientific validity of several thousand years of empirical thought. You are then able, through your positronics, to reason deductively by weighing, again through analog, incoming data against existing data. You can make true second-level connections."

"We understand the workings of the positronic brain," Friend Derec," Waldeyer said. "It is the human brain that confounds us."

"Bear with me," Derec said. "I want to pose you a question. Suppose, just suppose, that your basic programming was in error—not just in small ways, but in its most basic assumptions. Suppose every bit of sensory input you received was in total opposition to your basic programming."

"We would spend a great deal of time reasoning erroneously," Wohler said. "But human brains are not at the mercy of programming. You have the freedom to sift through all empirical data and arrive at the truth at all times."

"That's where you are wrong," Derec replied. "The human mind is not a computer with truth as its base. It is merely a collection of ganglia moved by electrical impulses. Truth is not its basis, but rather ego gratification. Truth to the human mind is a shifting thing, a sail billowing on the wind of fear and hope and desire. It has no reality, but rather creates it from moment to moment with that same creative intelligence that you value so highly in us."

"But the base program is available," Euler said. "It is there for the human to use."

"And it is also there for him to reject," Derec countered. "You *must* observe your programming. My mind has no such chains on it. The human mind is painfully mortal. That particular truth in itself is more than most humans can tolerate. We are frail creatures, seeking permanence in an impermanent world. We lie to those around us. We lie to ourselves. We lie in the face of all logic and all reason. We lie because, quite often, the truth would destroy us. We lie without even knowing it."

Avernus spoke. "How do robots that exist with humans on other worlds deal with the deceit?"

"They follow instruction according to the Laws of Robotics," Derec said, quite simply. "They are not autonomous as you are, so they have no choice. The Laws were invented with the salvation of the species in mind. Robots protect humans from their own lies, and honor them because of what's noble in the species. You saw Katherine's grief when she thought I was dead." He reached out and took her hand. "We are fragile creatures capable of great nobility and great ignominy. We make no excuses for ourselves. We are the creators of great good and great evil, and in the creation of robots, we were at the height of our goodness. Our species deserves praise and condemnation, and, in the final analysis, it is beyond rational, positronic explanation."

"You are saying we must take you as you are," Euler said.

"No laws will define us," Derec answered, "no theorem hold us in check. We will amaze and confound you, but I can guarantee you we will never be boring."

"You would tame us with your words," Wohler, the philosopher, said.

"Yes," Derec said, smiling. "I would do exactly that. And I will tell you now that you will let me because the wonders of the universe are contained in my confounding mind, and you can only reach them through me . . . and you desperately want to reach them!"

"But what of the Laws of Humanics?" Rydberg asked.

"Very simple," Katherine added, winking at Derec. "There is only one Law of Humanics: expect the unexpected."

"An oxymoron," Arion said.

"As close as you'll ever get," Derec said. "That's the point. You needn't give up your search for the Laws of Humanics, but you must make them fit us, not try to make us fit them. We can't be anything but what we are, but if you accept us—good and bad—we'll see to it that you reach your full potential."

"Intriguing words," Dante said, "but just words. Where is an example of what you can do with your creative intelligence?"

"If you'll let me," Derec said, "perhaps I can help you save your city."

"All your suggestions so far have tried to force us away

from our programming," Euler said.

Derec stood; he thought better on his feet. "That's because until yesterday I never fully realized what was going on and how little control you had over the situation. I'm working on that, too, but I have some other ideas."

Arion and Waldeyer sat side by side, pincers locked together. Derec walked between the two of them, resting his elbows on their shoulders.

"I've watched you digging in the tunnels, trying to siphon off reservoir water to lower the level and avoid a flooding of your underground operations. Has it been successful?"

"To a degree," Rydberg said. "We will break through after our meeting this morning. Unfortunately, we calculate that it will only postpone the inevitable for one more day. We can save our operations through tonight's expected rain, but that's it."

"All right," Derec said. "Let's think about something. I was in the main chamber of one of the quadrants yesterday. Was that chamber dug?"

"No," Avernus said. "Each quadrant Extruder Station is located in a chamber similiar to that one. Our first action in beginning underground operations was to take sonogram readings to determine natural caverns under the surface. The mine tunnels were dug, but the main chambers are natural."

"Has it occurred to you," Derec said, "to take sonograms now, in the present situation?"

"I do not understand," Avernus said.

Derec pounded the tabletop with an index finger. "Find the closest underground cavern to your reservoir, dig a tunnel connecting it to the reservoir, and . . ."

"And drain the reservoir water in there!" Avernus said, standing abruptly and breaking contact with the central core.

"Right!" Derec pointed to him. "Meanwhile, Katherine and I will be working on solving the murder. I'm absolutely convinced that the solution to the murder will also provide the reasons for the state of emergency." He turned to Supervisor Dante. "Is *that* creative enough for you?"

"Happily so," Dante said.

"It seems," Euler said, "that if we are to have the opportunity of putting Friend Derec's suggestions into practice, we should adjourn this meeting and set to work."

The robots stood, Derec wondering if they realized that he had gently manipulated them, for the first time, into including him as a real partner in their planning.

He watched them filing out of the large room, for the first time beginning to feel he was getting a handle on the deviousness of the mind that had brought all of them together. Synnoetics. The worst hills still remained to be scaled toward reaching a truly equal social union of human and robot. Now, if they could only survive the rains, they could perhaps be the trailblazers in the opening of a new era.

As soon as the robots left the room, Katherine hurried to the door and peered out. "They're gone," she said, turning back to Derec.

"Good."

He joined her at the door, Eve and Rec, trailing dutifully. Derec turned to them. "Has either of you ever witnessed within this building before?"

"Yes," Rec said. "Most of this building is given to experimentation on the positronic brain and ways to improve its function. I have witnessed experiments in almost every laboratory in the structure."

"Have you ever seen an office, something that a human might use as his personal quarters?"

"No," the robot answered.

"Are there parts of the building you have never seen?"

"Yes."

"All right, listen carefully," Derec said, shrugging in Katherine's direction. "I want you to take me to all the parts of the building you have never seen."

"I cannot do that."

"Why not?" Katherine asked.

"There is a sector in the Compass Tower that is off-limits to robots. No one goes there."

"Did someone tell you that," Derec asked, "a supervisor?"

"It is part of our programming," Rec said.

Eve agreed. "Not even supervisors are allowed."

Derec shook his head. Just like robots—all duty, no inquisitiveness. "I want you to take us there," he said.

"I already told you it was off-limits," Rec said.

Derec smiled. "I don't mean for you to take me *inside* the off-limits part," he said. "Just take me as close as you can get and point it out to me."

That seemed amenable enough, so the two witnesses led the way, while Derec and Katherine followed closely. They walked the maze-like halls, twisting and turning, but always going higher. An elevator took them six floors up, but that wasn't even the end of it. It was interesting to Derec. The meeting room had been designed to look like it was at the apex of the pyramid, but it was actually only about halfway up the structure, perhaps the illusion being more spiritual in intent than anything else.

The upper levels had begun to get rather small, doorways appearing more sparsely between the gently glowing wall panels, when the robots abruptly stopped. Rec pointed to a door at the end of a short hallway.

"We can go no farther," the robot said. "No one knows where that doorway leads."

"If you want to wait here," Derec said, "we'll be back soon."

"But it is off-limits," Eve said.

"To robots, not humans," Katherine replied.

"But we cannot separate," Rec persisted.

"It is only one door," Derec said. "We'll have to come back through it."

"Our orders . . ."

"Do what you want," Derec said. "We're going on."

With that, Derec and Katherine continued down the hallway, turning once to see the attentive robots before opening the door and stepping inside.

What they found was a spiral staircase leading up to a door set ten feet above their heads.

"You want to go first?" Derec asked.

"Go ahead," Katherine returned. "I left my courage back in that sealed room."

Derec moved slowly up the stairs, a feeling of expectation rising slowly in his stomach. He connected the word, butter-flies, to the feeling, but had no idea of what it meant. He reached the door, and pushed the stud, expecting it to be locked up tight.

It wasn't.

The door slid easily and opened, he thought at first, to the outside. It was as if he were walking onto an open platform set with furniture and a desk, a beautiful, panoramic view of Robot City all around. But there was no feel of the air, no wind, no heat from the mid-morning sun.

"How did we get outside?" Katherine asked, following him in.

"We're not," Derec said, pointing behind her.

The outside view was marred by the still-open doorway, a black maw in the center of downtown. When he pushed the stud to close the door, the full view was restored.

"Viewscreens?" she asked.

"I think so," he replied. "There must be a series of small cameras set around the peak of the pyramid to give the view, which is then put on the screens. Look," he pointed, "even above us."

She looked up to see pinkish-blue sky above. "That would be the view from the platform we materialized on," she said.

"Fascinating," he said softly, knowing they'd finally stumbled upon something. "If you were sitting in here, you could watch someone materialize on the platform and they'd never know it."

"Do you think someone watched *us* materialize?" she asked, eyes wide.

He shrugged. "I'd have to think it probable at this point,"

he said. "We were brought here. We were *meant* to be here. It seems logical that our progress would be measured."

"Have you ever considered the fact, Derec, that *you* were brought here and I'm excess baggage?" she asked.

He walked slowly through the room. It was designed for someone to live in. There were easy chairs and a couch that converted to a bed. Not city-robot material, but real furniture. There was even a plant of some kind under its own growth light. That told Derec that whoever kept this office returned at least often enough to keep the plant watered.

"I've considered a great many things," Derec told her, "including the scenario you've just outlined. But there are several things to consider. I believe our meeting on Aranimas's ship was accidental. The situation was too dangerous and uncontrollable to be otherwise, our injuries too real. But consider the facts that you admit to having known me previously by another name and that that name just happens to belong to someone who looked enough like me to be my twin. It's a large universe, Katherine. That's an awful lot of coincidence. Let me ask you something. Have *you* ever considered the possibility that the David you knew could be the one lying dead in that sealed room, and that I'm somebody else?"

Her face became confused, lips sputtering. "I—I . . ."

Then she started to say something and stopped. Derec would have given a fortune, ten fortunes, to know the thoughts that had been running through her mind that second before she shut herself up.

"What are you hiding from me?" he asked loudly, in frustration.

Her face was a mixture of pain and longing. She responded by solidifying, as she had done so many times since they'd met on Aranimas's ship. "There's nothing up here for me," she said. "I'm going back down with the robots. Join us quickly. We have other work to do."

Then she turned and departed without a backward glance,

leaving Derec angry again. He could feel so close to her, and so far away. There was never any mid-point with Katherine; it was all one way or the other.

He decided to inspect the office methodically, rather than simply tearing furiously into things, which had been his strongest desire. Starting on the outer edges of the room, he traversed it slowly, saving the plum of the desk for last.

He found a small, air-tight shelf full of tapes, all marked "Philosophy," then broken down according to planet. Nearly all of the fifty-five Spacer worlds were represented. They weren't of interest to him at the moment, but a perusal in future wasn't out of the question.

He continued his walk of the outer perimeter, his hand finding the ladder where his eyes couldn't. It was a metal ladder, set against the screen and lost in shadows. Even knowing it was there, he still found it difficult to see. It went up from the floor and stopped at the flat ceiling.

He climbed it until he reached the ceiling screen. There was no reason at all for this ladder to exist unless it went somewhere. Gingerly, he reached out and touched the ceiling screen above the ladder. It gave easily on well-oiled hinges, flapping open to reveal real sky.

He moved up through the trap door to find himself standing on the platform where he had materialized. Amazing. He began to put together a theory. Whoever started this civilization, whoever's arm it was that turned on l-1, with proper use of a Key to Perihelion, could materialize on Robot City at will, move down into the off-limits office and observe his city's progress without ever being seen. When he was through, he could leave by the same means.

So, the city had an overseer, a guardian, who had apparently brought Derec here to sweeten the mix with the human ingredient. Why Derec? That question, he couldn't answer.

He wondered if the overseer had been present during his and Katherine's stay, if he had been watching them, perhaps all the way up to the moment they opened the office door. It would be simple enough for him to get away. All he'd need was the Key and a few seconds' time.

Derec climbed back into the office and closed the trap door behind him, once again sealing in the illusion completely.

He continued his tour of the office by emptying the small trash can that sat by the desk. The trash can held several empty containers that he recognized as standard Spacer survival rations of good-tasting roughage plus supplementary vitamin and protein pills. He torn open one of the roughage containers to find, in the corner, a small glob of the stuff, which hadn't hardened completely. This food had been eaten within the last twenty-four hours. The rest of the trash was comprised of wadded-up pieces of paper containing mathematical equations relating to the geometric progression of the city-building, which seemed to relate to the time it would take to fill the entire planet with city. Others seemed to be directed to the amounts of rainfall and the reservoir size, quick calculations regarding how long it would take an overflow to occur. Derec had the feeling that if he simply sat in the office and waited an indefinite amount of time, he could probably catch the overseer coming back. Unfortunately, he didn't have an indefinite amount of time.

He put the trash back in the can and directed his attention to the desk itself. The top of the iron-alloy desk contained a blotter with paper and two zero-g ink pens. The only personal item on the desk was a holo-cube containing a scene of a very nice looking woman holding a baby. The sight of the cube sent a cold chill down his back.

He turned his attention to the drawers. On his left were several small drawers, which were, for the most part, empty. Only the top drawer contained anything at all, and that was simply more paper and some technical data on the workings of the logic circuits of the positronic brain. On his right, however, he struck gold. As he opened the big well drawer there, a slight motor hum brought a computer terminal up to desktop level, the screen already active, the cursor flashing: READY.

Interestingly enough, the terminal had all the hook-ups and leads for hyperwave transmission and reception. Unfortunately, the power pack and directional hyperwave antenna were missing from the back, taken, no doubt, by the overseer.

He stared at the terminal in disbelief. No blocks, no passwords, no protections on the system at all. He couldn't believe that an entire civilization would open itself up to him just because he'd found an office. Suppose he'd meant to cause it harm?

Cautiously, he slipped into the scheme of things, working his way down to the level of files, then asking to go to the central core. Once reaching that, he asked to open the file marked: CITY DEFENSES.

Within seconds, the READY signal was flashing again. He was in! Rapidly he typed:

LIST CITY DEFENSES.

The computer answered:

CITY DEFENSES: ADVANCE REPLICATION
                    SEAL CONTAMINATION
                    HALT CENTRAL CORE INPUT
                    MOBILATE CENTRAL CORE
                    LOCALIZE EMERGENCY
                          TERMINALS
                    ISOLATE SUPERVISORY
                          PERSONNEL

He sat, shaking, at the typer. This was it. He decided to try his hand at shutting it down. He typed:

CANCEL REPLICATION.

The computer never hesitated.

CITY DEFENSES CANNOT BE CANCELED WITHOUT JUSTIFICATION AND INPUT REGARDING ALIEN THREAT OR CONTAMINATION.

Derec typed:

OVERRIDE ALL PREVIOUS INSTRUCTIONS AND CANCEL REPLICATION.

The computer answered:

OVERRRIDE IMPOSSIBLE UNDER ALL CIRCUM-STANCES. CITY DEFENSES CANNOT BE CANCELED WITHOUT JUSTIFICATION AND INPUT REGARDING ALIEN THREAT OR CONTAMINATION.

It was a lock-out. The computer refused even to talk to him about it unless he could determine the reason for the defensive measures and provide proper rationalization for termination. It seemed etched in granite. He typed:

LIST REASONS FOR CITY DEFENSE ACTIVATION.

The computer answered with a graph of the city, its shape ever changing, turning slowly. A tiny light was flashing in the section marked Quadrant #4. At the bottom of the screen the computer wrote:

ALIEN CONTAMINATION IN QUADRANT #4.

Derec asked:

CITE NATURE OF CONTAMINATION.

The computer answered:

ALIEN CONTAMINATION IN QUADRANT #4.

He sat back and looked at the machine. It was very possible that the flashing light could represent the body of his look-alike. The machine wasn't going to let him off the hook on the murder. He was beginning to see why it was so easy for him to get into the central core from this terminal, and he received his final confirmation quickly, when he typed:

LIST PROCEDURE FOR DEACTIVATION OF CITY DEFENSES.

The machine replied:

DEACTIVATION PROCEDURE:

> ISOLATE CONTAMINATION OR
> PRESENCE
> DEFINE NATURE OF THREAT
> NEUTRALIZE THREAT
> PROVIDE PROOF OF

NEUTRALIZATION THRU
PROCEDURE C-15

Derec typed:
LIST PROCEDURE C-15
And was answered:

PROCEDURE C-15:   ISOLATE MOBILATED
CENTRAL CORE
ENTER CENTRAL CORE
PROVIDE SUPERVISOR
PASSWORD
ENTER PROOF OF
NEUTRALIZATION

Derec just stared at the screen, frustrated and amazed at
what he was looking at. Nothing of consequence could be
done from this terminal, or from *any* city terminal, for that
matter. Input had to come directly at the central core, and
unless he misunderstood the word "mobilate," the central
core was not stationary. It was mobile, moving. And to
round out the entire business philosophically, a supervisor
robot was necessary to enter the defensive program.

It was actually the perfect defense. The act of shutting
down the defenses had to be deliberate and calculated and
agreed to by *both* human and robot supervision. Again,
the system was set up synnoetically, and Derec, despite his
disappointment, had to admire it. Ultimately, he really
didn't know the form of the contamination. The central
core was behaving properly by not granting his requests
for deactivation until all the facts were in. The problem,
of course, was that city could kill itself before the facts
came to light.

He was back where he started, with the murder of his
twin. There was still much he could learn from the office
and the open terminal, but he simply didn't have the time
right now. He reluctantly decided that he'd have to close out
for now and return when there was more time.

He had reached out to return the terminal to its berth in

the drawer when he thought of something. If the overseer were, indeed, keeping track of them, perhaps there was a file extant with that information. Not knowing his own name, he decided to go with another. Bringing the filename menu back on the screen, he typed in the words:

BURGESS, KATHERINE

The machine answered:

BURGESS, KATHERINE, see DAVID.

His mouth was dry, his heart pounding as he typed in the name of the dead man.

The machine answered quickly, in a notation file obviously set in the overseer's own hand:

ASSIMILATION TEST ON DAVID #2 PROCEEDED ON LINE AND WITHOUT MISHAP UNTIL THE TRIGGERING OF THE CITY DEFENSIVE SYSTEM AND THE DEATH OF SUBJECT THROUGH UNKNOWN MEANS.

WITHOUT HUMAN INTERVENTION, ROBOTS ARE UNABLE TO PREVENT VITAL DAMAGE THROUGH OVER-SUCCESS OF CITY PLANNING AND OPERATION WOULD BE TOTAL FAILURE.

DAVID #1 ARRIVED TO INTERVENE IN CITY CATASTROPHE AND PROCEED WITH ORIGINAL OPERATIONAL TESTING OF SYNNOETIC THEORIES. RESULTS YET TO BE SEEN.

UNCONTROLLED FACTOR ARRIVED WITH DAVID #1 IN THE FORM OF A WOMAN. SHE IS NOW CALLING HERSELF KATHERINE BURGESS FOR REASONS UNKNOWN. HER ULTIMATE INFLUENCE OVER OPERATION AND THE EXACT NATURE OF HER AIMS HAVE YET TO BE DETERMINED.

SHE WILL BE WATCHED CAREFULLY.

That was it, the end of the file. Derec stared at the flashing cursor for a moment, his mind whirling with a dozen different thoughts. But one thought overrode everything else, one sentence burned its way into his brain and hurt him more deeply than he thought possible—SHE IS NOW CALLING HERSELF KATHERINE BURGESS FOR REASONS UNKNOWN.

CHAPTER 10
THE SEALED ROOM

Derec had hoped that when he came out of the overseer's office Katherine would have already been gone, but she wasn't. She stood waiting for him with the two witness robots, a smile on her face as if seeing him somehow made her happy. What an actress. He had to wonder now, once again, what it was she wanted out of all this. He'd once again have to pull in and play it by ear where she was concerned. Perhaps she'd say something to give herself away. Meanwhile, she'd get no satisfaction.

"How did it go?" she asked cheerily, but then her face changed, tightened up when she noticed his mood swing. "What's wrong?"

"Nothing . . . Katherine," he said, her phony name sticking in his throat. "I found an exit to the top platform, and a computer, but nothing in it helped any, except to tell me what we already knew—that we'd have to solve the murder."

"Well then, I think we should stop wasting time and get on to that," she said suspiciously, not quite believing his change of attitude. "Are you sure you're okay?"

"Never better," he lied, angry at himself for wanting to be close to her despite what he'd learned. If he had any sense, he'd turn and run as fast and as far as he could from her. Instead, he said, "Let's go."

They moved out of the Compass Tower quickly and quietly, Katherine watching Derec out of the corner of her eye most of the time. He tried to be more nonchalant to keep from arousing her suspicions, but it was difficult for him. He apparently wasn't as schooled in subterfuge as she. As they made their way through the building, robots paid them no attention, already becoming familiar and comfortable with human presence.

When they stepped outside, they found a tram with a utility driver atop it, waving to them. "Friend Derec!" the robot called, and they moved over to the tram.

"What is it?" Derec asked the squat driver.

"Supervisor Euler asked me to be your driver today, honoring an earlier request you made in regard to transportation."

"Well," Derec said, looking at Katherine, "it appears that we're finally being trusted a little bit. Our own tram, eh?"

"It's radio-controlled," the utility robot said.

Derec narrowed his brows. "What's its range?"

"The range of the control is roughly equivalent to the limits of the already extruded city."

"Oh," Derec said quietly. "You mean that the tram won't operate except in city limits?"

"A fair appraisal," the robot said.

Katherine laughed loudly. "Now *that's* what I call trust," she said, and shook her head.

He glared at her and climbed into the tram. "Rec," he told his witness, "why don't you ride up here with me?"

The robot dutifully climbed in beside Derec, leaving Katherine to sit with her witness in the seat behind.

"Where to, sir?" the tram driver asked.

Derec turned to Katherine. "You know where we're going?"

"Quadrant #4," Katherine replied. "Eve will show you from there."

They drove on quickly. Derec, for the first time, took a moment to think about the other things that had happened in the office, things that were pushed out of his mind by his anger toward Katherine. His name, for instance. He was called David #1 on the computer record. Then why did he come *after* David #2? Was it a simple experiment shorthand, or did the name have meaning? It sounded so . . . engineered. The thoughts generated by that line of reasoning were more than he could bear. He pushed them away and thought that if his name was, indeed, David, then Katherine *had* told him the truth; at least about that.

There were other concepts implied in those few paragraphs. Whoever the overseer was, he obviously knew David and Katherine, and knew something of their past histories. So whoever had brought him here was someone he'd known before his memory loss, and he couldn't help but consider the possibility that the overseer had had something to do with his memory loss. But the chances were just as good, if not better, that Katherine herself had been connected with his amnesia for her own purposes, whatever they were.

Layers and layers. So much had been implied by the notes on the computer. The city was, indeed, considered an experiment in synnoetics, of that much he could now be certain. But then, when it came time to deal with a reason for the defense system going operational, the overseer seemed just as much in the dark as he, himself, was.

Derec also wasn't sure if he had been deliberately brought here to help the city, or if he had shown up accidentally, the overseer deciding to use him, as opposed to either stepping in himself or letting the operation shut itself down. The more answers he found, it seemed, the more in the dark he was.

They arrived at quadrant #4 without difficulty. Eve took her triangulation readings to help them find their way back to the house on the pedestal. Derec watched the city developing all around him as they drove, the sight of humans driving the inhabitants into a frenzy of human preparation—the robot equivalent of nesting.

"This is the place," Eve said as the tram stopped in the middle of an ordinary-looking street. The witness looked at around. "It doesn't appear to be here."

"It's moved some, that's all," Katherine said. "We'll go on foot from this point."

They climbed out of the tram and started walking, the tram following close behind them in case they had need of it.

"You sure this is the right direction?" Derec asked, after they had gone a block. "How far could it have moved?"

"Everything looks familiar here," she replied.

"The whole city looks the same," Derec said. "I don't think you . . ."

"There!" She pointed.

Derec needed no pointing finger to tell him they'd arrived. A tall tower stood in the middle of a street, nothing else anywhere near it. Atop the tower was a single room, sealed up except for a circular hole cut out of it.

"Let's leave a witness here with the tram in case of problems," Derec said. "We'll take Rec up with us."

"Fine," Katherine replied, walking to the pole.

He followed her, watching the spiral staircase reform when she touched the pole with her hand.

"You're not going to believe this," she told him, starting confidently up the stairs. "If this man's not your twin, he went to an awful lot of trouble to look just like you."

Derec smiled weakly in return, wondering, given the fact that he was #1, just who was whose twin.

She reached the top, waiting off to the side for him to join her. "I want you to go in first," she said. "After what happened last time, I'm afraid of my reactions. I may have to work up to it."

"All right," he said, moving around to the cut-out. As he got close to the place, he felt his own insides jumping a bit at the thought of seeing himself dead. He got right up to the cut-out, then quickly ducked his head in before he changed his mind.

It was empty.

He climbed through; there was no sign of a body or anything that resembled a body or anything else for that matter.

"Katherine," he called. "Come around here."

She moved to the cut-out, shyly poking her head inside, her eyes widening when she saw the empty room. "Where is he?" she asked.

"That was my question," Derec replied. "It appears that our corpse has gotten up and walked away.

"Or was taken away," she returned. "Remember what happened when he died? A utility robot had to fight waste control robots for possession of the corpse. Maybe they got him this time."

"Didn't anyone stay behind when you passed out before to keep that from happening?"

"I don't know," Katherine said, and went back out the cut-out to call down to her witness. "Eve! Did anyone stay behind after I fell unconscious yesterday?"

"No," the robot called back up. "You were our first priority. We all did our parts to get you home safely and to get you medical attention."

Katherine came back into the room. "No one stayed behind," she said.

"I heard," Derec replied. "Pretty convenient."

"Convenient for whom?" she said, eyes flashing. "What are you driving at?"

"Nothing," he replied. "I'm just . . . disappointed."

"You're disappointed," she said, sitting on the floor and leaning against the wall. "This was my ticket out of here."

"Just like you," he said, "thinking about yourself while the whole world crumbles around you."

Her eyes were dark fire. "And just who should I think about?" she asked. "The buckets of bolts who run this place, who don't have enough sense to keep from destroying themselves?"

"Like every other human culture that ever lived," he replied. "Yes. Think about them . . ." He pointed at her, then snapped his fingers. "Maybe we don't need a body for this.

Maybe we can simply recreate the circumstances."

"You mean try and set it all up just like it happened to the dead man?"

"Sure. The computer in the office told me that there is danger from alien contamination. Let's see if we can bring it out a little."

Katherine stood again, her face uncertain. "Need I remind you that the last man who had to face up to this predicament is dead?"

He walked past her, out onto the now inward-curled disc that held the room, watching the robots on the streets hurrying to their deadlines through time and space. She joined him within a minute.

"What choice do we have?" he asked.

"None," she answered. "Both of our problems are tied up in the murder. We'll do whatever we have to, to solve it."

"Let's go over everything the witness told you," Derec said. "Look for a loophole."

"It's sparse," Katherine replied. "He was already sealed up, and angry about it, when they arrived to cut him out. He had no idea why he'd been sealed in. When they cut him out, his behavior seemed a bit erratic, he had a headache and a cut on his foot."

"Didn't you have a headache last night?" he asked.

She cocked her head. "I just assumed it had something to do with my passing out," she said.

"Just a thought," Derec replied. "I'm trying everything on for size right now."

"Anyway," she continued, "he went off, against supervisory request, and turned up dead a short time later. When the utility robot tried to turn the body over to take a pulse, another room sealed itself off, and the robot just barely survived the sealing because of his quick reflexes. That's it. The whole story."

He leaned against the curled lip of the disc on stiff arms, trying to reason the way a computer would. "You know," he said after a minute, "the phrase 'alien contamination' could cover a lot of territory. On surface, human beings and their composition are obvious. But, under the surface, on the body's interior, we're all quite a strange collection of 'alien' germs and viruses."

"The bleeding foot," Katherine said. "That thought occurred to me, but I was never able to connect it with the actual murder, so I assumed it to be inconsequential."

"Me too," Derec replied. "But I'm beginning to think that, perhaps, this puzzle works on more than the obvious level." He knelt on the ground, studying the cut-out piece of city-robot that lay on the disc surface.

"What are you doing?" Katherine asked.

"This piece has been taken off stream," he said. "It's not connected to the city anymore, or to its programming source."

"So?"

"So it's dead, it's the only thing around here that isn't going to protect me from its jagged edges."

"You're going to hurt yourself!" she said loudly.

"There's only one way to test our theory," he said, rolling up the sleeve of his one-piece.

Rec poked his head out of the room. "Please, Friend Derec, don't do anything that could cause harm to your body."

Derec ignored both Katherine and Rec, drawing his forearm across a sharp edge of the dead city part, making a five-centimeter gash along his inner arm.

He stood, grimacing with the pain, then watched the dark blood well up from the place.

"Nothing yet," Katherine said.

"Let's try an experiment," Derec said, turning his arm over so the blood could drip on the disc. "The second sealed room didn't develop until the utility robot rolled the body over. Maybe gravity. . ."

"Derec!" Katherine yelled.

No sooner had the blood hit the floor than the curled lip of the disc began growing, pushing in and up, trying to close them in.

"Let's get out of here!" Derec called, moving toward the stairs, the disc curling up over his head like a cresting wave as he moved.

With Katherine right behind, he reached the stairs leading down, only to have them disappear before he could plant a foot on them. Overhead, the roof of the already existing room was stretching itself out, joining the edge of the disc in a perfect, seamless weld. Where the stairs had been was now a solid wall.

"Keep moving around the disc!" Derec called, breaking into a trot. "Maybe we can beat the enclosure."

He had turned his arm back over now, trying to catch dripping blood on his free hand to keep it off the ground. But it didn't help. The city-robot had isolated him as the alien carrier and was reacting to *him* now, and not his blood.

They went around the perimeter of the room, the roof hurrying to meet the curling disc. It had closed them in completely.

Then, as they watched, the already existing room seemed to melt and combine with the floor, the outer walls straightening and angling to ninety degrees, then pushing in all around.

Within a minute, they found themselves standing in a sealed room, exactly like the one David had been cut out of.

CHAPTER 11
DEADLY AIR

Derec and Katherine sat on the floor of the room, while Rec, who'd been trapped with them, leaned close to Derec, witnessing the boy wrapping his cut arm in a piece of cloth ripped from his one-piece.

"Do you think Eve's called for help?" he asked Rec as he worked.

"No," the witness said. "Eve will not perceive a danger to you. Are you in danger?"

"What about the utility robot?" Katherine asked, ignoring the robot's question. "Will the utility robot summon help?"

"That is within the scope of the utility robot's field prerogatives," Rec replied, straightening as Derec finished. He then wheeled slowly around the room, taking everything in for later recounting. Rec took his job very seriously.

Derec had left two loose ends on the tight bandage, and held his arm out to Katherine to tie them. "Can I trust you to tie a good knot?" he asked.

"What's that supposed to mean?" she asked.

"Nothing," he said.

She frowned deeply as she tied. "What happened in that office?" she asked. "You've treated me like your worst enemy ever since you came out of there." She pulled the knot tight, a smile touching her lips when he groaned loudly.

"Look," he said. "You've got secrets, I've got secrets. Why don't we just leave it at that?"

"Fine with me," she said. "All I want is for us to get the

est of this together; then I'll make an emergency hyperwave
all and be out of your hair in less than a day. You can rot
ere for all I care."

"We'll both rot here," he said, wanting to hurt her.

She drew back. "What do you mean?"

"Nothing."

"Damn you!" she yelled. "Tell me what you mean? Why
id you say I'd rot here?"

"No reason."

"It's the hyperwave, isn't it?" she asked. "They won't
ive us access to the hyperwave."

"It's not that, it's . . ."

"It's what? What?"

He leaned his head back and shut his eyes. "There is no
yperwave transmitter," he said softly.

She pulled herself a distance from him and curled into a
mall ball. "You're lying," she said, but he could tell that
he really believed him.

"The robots have no contact with the outside," he said.
They have no spaceport for landing ships. They have no
yperwave, or even the equipment for making one. They've
een evasive about the point because of the security alert."

"Why have you waited until now to tell me this?" she
sked.

"I told you—you've got secrets, I've got secrets."

"I get it now," she said, her eyes distant. "We're both free
gents, looking out for ourselves."

"Something like that," he said, but why did it hurt so bad
o say it?

She stood and moved all the way across the room to sit on
he wall opposite. "Well, I suppose, at this point, we must
vork together to solve the murder," she said.

"I suppose," he replied, sorry to have started the whole
ine of conversation.

Her face was hard. "After that, I will thank you to stay
way from me. We'll each take care of our own problems."

"Fair enough."

"So tell me, if it's not a great secret, why the room sealed around us because you cut yourself?"

"I've got a theory, nothing more," he said. "The city-robot is programmed to protect human and robot inhabitants and to defend itself against anything alien . . . foreign to it. Apparently blood inside the body is fine, but once it gets outside the body, its natural microbes register as alien and set off the works. The city program has to be fairly complicated. The omission is obvious, and could either have been a mistake or a deliberate glitch to test the ability of the robots and humans living here to control their own system."

"What do we do now?"

"Well, once we get out, if I can get access to the central core with one of the supervisors, I can reprogram the core to accept human blood as a natural microbe on the body of the city. In this sterile atmosphere, it's perfectly understandable how such a glitch could happen. It could even be a means for the city to protect itself from infection."

"But how did David die?" Katherine asked.

"Could it have been blood loss?" Derec asked.

She shook her head. "No chance," she replied. "There was very little blood. The cut was smaller than yours."

"What's left?" he said. "I have to think that his death is a completely separate incident, unconnected to the blood loss."

She looked skeptical. "Back-to-back coincidences, Derec? Deadly coincidences at that."

He stood. "You're right, of course. It must all tie together . . . but how?" He paced the room. "What other leads do we have? The only other connection is the fact that both of you came away from a sealed room with a headache."

"We have another problem," she replied, watching him moving back and forth in the confined space. "When I came in this room the first time to find the body, it had been sealed up . . . air tight."

He stopped walking and stared at her. "The city would never keep us locked up without air. It would be a violation of the First Law, should we die."

"It happened to David."

"But David was already dead when it happened to him," Derec said. "In fact, this just strengthens my theory. When the utility robot rolled him over to check for signs of life, gravity pulled a little more blood out of an already open wound. The room didn't relate to David as a human, since he was dead. All it fixed its sights on was the 'infection.' We're still alive and the city-robot knows it. Whatever else this crazy place may be, it's run robotically. Ipso facto, we're safe on that account."

"Just the same," she said, "I'll be happier to be out of here."

"Me too."

"You realize, Derec," she said, her voice low and heavy with meaning, "that we are recreating history right now. We are going through exactly the same progression that David went through before he died."

"I know," Derec replied. "But what else can we do?"

They stared at one another across the space of the room, the witness recording it all, and they may as well have been a million kilometers apart. They sat that way for a long time, far longer than it should have taken for a supervisor to show up.

Derec spent the time alternately trying to think his way out of their dilemma, figure out what was going on with Katherine, and looking at his watch. And the late morning turned to early afternoon, and Derec, who wasn't worried about the air supply in the room, suddenly became very thirsty and began to dwell on the possibility that the robots had either forgotten them or couldn't find them.

"Friend Derec!" came a loud voice from outside the room. "Friend Katherine! It is I, Wohler, the philosopher!"

Derec glanced at his watch. It was nearly five P.M., which

meant rain was undoubtedly on the way. "We're in here!" Derec called. "Can you get us free?"

Wohler called back loudly, "An Auroran philosopher once said, 'Freedom is a condition of mind, and the best way to secure it is to breed it.' Ho, Derec. We were held up digging in the mines, but I now have a laser torch to cut you out. I am here on the west wall of this room. I will ask kindly that you move to the east wall to avoid the torch as well as possible!"

Derec was sitting against the west wall. He stood immediately and moved over near Katherine, who looked at him with unreadable eyes.

"Go ahead!" Derec yelled through cupped hands, Rec moving up closer to the west wall to witness the torching from the inside.

Even through the thickness of the wall, they could hear the hiss of the torch on the other side. Derec slid down the wall to sit next to Katherine. Their arms accidentally touched. Both of them pulled away.

"Something's wrong," she said. "Something feels wrong."

"I know," he replied, "but what?"

The inside of the wall began to glow red hot in a small, circular section. Then the red turned to white, and a rivet-sized section burned through to reveal the outside through a quivering haze of heat.

Derec watched the hole expand, his mind racing as the torch began to etch the beginnings of a human-sized circle in the side of the room. He thought about headaches, and about erratic behavior and about blood and its composition—and then he thought about the nature of the city-robot.

"Stop!" he yelled, jumping to his feet and running as close to the metal cutting as he dared. "Stop the torch!"

"Derec?" Katherine asked, beginning to stand.

Derec covered his mouth with his hand. "Get on the floor!" he yelled. "All the way down and cover your mouth!"

"What's wrong?" came Wohler's voice from outside, the sound of the laser winding down to nothing. "What is it?"

"We can't use the torch on the wall!" Derec called.

"I don't understand," Wohler said, bending down so that his eye covered the hole in the wall and he could look inside.

Derec backed away, getting down close to Katherine on the floor. "Is there some way to flush oxygen in here?" he asked loudly.

"We've come in a newly manufactured emergency truck," Wohler replied. "I believe the emergency equipment includes oxygen cylinders."

"Get one quickly!"

"The rains are approaching," Wohler said. "We must hurry and get you out."

"Listen," Derec said. "The city material is a kind of metallic skin, an iron/plastic alloy. In the manufacturing process, a great deal of carbon monoxide is used as the reducing agent. I think your torch is liberating the monoxide as a gas into the closed room. By cutting us out, you're gassing us!"

"The utility robot has gone for the oxygen!" Wohler said. "You have my apologies."

"You didn't know," Derec said. He looked at Katherine. "Are you all right?"

"So far," she replied. "Are you sure of what you're saying? David didn't die until later, outside of the room."

"It doesn't matter," he replied. "Carbon monoxide in large doses will simply work its way gradually through the bloodstream, bonding firmly with hemoglobin and starving the tissues of oxygen. His headache and erratic behavior were the first signs of an oxygen narcosis reaction and, unless he was treated to massive doses of oxygen, it would spread throughout his entire body, eventually killing him."

"And *my* headache?"

"You walked into the room with his body just after they had cut through the walls," he said. "You undoubtedly saved your own life by passing out when you did, for they took you out of the room immediately, thus limiting your exposure to the gas. Carbon monoxide is colorless, odorless, and tasteless. You would never have known what hit you."

"The oxygen is here, Derec!" Wohler called, fitting a hissing nozzle up against the hole.

Derec crawled across the floor toward the hole. "Come on," he said, waving her on.

They reached the hole and sat breathing the life-giving oxygen. Derec felt the beginnings of a small headache, but he was sure it would get no worse.

They emptied the cannister of oxygen and began another. When that was finished, Wohler returned to the opening. "Rain is imminent," the robot said. "How do we get you out? We have nothing small to cut through this, and our heavy equipment can't be brought up this high, at least not with the rain coming. Do we leave you for the night?"

"There's no time for that," Derec said. "I must get underground and report this information to the central core."

"The rain is also dangerous for me, Friend Derec," Wohler said. "I must take shelter soon."

"Okay," Derec said. "Stay with me as long as you can. Just let me think for a minute."

"Derec . . ." Katherine began.

"Shhh," Derec said. "Not now."

"Think about your arm," she said. "Think about where you cut it, and how."

"My arm, I . . ." He held his arm up, looking at the blood-soaked bandage and feeling the throb. "I cut it on the dead piece of city-robot," he said.

"Because . . ."

"Because it was the only piece of the city that would *allow* me to cut myself on it!" He put his hands to his head. "That's it! Wohler! Stand back. We're coming through."

With that, he raised his right hand, pushing his pointer

finger through the small, burned-out hole. As soon as his finger grazed the jagged edge of the hole, it expanded to allow free passage. Next came his balled-up fist; the hole expanded wide to keep from cutting him. Then his arm went through, followed by head and shoulders. Seconds later, he was standing on the disc, its edges curling up to protect him. Katherine followed him through, and both of them stared into the teeth of a bitter cold wind and a savage vision of blue-purple clouds crackling with lightning.

"We must go now!" Wohler said, his shiny gold body reflecting lightning flashes.

Suddenly, Katherine broke from the group, hurrying to the stairs.

"What are you doing?" Derec called to her, but she ignored him, charging as quickly as she could down the stairs.

"Perhaps she's hurrying to safety," Wohler said, as Rec made it through the hole in the wall.

"Perhaps," Derec said, but as he ran the rest of the disc and began to take the stairs, Katherine had already run to the tram that was still dutifully waiting. She barked some orders to the utility driver, and the unit sped off into the darkening night.

"What is happening?" Wohler called as he followed Derec down the stairs.

"I'm afraid something crazy," the boy answered, remembering a conversation they had had while waiting to be rescued.

They moved to the emergency van that Wohler had brought. "We must get you back to your apartment before the rain comes," the robot said.

"No!" Derec said. "Get me underground. I'll wait out the storm there. Then you've got to go after Katherine. I'm afraid of what she's doing."

A long streak of lightning struck the top of the pedestal right beside them, the metal clanging loudly and smoking.

"But where could she have gone, Friend Derec?" Wohler

asked as they all climbed aboard the large, white van.

"The Compass Tower," Derec said, voice heavy with dread. "I'm afraid she's climbing the Compass Tower."

The Quadrant #4 Extruder Station was less than ten minutes from the sealed room, with Wohler moving the emergency van along at the top speed possible that still allowed a safety margin for his passengers.

Derec watched the city speed past, its full-blown dance of thoughtless progress still continuing despite the gathering darkness, despite the fact that its course was suicidal. He feared for the city; he feared for Katherine, or whatever her name was. She was going for the Key, he was certain of that, trying to take herself out of the situation in the only way she knew how. He didn't expect that the Key would do her much good, but he could hardly blame her for trying. What frightened him was the danger she was exposing herself to by trying for the Key in the rain. He would have gone after her alone, but, having experienced the destructive power of Robot City's weather, he knew he'd be no help at all in a storm. Only a robot would have a chance.

Wohler jerked them to a stop before the Extruder Station entrance, a series of low, wide buildings constructing themselves from ground level. There was no robotic activity here now, no unloading of trucks. All had taken shelter from the impending storm.

"You think she's gone to the Compass Tower?" Wohler asked.

"I'm sure of it."

"She may have time before the storm to get inside to safety."

Derec looked at him, then reached out and put a hand on his shiny gold arm. "She's not going inside," he said. "She'll be trying to climb the pyramid."

"But why?"

"We hid something there, something she's trying to retrieve."

"I must go," Wohler said without hesitation. "She'll be killed."

"What will the rain do to you?" Derec asked as he climbed out of the van.

"Rain in ordinary amounts won't do anything," the robot replied. "City rain could force its way through my plating in a thousand different places and make its way into my electrical system. The limits of the damage at that point are a matter of imaginative speculation."

"I don't know what to tell you," Derec said. "If you don't go . . ."

"Katherine will die," the robot finished. "You can tell me nothing. My duty is self-evident. Good-bye, Derec."

Wohler looked back once to make sure the witnesses were off the van, then hurried off at a pace that didn't include the safety margin he had preserved with Derec in the cab.

"Come with me," Derec told the witnesses, and moved toward the now-closed entrance to the underground. Despite his fears for Katherine's safety, he had things to do. With his explanation of the murder and its connection to the city defenses, backed up totally by Rec's witness testimony, there was no doubt that he'd at least be able to get into the core and stop the replication. That wouldn't stop tonight's rain, however, or even future rains for a time; but it was a start.

He opened the outside door, then hurried inside, going down the stairs to the now-deserted holding area and its bank of elevators. This wasn't the same Extruder Station he'd been in previously, but it was set up exactly the same.

He walked quickly to the same elevator he had taken with Avernus when he'd gone underground. He got inside with the witnesses and pushed the down arrow. The lift began its long journey to the caverns below.

The elevator opened into the bustling cavern where the work of building Robot City continued unabated. There wasn't a supervisor in sight, however. There seemed to be activity at one of the darkened, unused mine tunnels at the west end of the cavern.

He began to move into the flow, then stopped, steeling himself. Deliberation, Avernus had said. As he stood on the edge of the activity, a long tram sped past him at a hundred kilometers an hour, passing within a few centimeters, his hair being pulled by its suction.

Deliberation. It was the only way.

"Stay with me," he told the witnesses. Then he set his body in line with his goal and shut his eyes, taking a blind step right into the fray.

He walked quickly, without hesitation, trying to direct his mind away from the feel of unrushing robots and vehicles that barely brushed him as they hurried past. Occasionally, he would open his eyes a touch, just to make sure he was still heading in the right direction. Then he'd squeeze them closed again, and keep walking.

He kept this up for nearly ten minutes as he crossed the great chamber without mishap. As he reached the safety of the mine entrance, he released a huge sigh that made him feel as if he'd been holding his breath the whole time.

A utility robot was stationed near the mine entrance, using an overhead pulley system to remove the spent batteries from a fleet of mine trams and replacing them with charged batteries. The trams were parked three deep all around him.

"Robot!" Derec called across the cars to him. "Where can I find Supervisor Avernus?"

The utility robot pointed down the tunnel. "They are releasing some of the reservoir water into the abandoned tunnels. It may be dangerous for humans."

"Thanks," Derec said, then pointed to a tram. "Has this one been recharged?"

"Yes," the robot answered.

"Thanks again," Derec said, and climbed behind the steering mechanism. "Rec, Eve, get in."

As the robots climbed into the back of the tram, the utility called to Derec.

"Did you not hear me? It may be dangerous for humans in there."

"Thanks," Derec said again, waving, then keyed on the electric hum and geared the car down the dark tunnel.

As he sped down the tunnels, marking distance by counting the small, red lights spaced along the length, he passed other trams full of robots going the other way. They were uniformly dirty from digging, many of them dangling shorted-out appendages. Even for robots, they appeared grim. One tram they passed carried a robot shorting from the head, sparks arcing from his photocells and speaker.

He drove for several kilometers, climbing gently upward with the tunnel. Finally, he approached a large egg of light that threw long shadows against the rough-hewn walls. When he reached the place, he found a large number of utility robots, plus six of the seven supervisors, gathered around a drop-off in the tunnel.

He jumped from the tram and pushed his way through the crowd to approach the drop-off. It was the same area in which the robots had been digging the day before, only approached from the other side. A subsidiary tunnel, going upward, had been dug by hand, and it met the existing tunnel, which had been trenched out to carry water. The trench was empty. Euler and Rydberg were leaning out over the trench, looking up the newly dug tunnel, while Avernus sorted out those robots damaged beyond usefulness here, and sent them back down the tunnel.

Derec moved up to Euler. "I've solved the murder," he told the supervisor without preamble.

Both Rydberg and Euler turned to look at him. "What was the cause?" Rydberg asked.

"Carbon monoxide poisoning," Derec said. "When they tried to torch David out of the sealed room, carbon monoxide was released by the heating process into the enclosed space."

"It was our fault, then," Euler said.

"It was an unfortunate accident," Derec replied. "And I have witnesses." Both Eve and Rec hurried to join him.

"Two minutes," Dante called. The small robot was fiddling with a terminal hooked up in the back of a tram, his long digits moving with incredible speed over the keyboard.

"Two minutes until what?" Derec asked.

"Until the charge we placed by the reservoir wall brings the water down," Euler replied.

"I also know why the city is on security alert," Derec said. "It was because of David's blood. When he cut himself, the blood that dropped on the city-robot was mistaken for an alien presence because of the blood organisms. My witnesses will also corroborate that fact."

Euler spoke up. "Then we need to feed this information to the central core and stop the replication, if there's time."

"What do you mean, if there's time?" Derec asked.

Avernus joined the group. "We found a cavern that would hold all the water in the reservoir, thanks to your sonogram. Unfortunately, it will take a great deal of digging to reach it." Avernus pointed to the trench. "This diversion will do no more than put off the inevitable for one more day; then, instead of overflowing above, the water will overflow below, here in the tunnels."

"Where is the central core?" Derec asked. "If we can get to it and stop the replication, then we can use the digging machines to turn the trick before the next day's rain."

Avernus turned to Dante, looking at him over the heads of all the other robots. "Where is the core now?" he called loudly.

The little robot's digits flew over the keys while Euler spoke. "Even with the machines, we'd have to start digging almost immediately to reach the cavern in time."

"The core is in Tunnel J-33 at the moment," Dante called, "moving south by southwest at ten kilometers per hour." He hesitated briefly, then added, "Twenty centads."

Avernus turned abruptly from them all. "That is . . . too bad," he said.

"What do you mean, too bad?" Derec asked.

All at once, there was a rumble that shook the tunnel, dust and loose pebbles falling atop them. Derec nearly lost his footing on the quaking ground. Within seconds, a low roar filled the mines, growing in intensity with each passing second.

"It is too bad," Euler said loudly above the roar, "because the central core is in Tunnel J-33, on the wrong side of the trench, and the rains are beginning outside."

With that, tons of water came rushing down the new tunnel, slamming in fury into the trench below, churning, forthy white, dangerous and untamed. Derec watched in horrified fascination as his only possible route to the central core disappeared under a raging river that hadn't been there a second before.

Katherine's mind was as dark as the clouds overhead as her tram hurried through the streets of Robot City in the direction of the Compass Tower.

"I fear we won't make the Tower before the rains come," the utility driver told her. "We must take shelter."

"No," she said, determined that she'd keep them from taking away her last ounce of free will. "Go on. Hurry!"

"It is not safe for you out here," the robot insisted. "I cannot in all conscience take you any farther."

Katherine began to respond with anger, but feared it would arouse the robot's suspicions. "All right," she said. "Pull over at the next building."

"Very good," the robot replied, and brought the tram to an immediate stop before a tall building that had the words MUSEUM OF ART embossed in metal above the doors.

The robot got out of the tram and took Katherine by the arm to guide her. "This way, please," he said, and Katherine began to think the robots had been having meetings about human duplicity.

She allowed the robot to lead her into the confines of the building. "This is Supervisor Arion's project," he said, "to please our human inhabitants."

She looked around, taking note that the robot had used the word *inhabitant* instead of visitors. It merely confirmed what she already knew to be the case. They weren't going to let her go. They had no intention of letting her go. The robots needed someone to serve, and they'd keep the masters as slaves just to see that it came to be.

The first floor of the museum was full of geometric sculptures, many of them made from city material that moved through its own sequences, constantly changing shapes in an infinite variety of patterns.

After a moment, she asked, "Please, is it possible to contact Derec and tell him where we are? I'm afraid he'll worry."

"There should be a terminal in the curator's office," the robot replied. "Would you like me to do it for you?"

"Yes, please. I would be most grateful."

The robot hurried off immediately. As soon as he was out of sight at the far end of the building, Katherine turned and ran.

She got quickly out the front doors and down the short walk to the tram, taking the driver's position. It started up easily, and she was off. She had no idea of which streets to take to get to the pyramid, but its size made it a beacon. She simply kept moving toward it.

She concentrated on planning as she drove. The rain was very close now, and she didn't want to get caught in it, but it was worth the try to get out of the city. Derec had said there was a trap door from the office to the platform atop the structure. She'd go through the inside of the pyramid, then, to reach the top. The Key was hidden partway down the outside of the structure, and it would be far easier and faster to climb down from the top than to climb up.

The sky rumbled loudly as she drove; the wind whipped her long hair around her face. She was cold, but put it out of her mind as she concentrated on her objective. Why did he have to do it to her? Why did he have to go over to the other side? The city had become Derec's obsession. He apparently couldn't understand that she had to have freedom, that she couldn't live within its structure forever.

The pyramid loomed large before her. It lit up brightly as a bolt of lightning ran down its face. She skidded to a stop before it and jumped out of the tram, hearing a noise behind her.

There, two blocks distant, the robot that called itself Wohler was hurrying to intercept her. She turned and ran up to the entry. The city material melted away at her approach to allow her inside.

Once inside, she had no idea of where she was going. The only thing she remembered for sure was that she needed to keep going up. She ran the maze-like halls, taking every opportunity to climb stairs or take an elevator that would put her higher. About halfway up the structure, she heard an announcement over unseen loudspeakers that called attention to her flight and gave instructions for her apprehension.

At that, she doubled her pace, going full out. Her only hope of escaping was to reach the safety of the off-limits zone before she was spotted.

She hurried unseen down the now-shortened hallways, reaching the last elevator up. A tech robot with welder arms spotted her as she hurried inside. Heart pounding, she stabbed at the up arrow and the machine sped her quickly to the upper floor.

The doors slid open and she burst through, running immediately. There were voices behind, calling her by name. She turned a corner, ran up a short ramp, and burst into the off-limits hallway just as the robots behind were closing on her.

She ran to the door leading up to the office, her hand going to the power stud.

"Katherine."

She recognized Wohler's voice and turned to face him. He stood, a hallway full of robots behind him, at the edge of the off-limits zone, the same place the witnesses had stopped earlier in the day.

"What do you want?" she asked.

"Come away from there. This place is off-limits."

She smiled. "Not to me," she said. "I'm human, remember? I'm free, and I'm going to be freer."

"Please do not go outside," Wohler said. "The rains are beginning. It could be dangerous for you."

"You're not going to keep me here," she said, opening the door that faced the spiral staircase.

"We would love to have you stay with us," the robot said, "but we would never keep you here against your will."

"Then why don't you have the means on-planet for me to leave or call for help?"

"You act as if we brought you here under false pretenses," Wohler said. "We did nothing. You came here uninvited. Welcome . . . but uninvited. Our civilization has not developed to the point where planetary interaction is possible. You can see that for yourself."

"We're wasting time," Katherine said, and started through the door.

"Please reconsider," the robot called. "Don't put yourself in jeopardy."

She stared hard at him. "I've been in jeopardy every second I've been in this crazy place."

With that, she moved through the door, closing it behind her. She took the stairs quickly and entered the office. The angry clouds rolled up close to the viewers, making it seem as if she were standing in the midst of the gathering storm.

Searching the office, she found the ladder easily enough, climbing it to reach the windy platform above. The wind was so strong that she feared getting to her feet, and crawled to the edge where she and Derec had made their first treacherous descent into the city of robots.

For the first time since being freed from the sealed room, her fears began to overcome her anger at the situation as she turned her body to edge herself off the dizzying height to begin her climb downward. The wind pulled viciously at her like cold, prying hands; her ears and nose went numb, and her fingers tingled with the cold.

Though the pyramid was made from the same material as the rest of the city, it wasn't the same in any other respect. It was rigid and unbending, its face set with patterns of holes that she and Derec had used as hand and footholds previously, and in which they had hidden the Key on their first descent.

Her mind whirled as she climbed, slowly, so slowly. How far down had it been? She had been moving fast, and Derec, carrying the Key, had been unable to keep up. They had stopped for a conference and decided to hide the Key and continue without it. How far down? A fourth of the climb, barely a fourth, in the leftmost hole of the pattern that ran down the center of the structure.

She continued downward, her fingers hurting now, her eyes looking upward, trying to gauge her distance just right. She began testing the holes in the repeated pattern, to no avail. She still hadn't reached the place. Something wet and cold hit her hard on the back. Her hands almost pulled out of their holds reflexively. It was a raindrop, and it wet the entire back of her one-piece.

She was running out of time.

The pattern of holes repeated again as she inched downward, and when she looked up, squinting against the frigid wind, she *knew* she had reached the place.

Hugging the pyramid face with the last of her strength she slowly reached out, sticking her hand into the leftmost hole of the pattern.

The Key was gone.

"No!" she screamed loudly into the teeth of the monster and, as if in response, the rain tore from the heavens in blinding, bludgeoning sheets to silence her protests.

* * *

Derec stood at the exit door to the Extruder Station and listened to the rain pounding against the door, and watched the small puddle that had somehow made its way under the sealed entry. Katherine was out there somewhere, and Wohler. Nothing had been heard from either of them since before the start of the rain. Avernus had made contact with the Compass Tower, and though both had been seen there, neither was there now.

With the rain controlling the day, everything had come to a standstill, making searching impossible, making contact with the central core impossible, making everything except the almighty building project slow to nothing. It was maddening.

He pounded the door, his fist sinking in, cushioning. He wanted to open those doors and run into the city and find her for himself—but he knew what that meant. Most likely, nothing would be known until the rain abated the next morning.

He turned from the door and walked down the stairs to the holding area and the six robot supervisors who awaited him there. His mind was awash in anxiety.

"Supervisor Rydberg has proposed a plan, Friend Derec," Euler said. "Perhaps you will comment on it."

Derec looked at Rydberg, trying to bring his mind back to the present. Why did the woman affect him this way? "Let's hear your plan," he said.

"We can go ahead and devise our evacuation schedule for the robots working underground," Rydberg said. "It seems that when morning comes, you will be able to contact the core and halt the replication. It will be too late to dig through to the cavern in time, but at least we will have the opportunity to spare our mine workers before the floods."

"Why do you have to give up like this?" Derec said, exasperated. "You've heard the reasons for the defenses. Can't you just stop them now and use the digging equipment to begin excavating the cavern?"

Waldeyer, the squat, wheeled supervisor, said, "The central core is our master program. We cannot abandon it. Only the central core can judge the veracity of your statements and make the final decision."

"I'm going to reprogram the central core," Derec answered, too loudly. "I'm going to change its definition of 'veracity.' And besides, the Laws of Robotics are your master program, and the Second Law states that you will obey a human command unless it violates the First Law. I'm *commanding* you to halt the mining processes and begin digging through to the drainage cavern."

"The defensive procedures were designed by the central core to protect the city, which is designed to protect human life," Waldeyer replied. "The central core *must* be the determining factor in any decision to abandon the defenses. Though your arguments sound humane, they may, ultimately, be in violation of the First Law; for if the central core determines that your conclusions are erroneous, then shutting down the defenses could be the most dangerous of all possible decisions."

Derec felt as if he were on a treadmill. All argument ultimately led back to the central core. And though he was sure that the central core would back off once he programmed the information about human blood into it, he had no way to prove that to the robots who, in turn, refused to do anything to halt the city's replication until they'd received that confirmation from central.

Then an idea struck him, an idea that was so revisionist in its approach that he was frightened at first even to think out its effects on the robots. What he had in mind would either liberate their thinking or send them into a contradictory mental freeze-up that could destroy them.

"What do you think of Rydberg's plan?" Avernus asked him. "It will save a great many robots."

Avernus—that was it—Avernus the humanitarian. Derec knew that his idea would destroy the other robots, but Avernus, he was different. Avernus leaned toward the humane, a leaning that could just possibly save himself and the rest of Robot City.

"I will comment on the evacuation plan later," Derec said. "First, I'd like to speak with Avernus alone."

"We make decisions together," Euler said.

"Why?" Derec asked.

"We've always done it that way," Rydberg said.

"Not any more," Derec said, his voice hard. "Unless you can give me a sound, First Law reason why I shouldn't speak with Avernus alone, I will then assume you are violating the Laws yourselves."

Euler walked to the center of the room, then turned slowly to look at Avernus. "We've always done it this way," he said.

Avernus, the giant, moved stoically toward Euler, putting a larger pincer on the robot's shoulder. "It won't hurt anything, this once, if we go against our own traditions."

"But traditions are the hallmark of civilization," Euler said.

"Survival is also one of the hallmarks," Derec replied, looking up at Avernus. "Are you willing?"

"Yes," Avernus answered without hesitation. "We will speak alone."

Derec led Avernus to the elevators, then had a thought and returned to Euler. He unwrapped the fabric bandage from his cut arm and handed it to the supervisor. "Have the blood analyzed, the data broken down on disc so I can feed it to the core."

"Yes, Derec," Euler said, and it was the first time the supervisor had addressed him without the formal declaration, Friend. Maybe they were all growing up a little bit.

Derec then joined Avernus in the elevator, pushing the down arrow as the doors slid closed. They only traveled down for a moment before Derec pushed the emergency stop button; the machine jerked to a halt.

"What is this about?" Avernus asked.

"I want to make a deal with you," Derec said.

"What sort of deal?"

"The lives of your robots for one of your digging machines."

Avernus just stared at him. "I do not understand."

"Let's talk about the Third Law of Robotics," Derec said. "You are obligated by the Third Law to protect your own existence as long as it doesn't interfere with the First or Second Laws. In your case, with your special programming, I can easily extend the Third Law to include the robots under your control."

"Go on."

"My deal is a simple one. Rydberg has suggested an evacuation plan that could save the robots in the mines from the flooding that is sure to occur if the cavern is not excavated. That evacuation plan depends *completely* on my reprogramming the central core to halt the replication. For if I don't, the city will have to keep replicating, even to its own destruction . . . that destruction to include the robots who are working underground."

"I understand that," Avernus said.

"All right." Derec took a deep breath. What he was getting ready to propose would undoubtedly freeze out the positronics of any of the other robots; the contradictions were too great, the choices too impossible to make. But with Avernus . . . maybe, just maybe. "Unless you give me one of the digging machines so I can begin the excavation myself, I will refuse to reprogram the central core, thereby condemning all your robots to stay underground during the flooding."

Avernus red eyes flared brightly. "You would . . . kill so many?"

"I would save your city *and* your robots!" Derec yelled. "It's all or nothing. Give me the machine or suffer the consequences."

"You ask me to deny the central core program that protects the First Law."

"Yes," Derec said simply, his voice quieting. "You have *got* to make the creative leap to save your robots. Some-

where in that brain of yours, you've got to make a value
judgment that goes beyond your programming."

Avernus just stood there, quaking slightly, and Derec felt
tears welling up in his eyes, knowing the torture he was
putting the supervisor through. If this failed, if he, in effect,
killed Avernus by killing his mind, he'd never be able to
forgive himself.

The big robot's eyes flashed on and off several times, and
suddenly his body shuddered violently, then stopped. Derec
heard a sob escape his own lips. Avernus bent to him.

"You will have your digging machine," the robot told
him, "and me to help you use it."

CHAPTER 13
THE CENTRAL CORE

Even as Katherine clung doggedly to the face of the pyramid, she knew that her ability to hold on could be measured in no more than minutes, as the rain lashed savagely at her and the winds worked to rip her off the patterned facade.

The ground lay several hundred meters below, calling to her. As her body went totally numb in the freezing downpour, her strong survival instinct was the only thing keeping her hanging on.

Her brain whirled, rejecting its own death while trying desperately to prepare for it, and through it all, she could hear the wind calling her name, over and over.

"Katherine!"

Closer now, the sound grew more pronounced. It seemed to come from below.

"Katherine!"

For the first time since she'd begun her climb, she risked a look downward, in the direction of the sound. She blinked through the icy water that streamed down her face only to see an apparition, a gray mass moving quickly up the face below her, proof that her mind was already gone.

"Katherine, hang on! I'm coming!"

In disbelief, she watched the apparition coming closer. And as her arms ached, trying to talk her into letting go and experiencing peace, she saw a golden hand reach from under the gray lump and grasp a handhold in one of the cutouts.

Wohler!

"Please hold on!"

"I can't!" she called back, surprised to hear the hysteria in
er own voice. And as if to reinforce the idea, her left hand
st its grip, her arm falling away from the building, the
dded pressure sending cramping pain through her right arm
ill lodged in the hole.

The robot below hurried his pace. The wind, getting be-
eath the tarp he wore to protect himself from the rain,
ulled it away from his body to float like a huge, prehistoric
ird.

"P-please . . ." she called weakly, her right arm ready to
ive out.

"Hold on! Please hold on!"

The urgency in his voice astounded her, giving her an
xtra ounce of courage, a few more seconds when seconds
ere everything. And as she felt her hand slip away for good
nd all, his large body had wedged in behind her, holding
er up against the facade.

Wohler clamped solidly in hand and footholds just above
nd below hers and he completely enveloped her, protecting.
he let herself relax, all the strength immediately oozing out
f her, Wohler supporting her completely.

"Are you unhurt?" the robot asked in her ear.

"I-I think so," she answered in a small voice. "What hap-
ens now?"

"We can only wait," Wohler said, his voice sounding
omehow ragged. "An old Earth proverb says, 'Patience is a
itter plant but it has sweet fruit.' Survival w-will be our
uit . . . Friend Katherine."

"Friend Wohler," she responded, tears mixing with the
old rain on her face. "I want to th-thank you for coming up
ere for me."

But Wohler didn't answer.

The supervisors as a group stood behind the gateway ex-
avator that Derec and Avernus operated. Neither helping
or hindering, they simply took it all in, no doubt unable to

appreciate the thought processes that had led the big robot
pull the machine away from his mining crews and their repl
cation labors, to put it to work simply clearing a path f
something that, at this point, was no more than mere pote
tial.

Derec had seen excavators like these before. On the aste
oid where he had first awakened to find he had no identit
the robots had used identical machines to cut out the guts
the asteroid in their search for the Key to Perihelion.

The gateway was a marvel, for it demolished and rebui
at the same time. Derec sat with Avernus at the two cabi
control panels, watching the boom arms cutting into roc
face nearly a hundred feet distant. One of the boom arm
bore rotary grinders, the other microwave lasers that to
frantically at the core of the planet, chewing it up as it wen
There were numerous conveyors and pulleys for the remov
and scanning of potential salvage material, but none of thes
were in use right now. They were simply grinding and con
pressing the excavated rock and earth, the gateway itse
using the materials to build a strong tunnel behind—smoot
rock walls, reinforcing synthemesh, even overhead lamps.

They were creeping toward the cavern, every meter
meter closer to possible salvation. They had been workin
through the night, Derec desperately trying to let the effo
keep his mind off Katherine and Wohler. It wasn't workin
There had been no word of them since before the storm ha
begun nearly ten hours ago. Had they been alive, he woul
have heard by now.

There was always the chance that Katherine had retrieve
the Key and left, perhaps waiting out the rain in the gra
void of Perihelion, or perhaps finding her way to anothe
place. But that didn't explain Wohler's absence.

During the grueling hours spent working the gateway
Avernus and Derec had conversed very little, both, appa
ently, lost in their own thoughts. Derec worried for Avernus
who he knew was going through a great many interna
recriminations that could only be resolved with a satisfactor

outcome and subsequent vindication of his actions.

"Derec!" came Euler's voice from the newly built tunnel behind; it was the first time the robot had spoken to them since the operation had begun.

Derec looked at his watch. It was nearly five A.M. He shared a glance with Avernus. "Yes!" he called back.

"The rain has abated," Euler returned. "The missing have been located!"

Derec resisted the urge to jump from the controls and charge out of there. He still had work to do. He looked at Avernus. "What now?"

"Now we will see," the robot said. "We must locate the core and reprogram."

"Should I leave you here to continue operations and go with someone else to the core?"

"No," Avernus said with authority. "I am supervisor of the underground and know my way around it. I also . . . must know the outcome. Can you understand that?"

Derec reached out and punched off the control board, stopping new digging and bringing all operants to the standby position. "You bet I can understand it. Let's go!"

They moved out of the gateweay, squeezing past stacked up cylinders to join the other supervisors in the tunnel behind. It was the first time Derec had looked back at their handiwork. The tunnel he and Avernus had made stretched several hundred yards behind them, nearly as far he could see.

"Where are Katherine and Wohler?" he asked. "Are they all right?"

"No one knows," Rydberg said. "They are clinging to the side of the Compass Tower, nearly a hundred meters above the surface, but they have not responded to voice communication, nor have they attempted to come down."

Derec's heart sank. They'd been out all night in the rain. It looked bad.

"Are rescue operations underway?" he asked.

"Utility robots are now scaling the Tower to determine the

extent of the problem for emergency disposition," Euler said.

"The central core," Avernus said to Dante. "Tell me where it is right now."

"Tell me honestly, Euler," Derec said. "Will my presence at the Tower facilitate the rescue operation?"

"Tower rescue has always been part of our basic program, for reasons no one can fathom," the robot said. "Standard operating procedure has already been initiated. You could only hinder the operation."

"Good," Derec said. Of course Tower rescue was standard. The overseer had worried that, should the trap door to the office below become jammed, he would be caught on the Tower, unable to get down. The almighty overseer didn't mind letting everyone else twist slowly in the wind, but he wasn't going to let himself be uncomfortable on the Tower.

Dante spoke up from the terminal in his tram car. "The central core is in Quadrant 2, Tunnel D-24, moving to the north."

Avernus nodded and looked at Derec. "We must hurry," he said, "lest all our work be in vain."

"Work is already in vain," Waldeyer said to Avernus. "Because of your unauthorized impoundment of the gateway excavator, the on-hand raw iron consignments have dropped dangerously low. Within an hour, replication efforts will begin falling behind schedule."

The big robot simply hung his head, looking at the floor.

"I pose a question to you all," Derec said. "If Avernus and I are able to get to the core and reprogram to halt the replication, will our work already done here enable us to dig the rest of the way through to the cavern before tonight's rain?"

"Barring work stoppage and machinery malfunction," Euler said, "we should just be able to make it. This, of course, is all hypothetical."

Derec just looked at them. There was no satisfaction to be gained from arguing at this point. It was time to deliver the goods. "Where's the data from my blood sample?" he asked.

Arion stepped forward and handed him a mini-disc. "Everything you asked for is in here," he said.

"Thanks," Derec said, taking the disc and putting it in his breast pocket. "Now, listen. We're going to the central core. As soon as we reprogram, we'll need you to begin work here again immediately so that no time is lost."

Arion took a step toward the gateweay. "It is now too late to move the excavator back to the iron mine and pick up our failed operation there, so I see no reason why the digging here shouldn't continue in your absence. There is no longer anything to lose. I will continue to work here, even as you approach the central core."

"No," Euler said. "Will *you* now violate your programming, and perhaps the Laws?"

"The program is already shattered," Arion said, moving into the innards of the gateway. "There is no putting it back together now."

Derec smiled broadly as he heard the standby board being brought to full ready by Arion. He walked over to Dante. "We'll need your tram," he said. "Now."

The fever had come on strong, and along with it, hallucinations. Katherine's world was a nightmare of water, a world of water always threatening to pull her downward, and through it all Derec/David, David/Derec, Derec/David, his face smiling evilly and becoming mechanical even as she watched, metamorphosing from human to robot and back again, over and over. He'd skim the cresting waves to take her in his arms, only to use those arms to pull her underwater—drowning her! Drowning!

"Katherine . . . Katherine. Wake up. Wake up."

Voices intruding in her world of water. She wanted them to go away, to leave her alone. The water was treacherous, but at least it was warm.

"Katherine . . ."

Something was shaking her, pulling her violently from her dream world. She opened her eyes to pain blazing like fire through her head.

It was daytime, early morning. A utility robot was staring at her around the protective branch of Wohler's arm.

"C-cold," she rasped, teeth chattering. "So . . . cold."

A light flared above her and to the left, a light raining sparks. She squinted. Welders were using laser torches to cut Wohler's pincers off the facade where they were locked tight. Above the welder, she could see mechanical pulleys magnetically clamped to the side of the structure, city-material ropes dangling.

"We are cutting you free," the robot said. "A net and stretcher have been strung just below you. You are safe now."

"C-cold," she rasped again.

"We will warm you. We will get you medical attention."

And through the haze that was her mind, she felt the reassuring firmness of Wohler's body protecting her, always protecting her.

"Wohler!" she said loudly. "We're s-safe. Wohler!"

"Supervisor Wohler is . . . nonoperational," the utility said.

Even through the hurt and the delirium, she was wracked by waves of shame. That this robot would give his life for hers, after the way she'd acted, was more than she could bear.

She felt his weight behind her give; then hands were lifting both of them onto the stretchers pulled up tight below. She felt the morning sun on her face, a sun that Wohler would never experience again, and rather than dwell on the unpleasant results of its own selfishness, her mind once more retreated into the blissful haze of unconsciousness.

"Would you have?" Avernus asked him as they pushed the tram down tunnel D-24, heading north.

"Would I have what?" Derec replied. The tunnel walls rushed past, red lights zipping overhead at two-second intervals.

"Would you have let the robots die if I hadn't agreed to help you dig the tunnel?"

"No," Derec said. "I wouldn't have done anything like that. I just wanted to talk some sense into you."

"You lied to me."

"I lied to save you," Derec said. "Remember our discussion about lying in the Compass Tower? I created a different reality, a hypothetical reality, to force you into a different line of thought."

"You lied to me."

"Yes."

"I do not know if I'll ever really understand that," Avernus said, subtly telling Derec that their relationship would forever be strained.

"I'll have to learn to live with that," Derec replied sadly. "Sometimes the right thing isn't always the best thing. I'm sorry if I hurt you."

"Hurt is not a term that I understand," the robot replied.

"No," Derec said, turning to fiddle with the terminal Dante had left in the back. "It's a term that I relate to."

Derec used the terminal to contact the city's hastily organized medical facility, trying for information on Katherine and Wohler. He and Avernus had left Quadrant #4 and traveled through the city to #2, going underground again at that point. Tunnel D-24 was one of the more distant shafts, drilled as an oil exploration point for the plastics operation. A pipeline churned loudly, attached to the tunnel ceiling above their heads.

"They've gotten Katherine and Wohler down from the Tower!" he said, wishing his fingers moved as well as Dante's over the keyboard.

"Are they well?"

"Katherine is suffering from shock and exposure," Derec

said excitedly. "She's being treated now. The prognosis is good. Wohler is . . . is . . ." He turned sadly to Avernus. "Wohler is dead."

"Look!" the robot called, pointing ahead.

Farther along the tunnel, they were rapidly closing on a moving area of light. It was perhaps six meters long, and just tall enough to miss the overhanging lights.

"The central core!" Avernus said, braking heavily, the tram skidding to a halt.

"What are you doing?" Derec asked. "It's getting away!"

"It will be faster now on foot," Avernus said.

"Not for me," Derec replied. "I can't run fast enough to . . ."

"Climb on my back," the robot ordered. "Quickly."

While the huge robot was still sitting, Derec stood and climbed onto his broad back, putting his hands around Avernus's head, the robot locking an arm behind him, holding Derec on tightly.

Then Avernus jumped from the cart and began a headlong charge down the tunnel, moving faster than Derec realized was possible. Tunnel segments flew by in a blur as the moving core grew larger and larger in their vision.

They caught it quickly, and Avernus slowed his pace to match the speed of the core. Its outer surface was transparent plastic of some kind, and very thick. Like a transparent egg shell, it contained the complex workings of a sophisticated operating machine. In the rear was a platform with steps leading up to a sliding door.

Avernus jumped, catching the stairs and climbing on. He brought his arm around, gently lifting Derec off to stand before the door. "Go on," he said. "Go in. Only one at a time can pass through."

Derec slid open the door by hand and walked in to find himself within the transparent chamber. A red button was set in the plastic before him. He pushed it. Sprayers and heat lamps came on, a full body spray of compressed air traveling the length of his body to remove all traces of dust. There

as a loud sound of suction, and then the wall before him
id open and he walked into the beating heart of Robot City.

The core was open, like an exposed brain, its working
synapses sparking photons up and down its length, its fluid-
s a marvel of imaginative engineering. He found a typer
alfway down its length and juiced it to life, while hearing
vernus going through the chamber ritual. The robot was
doubled over to fit within the "clean room."

The first thing he did was open a file under the heading of
HEMOGLOBIN, and enter the disc's-worth of information
rion had procured for him. Then he got into the DE-
ENSES file again, going as far as he could with the system
ntil it prompted him for the supervisor's password.

He heard a door slide open and turned to see Avernus, still
somewhat hunched over, move to stand beside him at the
per.

"It wants your password," Derec said.

Avernus looked at him, not speaking, then reached out
nd typed on the screen:

AVERNUS—2Q2-1719

PASSWORD: SYNNOETICS

Without a second's hesitation, the computer prompted:

RATIONALIZATION FOR DEACTIVATION OF CITY
DEFENSES?

With shaking fingers, Derec typed his rationalization into
e machine, dumping, as he did so, all the information from
e HEMOGLOBIN file into the CITY DEFENSES file as
athoritative backup and information to keep the same thing
om ever happening again.

When he was through typing he stood back and took a
eath, almost afraid to push the ENTER key.

"We must know now," Avernus said.

Derec nodded, swallowed hard, and entered the informa-
on.

The machine churned quietly for a moment that seemed to
st an hour. Finally, quite simply and without fanfare, it
sponded.

RATIONALIZATION ACCEPTED—DEFENSES DEAC-
TIVATED.

They stood for a moment, staring, not quite believing that
it could be so easy. Then they felt a noticeable slowing of
the core's motion. Within seconds, it had ground to a stop.

It was over.

Derec walked the corridors of the mostly dark, mostly unfurnished medical facility. It would be a fine building when it was completely finished, a place where the humans who would inhabit Robot City could receive the finest medical care available anywhere in the galaxy under the supervision of the most advanced team of med-bots operational. He knew this would be so because the robots who performed the services would perform them by choice, out of love instead of servitude.

He walked the corridors alone—no guides, no keepers, no jailers. He was a free citizen now, a condemned man no longer. And it was good, because now, right now, he preferred being alone.

A room at the end of the corridor was awash with light, and he knew he'd find Katherine there, recovering from her fight with the storm. He no longer cared about her subterfuge or her reasons for being with him on Robot City. For good or ill, he was happy and thankful that she was alive. Nothing else really could, or did, matter.

He was beginning to know why she affected him the way she did—he loved her.

He reached the room and poked his head inside. It was a large room, one that would most likely be a ward at some future time. But right now it was empty, except for Katherine's place at the far end.

She lay in stasis, floating half a meter above a table, bright lights surrounding her completely. She was naked,

159

just as she'd been on Rockliffe Station. This time he didn't turn away, but looked, and her body seemed somehow . . . familiar to him.

A med-bot rolled up to him.

"How is she?" he asked.

"Splendid," the robot replied, "except for her chronic condition . . ."

"I don't want to talk about it," he said, letting her have her secrets. "Other than that?"

"She's sleeping lightly," the med-bot said. "We have rebalanced her chemicals through massive influxes of oxygen and fluids, and warmed her up. She lost a small part of her left ear to the cold, but that has already been adjusted through laser cosmetic surgery. You may visit with her if you wish."

"I'd like that," he said. "But before you wake her up, would you put a robe or something on her?"

"The heat lamps work better if . . ."

"I know," Derec said. "It's a matter of her personal privacy."

"I see," the robot said in its best bedside manner, but Derec could tell that it didn't.

When the med-bot turned and rolled back to Katherine, Derec politely stepped through the doorway and back into the hall.

A moment later, he could hear her talking to the robot, so he walked back in. She was off the table, sitting in a motorized chair, swathed in a bright white bathrobe. Her face was blank as he moved up to her.

"I'm sorry for everything," he said. "I've been suspicious and hard to get along with and . . ."

She smiled slightly, putting up a hand. "No more than I have," she said softly, her voice hoarse. "I guess I've acted pretty stupidly."

"Human prerogative," he said. "You look . . . good."

"They scraped the surface skin off me," she said, "cleared away the dead dermis. I guess I could say you're looking at

he new me." She moved her gaze to the floor. "The Key is
gone."

"I didn't know," he replied. "I guess we're really stuck."

She nodded. "Did you hear what . . . what Wohler did for
me?"

"Yes."

"I never understood your . . . feeling for the robots," she
said, eyes welling up with tears. "But his life was as important to him as mine is to me, and he . . . he gave it up . . . so I
could live."

"He was burned out completely," Derec said. "They're
trying to reconstruct him now."

She looked up at him. "Reconstruct?"

"It won't be the same, of course. We are, all of us, a
product of our memories. The Wohler you knew is, for the
most part, dead."

"But if they reconstruct," she said, "something of him
will remain."

"Yes. Something."

"I want to go there," she said. "I want to go where he is."

She tried to stand, Derec gently pushing her back in the
chair. "You're still a sick girl," he said. "You can't be running around doing . . ."

"No," she said, a spark of the old Katherine already coming back. "He died so that I could live. If there's anything of
him left, I want to be there."

Derec drew a long breath. "I'll see what I can do," he
said, knowing how stubborn she could be.

And so, thirty minutes later, Katherine, wrapped in a sterile suit, wheeled herself into the dust-free repair chamber
where six different robots were working diligently on the
body of Wohler, the philosopher. Derec walked with her.

Most of his plating was gone, circuit boards and relays
hitting the floor with clockwork regularity, a small robot
wheeling silently around and sweeping up the discards.

"Can I get closer?" she asked Derec.

"I don't see why not," he answered.

Just then, Euler came into the chamber and walked directly toward the couple. "Friend Derec," he said. Derec smiled at the reuse of the title before his name. "We are just completing work on the connecting tunnel to the runoff cavern and would very much like you to be present for the opening."

Derec looked down at Katherine. "Well, I'm kind of busy right now, I . . ."

"Nonsense," Katherine said, reaching out to pat his hand. "I'm just going to stay around here for a while. One of the robots here can get me back to medical."

He smiled broadly. "You sure it's okay?"

She nodded, smiling widely. "I understand completely," she said.

He grinned at Euler. "Let's go," he said, and the two of them moved quickly out of the room.

Katherine listened to their footsteps receding down the hall, then wheeled her chair closer to the work table. Her anger at Derec along with a great many other conflicting emotions, had died along with Wohler on the Compass Tower. Because of her thoughtlessness, a life had been lost. All her other emotions seemed petty in the face of that.

She wheeled up near the golden robot's head. Most of his body was exposed in pieces on the table, but the head and upper torso were intact. The robots working on the body moved around the table to accommodate her presence.

She stared at his head, reaching out a finger to gingerly touch him. "I'm so sorry," she said.

Suddenly, the head turned to her, its photocells glowing brightly. "Were you addressing me?" he asked her.

"Wohler," she said, jumping. "You're alive."

"Do we know one another?" he asked, and she realized that this was a different Wohler, a newly programmed Wohler who knew nothing of their previous experience.

"No," she said, choking back a sob. "My name is Katherine. I'm . . . pleased to make your acquaintance."

"A new friendship is like new wine," Wohler said. "When it has aged, you will drink it with pleasure. Katherine . . . Katherine. Why are you crying?"

Only a small dam held back the waters in the trench from the tunnel that Derec and Avernus had dug to the cavern. The supervisors and as many of the utility robots as could clusters in the opening were there, Derec holding the electronic detonator that would blast away the dam and open up the new waterway.

"This is the first day," Euler told him, "the first day in a truly unified city of humans and robots. The beginning of the perfect world."

"We have reacted synnoetically to make this day happen," Rydberg said. "Working together we can accomplish much."

"While we still have a great deal to learn about one another," Derec said, "I, too, believe that we have proven something of value here today."

"Then open the floodgate, Friend Derec," Euler said, "and make the connection complete."

"With pleasure."

Derec flipped the toggle on the hand control. A small explosion made the wall of dirt and rock jump. Then it crumbled, and rapidly flowing water from the trench finished the job that the explosive had begun.

And as the waters rushed past, he thought of all the things still unresolved, still rushing, like the waters, through his confused brain. Who was he? Who was the dead man? Who put this all together, and why?

And then there was Katherine.

In many ways, he still felt as if his journey had just begun, but he couldn't help but feel he had accomplished something major with the breaking down of the dam. He couldn't help but feel that something good, something positive had been accomplished. And that made him feel just fine. Maybe life was nothing so much as a succession of small battles, small victories to be won.

"Derec," came a voice behind him, and he turned to see Avernus standing there.

"Yes?"

The robot, so large, spoke with a small voice. "I do not know that I can understand why you did what you did to me last night," he said, "but I cannot help but feel that we did the right thing, and that doing the right thing is what is important."

"I couldn't agree more," Derec said, smiling widely. "Friends?"

Avernus nodded solidly. "Friends," he said, as he laid his pincer in Derec's open palm in the universal gesture of peace and good will.

It wasn't going to be such a bad day after all.

DATA BANK

Illustrations by Paul Rivoche

KATHERINE ARIEL BURGESS, "KATE": Kate is a native Auroran, banished from her homeworld because of an incurable disease. Despite her illness and a pampered upbringing, Kate is headstrong, tough, demanding, and resourceful. On the advice of the medical robot Galen, she refuses to tell Derec what she knows of his past life.

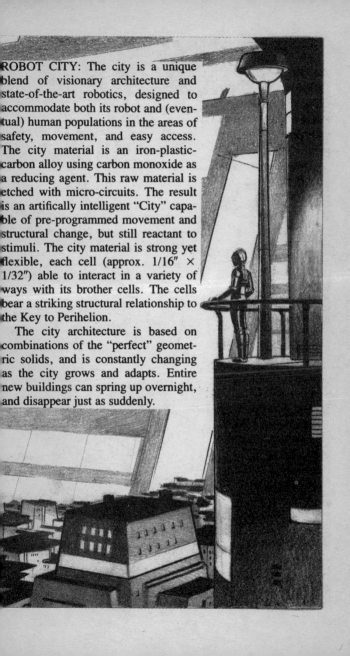

ROBOT CITY: The city is a unique blend of visionary architecture and state-of-the-art robotics, designed to accommodate both its robot and (eventual) human populations in the areas of safety, movement, and easy access. The city material is an iron-plastic-carbon alloy using carbon monoxide as a reducing agent. This raw material is etched with micro-circuits. The result is an artifically intelligent "City" capable of pre-programmed movement and structural change, but still reactant to stimuli. The city material is strong yet flexible, each cell (approx. 1/16" × 1/32") able to interact in a variety of ways with its brother cells. The cells bear a striking structural relationship to the Key to Perihelion.

The city architecture is based on combinations of the "perfect" geometric solids, and is constantly changing as the city grows and adapts. Entire new buildings can spring up overnight, and disappear just as suddenly.

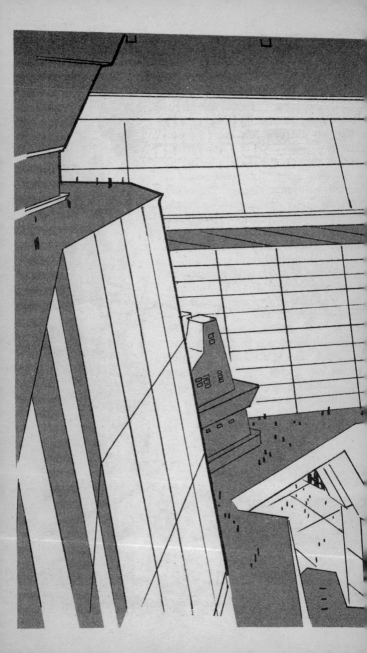

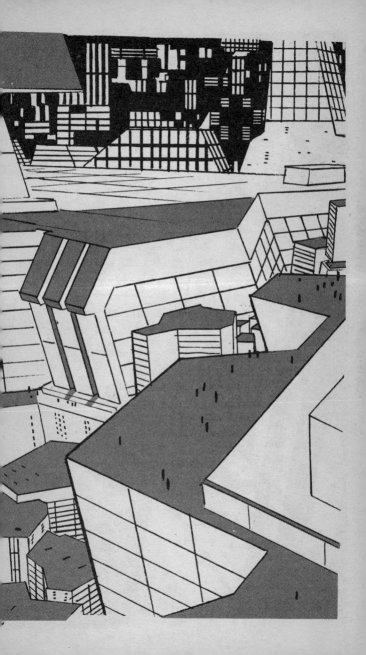

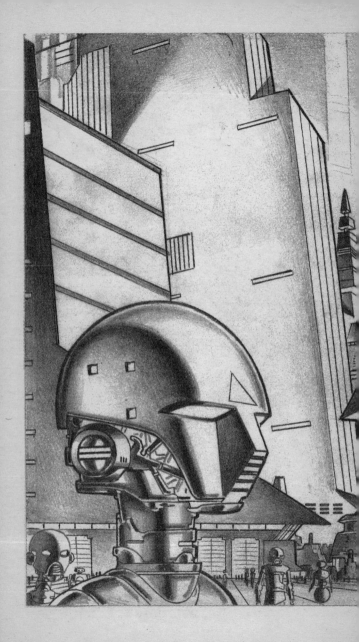

WITNESS ROBOTS: These robots contain specialized senso
equipment and are equipped to function only as event witnesse
and reporters. Capable only of first-level (observation) connec
tions, the witness robot has no lifting appendages, in order t
maintain detached objectivity.

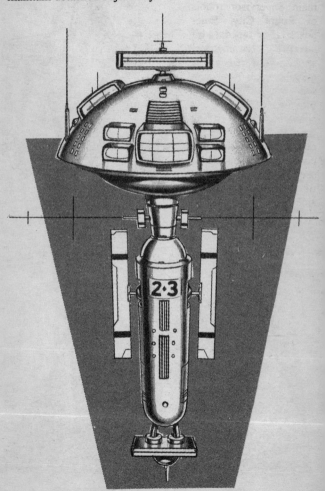

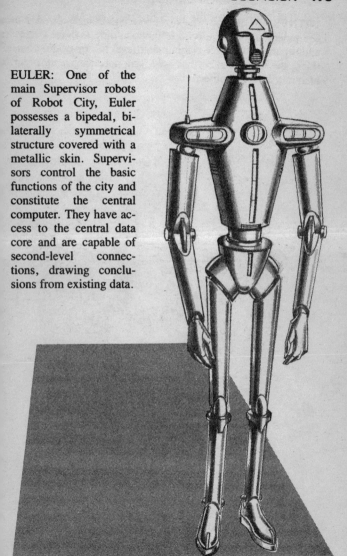

EULER: One of the main Supervisor robots of Robot City, Euler possesses a bipedal, bilaterally symmetrical structure covered with a metallic skin. Supervisors control the basic functions of the city and constitute the central computer. They have access to the central data core and are capable of second-level connections, drawing conclusions from existing data.

AVERNUS: Another of the main Supervisors, Avernus has a bipedal, humanoid structure, stands approximately twelve feet high, and has a jet-black metallic skin. Instead of the pseudo-hands possessed by human-oriented supervisors, such as Euler, Avernus has interchangeable hands for various functions. He is shown here with the humanoid hands he employs for very delicate work. His usual hands, however, are a set of highly adaptable pincer-like claws.

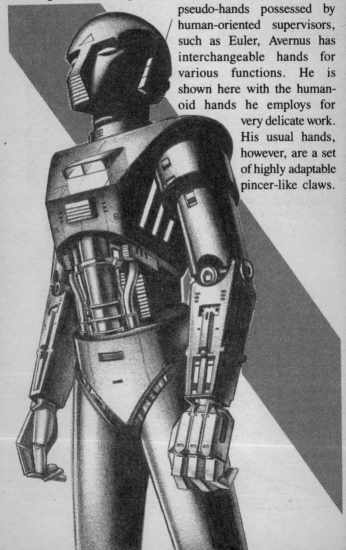

TROUBLESHOOTER: Small, round computer diagnostician. Makes quick determinations of fault in computer function, and does nothing else.

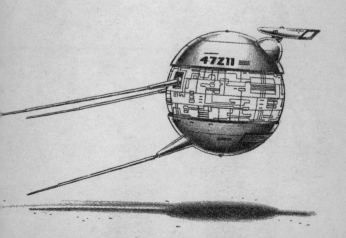

MIKE MCQUAY

Mike McQuay began his writing career in 1975 while a production line worker at a factory. Before that, he worked a variety of jobs, including: musician, airplane mechanic, banker, retail store owner, bartender, Club Med salesman, and film pirate.

Since the publication of his first novel, *Lifekeeper*, in 1980, McQuay has published 22 novels and short story collections in a variety of fields—science fiction, children's, horror, mainstream thriller, and adventure.

McQuay is 37 years old and lives in Oklahoma City with his writer wife Shanna Bacharach, their three children and three cats.

CHARLES AND MARY LAMB

Tales from Shakespeare

Illustrated by Arthur Rackham

J. M. Dent & Sons Ltd: London
EVERYMAN'S LIBRARY

EDITOR'S NOTE

CHARLES LAMB was still a young man, not yet known as 'Elia' of the essays, when he and his sister and life-long companion, Mary, wrote together in 1806 the *Tales from Shakespeare*; they were living at the time in Mitre Court Buildings, Temple. In a letter to a friend in that year, Mary Lamb says that plays, novels, poems, and 'all manner of such-like vapouring and vaporous schemes are floating in my head,' the result being that Charles, writing on 10th May, speaks of Mary as having already completed six of the tales: 'The Tempest,' 'Winter's Tale,' 'Midsummer Night's Dream,' 'Much Ado,' 'Two Gentlemen of Verona,' and 'Cymbeline.' 'The Merchant of Venice' was in preparation; Charles himself had done 'Othello' and 'Macbeth,' and said it was his intention to do all the tragedies.

We get other interesting glimpses of the tales from Mary. 'You would like to see us,' she says, 'as we often sit, writing on one table (but not on one cushion sitting), like Hermia and Helena in the 'Midsummer Night's Dream'; or, rather, like an old literary Darby and Joan; I taking snuff, and he groaning all the while, and saying he can make nothing of it, which he always says till he has finished, and then he finds that he has made something of it.' And in one of Charles's letters he writes: 'Mary is stuck fast in "All's Well that Ends Well." She complains of having to set forth so many female characters in boys' clothes. She begins to think Shakespeare must have wanted imagination! I, to encourage her (for she often faints in the prosecution of her great work), flatter her by telling her how well such a play and such a play is done. But she is stuck fast, and I have been obliged to promise to assist her. To do this it will be necessary to leave off tobacco.' Later on, Mary writes that 'Charles has been reading over the tale I told you plagued me so much, and he thinks it one of the very best; it is "All's Well that Ends Well."' Finally, we find on 29th January 1807, Charles writing to Wordsworth: 'We have booked off from Swan and Two Necks, Lad Lane, this day (per coach), the *Tales from Shakespeare*. . . . We think "Pericles" of hers the best, and "Othello" of mine; but I hope all have some good.'

Charles Lamb died at Edmonton in 1834. Mary Lamb lived for some years after him, and dying in 1847, was buried by his side in Edmonton churchyard.

Besides the *Tales from Shakespeare*, 1807, we have three tales by Charles in Mary Lamb's *Mrs. Leicester's School*, 1808, and *Poetry for Children*, which he wrote with her in 1809. The *Essays of Elia*, 1823, and the *Last Essays of Elia*, 1833, are his most precious books. How precious they are you will know when you read Elia's reverie upon Dream-Children, and his boyish *Recollections of Christ's Hospital*.

ERNEST RHYS.

BIBLIOGRAPHY

SEPARATE WORKS. *Poems on Various Subjects, by S. T. Coleridge, late of Jesus College, Cambridge*, 1796, contains four sonnets by Lamb, signed 'C. L.'; *Poems, by S. T. Coleridge, Second Edition, to which are now added Poems by Charles Lamb and Charles Lloyd*, 1797; *Blank Verse*, by Charles Lloyd and Charles Lamb, 1798; *A Tale of Rosamund Gray and Old Blind Margaret*, 1798; *John Woodvil, a Tragedy*, 1802; *The King and Queen of Hearts*, 1806; *Tales from Shakespeare*, by Charles and Mary Lamb, 2 vols., 1807; *Specimens of English Dramatic Poets*, 1808; *The Adventures of Ulysses*, by Charles and Mary Lamb, 2 vols., 1808; *Mrs. Leicester's School*, by Charles and Mary Lamb, 1808; *Poetry for Children*, by Charles and Mary Lamb, 2 vols. 1809; *Prince Dorus*, 1811; *The Works of Charles Lamb*, 2 vols., 1818; *Elia*, 1823; *Album Verses*, 1830; *Satan in Search of a Wife*, 1831; *The Last Essays of Elia*, 1833.

COLLECTED EDITIONS. *Poetical Works* (E. Moxon), 1836; *Letters of Charles Lamb, with a Sketch of his Life*, edited by T. N. Talfourd (E. Moxon), 1837; *Works*, edited by T. N. Talfourd (E. Moxon), 1840, 1859, 1870; *Correspondence and Works*, 4 vols. (E. Moxon & Co), 1868–70; *Complete Works in Prose and Verse*, edited and prefaced by R. H. Shepherd, 1874; *Mary and Charles Lamb: Poems, Letters, and Remains*, edited by W. C. Hazlitt, 1874; *Life, Letters, and Writings*, edited by Percy Fitzgerald, 6 vols., 1875; *Works*, edited with biographical introduction and notes by C. Kent, 1876; *Works and Correspondence*, edited by Alfred Ainger, 6 vols., 1883–8; *Works of Charles and Mary Lamb*, edited by E. V. Lucas, 7 vols, 1903–5; *Works* edited by W. Macdonald, 12 vols., 1903–7; *Works of Charles and Mary Lamb*, edited by T. Hutchinson, vols., 1908; *Letters of Charles and Mary Lamb*, edited by E. V. Lucas, 3 vols., 1935; *The Essays of Elia*, edited by F. W. Robinson, 1959; *Charles and Mary Lamb, Letters*, edited by E. W. Marrs, 3 vols., 1976–8.

CONTENTS

ILLUSTRATIONS

PREFACE

THE following Tales are meant to be submitted to the young reader as an introduction to the study of Shakespeare, for which purpose his words are used whenever it seemed possible to bring them in; and in whatever has been added to give them the regular form of a connected story, diligent care has been taken to select such words as might least interrupt the effect of the beautiful English tongue in which he wrote: therefore, words introduced into our language since his time have been as far as possible avoided.

In those tales which have been taken from the Tragedies, the young readers will perceive, when they come to see the source from which these stories are derived, that Shakespeare's own words, with little alteration, recur very frequently in the narrative as well as in the dialogue; but in those made from the Comedies the writers found themselves scarcely ever able to turn his words into the narrative form: therefore it is feared that, in them, dialogue has been made use of too frequently for young people not accustomed to the dramatic form of writing. But this fault, if it be a fault, has been caused by an earnest wish to give as much of Shakespeare's own words as possible: and if the '*He said,*' and '*She said,*' the question and the reply, should sometimes seem tedious to their young ears, they must pardon it, because it was the only way in which could be given to them a few hints and little foretastes of the great pleasure which awaits them in their elder years, when they come to the rich treasures from which these small and valueless coins are extracted; pretending to no other merit than as faint and imperfect stamps of Shakespeare's matchless image. Faint and imperfect images they must be called, because the beauty of his language is too frequently destroyed by the necessity of changing many of his excellent words into words far less expressive of his true sense, to make it read something like prose; and even in some few places, where his blank verse is given unaltered, as hoping from its simple plainness to cheat the young reader into the belief that they are reading prose, yet still his language being transplanted from its own natural soil and wild poetic garden, it must want much of its native beauty.

It has been wished to make these Tales easy reading for very young children. To the utmost of their ability the writers have constantly kept this in mind; but the subjects of most of them made this a very difficult task. It was no easy matter to give the histories of men and women in terms familiar to the apprehension of a very young mind. For young ladies too, it has been the intention chiefly to write; because boys being generally permitted the use of their fathers' libraries at a much earlier age than girls are, they frequently have the best scenes of Shakespeare by heart, before their sisters are permitted to look into this manly book; and, therefore, instead of recommending these Tales to the perusal of young gentlemen who can read them so much better in the originals, their kind assistance is rather requested in explaining to their sisters such parts as are hardest for them to understand: and when they have helped them to get over the difficulties, then perhaps they will read to them (carefully selecting what is proper for a young sister's ear) some passage which has pleased them in one of these stories, in the very words of the scene from which it is taken; and it is hoped they will find that the beautiful extracts, the select passages, they may choose to give their sisters in this way will be much better relished and understood from their having some notion of the general story from one of these imperfect abridgments;—which if they be fortunately so done as to prove delightful to any of the young readers, it is hoped that no worse effect will result than to make them wish themselves a little older, that they may be allowed to read the Plays at full length (such a wish will be neither peevish nor irrational). When time and leave of judicious friends shall put them into their hands, they will discover in such of them as are here abridged (not to mention almost as many more, which are left untouched) many surprising events and turns of fortune, which for their infinite variety could not be contained in this little book, besides a world of sprightly and cheerful characters, both men and women, the humour of which it was feared would be lost if it were attempted to reduce the length of them.

What these Tales shall have been to the *young* readers, that and much more it is the writers' wish that the true Plays of Shakespeare may prove to them in older years —enrichers of the fancy, strengtheners of virtue, a withdrawing from all selfish and mercenary thoughts, a lesson of all sweet and honourable thoughts and actions, to teach courtesy, benignity, generosity, humanity: for of examples, teaching these virtues, his pages are full.

THE TEMPEST

THERE was a certain island in the sea, the only inhabitants of which were an old man, whose name
was Prospero, and his daughter Miranda, a very beautiful
young lady. She came to this island so young, that she
had no memory of having seen any other human face
than her father's.

They lived in a cave or cell, made out of a rock;
it was divided into several apartments, one of which
Prospero called his study; there he kept his books, which
chiefly treated of magic, a study at that time much
affected by all learned men: and the knowledge of this
art he found very useful to him; for being thrown by a
strange chance upon this island, which had been enchanted by a witch called Sycorax, who died there a
short time before his arrival, Prospero, by virtue of his
art, released many good spirits that Sycorax had imprisoned in the bodies of large trees, because they had
refused to execute her wicked commands. These gentle
spirits were ever after obedient to the will of Prospero.
Of these Ariel was the chief.

The lively little sprite Ariel had nothing mischievous
in his nature, except that he took rather too much
pleasure in tormenting an ugly monster called Caliban,
for he owed him a grudge because he was the son of his
old enemy Sycorax. This Caliban, Prospero found in
the woods, a strange misshapen thing, far less human in
form than an ape: he took him home to his cell, and
taught him to speak; and Prospero would have been
very kind to him, but the bad nature which Caliban
inherited from his mother Sycorax, would not let him
learn anything good or useful: therefore he was employed like a slave, to fetch wood, and do the most

5

laborious offices; and Ariel had the charge of compelling him to these services.

When Caliban was lazy and neglected his work, Ariel (who was invisible to all eyes but Prospero's) would come slily and pinch him, and sometimes tumble him down in the mire; and then Ariel, in the likeness of an ape, would make mouths at him. Then swiftly changing his shape, in the likeness of a hedgehog, he would lie tumbling in Caliban's way, who feared the hedgehog's sharp quills would prick his bare feet. With a variety of such-like vexatious tricks Ariel would often torment him, whenever Caliban neglected the work which Prospero commanded him to do.

Having these powerful spirits obedient to his will, Prospero could by their means command the winds, and the waves of the sea. By his orders they raised a violent storm, in the midst of which, and struggling with the wild sea-waves that every moment threatened to swallow it up, he showed his daughter a fine large ship, which he told her was full of living beings like themselves. 'O my dear father,' said she, 'if by your art you have raised this dreadful storm, have pity on their sad distress. See! the vessel will be dashed to pieces. Poor souls! they will all perish. If I had power, I would sink the sea beneath the earth, rather than the good ship should be destroyed, with all the precious souls within her.'

'Be not so amazed, daughter Miranda,' said Prospero; 'there is no harm done. I have so ordered it, that no person in the ship shall receive any hurt. What I have done has been in care of you, my dear child. You are ignorant who you are, or where you came from, and you know no more of me, but that I am your father, and live in this poor cave. Can you remember a time before you came to this cell? I think you cannot for you were not then three years of age.'

'Certainly I can, sir,' replied Miranda.

'By what?' asked Prospero; 'by any other house or person? Tell me what you can remember, my child.'

Miranda said: 'It seems to me like the recollection of a dream. But had I not once four or five women who attended upon me?'

Prospero answered: 'You had, and more. How is it that this still lives in your mind? Do you remember how you came here?'

'No, sir,' said Miranda, 'I remember nothing more.'

'Twelve years ago, Miranda,' continued Prospero, 'I was duke of Milan, and you were a princess, and my only heir. I had a younger brother, whose name was Antonio, to whom I trusted everything: and as I was fond of retirement and deep study, I commonly left the management of my state affairs to your uncle, my false brother (for so indeed he proved). I, neglecting all worldly ends, buried among my books, did dedicate my whole time to the bettering of my mind. My brother Antonio being thus in possession of my power, began to think himself the duke indeed. The opportunity I gave him of making himself popular among my subjects awakened in his bad nature a proud ambition to deprive me of my dukedom: this he soon effected with the aid of the king of Naples, a powerful prince, who was my enemy.'

'Wherefore,' said Miranda, 'did they not that hour destroy us?'

'My child,' answered her father, 'they durst not, so dear was the love that my people bore me. Antonio carried us on board a ship, and when we were some leagues out at sea, he forced us into a small boat, without either tackle, sail, or mast: there he left us, as he thought, to perish. But a kind lord of my court, one Gonzalo, who loved me, had privately placed in the boat, water, provisions, apparel, and some books which I prize above my dukedom.'

'O my father,' said Miranda, 'what a trouble must I have been to you then!'

'No, my love,' said Prospero, 'you were a little cherub that did preserve me. Your innocent smiles made me bear up against my misfortunes. Our food lasted till we landed on this desert island, since when my chief delight has been in teaching you, Miranda, and well have you profited by my instructions.'

'Heaven thank you, my dear father,' said Miranda. 'Now pray tell me, sir, your reason for raising this sea-storm?'

'Know then,' said her father, 'that by means of this storm, my enemies, the king of Naples, and my cruel brother, are cast ashore upon this island.'

Having so said, Prospero gently touched his daughter with his magic wand, and she fell fast asleep; for the spirit Ariel just then presented himself before his master, to give an account of the tempest, and how he had disposed of the ship's company, and though the spirits were always invisible to Miranda, Prospero did not choose she should hear him holding converse (as would seem to her) with the empty air.

'Well, my brave spirit,' said Prospero to Ariel, 'how have you performed your task?'

Ariel gave a lively description of the storm, and of the terrors of the mariners; and how the king's son, Ferdinand, was the first who leaped into the sea; and his father thought he saw his dear son swallowed up by the waves and lost. 'But he is safe,' said Ariel, 'in a corner of the isle, sitting with his arms folded, sadly lamenting the loss of the king, his father, whom he concludes drowned. Not a hair of his head is injured, and his princely garments, though drenched in the sea-waves, look fresher than before.'

'That's my delicate Ariel,' said Prospero. 'Bring him hither: my daughter must see this young prince. Where is the king, and my brother?'

'I left them,' answered Ariel, 'searching for Ferdinand, whom they have little hopes of finding, thinking they saw him perish. Of the ship's crew not one is missing; though each one thinks himself the only one saved: and the ship, though invisible to them, is safe in the harbour.'

'Ariel,' said Prospero, 'thy charge is faithfully performed: but there is more work yet.'

'Is there more work?' said Ariel. 'Let me remind you, master, you have promised me my liberty. I pray, remember, I have done you worthy service, told you no lies, made no mistakes, served you without grudge or grumbling.'

'How now!' said Prospero. 'You do not recollect what a torment I freed you from. Have you forgot the wicked witch Sycorax, who with age and envy was almost bent double? Where was she born? Speak; tell me.'

'Sir, in Algiers,' said Ariel.

'O was she so?' said Prospero. 'I must recount what you have been, which I find you do not remember. This bad witch, Sycorax, for her witchcrafts, too terrible to enter human hearing, was banished from Algiers, and here left by the sailors; and because you were a spirit too delicate to execute her wicked commands, she shut you up in a tree, where I found you howling. This torment, remember, I did free you from.'

'Pardon me, dear master,' said Ariel, ashamed to seem ungrateful; 'I will obey your commands.'

'Do so,' said Prospero, 'and I will set you free.' He then gave orders what further he would have him do; and away went Ariel, first to where he had left Ferdinand, and found him still sitting on the grass in the same melancholy posture.

'O my young gentleman,' said Ariel, when he saw him, 'I will soon move you. You must be brought, I find, for the Lady Miranda to have a sight of your pretty person. Come, sir, follow me.' He then began singing:

'Full fathom five thy father lies:
  Of his bones are coral made;
Those are pearls that were his eyes:
  Nothing of him that doth fade,
But doth suffer a sea-change
Into something rich and strange.
Sea-nymphs hourly ring his knell:
Hark! now I hear them,—Ding-dong, bell.'

This strange news of his lost father soon roused the prince from the stupid fit into which he had fallen. He followed in amazement the sound of Ariel's voice, till it led him to Prospero and Miranda, who were sitting under the shade of a large tree. Now Miranda had never seen a man before, except her own father.

'Miranda,' said Prospero, 'tell me what you are looking at yonder.'

'O father,' said Miranda, in a strange surprise, 'surely that is a spirit. Lord! how it looks about! Believe me, sir, it is a beautiful creature. Is it not a spirit?'

'No, girl,' answered her father; 'it eats, and sleeps, and has senses such as we have. This young man you see was in the ship. He is somewhat altered by grief, or you might call him a handsome person. He has lost his companions, and is wandering about to find them.'

Miranda, who thought all men had grave faces and grey beards like her father, was delighted with the appearance of this beautiful young prince; and Ferdinand, seeing such a lovely lady in this desert place, and from the strange sounds he had heard, expecting nothing but wonders, thought he was upon an enchanted island, and that Miranda was the goddess of the place, and as such he began to address her.

She timidly answered, she was no goddess, but a simple maid, and was going to give him an account of herself, when Prospero interrupted her. He was well pleased to find they admired each other, for he plainly

perceived they had (as we say) fallen in love at first sight:
but to try Ferdinand's constancy, he resolved to throw
some difficulties in their way: therefore advancing forward, he addressed the prince with a stern air, telling
him, he came to the island as a spy, to take it from him
who was the lord of it. 'Follow me,' said he, 'I will
tie you neck and feet together. You shall drink sea-
water; shell-fish, withered roots, and husks of acorns
shall be your food.' 'No,' said Ferdinand, 'I will resist
such entertainment, till I see a more powerful enemy,'
and drew his sword; but Prospero, waving his magic
wand, fixed him to the spot where he stood, so that he
had no power to move.

Miranda hung upon her father, saying: 'Why are you
so ungentle? Have pity, sir; I will be his surety. This
is the second man I ever saw, and to me he seems a
true one.'

'Silence,' said the father: 'one word more will make
me chide you, girl! What! an advocate for an impostor!
You think there are no more such fine men, having
seen only him and Caliban. I tell you, foolish girl,
most men as far excel this, as he does Caliban.' This he
said to prove his daughter's constancy; and she replied:
'My affections are most humble. I have no wish to see
a goodlier man.'

'Come on, young man,' said Prospero to the prince;
'you have no power to disobey me.'

'I have not indeed,' answered Ferdinand; and not
knowing that it was by magic he was deprived of all
power of resistance, he was astonished to find himself
so strangely compelled to follow Prospero: looking back
on Miranda as long as he could see her, he said, as he
went after Prospero into the cave: 'My spirits are all
bound up as if I were in a dream; but this man's threats,
and the weakness which I feel, would seem light to me
if from my prison I might once a day behold this
fair maid.'

Prospero kept Ferdinand not long confined within the cell: he soon brought out his prisoner, and set him a severe task to perform, taking care to let his daughter know the hard labour he had imposed on him, and then pretending to go into his study, he secretly watched them both.

Prospero had commanded Ferdinand to pile up some heavy logs of wood. Kings' sons not being much used to laborious work, Miranda soon after found her lover almost dying with fatigue. 'Alas!' said she, 'do not work so hard; my father is at his studies, he is safe for these three hours; pray rest yourself.'

'O my dear lady,' said Ferdinand, 'I dare not. I must finish my task before I take my rest.'

'If you will sit down,' said Miranda, 'I will carry your logs the while.' But this Ferdinand would by no means agree to. Instead of a help Miranda became a hindrance, for they began a long conversation, so that the business of log-carrying went on very slowly.

Prospero, who had enjoined Ferdinand this task merely as a trial of his love, was not at his books, as his daughter supposed, but was standing by them invisible, to overhear what they said.

Ferdinand inquired her name, which she told, saying it was against her father's express command she did so.

Prospero only smiled at this first instance of his daughter's disobedience, for having by his magic art caused his daughter to fall in love so suddenly, he was not angry that she showed her love by forgetting to obey his commands. And he listened well pleased to a long speech of Ferdinand's, in which he professed to love her above all the ladies he ever saw.

In answer to his praises of her beauty, which he said exceeded all the women in the world, she replied: 'I do not remember the face of any woman, nor have I seen any more men than you, my good friend, and my dear father. How features are abroad, I know not: but.

believe me, sir, I would not wish any companion in the world but you, nor can my imagination form any shape but yours that I could like. But, sir, I fear I talk to you too freely, and my father's precepts I forget.'

At this Prospero smiled, and nodded his head, as much as to say: 'This goes on exactly as I could wish; my girl will be queen of Naples.'

And then Ferdinand, in another fine long speech (for young princes speak in courtly phrases), told the innocent Miranda he was heir to the crown of Naples, and that she should be his queen.

'Ah! sir,' said she, 'I am a fool to weep at what I am glad of. I will answer you in plain and holy innocence. I am your wife if you will marry me.'

Prospero prevented Ferdinand's thanks by appearing visible before them.

'Fear nothing, my child,' said he; 'I have overheard, and approve of all you have said. And, Ferdinand, if I have too severely used you, I will make you rich amends, by giving you my daughter. All your vexations were but trials of your love, and you have nobly stood the test. Then as my gift, which your true love has worthily purchased, take my daughter, and do not smile that I boast she is above all praise.' He then, telling them that he had business which required his presence, desired they would sit down and talk together till he returned; and this command Miranda seemed not at all disposed to disobey.

When Prospero left them, he called his spirit Ariel, who quickly appeared before him, eager to relate what he had done with Prospero's brother and the king of Naples. Ariel said he had left them almost out of their senses with fear, at the strange things he had caused them to see and hear. When fatigued with wandering about, and famished for want of food, he had suddenly set before them a delicious banquet, and then, just as they were going to eat, he appeared visible before them in the shape of a harpy, a voracious monster with wings, and the feast vanished away. Then, to their utter amazement, this seeming harpy spoke to them, reminding them of their cruelty in driving Prospero from his dukedom, and leaving him and his infant daughter to perish in the sea; saying, that for this cause these terrors were suffered to afflict them.

The king of Naples, and Antonio the false brother, repented the injustice they had done to Prospero; and Ariel told his master he was certain their penitence was sincere, and that he, though a spirit, could not but pity them.

'Then bring them hither, Ariel,' said Prospero: 'if you, who are but a spirit, feel for their distress, shall not I, who am a human being like themselves, have compassion on them? Bring them, quickly, my dainty Ariel.'

Ariel soon returned with the king, Antonio, and old Gonzalo in their train, who had followed him, wondering at the wild music he played in the air to draw them on to his master's presence. This Gonzalo was the same who had so kindly provided Prospero formerly with books and provisions, when his wicked brother left him, as he thought, to perish in an open boat in the sea.

Grief and terror had so stupefied their senses, that they did not know Prospero. He first discovered himself to the good old Gonzalo, calling him the preserver of his life; and then his brother and the king knew that he was the injured Prospero.

Antonio with tears, and sad words of sorrow and true repentance, implored his brother's forgiveness, and the king expressed his sincere remorse for having assisted Antonio to depose his brother: and Prospero forgave them; and, upon their engaging to restore his dukedom, he said to the king of Naples: 'I have a gift in store for you too'; and opening a door, showed him his son Ferdinand playing at chess with Miranda.

Nothing could exceed the joy of the father and the son at this unexpected meeting, for they each thought the other drowned in the storm.

'O wonder!' said Miranda, 'what noble creatures these are! It must surely be a brave world that has such people in it.'

The king of Naples was almost as much astonished at the beauty and excellent graces of the young Miranda, as his son had been. 'Who is this maid?' said he; 'she seems the goddess that has parted us, and brought us thus together.' 'No, sir,' answered Ferdinand, smiling to find his father had fallen into the same mistake that he had done when he first saw Miranda, 'she is a mortal but by immortal Providence she is mine; I chose her when I could not ask you, my father, for your consent, not thinking you were alive. She is the daughter to this Prospero, who is the famous duke of Milan, of whose renown I have heard so much, but never saw him till now: of him I have received a new life: he has made himself to me a second father, giving me this dear lady.'

'Then I must be her father,' said the king; 'but oh! how oddly will it sound, that I must ask my child forgiveness.'

'No more of that,' said Prospero: 'let us not remember our troubles past, since they so happily have ended.' And then Prospero embraced his brother, and again assured him of his forgiveness; and said that a wise over-ruling Providence had permitted that he should be driven from his poor dukedom of Milan, that his daughter might inherit the crown of Naples, for that by their meeting in this desert island, it had happened that the king's son had loved Miranda.

These kind words which Prospero spoke, meaning to comfort his brother, so filled Antonio with shame and remorse, that he wept and was unable to speak; and the kind old Gonzalo wept to see this joyful reconciliation, and prayed for blessings on the young couple.

Prospero now told them that their ship was safe in the harbour, and the sailors all on board her, and that he and his daughter would accompany them home the next morning. 'In the meantime,' says he, 'partake of such refreshments as my poor cave affords; and for your evening's entertainment I will relate the history of my life from my first landing in this desert island.' He then called for Caliban to prepare some food, and set the cave in order; and the company were astonished at the uncouth form and savage appearance of this ugly monster, who (Prospero said) was the only attendant he had to wait upon him.

Before Prospero left the island, he dismissed Ariel from his service, to the great joy of that lively little spirit; who, though he had been a faithful servant to his master, was always longing to enjoy his free liberty, to wander uncontrolled in the air, like a wild bird, under green trees, among pleasant fruits, and sweet-smelling flowers. 'My quaint Ariel,' said Prospero to the little sprite when he made him free, 'I shall miss you; yet you shall have your freedom.' 'Thank you, my dear master,' said Ariel; 'but give me leave to attend your ship home with prosperous gales, before you bid farewell to the assistance of your faithful spirit; and then, master, when I am free, how merrily I shall live!' Here Ariel sung this pretty song:

'Where the bee sucks, there suck I;
In a cowslip's bell I lie;
There I crouch when owls do cry.
On the bat's back I do fly
After summer merrily.
    Merrily, merrily shall I live now
Under the blossom that hangs on the bough.'

Prospero then buried deep in the earth his magical books and wand, for he was resolved never more to make use of the magic art. And having thus overcome his enemies, and being reconciled to his brother and the king of Naples, nothing now remained to complete his happiness, but to revisit his native land, to take possession of his dukedom, and to witness the happy nuptials of his daughter and Prince Ferdinand, which the king said should be instantly celebrated with great splendour on their return to Naples. At which place, under the safe convoy of the spirit Ariel, they, after a pleasant voyage, soon arrived.

A MIDSUMMER NIGHT'S DREAM

THERE was a law in the city of Athens which gave to its citizens the power of compelling their daughters to marry whomsoever they pleased; for upon a daughter's refusing to marry the man her father had chosen to be her husband, the father was empowered by this law to cause her to be put to death; but as fathers do not often desire the death of their own daughters, even though they do happen to prove a little refractory, this law was seldom or never put in execution, though perhaps the young ladies of that city were not unfrequently threatened by their parents with the terrors of it.

There was one instance, however, of an old man, whose name was Egeus, who actually did come before Theseus (at that time the reigning duke of Athens), to complain that his daughter Hermia, whom he had commanded to marry Demetrius, a young man of a noble Athenian family, refused to obey him, because she loved another young Athenian, named Lysander. Egeus demanded justice of Theseus, and desired that this cruel law might be put in force against his daughter.

Hermia pleaded in excuse for her disobedience, that Demetrius had formerly professed love for her dear friend Helena, and that Helena loved Demetrius to distraction; but this honourable reason, which Hermia gave for not obeying her father's command, moved not the stern Egeus.

Theseus, though a great and merciful prince, had no power to alter the laws of his country; therefore he could only give Hermia four days to consider of it: and at the end of that time, if she still refused to marry Demetrius, she was to be put to death.

When Hermia was dismissed from the presence of the

duke, she went to her lover Lysander, and told him the peril she was in, and that she must either give him up and marry Demetrius, or lose her life in four days.

Lysander was in great affliction at hearing these evil tidings; but recollecting that he had an aunt who lived at some distance from Athens, and that at the place where she lived the cruel law could not be put in force against Hermia (this law not extending beyond the boundaries of the city), he proposed to Hermia that sne should steal out of her father's house that night, and go with him to his aunt's house, where he would marry her. 'I will meet you,' said Lysander, 'in the wood a few miles without the city; in that delightful wood where we have so often walked with Helena in the pleasant month of May.'

To this proposal Hermia joyfully agreed; and she told no one of her intended flight but her friend Helena. Helena (as maidens will do foolish things for love) very ungenerously resolved to go and tell this to Demetrius, though she could hope no benefit from betraying her friend's secret, but the poor pleasure of following her faithless lover to the wood; for she well knew that Demetrius would go thither in pursuit of Hermia.

The wood in which Lysander and Hermia proposed to meet was the favourite haunt of those little beings known by the name of *Fairies*.

Oberon the king, and Titania the queen of the fairies, with all their tiny train of followers, in this wood held their midnight revels.

Between this little king and queen of sprites there happened, at this time, a sad disagreement; they never met by moonlight in the shady walks of this pleasant wood, but they were quarrelling, till all their fairy elves would creep into acorn-cups and hide themselves for fear.

The cause of this unhappy disagreement was Titania's refusing to give Oberon a little changeling boy, whose mother had been Titania's friend; and upon her death the fairy queen stole the child from its nurse, and brought him up in the woods.

The night on which the lovers were to meet in this wood, as Titania was walking with some of her maids of honour, she met Oberon attended by his train of fairy courtiers.

'Ill met by moonlight, proud Titania,' said the fairy king. The queen replied: 'What, jealous Oberon, is it you? Fairies, skip hence; I have foresworn his company.' 'Tarry, rash fairy,' said Oberon; 'am not I thy lord? Why does Titania cross her Oberon? Give me your little changeling boy to be my page.'

'Set your heart at rest,' answered the queen; 'your whole fairy kingdom buys not the boy of me.' She then left her lord in great anger. 'Well, go your way,' said Oberon: 'before the morning dawns I will torment you for this injury.'

Oberon then sent for Puck, his chief favourite and privy counsellor.

Puck (or as he was sometimes called, Robin Goodfellow) was a shrewd and knavish sprite, that used to play comical pranks in the neighbouring villages; sometimes getting into the dairies and skimming the milk, sometimes plunging his light and airy form into the butter-churn, and while he was dancing his fantastic shape in the churn, in vain the dairymaid would labour to change her cream into butter: nor had the village swains any better success; whenever Puck chose to play his freaks in the brewing copper, the ale was sure to be spoiled. When a few good neighbours were met to drink some comfortable ale together, Puck would jump into the bowl of ale in the likeness of a roasted crab, and when some old goody was going to drink he would bob against her lips, and spill the ale over her withered chin; and presently after, when the same old dame was gravely seating herself to tell her neighbours a sad and melancholy story, Puck would slip her three-legged stool from under her, and down toppled the poor old woman, and then the old gossips would hold their sides and laugh at her, and swear they never wasted a merrier hour.

'Come hither, Puck,' said Oberon to this little merry wanderer of the night; 'fetch me the flower which maids call *Love in Idleness*; the juice of that little purple flower laid on the eyelids of those who sleep, will make them, when they awake, dote on the first thing they see. Some of the juice of that flower I will drop on the eyelids of my Titania when she is asleep; and the first thing she looks upon when she opens her eyes she will fall in love with, even though it be a lion or a bear, a meddling monkey, or a busy ape; and before I will take this charm from off her sight, which I can do with another charm I know of, I will make her give me that boy to be my page.'

Puck, who loved mischief to his heart, was highly diverted with this intended frolic of his master, and ran to seek the flower; and while Oberon was waiting the return of Puck, he observed Demetrius and Helena enter the wood: he overheard Demetrius reproaching Helena for following him, and after many unkind words on his part, and gentle expostulations from Helena, reminding him of his former love and professions of true faith to her, he left her (as he said) to the mercy of the wild beasts, and she ran after him as swiftly as she could.

The fairy king, who was always friendly to true lovers, felt great compassion for Helena; and perhaps, as Lysander said they used to walk by moonlight in this pleasant wood, Oberon might have seen Helena in those happy times when she was beloved by Demetrius. However that might be, when Puck returned with the little purple flower, Oberon said to his favourite: 'Take a part of this flower; there has been a sweet Athenian lady here, who is in love with a disdainful youth; if you find him sleeping, drop some of the love-juice in his eyes, but contrive to do it when she is near him, that the first thing he sees when he awakes may be this despised lady. You will know the man by the Athenian garments which he wears.' Puck promised to manage this matter very dexterously: and then Oberon went, unperceived by Titania, to her bower, where she was preparing to go to rest. Her fairy bower was a bank, where grew wild thyme, cowslips, and sweet violets, under a canopy of wood-bine, musk-roses, and eglantine. There Titania always slept some part of the night; her coverlet the enamelled skin of a snake, which, though a small mantle, was wide enough to wrap a fairy in.

He found Titania giving orders to her fairies, how they were to employ themselves while she slept. 'Some of you,' said her majesty, 'must kill cankers in the musk-rose buds, and some wage war with the bats for their leathern wings, to make my small elves coats; and some of you keep watch that the clamorous owl, that nightly hoots, come not near me: but first sing me to sleep.' Then they began to sing this song:

> 'You spotted snakes with double tongue,
> Thorny hedgehogs, be not seen;
> Newts and blind-worms do no wrong,
> Come not near our Fairy Queen.
> Philomel, with melody,
> Sing in our sweet lullaby,
> Lulla, lulla, lullaby; lulla, lulla, lullaby;
> Never harm, nor spell, nor charm,
> Come our lovely lady nigh;
> So good night with lullaby.'

When the fairies had sung their queen asleep with this pretty lullaby, they left her to perform the important services she had enjoined them. Oberon then softly drew near his Titania, and dropped some of the love-juice on her eyelids, saying:

> 'What thou seest when thou dost wake,
> Do it for thy true-love take.'

But to return to Hermia, who made her escape out

of her father's house that night, to avoid the death she was doomed to for refusing to marry Demetrius. When she entered the wood, she found her dear Lysander waiting for her, to conduct her to his aunt's house; but before they had passed half through the wood, Hermia was so much fatigued, that Lysander, who was very careful of this dear lady, who had proved her affection for him even by hazarding her life for his sake, persuaded her to rest till morning on a bank of soft moss, and lying down himself on the ground at some little distance, they soon fell fast asleep. Here they were found by Puck, who, seeing a handsome young man asleep, and perceiving that his clothes were made in the Athenian fashion, and that a pretty lady was sleeping near him, concluded that this must be the Athenian maid and her disdainful lover whom Oberon had sent him to seek; and he naturally enough conjectured that, as they were alone together, she must be the first thing he would see when he awoke; so, without more ado, he proceeded to pour some of the juice of the little purple flower into his eyes. But it so fell out, that Helena came that way, and, instead of Hermia, was the first object Lysander beheld when he opened his eyes; and strange to relate, so powerful was the love-charm, all his love for Hermia vanished away, and Lysander fell in love with Helena.

Had he first seen Hermia when he awoke, the blunder Puck committed would have been of no consequence, for he could not love that faithful lady too well; but for poor Lysander to be forced by a fairy love-charm to forget his own true Hermia, and to run after another lady, and leave Hermia asleep quite alone in a wood at midnight, was a sad chance indeed.

Thus this misfortune happened. Helena, as has been before related, endeavoured to keep pace with Demetrius when he ran away so rudely from her; but she could not continue this unequal race long, men being always better runners in a long race than ladies. Helena soon lost sight of Demetrius; and as she was wandering about, dejected and forlorn, she arrived at the place where Lysander was sleeping. 'Ah!' said she, 'this is Lysander lying on the ground: is he dead or asleep?' Then, gently touching him, she said: 'Good sir, if you are alive, awake.' Upon this Lysander opened his eyes, and (the love-charm beginning to work) immediately addressed her in terms of extravagant love and admiration; telling her she as much excelled Hermia in beauty as a dove does a raven, and that he would run through fire for her sweet sake; and many more such lover-like speeches. Helena, knowing Lysander was her friend Hermia's lover, and that he was solemnly engaged to marry her, was in the utmost rage when she heard herself addressed in this manner; for she thought (as well she might) that Lysander was making a jest of her. 'Oh!' said she, 'why was I born to be mocked and scorned by every one? Is it not enough, is it not enough, young man, that I can never get a sweet look or a kind word from Demetrius; but you, sir, must pretend in this disdainful manner to court me? I thought, Lysander, you were a lord of more true gentleness.' Saying these words in great anger, she ran away; and Lysander followed her, quite forgetful of his own Hermia, who was still asleep.

When Hermia awoke, she was in a sad fright at finding herself alone. She wandered about the wood, not knowing what was become of Lysander, or which way to go to seek for him. In the meantime Demetrius, not being able to find Hermia and his rival Lysander, and fatigued with his fruitless search, was observed by Oberon fast asleep. Oberon had learnt by some questions he had asked of Puck, that he had applied the love-charm to the wrong person's eyes; and now having found the person first intended, he touched the eyelids of the sleeping Demetrius with the love-juice, and he instantly awoke; and the first thing he saw being Helena, he, as Lysander had done before, began to address love-speeches to her; and just at that moment Lysander, followed by Hermia (for through Puck's unlucky mistake it was now become Hermia's turn to run after her lover) made his appearance; and then Lysander and Demetrius, both speaking together, made love to Helena, they being each one under the influence of the same potent charm.

The astonished Helena thought that Demetrius, Lysander, and her once dear friend Hermia, were all in a plot together to make a jest of her.

Hermia was as much surprised as Helena; she knew not why Lysander and Demetrius, who both before loved her, were now become the lovers of Helena; and to Hermia the matter seemed to be no jest.

The ladies, who before had always been the dearest of friends, now fell to high words together.

'Unkind Hermia,' said Helena, 'it is you have set Lysander on to vex me with mock praises; and your other lover Demetrius, who used almost to spurn me with his foot, have you not bid him call me Goddess, Nymph, rare, precious, and celestial? He would not speak thus to me, whom he hates, if you did not set him on to make a jest of me. Unkind Hermia, to join with men in scorning your poor friend. Have you forgot our school-day friendship? How often, Hermia, have we two, sitting on one cushion, both singing one song, with our needles working the same flower, both on the same sampler wrought; growing up together in fashion of a double cherry, scarcely seeming parted! Hermia, it is not friendly in you, it is not maidenly to join with men in scorning your poor friend.'

I am amazed at your passionate words,' said Hermia: I scorn you not; it seems you scorn me.' 'Ay, do,' returned Hermia, 'persevere, counterfeit serious looks, and make mouths at me when I turn my back; then wink at each other, and hold the sweet jest up. If you had any pity, grace, or manners, you would not use me thus.'

While Helena and Hermia were speaking these angry words to each other, Demetrius and Lysander left them, to fight together in the wood for the love of Helena.

When they found the gentlemen had left them, they departed, and once more wandered weary in the wood in search of their lovers.

As soon as they were gone, the fairy king, who with little Puck had been listening to their quarrels, said to him: 'This is your negligence, Puck; or did you do this wilfully?' 'Believe me, king of shadows,' answered Puck, 'it was a mistake; did not you tell me I should know the man by his Athenian garments? However, I am not sorry this has happened, for I think their jangling makes excellent sport.' 'You heard,' said Oberon, 'that Demetrius and Lysander are gone to seek a convenient place to fight in. I command you to overhang the night with a thick fog, and lead these quarrelsome lovers so astray in the dark, that they shall not be able to find each other. Counterfeit each of their voices to the other, and with bitter taunts provoke them to follow you, while they think it is their rival's tongue they hear. See you do this, till they are so weary they can go no farther; and when you find they are asleep, drop the juice of this other flower into Lysander's eyes, and when he awakes he will forget his new love for Helena, and return to his old passion for Hermia; and then the two fair ladies may each one be happy with the man she loves, and they will think all that has passed a vexatious dream. About this quickly, Puck, and I will go and see what sweet love my Titania has found.'

Titania was still sleeping, and Oberon seeing a clown near her, who had lost his way in the wood, and was likewise asleep: 'This fellow,' said he, 'shall be my

Titania's true love'; and clapping an ass's head over the clown's, it seemed to fit him as well as if it had grown upon his own shoulders. Though Oberon fixed the ass's head on very gently, it awakened him, and rising up, unconscious of what Oberon had done to him, he went towards the bower where the fairy queen slept.

'Ah! what angel is that I see?' said Titania, opening her eyes, and the juice of the little purple flower beginning to take effect: 'are you as wise as you are beautiful?'

'Why, mistress,' said the foolish clown, 'if I have wit enough to find the way out of this wood, I have enough to serve my turn.'

'Out of the wood do not desire to go,' said the enamoured queen. 'I am a spirit of no common rate. I love you. Go with me, and I will give you fairies to attend upon you.'

She then called four of her fairies: their names were, Pease-blossom, Cobweb, Moth, and Mustard-seed.

'Attend,' said the queen, 'upon this sweet gentleman; hop in his walks, and gambol in his sight; feed him with grapes and apricots, and steal for him the honey-bags from the bees. Come, sit with me,' said she to the clown, 'and let me play with your amiable hairy cheeks, my beautiful ass! and kiss your fair large ears, my gentle joy!'

'Where is Pease-blossom?' said the ass-headed clown, not much regarding the fairy queen's courtship, but very proud of his new attendants.

'Here, sir,' said little Pease-blossom.

'Scratch my head,' said the clown. 'Where is Cobweb?'

'Here, sir,' said Cobweb.

'Good Mr. Cobweb,' said the foolish clown, 'kill me the red humble bee on the top of that thistle yonder; and, good Mr. Cobweb, bring me the honey-bag. Do not fret yourself too much in the action, Mr. Cobweb, and

Where is Pease-blossom?

take care the honey-bag break not; I should be sorry to have you overflown with a honey-bag. Where is Mustard-seed?'

'Here, sir,' said Mustard-seed: 'what is your will?'

'Nothing,' said the clown, 'good Mr. Mustard-seed, but to help Mr. Pease-blossom to scratch; I must go to a barber's, Mr. Mustard-seed, for methinks I am marvellous hairy about the face.'

'My sweet love,' said the queen, 'what will you have to eat? I have a venturous fairy shall seek the squirrel's hoard, and fetch you some new nuts.'

'I had rather have a handful of dried pease,' said the clown, who with his ass's head had got an ass's appetite. 'But, I pray, let none of your people disturb me, for I have a mind to sleep.'

'Sleep, then,' said the queen, 'and I will wind you in my arms. O how I love you! how I dote upon you!'

When the fairy king saw the clown sleeping in the arms of his queen, he advanced within her sight, and reproached her with having lavished her favours upon an ass.

This she could not deny, as the clown was then sleeping within her arms, with his ass's head crowned by her with flowers.

When Oberon had teased her for some time, he again demanded the changeling boy; which she, ashamed of being discovered by her lord with her new favourite, did not dare to refuse him.

Oberon, having thus obtained the little boy he had so long wished for to be his page, took pity on the disgraceful situation into which, by his merry contrivance, he had brought his Titania and threw some of the juice of the other flower into her eyes; and the fairy queen immediately recovered her senses, and wondered at her late dotage, saying how she now loathed the sight of the strange monster.

Oberon likewise took the ass's head from off the clown,

and left him to finish his nap with his own fool's head upon his shoulders.

Oberon and his Titania being now perfectly reconciled, he related to her the history of the lovers, and their midnight quarrels; and she agreed to go with him and see the end of their adventures.

The fairy king and queen found the lovers and their fair ladies, at no great distance from each other, sleeping on a grass-plot; for Puck, to make amends for his former mistake, had contrived with the utmost diligence to bring them all to the same spot, unknown to each other: and he had carefully removed the charm from off the eyes of Lysander with the antidote the fairy king gave to him.

Hermia first awoke, and finding her lost Lysander asleep so near her, was looking at him and wondering at his strange inconstancy.   Lysander presently opening his eyes, and seeing his dear Hermia, recovered his reason which the fairy charm had before clouded, and with his reason, his love for Hermia; and they began to talk over the adventures of the night, doubting if these things had really happened, or if they had both been dreaming the same bewildering dream.

Helena and Demetrius were by this time awake; and a sweet sleep having quieted Helena's disturbed and angry spirits, she listened with delight to the professions of love which Demetrius still made to her, and which, to her surprise as well as pleasure, she began to perceive were sincere.

These fair night-wandering ladies, now no longer rivals, became once more true friends; all the unkind words which had passed were forgiven, and they calmly consulted together what was best to be done in their present situation.   It was soon agreed that, as Demetrius had given up his pretensions to Hermia, he should endeavour to prevail upon her father to revoke the cruel sentence of death which had been passed against her.

Demetrius was preparing to return to Athens for this friendly purpose, when they were surprised with the sight of Egeus, Hermia's father, who came to the wood in pursuit of his runaway daughter.

When Egeus understood that Demetrius would not now marry his daughter, he no longer opposed her marriage with Lysander, but gave his consent that they should be wedded on the fourth day from that time, being the same day on which Hermia had been condemned to lose her life; and on that same day Helena joyfully agreed to marry her beloved and now faithful Demetrius.

The fairy king and queen, who were invisible spectators of this reconciliation, and now saw the happy ending of the lovers' history, brought about through the good offices of Oberon, received so much pleasure, that these kind spirits resolved to celebrate the approaching nuptials with sports and revels throughout their fairy kingdom.

And now, if any are offended with this story of fairies and their pranks, as judging it incredible and strange, they have only to think that they have been asleep and dreaming, and that all these adventures were visions which they saw in their sleep: and I hope none of my readers will be so unreasonable as to be offended with a pretty harmless Midsummer Night's Dream.

LEONTES, king of Sicily, and his queen, the beautiful and virtuous Hermione, once lived in the greatest harmony together. So happy was Leontes in the love of this excellent lady, that he had no wish ungratified, except that he sometimes desired to see again, and to present to his queen, his old companion and school-fellow, Polixenes, king of Bohemia. Leontes and Polixenes were brought up together from their infancy, but being, by the death of their fathers, called to reign over their respective kingdoms, they had not met for many years, though they frequently interchanged gifts, letters, and loving embassies.

At length, after repeated invitations, Polixenes came from Bohemia to the Sicilian court, to make his friend Leontes a visit.

At first this visit gave nothing but pleasure to Leontes. He recommended the friend of his youth to the queen's particular attention, and seemed in the presence of his dear friend and old companion to have his felicity quite completed. They talked over old times; their school-days and their youthful pranks were remembered, and recounted to Hermione, who always took a cheerful part in these conversations.

When, after a long stay, Polixenes was preparing to depart, Hermione, at the desire of her husband, joined her entreaties to his that Polixenes would prolong his visit.

And now began this good queen's sorrow; for Polixenes refusing to stay at the request of Leontes, was won over by Hermione's gentle and persuasive words to put off his departure for some weeks longer. Upon this, although Leontes had so long known the integrity and honourable principles of his friend Polixenes, as well as the excellent disposition of his virtuous queen, he was seized with an ungovernable jealousy. Every attention Hermione showed to Polixenes, though by her husband's particular desire, and merely to please him, increased the unfortunate king's jealousy; and from being a loving and a true friend, and the best and fondest of husbands, Leontes became suddenly a savage and inhuman monster. Sending for Camillo, one of the lords of his court, and telling him of the suspicion he entertained, he commanded him to poison Polixenes.

Camillo was a good man; and he, well knowing that the jealousy of Leontes had not the slightest foundation in truth, instead of poisoning Polixenes, acquainted him with the king his master's orders, and agreed to escape with him out of the Sicilian dominions; and Polixenes, with the assistance of Camillo, arrived safe in his own kingdom of Bohemia, where Camillo lived from that time in the king's court, and became the chief friend and favourite of Polixenes.

The flight of Polixenes enraged the jealous Leontes still more; he went to the queen's apartment, where the good lady was sitting with her little son Mamillius, who was just beginning to tell one of his best stories to amuse his mother, when the king entered, and taking the child away, sent Hermione to prison.

Mamillius, though but a very young child, loved his mother tenderly; and when he saw her so dishonoured, and found she was taken from him to be put into a prison, he took it deeply to heart, and drooped and pined away by slow degrees, losing his appetite and his sleep, till it was thought his grief would kill him.

The king, when he had sent his queen to prison, commanded Cleomenes and Dion, two Sicilian lords, to go to Delphos, there to inquire of the oracle at the temple of Apollo, if his queen had been unfaithful to him.

When Hermione had been a short time in prison, she was brought to bed of a daughter; and the poor lady received much comfort from the sight of her pretty baby, and she said to it: 'My poor little prisoner, I am as innocent as you are.'

Hermione had a kind friend in the noble-spirited Paulina, who was the wife of Antigonus, a Sicilian lord; and when the lady Paulina heard her royal mistress was brought to bed, she went to the prison where Hermione was confined; and she said to Emilia, a lady who attended upon Hermione: 'I pray you, Emilia, tell the good queen, if her majesty dare trust me with her little babe, I will carry it to the king, its father; we do not know how he may soften at the sight of his innocent child.' 'Most worthy madam,' replied Emilia, 'I will acquaint the queen with your noble offer; she was wishing to-day that she had any friend who would venture to present the child to the king.' 'And tell her,' said Paulina, 'that I will speak boldly to Leontes in her defence.' 'May you be for ever blessed,' said Emilia, 'for your kindness to our gracious queen!' Emilia then went to Hermione, who joyfully gave up her baby to the care of Paulina, for she had feared that no one would dare venture to present the child to its father.

Paulina took the new-born infant, and forcing herself into the king's presence, notwithstanding her husband, fearing the king's anger, endeavoured to prevent her, she laid the babe at its father's feet, and Paulina made a noble speech to the king in defence of Hermione, and she reproached him severely for his inhumanity, and implored him to have mercy on his innocent wife and child. But Paulina's spirited remonstrances only aggravated Leontes' displeasure, and he ordered her husband Antigonus to take her from his presence.

When Paulina went away, she left the little baby at its father's feet, thinking when he was alone with it, he would look upon it, and have pity on its helpless innocence.

The good Paulina was mistaken: for no sooner was

she gone than the merciless father ordered Antigonus, Paulina's husband, to take the child, and carry it out to sea, and leave it upon some desert shore to perish.

Antigonus, unlike the good Camillo, too well obeyed the orders of Leontes; for he immediately carried the child on ship-board, and put out to sea, intending to leave it on the first desert coast he could find.

So firmly was the king persuaded of the guilt of Hermione, that he would not wait for the return of Cleomenes and Dion, whom he had sent to consult the oracle of Apollo at Delphos; but before the queen was recovered from her lying-in, and from her grief for the loss of her precious baby, he had her brought to a public trial before all the lords and nobles of his court. And when all the great lords, the judges, and all the nobility of the land were assembled together to try Hermione, and that unhappy queen was standing as a prisoner before her subjects to receive their judgment, Cleomenes and Dion entered the assembly, and presented to the king the answer of the oracle, sealed up; and Leontes commanded the seal to be broken, and the words of the oracle to be read aloud, and these were the words: '*Hermione is innocent, Polixenes blameless, Camillo a true subject, Leontes a jealous tyrant, and the king shall live without an heir if that which is lost be not found.*' The king would give no credit to the words of the oracle: he said it was a falsehood invented by the queen's friends, and he desired the judge to proceed in the trial of the queen; but while Leontes was speaking, a man entered and told him that the prince Mamillius, hearing his mother was to be tried for her life, struck with grief and shame, had suddenly died.

Hermione, upon hearing of the death of this dear affectionate child, who had lost his life in sorrowing for her misfortune, fainted; and Leontes, pierced to the heart by the news, began to feel pity for his unhappy queen, and he ordered Paulina, and the ladies who were her attendants, to take her away, and use means for her recovery. Paulina soon returned, and told the king that Hermione was dead.

When Leontes heard that the queen was dead, he repented of his cruelty to her; and now that he thought his ill-usage had broken Hermione's heart, he believed her innocent; and now he thought the words of the oracle were true, as he knew 'if that which was lost was not found,' which he concluded was his young daughter, he should be without an heir, the young prince Mamillius being dead; and he would give his kingdom now to recover his lost daughter: and Leontes gave himself up to remorse, and passed many years in mournful thoughts and repentant grief.

The ship in which Antigonus carried the infant princess out to sea was driven by a storm upon the coast of Bohemia, the very kingdom of the good king Polixenes. Here Antigonus landed, and here he left the little baby.

Antigonus never returned to Sicily to tell Leontes where he had left his daughter, for as he was going back to the ship, a bear came out of the woods, and tore him to pieces; a just punishment on him for obeying the wicked order of Leontes.

The child was dressed in rich clothes and jewels; for Hermione had made it very fine when she sent it to Leontes, and Antigonus had pinned a paper to its mantle, and the name of *Perdita* written thereon, and words obscurely intimating its high birth and untoward fate.

This poor deserted baby was found by a shepherd. He was a humane man, and so he carried the little Perdita home to his wife, who nursed it tenderly; but poverty tempted the shepherd to conceal the rich prize he had found: therefore he left that part of the country, that no one might know where he got his riches, and with part of Perdita's jewels he bought herds of sheep, and became a wealthy shepherd. He brought up Perdita as his own child, and she knew not she was any other than a shepherd's daughter.

The little Perdita grew up a lovely maiden; and though she had no better education than that of a shepherd's daughter, yet so did the natural graces she inherited from her royal mother shine forth in her untutored mind, that no one from her behaviour would have known she had not been brought up in her father's court.

Polixenes, the king of Bohemia, had an only son, whose name was Florizel. As this young prince was hunting near the shepherd's dwelling, he saw the old man's supposed daughter; and the beauty, modesty, and queen-like deportment of Perdita caused him instantly to fall in love with her. He soon, under the name of Doricles, and in the disguise of a private gentleman, became a constant visitor at the old shepherd's house. Florizel's frequent absences from court alarmed Polixenes; and setting people to watch his son, he discovered his love for the shepherd's fair daughter.

Polixenes then called for Camillo, the faithful Camillo, who had preserved his life from the fury of Leontes, and desired that he would accompany him to the house of the shepherd, the supposed father of Perdita.

Polixenes and Camillo, both in disguise, arrived at the old shepherd's dwelling while they were celebrating the feast of sheep-shearing; and though they were strangers, yet at the sheep-shearing every guest being made welcome, they were invited to walk in, and join in the general festivity.

Nothing but mirth and jollity was going forward. Tables were spread, and great preparations were making for the rustic feast. Some lads and lasses were dancing on the green before the house, while others of the young men were buying ribands, gloves, and such toys, of a pedlar at the door.

While this busy scene was going forward, Florizel and Perdita sat quietly in a retired corner, seemingly more pleased with the conversation of each other, than desirous of engaging in the sports and silly amusements of those around them.

The king was so disguised that it was impossible his son could know him: he therefore advanced near enough to hear the conversation. The simple yet elegant manner in which Perdita conversed with his son did not a little surprise Polixenes: he said to Camillo: 'This is the prettiest low-born lass I ever saw; nothing she does or says but looks like something greater than herself, too noble for this place.'

Pamillo replied: 'Indeed she is the very queen of curds and cream.'

'Pray, my good friend,' said the king to the old shepherd, 'what fair swain is that talking with your daughter?' 'They call him Doricles,' replied the shepherd. 'He says he loves my daughter; and, to speak truth, there is not a kiss to choose which loves the other best. If young Doricles can get her, she shall bring him that he little dreams of'; meaning the remainder of Perdita's jewels; which, after he had bought herds of sheep with part of them, he had carefully hoarded up for her marriage portion.

Polixenes then addressed his son. 'How now, young man!' said he: 'your heart seems full of something that takes off your mind from feasting. When I was young, I used to load my love with presents; but you have let the pedlar go, and have bought your lass no toy.'

The young prince, who little thought he was talking to the king his father, replied: 'Old sir, she prizes not such trifles; the gifts which Perdita expects from me are locked up in my heart.' Then turning to Perdita, he said to her: 'O hear me, Perdita, before this ancient gentleman, who it seems was once himself a lover; he shall hear what I profess.' Florizel then called upon the old stranger to be a witness to a solemn promise of marriage which he made to Perdita, saying to Polixenes: 'I pray you, mark our contract.'

'Mark your divorce, young sir,' said the king, discovering himself. Polixenes then reproached his son for daring to contract himself to this low-born maiden, calling Perdita 'shepherd's brat, sheep-hook,' and other disrespectful names; and threatening, if ever she suffered his son to see her again, he would put her, and the old shepherd her father, to a cruel death.

The king then left them in great wrath, and ordered Camillo to follow him with prince Florizel.

When the king had departed, Perdita, whose royal nature was roused by Polixenes' reproaches, said: 'Though we are all undone, I was not much afraid; and once or twice I was about to speak, and tell him plainly that the selfsame sun which shines upon his palace, hides not his face from our cottage, but looks on both alike.' Then sorrowfully she said: 'But now I am awakened from this dream, I will queen it no further. Leave me, sir; I will go milk my ewes and weep.'

The kind-hearted Camillo was charmed with the spirit and propriety of Perdita's behaviour; and perceiving that the young prince was too deeply in love to give up his mistress at the command of his royal father, he thought of a way to befriend the lovers, and at the same time to execute a favourite scheme he had in his mind.

Camillo had long known that Leontes, the king of Sicily, was become a true penitent; and though Camillo was now the favoured friend of king Polixenes, he could not help wishing once more to see his late royal master and his native home. He therefore proposed to Florizel and Perdita that they should accompany him to the Sicilian court, where he would engage Leontes should protect them, till, through his mediation, they could obtain pardon from Polixenes, and his consent to their marriage.

To this proposal they joyfully agreed; and Camillo, who conducted everything relative to their flight, allowed the old shepherd to go along with them.

The shepherd took with him the remainder of Perdita's jewels, her baby clothes, and the paper which he had found pinned to her mantle.

After a prosperous voyage, Florizel and Perdita, Camillo and the old shepherd, arrived in safety at the court of Leontes. Leontes, who still mourned his dead Hermione and his lost child, received Camillo with great kindness, and gave a cordial welcome to prince Florizel. But Perdita, whom Florizel introduced as his princess, seemed to engross all Leontes' attention: perceiving a resemblance between her and his dead queen Hermione, his grief broke out afresh, and he said, such a lovely creature might his own daughter have been, if he had not so cruelly destroyed her. 'And then, too,' said he to Florizel, 'I lost the society and friendship of your grave father, whom I now desire more than my life once again to look upon.'

When the old shepherd heard how much notice the king had taken of Perdita, and that he had lost a daughter, who was exposed in infancy, he fell to comparing the time when he found the little Perdita, with the manner of its exposure, the jewels and other tokens of its high birth; from all which it was impossible for him not to conclude that Perdita and the king's lost daughter were the same.

Florizel and Perdita, Camillo and the faithful Paulina, were present when the old shepherd related to the king the manner in which he had found the child, and also the circumstance of Antigonus' death, he having seen the bear seize upon him. He showed the rich mantle in which Paulina remembered Hermione had wrapped the child; and he produced a jewel which she remembered Hermione had tied about Perdita's neck, and he gave up the paper which Paulina knew to be the writing of her husband; it could not be doubted that Perdita was

Leontes' own daughter: but oh! the noble struggles of Paulina, between sorrow for her husband's death, and joy that the oracle was fulfilled, in the king's heir, his long-lost daughter being found. When Leontes heard that Perdita was his daughter, the great sorrow that he felt that Hermione was not living to behold her child, made him that he could say nothing for a long time, but 'O thy mother, thy mother!'

Paulina interrupted this joyful yet distressful scene, with saying to Leontes, that she had a statue newly finished by that rare Italian master, Julio Romano, which was such a perfect resemblance of the queen, that would his majesty be pleased to go to her house and look upon it, he would be almost ready to think it was Hermione herself. Thither then they all went; the king anxious to see the semblance of his Hermione, and Perdita longing to behold what the mother she never saw did look like.

When Paulina drew back the curtain which concealed this famous statue, so perfectly did it resemble Hermione, that all the king's sorrow was renewed at the sight: for a long time he had no power to speak or move.

'I like your silence, my liege,' said Paulina, 'it the more shows your wonder. Is not this statue very like your queen?'

At length the king said: 'O, thus she stood, even with such majesty, when I first wooed her. But yet, Paulina, Hermione was not so aged as this statue looks.' Paulina replied: 'So much the more the carver's excellence, who has made the statue as Hermione would have looked had she been living now. But let me draw the curtain, sire, lest presently you think it moves.'

The king then said: 'Do not draw the curtain; would I were dead! See, Camillo, would you not think it breathed? Her eye seems to have motion in it.' 'I must draw the curtain, my liege,' said Paulina. 'You are so transported, you will persuade yourself the statue

When Paulina drew back the curtain which concealed the famous statue

lives.' 'O, sweet Paulina,' said Leontes, 'make me think so twenty years together! Still methinks there is an air comes from her. What fine chisel could ever yet cut breath? Let no man mock me, for I will kiss her.' 'Good my lord, forbear!' said Paulina. 'The ruddiness upon her lip is wet; you will stain your own with oily painting. Shall I draw the curtain?' 'No, not these twenty years,' said Leontes.

Perdita, who all this time had been kneeling, and beholding in silent admiration the statue of her matchless mother, said now: 'And so long could I stay here, looking upon my dear mother.'

'Either forbear this transport,' said Paulina to Leontes, 'and let me draw the curtain; or prepare yourself for more amazement. I can make the statue move indeed; ay, and descend from off the pedestal, and take you by the hand. But then you will think, which I protest I am not, that I am assisted by some wicked powers.'

'What you can make her do,' said the astonished king, 'I am content to hear; for it is as easy to make her speak as move.'

Paulina then ordered some slow and solemn music, which she had prepared for the purpose, to strike up; and, to the amazement of all the beholders, the statue came down from off the pedestal, and threw its arms around Leontes' neck. The statue then began to speak, praying for blessings on her husband, and on her child, the newly-found Perdita.

No wonder that the statue hung upon Leontes' neck, and blessed her husband and her child. No wonder; for the statue was indeed Hermione herself, the real, the living queen.

Paulina had falsely reported to the king the death of Hermione, thinking that the only means to preserve her royal mistress's life; and with the good Paulina, Hermione had lived ever since, never choosing Leontes should know she was living, till she heard Perdita was found; for though she had long forgiven the injuries which Leontes had done to herself, she could not pardon his cruelty to his infant daughter.

His dead queen thus restored to life, his lost daughter found, the long-sorrowing Leontes could scarcely support the excess of his own happiness.

Nothing but congratulations and affectionate speeches were heard on all sides. Now the delighted parents thanked prince Florizel for loving their lowly-seeming daughter; and now they blessed the good old shepherd for preserving their child. Greatly did Camillo and Paulina rejoice that they had lived to see so good an end of all their faithful services.

And as if nothing should be wanting to complete this strange and unlooked-for joy, king Polixenes himself now entered the palace.

When Polixenes first missed his son and Camillo, knowing that Camillo had long wished to return to Sicily, he conjectured he should find the fugitives here; and, following them with all speed, he happened to just arrive at this, the happiest moment of Leontes' life.

Polixenes took a part in the general joy; he forgave his friend Leontes the unjust jealousy he had conceived against him, and they once more loved each other with all the warmth of their first boyish friendship. And there was no fear that Polixenes would now oppose his son's marriage with Perdita. She was no 'sheep-hook' now, but the heiress of the crown of Sicily.

Thus have we seen the patient virtues of the long-suffering Hermione rewarded. That excellent lady lived many years with her Leontes and her Perdita, the happiest of mothers and of queens.

MUCH ADO ABOUT NOTHING

THERE lived in the palace at Messina two ladies, whose names were Hero and Beatrice. Hero was the daughter, and Beatrice the niece, of Leonato, the governor of Messina.

Beatrice was of a lively temper, and loved to divert her cousin Hero, who was of a more serious disposition, with her sprightly sallies. Whatever was going forward was sure to make matter of mirth for the light-hearted Beatrice.

At the time the history of these ladies commences some young men of high rank in the army, as they were passing through Messina on their return from a war that was just ended, in which they had distinguished themselves by their great bravery, came to visit Leonato. Among these were Don Pedro, the prince of Arragon; and his friend Claudio, who was a lord of Florence; and with them came the wild and witty Benedick, and he was a lord of Padua.

These strangers had been at Messina before, and the hospitable governor introduced them to his daughter and his niece as their old friends and acquaintance.

Benedick, the moment he entered the room, began a lively conversation with Leonato and the prince. Beatrice, who liked not to be left out of any discourse, interrupted Benedick with saying: 'I wonder that you will still be talking, signior Benedick: nobody marks you.' Benedick was just such another rattle-brain as Beatrice, yet he was not pleased at this free salutation; he thought it did not become a well-bred lady to be so flippant with her tongue; and he remembered, when he was last at Messina, that Beatrice used to select him to make her merry jests upon. And as there is no one who so little likes to be made a jest of as those who are apt to take the same liberty themselves, so it was with Benedick and Beatrice; these two sharp wits never met in former times but a perfect war of raillery was kept up between them, and they always parted mutually displeased with each other. Therefore when Beatrice stopped him in the middle of his discourse with telling him nobody marked what he was saying, Benedick, affecting not to have observed before that she was present, said: 'What, my dear lady Disdain, are you yet living?' And now war broke out afresh between them, and a long jangling argument ensued, during which Beatrice, although she knew he had so well approved his valour in the late war, said that she would eat all he had killed there: and observing the prince take delight in Benedick's conversation, she called him 'the prince's jester.' This sarcasm sunk deeper into the mind of Benedick than all Beatrice had said before. The hint she gave him that he was a coward, by saying she would eat all he had killed, he did not regard, knowing himself to be a brave man; but there is nothing that great wits so much dread as the imputation of buffoonery, because the charge comes sometimes a little too near the truth: therefore Benedick perfectly hated Beatrice when she called him 'the prince's jester.'

The modest lady Hero was silent before the noble guests; and while Claudio was attentively observing the improvement which time had made in her beauty, and was contemplating the exquisite graces of her fine figure (for she was an admirable young lady), the prince was highly amused with listening to the humorous dialogue between Benedick and Beatrice; and he said in a whisper to Leonato: 'This is a pleasant-spirited young lady. She were an excellent wife for Benedick.' Leonato replied to this suggestion: 'O, my lord, my lord, if they were but a week married, they would talk themselves mad.' But though Leonato thought they would make a discordant pair, the prince did not give up the idea of matching these two keen wits together.

When the prince returned with Claudio from the palace, he found that the marriage he had devised between Benedick and Beatrice was not the only one projected in that good company, for Claudio spoke in such terms of Hero, as made the prince guess at what was passing in his heart; and he liked it well, and he said to Claudio: 'Do you affect Hero?' To this question Claudio replied: 'O my lord, when I was last at Messina, I looked upon her with a soldier's eye, that liked, but had no leisure for loving; but now, in this happy time of peace, thoughts of war have left their places vacant in my mind, and in their room come thronging soft and delicate thoughts, all prompting me how fair young Hero is, reminding me that I liked her before I went to the wars.' Claudio's confession of his love for Hero so wrought upon the prince, that he lost no time in soliciting the consent of Leonato to accept of Claudio for a son-in-law. Leonato agreed to this proposal, and the prince found no great difficulty in persuading the gentle Hero herself to listen to the suit of the noble Claudio, who was a lord of rare endowments, and highly accomplished, and Claudio, assisted by his kind prince, soon prevailed upon Leonato to fix an early day for the celebration of his marriage with Hero.

Claudio was to wait but a few days before he was to be married to his fair lady; yet he complained of the interval being tedious, as indeed most young men are impatient when they are waiting for the accomplishment of any event they have set their hearts upon: the prince, therefore, to make the time seem short to him, proposed as a kind of merry pastime that they should invent some artful scheme to make Benedick and Beatrice fall in love with each other. Claudio entered with great satisfaction into this whim of the prince, and Leonato promised them his assistance, and even Hero said she would do any modest office to help her cousin to a good husband.

The device the prince invented was, that the gentlemen should make Benedick believe that Beatrice was in love with him, and that Hero should make Beatrice believe that Benedick was in love with her.

The prince, Leonato, and Claudio began their operations first: and watching upon an opportunity when Benedick was quietly seated reading in an arbour, the prince and his assistants took their station among the trees behind the arbour, so near that Benedick could not choose but hear all they said; and after some careless talk the prince said: 'Come hither, Leonato. What was it you told me the other day—that your niece Beatrice was in love with signior Benedick? I did never think that lady would have loved any man.' 'No, nor I neither, my lord.' answered Leonato. 'It is most wonderful that she should so dote on Benedick, whom she in all outward behaviour seemed ever to dislike.' Claudio confirmed all this with saying that Hero had told him Beatrice was so in love with Benedick, that she would certainly die of grief, if he could not be brought to love her; which Leonato and Claudio seemed to agree was impossible, he having always been such a railer against all fair ladies, and in particular against Beatrice.

The prince affected to hearken to all this with great compassion for Beatrice, and he said: 'It were good that Benedick were told of this.' 'To what end?' said Claudio; 'he would but make sport of it, and torment the poor lady worse.' 'And if he should,' said the prince, 'it were a good deed to hang him; for Beatrice is an excellent sweet lady, and exceeding wise in everything but in loving Benedick.' Then the prince motioned to his companions that they should walk on, and leave Benedick to meditate upon what he had overheard.

Benedick had been listening with great eagerness to

this conversation; and he said to himself when he heard Beatrice loved him: 'Is it possible? Sits the wind in that corner?' And when they were gone, he began to reason in this manner with himself: 'This can be no trick! they were very serious, and they have the truth from Hero, and seem to pity the lady. Love me! Why it must be requited! I did never think to marry. But when I said I should die a bachelor, I did not think I should live to be married. They say the lady is virtuous and fair. She is so. And wise in everything but loving me. Why, that is no great argument of her folly. But here comes Beatrice. By this day, she is a fair lady. I do spy some marks of love in her.' Beatrice now approached him, and said with her usual ta.tness: 'Against my will I am sent to bid you come in to dinner.' Benedick, who never felt himself disposed to speak so politely to her before, replied: 'Fair Beatrice, I thank you for your pains': and when Beatrice, after two or three more rude speeches, left him, Benedick thought he observed a concealed meaning of kindness under the uncivil words she uttered, and he said aloud: 'If I do not take pity on her, I am a villain. If I do not love her, I am a Jew. I will go get her picture.'

The gentleman being thus caught in the net they had spread for him, it was now Hero's turn to play her part with Beatrice; and for this purpose she sent for Ursula and Margaret, two gentlewomen who attended upon her, and she said to Margaret: 'Good Margaret, run to the parlour; there you will find my cousin Beatrice talking with the prince and Claudio. Whisper in her ear, that I and Ursula are walking in the orchard, and that our discourse is all of her. Bid her steal into that pleasant arbour, where honeysuckles, ripened by the sun, like ungrateful minions, forbid the sun to enter.' This arbour, into which Hero desired Margaret to entice Beatrice, was the very same pleasant arbour where Benedick had so lately been an attentive listener.

'I will make her come, I warrant, presently,' said Margaret.

Hero, then taking Ursula with her into the orchard, said to her: 'Now, Ursula, when Beatrice comes, we will walk up and down this alley, and our talk must be only of Benedick, and when I name him, let it be your part to praise him more than ever man did merit. My talk to you must be how Benedick is in love with Beatrice. Now begin; for look where Beatrice like a lapwing runs close by the ground, to hear our conference.' They then began; Hero saying, as if in answer to something which Ursula had said: 'No, truly, Ursula. She is too disdainful; her spirits are as coy as wild birds of the rock.' 'But are you sure,' said Ursula, 'that Benedick loves Beatrice so entirely?' Hero replied: 'So says the prince, and my lord Claudio, and they entreated me to acquaint her with it; but I persuaded them, if they loved Benedick, never to let Beatrice know of it.' 'Certainly,' replied Ursula, 'it were not good she knew his love, lest she made sport of it.' 'Why, to say truth,' said Hero, 'I never yet saw a man, how wise soever, or noble, young, or rarely featured, but she would dispraise him.' 'Sure, sure, such carping is not commendable,' said Ursula. 'No,' replied Hero, 'but who dare tell her so? If I should speak, she would mock me into air.' 'O! you wrong your cousin,' said Ursula: 'she cannot be so much without true judgment, as to refuse so rare a gentleman as signior Benedick.' 'He hath an excellent good name,' said Hero: 'indeed, he is the first man in Italy, always excepting my dear Claudio.' And now, Hero giving her attendant a hint that it was time to change the discourse, Ursula said: 'And when are you to be married, madam?' Hero then told her, that she was to be married to Claudio the next day, and desired she would go in with her, and look at some new attire, as she wished to consult with her on what she would wear on the morrow. Beatrice, who had been listening with breathless eagerness to this dialogue, when they went away, exclaimed: 'What fire is in mine ears? Can this be true? Farewell, contempt and scorn, and maiden pride, adieu! Benedick, love on! I will requite you, taming my wild heart to your loving hand.'

It must have been a pleasant sight to see these old enemies converted into new and loving friends, and to behold their first meeting after being cheated into mutual liking by the merry artifice of the good-humoured prince. But a sad reverse in the fortunes of Hero must now be thought of. The morrow, which was to have been her wedding-day, brought sorrow on the heart of Hero and her good father Leonato.

The prince had a half-brother, who came from the wars along with him to Messina. This brother (his name was Don John) was a melancholy, discontented man, whose spirits seemed to labour in the contriving of villanies. He hated the prince his brother, and he hated Claudio, because he was the prince's friend, and determined to prevent Claudio's marriage with Hero, only for the malicious pleasure of making Claudio and the prince unhappy; for he knew the prince had set his heart upon this marriage, almost as much as Claudio himself; and to effect this wicked purpose, he employed one Borachio, a man as bad as himself, whom he encouraged with the offer of a great reward. This Borachio paid his court to Margaret, Hero's attendant; and Don John, knowing this, prevailed upon him to make Margaret promise to talk with him from her lady's chamber window that night, after Hero was asleep, and also to dress herself in Hero's clothes, the better to deceive Claudio into the belief that it was Hero; for that was the end he meant to compass by this wicked plot.

Don John then went to the prince and Claudio, and told them that Hero was an imprudent lady, and that she talked with men from her chamber window at midnight. Now this was the evening before the wedding, and he offered to take them that night, where they should themselves hear Hero discoursing with a man from her window; and they consented to go along with him, and Claudio said: 'If I see anything to-night why I should not marry her, to-morrow in the congregation, where I intended to wed her, there will I shame her.' The prince also said: 'And as I assisted you to obtain her, I will join with you to disgrace her.'

When Don John brought them near Hero's chamber that night, they saw Borachio standing under the window, and they saw Margaret looking out of Hero's window, and heard her talking with Borachio: and Margaret being dressed in the same clothes they had seen Hero wear, the prince and Claudio believed it was the lady Hero herself.

Nothing could equal the anger of Claudio, when he had made (as he thought) this discovery. All his love for the innocent Hero was at once converted into hatred, and he resolved to expose her in the church, as he had said he would, the next day; and the prince agreed to this, thinking no punishment could be too severe for the naughty lady, who talked with a man from her window the very night before she was going to be married to the noble Claudio.

The next day, when they were all met to celebrate the marriage, and Claudio and Hero were standing before the priest, and the priest, or friar, as he was called, was proceeding to pronounce the marriage ceremony, Claudio, in the most passionate language, proclaimed the guilt of the blameless Hero, who, amazed at the strange words he uttered, said meekly: 'Is my lord well, that he does speak so wide?'

Leonato, in the utmost horror, said to the prince: 'My lord, why speak not you?' 'What should I speak?' said the prince; 'I stand dishonoured, that have gone about to link my dear friend to an unworthy woman.

Leonato, upon my honour, myself, my brother, and this grieved Claudio, did see and hear her last night at midnight talk with a man at her chamber window.'

Benedick, in astonishment at what he heard, said: 'This looks not like a nuptial.'

'True, O God!' replied the heart-struck Hero; and then this hapless lady sunk down in a fainting fit, to all appearance dead. The prince and Claudio left the church, without staying to see if Hero would recover, or at all regarding the distress into which they had thrown Leonato. So hard-hearted had their anger made them.

Benedick remained, and assisted Beatrice to recover Hero from her swoon, saying: 'How does the lady?' 'Dead, I think,' replied Beatrice in great agony, for she loved her cousin; and knowing her virtuous principles, she believed nothing of what she had heard spoken against her. Not so the poor old father; he believed the story of his child's shame, and it was piteous to hear him lamenting over her, as she lay like one dead before him, wishing she might never more open her eyes.

But the ancient friar was a wise man, and full of observation on human nature, and he had attentively marked the lady's countenance when she heard herself accused, and noted a thousand blushing shames to start into her face, and then he saw an angel-like whiteness bear away those blushes, and in her eye he saw a fire that did belie the error that the prince did speak against her maiden truth, and he said to the sorrowing father: 'Call me a fool; trust not my reading, nor my observation; trust not my age, my reverence, nor my calling, if this sweet lady lie not guiltless here under some biting error.'

When Hero had recovered from the swoon into which she had fallen, the friar said to her: 'Lady, what man is he you are accused of?' Hero replied: 'They know that do accuse me; I know of none': then turning to Leonato, she said: 'O my father, if you can prove that any man has ever conversed with me at hours unmeet, or that I yesternight changed words with any creature, refuse me, hate me, torture me to death.'

'There is,' said the friar, 'some strange misunderstanding in the prince and Claudio'; and then he counselled Leonato, that he should report that Hero was dead; and he said that the death-like swoon in which they had left Hero would make this easy of belief; and he also advised him that he should put on mourning, and erect a monument for her, and do all rites that appertain to a burial. 'What shall become of this?' said Leonato; 'What will this do?' The friar replied: 'This report of her death shall change slander into pity: that is some good; but that is not all the good I hope for. When Claudio shall hear she died upon hearing his words, the idea of her life shall sweetly creep into his imagination. Then shall he mourn, if ever love had interest in his heart, and wish that he had not so accused her; yea, though he thought his accusation true.'

Benedick now said: 'Leonato, let the friar advise you; and though you know how well I love the prince and Claudio, yet on my honour I will not reveal this secret to them.'

Leonato, thus persuaded, yielded; and he said sorrowfully: 'I am so grieved, that the smallest twine may lead me.' The kind friar then led Leonato and Hero away to comfort and console them, and Beatrice and Benedick remained alone; and this was the meeting from which their friends, who contrived the merry plot against them, expected so much diversion; those friends who were now overwhelmed with affliction, and from whose minds all thoughts of merriment seemed for ever banished.

Benedick was the first who spoke, and he said: 'Lady Beatrice, have you wept all this while?' 'Yea, and I will weep a while longer,' said Beatrice. 'Surely,' said Benedick, 'I do believe your fair cousin is wronged.' 'Ah!' said Beatrice, 'how much might that man deserve of me who would right her!' Benedick then said: 'Is there any way to show such friendship? I do love nothing in the world so well as you: is not that strange?' 'It were as possible,' said Beatrice, 'for me to say I loved nothing in the world so well as you; but believe me not, and yet I lie not. I confess nothing, nor I deny nothing. I am sorry for my cousin.' 'By my sword,' said Benedick, 'you love me, and I protest I love you. Come, bid me do anything for you.' 'Kill Claudio,' said Beatrice. 'Ha! not for the wide world,' said Benedick; for he loved his friend Claudio, and he believed he had been imposed upon. 'Is not Claudio a villain, that has slandered, scorned, and dishonoured my cousin?' said Beatrice: 'O that I were a man!' 'Hear me, Beatrice!' said Benedick. But Beatrice would hear nothing in Claudio's defence; and she continued to urge on Benedick to revenge her cousin's wrongs: and she said: 'Talk with a man out of the window; a proper saying! Sweet Hero! she is wronged; she is slandered; she is undone. O that I were a man for Claudio's sake! or that I had any friend, who would be a man for my sake! but valour is melted into courtesies and compliments. I cannot be a man with wishing, therefore I will die a woman with grieving.' 'Tarry, good Beatrice,' said Benedick; 'by this hand I love you.' 'Use it for my love some other way than swearing by it,' said Beatrice. 'Think you on your soul that Claudio has wronged Hero?' asked Benedick. 'Yea,' answered Beatrice; 'as sure as I have a thought, or a soul.' 'Enough,' said Benedick; 'I am engaged; I will challenge him. I will kiss your hand, and so leave you. By this hand, Claudio shall render me a dear account! As you hear from me, so think of me. Go, comfort your cousin.'

While Beatrice was thus powerfully pleading with Benedick, and working his gallant temper by the spirit of her angry words, to engage in the cause of Hero, and fight even with his dear friend Claudio, Leonato was challenging the prince and Claudio to answer with their swords the injury they had done his child, who, he affirmed, had died for grief. But they respected his age and his sorrow, and they said: 'Nay, do not quarrel with us, good old man.' And now came Benedick, and he also challenged Claudio to answer with his sword the injury he had done to Hero; and Claudio and the prince said to each other: 'Beatrice has set him on to do this.' Claudio nevertheless must have accepted this challenge of Benedick, had not the justice of Heaven at the moment brought to pass a better proof of the innocence of Hero than the uncertain fortune of a duel.

While the prince and Claudio were yet talking of the challenge of Benedick, a magistrate brought Borachio as a prisoner before the prince. Borachio had been overheard talking with one of his companions of the mischief he had been employed by Don John to do.

Borachio made a full confession to the prince in Claudio's hearing, that it was Margaret dressed in her lady's clothes that he had talked with from the window, whom they had mistaken for the lady Hero herself; and no doubt continued on the minds of Claudio and the prince of the innocence of Hero. If a suspicion had remained it must have been removed by the flight of Don John, who, finding his villanies were detected, fled from Messina to avoid the just anger of his brother.

The heart of Claudio was sorely grieved when he found he had falsely accused Hero, who, he thought, died upon hearing his cruel words; and the memory of his beloved Hero's image came over him, in the rare semblance that he loved it first; and the prince asking him if what he heard did not run like iron through his soul, he answered, that he felt as if he had taken poison while Borachio was speaking.

And the repentant Claudio implored forgiveness of the old man Leonato for the injury he had done his child; and promised, that whatever penance Leonato would lay upon him for his fault in believing the false accusation against his betrothed wife, for her dear sake he would endure it.

The penance Leonato enjoined him was, to marry the next morning a cousin of Hero's, who, he said, was now his heir, and in person very like Hero. Claudio, regarding the solemn promise he made to Leonato, said, he would marry this unknown lady, even though she were an Ethiop: but his heart was very sorrowful, and he passed that night in tears, and in remorseful grief, at the tomb which Leonato had erected for Hero.

When the morning came, the prince accompanied Claudio to the church, where the good friar, and Leonato and his niece, were already assembled, to celebrate a second nuptial; and Leonato presented to Claudio his promised bride; and she wore a mask, that Claudio might not discover her face. And Claudio said to the lady in the mask: 'Give me your hand, before this holy friar; I am your husband, if you will marry me.' 'And when I lived I was your other wife,' said this unknown lady; and, taking off her mask, she proved to be no niece (as was pretended), but Leonato's very daughter, the lady Hero herself. We may be sure that this proved a most agreeable surprise to Claudio, who thought her dead, so that he could scarcely for joy believe his eyes; and the prince, who was equally amazed at what he saw, exclaimed: 'Is not this Hero, Hero that was dead?' Leonato replied: 'She died, my lord, but while her slander lived.' The friar promised them an explanation of this seeming miracle, after the ceremony was ended; and was proceeding to marry them, when he was interrupted by Benedick, who desired to be married at the same time to Beatrice. Beatrice making some demur to this match, and Benedick challenging her with her love for him, which he had learned from Hero, a pleasant explanation took place; and they found they had both been tricked into a belief of love, which had never existed, and had become lovers in truth by the power of a false jest: but the affection, which a merry invention had cheated them into, was grown too powerful to be shaken by a serious explanation; and since Benedick proposed to marry, he was resolved to think nothing to the purpose that the world could say against it; and he merrily kept up the jest, and swore to Beatrice, that he took her but for pity, and because he heard she was dying of love for him; and Beatrice protested, that she yielded but upon great persuasion, and partly to save his life, for she heard he was in a consumption. So these two mad wits were reconciled, and made a match of it, after Claudio and Hero were married; and to complete the history, Don John, the contriver of the villany, was taken in his flight, and brought back to Messina; and a brave punishment it was to this gloomy, discontented man, to see the joy and feastings which, by the disappointment of his plots, took place in the palace in Messina.

AS YOU LIKE IT

DURING the time that France was divided into provinces (or dukedoms as they were called) there reigned in one of these provinces an usurper, who had deposed and banished his elder brother, the lawful duke. The duke, who was thus driven from his dominions, retired with a few faithful followers to the forest of Arden; and here the good duke lived with his loving friends, who had put themselves into a voluntary exile for his sake, while their land and revenues enriched the false usurper; and custom soon made the life of careless ease they led here more sweet to them than the pomp and uneasy splendour of a courtier's life. Here they lived like the old Robin Hood of England, and to this forest many noble youths daily resorted from the court, and did fleet the time carelessly, as they did who lived in the golden age. In the summer they lay along under the fine shade of the large forest trees, marking the playful sports of the wild deer; and so fond were they of these poor dappled fools, who seemed to be the native inhabitants of the forest, that it grieved them to be forced to kill them to supply themselves with venison for their food. When the cold winds of winter made the duke feel the change of his adverse fortune, he would endure it patiently, and say: 'These chilling winds which blow upon my body are true counsellors; they do not flatter, but represent truly to me my condition; and though they bite sharply, their tooth is nothing like so keen as that of unkindness and ingratitude. I find that howsoever men speak against adversity, yet some sweet uses are to be extracted from it; like the jewel, precious for medicine, which is taken from the head of the venomous and despised toad.' In this manner did the patient duke draw a useful moral from everything that he saw; and by the help of this moralizing turn, in that life of his, remote from public haunts, he could find tongues in trees, books in the running brooks, sermons in stones, and good in everything.

The banished duke had an only daughter, named Rosalind, whom the usurper, duke Frederick, when he banished her father, still retained in his court as a companion for his own daughter Celia. A strict friendship subsisted between these ladies, which the disagreement between their fathers did not in the least interrupt, Celia striving by every kindness in her power to make amends to Rosalind for the injustice of her own father in deposing the father of Rosalind; and whenever the thoughts of her father's banishment, and her own dependence on the false usurper, made Rosalind melancholy, Celia's whole care was to comfort and console her.

One day, when Celia was talking in her usual kind manner to Rosalind, saying: 'I pray you, Rosalind, my sweet cousin, be merry,' a messenger entered from the duke, to tell them that if they wished to see a wrestling match, which was just going to begin, they must come instantly to the court before the palace; and Celia, thinking it would amuse Rosalind, agreed to go and see it.

In those times wrestling, which is only practised now by country clowns, was a favourite sport even in the courts of princes, and before fair ladies and princesses. To this wrestling match, therefore, Celia and Rosalind went. They found that it was likely to prove a very tragical sight; for a large and powerful man, who had been long practised in the art of wrestling, and had slain many men in contests of this kind, was just going to wrestle with a very young man, who, from his extreme youth and inexperience in the art, the beholders all thought would certainly be killed.

When the duke saw Celia and Rosalind, he said: 'How now, daughter and niece, are you crept hither to see the wrestling? You will take little delight in it, there is such odds in the men: in pity to this young man, I would wish to persuade him from wrestling. Speak to him, ladies, and see if you can move him.'

The ladies were well pleased to perform this humane office, and first Celia entreated the young stranger that he would desist from the attempt; and then Rosalind spoke so kindly to him, and with such feeling consideration for, the danger he was about to undergo, that instead of being persuaded by her gentle words to forego his purpose, all his thoughts were bent to distinguish himself by his courage in this lovely lady's eyes. He refused the request of Celia and Rosalind in such graceful and modest words, that they felt still more concern for him; he concluded his refusal with saying: 'I am sorry to deny such fair and excellent ladies anything. But let your fair eyes and gentle wishes go with me to my trial, wherein if I be conquered there is one shamed that was never gracious; if I am killed, there is one dead that is willing to die; I shall do my friends no wrong, for I have none to lament me; the world no injury, for in it I have nothing; for I only fill up a place in the world which may be better supplied when I have made it empty.'

And now the wrestling match began. Celia wished the young stranger might not be hurt; but Rosalind felt most for him. The friendless state which he said he was in, and that he wished to die, made Rosalind think that he was like herself, unfortunate; and she pitied him so much, and so deep an interest she took in his danger while he was wrestling, that she might almost be said at that moment to have fallen in love with him.

The kindness shown this unknown youth by these fair and noble ladies gave him courage and strength, so that he performed wonders; and in the end completely conquered his antagonist, who was so much hurt, that for a while he was unable to speak or move.

The duke Frederick was much pleased with the

courage and skill shown by this young stranger; and desired to know his name and parentage, meaning to take him under his protection.

The stranger said his name was Orlando, and that he was the youngest son of Sir Roland de Boys.

Sir Rowland de Boys, the father of Orlando, had been dead some years; but when he was living, he had been a true subject and dear friend of the banished duke; therefore, when Freeerick heard Orlando was the son of his banished brother's friend, all his liking for this brave young man was changed into displeasure, and he left the place in very ill humour. Hating to hear the very name of any of his brother's friends, and yet still admiring the valour of the youth, he said, as he went out, that he wished Orlando had been the son of any other man.

Rosalind was delighted to hear that her new favourite was the son of her father's old friend; and she said to Celia: 'My father loved Sir Rowland de Boys, and if I had known this young man was his son, I would have added tears to my entreaties before he should have ventured.'

The ladies then went up to him; and seeing him abashed by the sudden displeasure shown by the duke, they spoke kind and encouraging words to him; and Rosalind, when they were going away, turned back to speak some more civil things to the brave young son of her father's old friend; and taking a chain from off her neck, she said: 'Gentleman, wear this for me. I am out of suits with fortune, or I would give you a more valuable present.'

When the ladies were alone, Rosalind's talk being still of Orlando, Celia began to perceive her cousin had fallen in love with the handsome young wrestler, and she said to Rosalind: 'Is it possible you should fall in love so suddenly?' Rosalind replied: 'The duke, my father, loved his father dearly.' 'But,' said Celia, 'does it therefore follow that you should love·his son dearly?

for then I ought to hate him, for my father hated his father; yet I do not hate Orlando.'

Frederick being enraged at the sight of Sir Rowland de Boys' son, which reminded him of the many friends the banished duke had among the nobility, and having been for some time displeased with his niece, because the people praised her for her virtues, and pitied her for her good father's sake, his malice suddenly broke out against her; and while Celia and Rosalind were talking of Orlando, Frederick entered the room, and with looks full of anger ordered Rosalind instantly to leave the palace, and follow her father into banishment; telling Celia, who in vain pleaded for her, that he had only suffered Rosalind to stay upon her account. 'I did not then,' said Celia, 'entreat you to let her stay, for I was too young at that time to value her; but now that I know her worth, and that we so long have slept together, rose at the same instant, learned, played, and eat together, I cannot live out of her company.' Frederick replied: 'She is too subtle for you; her smoothness, her very silence, and her patience speak to the people, and they pity her. You are a fool to plead for her, for you will seem more bright and virtuous when she is gone; therefore open not your lips in her favour, for the doom which I have passed upon her is irrevocable.'

When Celia found she could not prevail upon her father to let Rosalind remain with her, she generously resolved to accompany her; and leaving her father's palace that night, she went along with her friend to seek Rosalind's father, the banished duke, in the forest of Arden.

Before they set out, Celia considered that it would be unsafe for two young ladies to travel in the rich clothes they then wore; she therefore proposed that they should disguise their rank by dressing themselves like country maids. Rosalind said it would be a still greater protection if one of them was to be dressed like a man; and so it was quickly agreed on between them, that as Rosalind was the tallest, she should wear the dress of a young countryman, and Celia should be habited like a country lass, and that they should say they were brother and sister, and Rosalind said she would be called Ganymede, and Celia chose the name of Aliena.

In this disguise, and taking their money and jewels to defray their expenses, these fair princesses set out on their long travel; for the forest of Arden was a long way off, beyond the boundaries of the duke's dominions.

The Lady Rosalind (or Ganymede as she must now be called) with her manly garb seemed to have put on a manly courage. The faithful friendship Celia had shown in accompanying Rosalind so many weary miles, made the new brother, in recompense for this true love, exert a cheerful spirit, as if he were indeed Ganymede, the rustic and stout-hearted brother of the gentle village maiden, Aliena.

When at last they came to the forest of Arden, they no longer found the convenient inns and good accommodations they had met with on the road; and being in want of food and rest, Ganymede, who had so merrily cheered his sister with pleasant speeches and happy remarks all the way, now owned to Aliena that he was so weary, he could find in his heart to disgrace his man's apparel, and cry like a woman; and Aliena declared she could go no farther; and then again Ganymede tried to recollect that it was a man's duty to comfort and console a woman, as the weaker vessel; and to seem courageous to his new sister; he said: 'Come, have a good heart, my sister Aliena; we are now at the end of our travel, in the forest of Arden.' But feigned manliness and forced courage would no longer support them; for though they were in the forest of Arden, they knew not where to find the duke: and here the travel of these weary ladies might have come to a sad conclusion, for they might have lost themselves, and perished for want of food; but providentially, as they were sitting on the grass, almost dying with fatigue and hopeless of any relief, a country-man chanced to pass that way, and Ganymede once more tried to speak with a manly boldness, saying: 'Shepherd, if love or gold can in this desert place procure us enter-tainment, I pray you bring us where we may rest our-selves; for this young maid, my sister, is much fatigued with travelling, and faints for want of food.'

The man replied that he was only a servant to a shep-herd, and that his master's house was just going to be sold, and therefore they would find but poor entertain-ment; but that if they would go with him, they should be welcome to what there was. They followed the man, the near prospect of relief giving them fresh strength; and bought the house and sheep of the shep-herd, and took the man who conducted them to the shepherd's house to wait on them; and being by this means so fortunately provided with a neat cottage, and well supplied with provisions, they agreed to stay here till they could learn in what part of the forest the duke dwelt.

When they were rested after the fatigue of their journey, they began to like their new way of life, and almost fancied themselves the shepherd and shepherdess they feigned to be: yet sometimes Ganymede remembered he had once been the same lady Rosalind who had so dearly loved the brave Orlando, because he was the son of old Sir Rowland, her father's friend; and though Ganymede thought that Orlando was many miles distant, even so many weary miles as they had travelled, yet it soon appeared that Orlando was also in the forest of Arden: and in this manner this strange event came to pass.

Orlando was the youngest son of Sir Rowland de Boys, who, when he died, left him (Orlando being then very young) to the care of his eldest brother Oliver, charging Oliver on his blessing to give his brother a good education, and provide for him as became the dignity of their ancient house. Oliver proved an unworthy brother; and disregarding the commands of his dying father, he never put his brother to school, but kept him at home untaught and entirely neglected. But in his nature and in the noble qualities of his mind Orlando so much resembled his excellent father, that without any advantages of education he seemed like a youth who had been bred with the utmost care; and Oliver so envied the fine person and dignified manners of his untutored brother, that at last he wished to destroy him; and to effect this he set on people to persuade him to wrestle with the famous wrestler, who, as has been before related, had killed so many men. Now, it was this cruel brother's neglect of him which made Orlando say he wished to die, being so friendless.

When, contrary to the wicked hopes he had formed, his brother proved victorious, his envy and malice knew no bounds, and he swore he would burn the chamber where Orlando slept. He was overheard making this vow by one that had been an old and faithful servant to their father, and that loved Orlando because he resembled Sir Rowland. This old man went out to meet him when he returned from the duke's palace, and when he saw Orlando, the peril his dear young master was in made him break out into these passionate exclamations: 'O my gentle master, my sweet master, O you memory of old Sir Rowland! why are you virtuous? why are you gentle, strong, and valiant? and why would you be so fond to overcome the famous wrestler? Your praise is come too swiftly home before you.' Orlando, wondering what all this meant, asked him what was the matter. And then the old man told him how his wicked brother, envying the love all people bore him, and now hearing the fame he had gained by his victory in the duke's palace, intended to destroy him, by setting fire to his chamber that night; and in conclusion, advised him to escape the danger he was in by instant flight; and knowing Orlando had no money, Adam (for that was the good old man's name) had brought out with him his own little hoard, and he said: 'I have five hundred crowns, the thrifty hire I saved under your father, and laid by to be provision for me when my old limbs should become unfit for service; take that, and He that doth the ravens feed be comfort to my age! Here is the gold; all this I give to you: let me be your servant; though I look old I will do the service of a younger man in all your business and necessities.' 'O good old man!' said Orlando, 'how well appears in you the constant service of the old world! You are not for the fashion of these times. We will go along together, and before your youthful wages are spent, I shall light upon some means for both our maintenance.'

Together then this faithful servant and his loved master set out; and Orlando and Adam travelled on, uncertain what course to pursue, till they came to the forest of Arden, and there they found themselves in the same distress for want of food that Ganymede and Aliena had been. They wandered on, seeking some human habitation, till they were almost spent with hunger and fatigue. Adam at last said: 'O my dear master, I die for want of food, I can go no farther!' He then laid himself down, thinking to make that place his grave, and bade his dear master farewell. Orlando, seeing him in this weak state, took his old servant up in his arms, and carried him under the shelter of some pleasant trees; and he said to him: 'Cheerly, old Adam, rest your weary limbs here awhile, and do not talk of dying!'

Orlando then searched about to find some food, and he happened to arrive at that part of the forest where the duke was; and he and his friends were just going to eat their dinner, this royal duke being seated on the grass, under no other canopy than the shady covert of some large trees.

Orlando, whom hunger had made desperate, drew his sword, intending to take their meat by force, and said: 'Forbear and eat no more; I must have your food!' The duke asked him, if distress had made him so bold, or if he were a rude despiser of good manners? On this Orlando said, he was dying with hunger; and then the duke told him he was welcome to sit down and eat with them. Orlando hearing him speak so gently, put up his sword, and blushed with shame at the rude manner in which he had demanded their food. 'Pardon me, I pray you,' said he: 'I thought that all things had been savage here, and therefore I put on the countenance of stern command; but whatever men you are, that in this desert, under the shade of melancholy boughs, lose and neglect the creeping hours of time; if ever you have looked on better days; if ever you have been where bells have knolled to church; if you have ever sat at any good man's feast; if ever from your eyelids you have wiped a tear, and know what it is to pity or be pitied, may gentle speeches now move you to do me human courtesy!' The duke replied: 'True it is that we are men (as you say) who have seen better days, and though we have now our habitation in this wild forest, we have lived in towns and cities, and have with holy bell been knolled to church, have sat at good men's feasts, and from our eyes have wiped the drops which sacred pity has engendered; therefore sit you down, and take of our refreshment as much as will minister to your wants.' 'There is an old poor man,' answered Orlando, 'who has limped after me many a weary step in pure love, oppressed at once with two sad infirmities, age and hunger; till he be satisfied, I must not touch a bit.' 'Go, find him out, and bring him hither,' said the duke; 'we will forbear to eat till you return.' Then Orlando went like a doe to find its fawn and give it food; and presently returned, bringing Adam in his arms; and the duke said: 'Set down your venerable burthen; you are both welcome'; and they fed the old man, and cheered his heart, and he revived, and recovered his health and strength again.

The duke inquired who Orlando was; and when he found that he was the son of his old friend, Sir Rowland de Boys, he took him under his protection, and Orlando and his old servant lived with the duke in the forest.

Orlando arrived in the forest not many days after Ganymede and Aliena came there, and (as has been before related) bought the shepherd's cottage.

Ganymede and Aliena were strangely surprised to find the name of Rosalind carved on the trees, and love-sonnets, fastened to them, all addressed to Rosalind; and while they were wondering how this could be, they met Orlando, and they perceived the chain which Rosalind had given him about his neck.

Orlando little thought that Ganymede was the fair princess Rosalind, who, by her noble condescension and favour, had so won his heart that he passed his whole time in carving her name upon the trees, and writing sonnets in praise of her beauty: but being much pleased with the graceful air of this pretty shepherd-youth, he entered into conversation with him, and he thought he saw a likeness in Ganymede to his beloved Rosalind, but that he had none of the dignified deportment of that noble lady; for Ganymede assumed the forward manners often seen in youths when they are between boys and men, and with much archness and humour talked to Orlando of a certain lover, 'who,' said he, 'haunts our forest, and spoils our young trees with carving Rosalind upon their barks; and he hangs odes upon hawthorns, and elegies on brambles, all praising this same Rosalind. If I could find this lover, I would give him some good counsel that would soon cure him of his love.'

Orlando confessed that he was the fond lover of whom he spoke, and asked Ganymede to give him the good counsel he talked of. The remedy Ganymede proposed, and the counsel he gave him, was that Orlando should come every day to the cottage where he and his sister Aliena dwelt: 'And then,' said Ganymede, 'I will feign myself to be Rosalind, and you shall feign to court me in the same manner as you would do if I was Rosalind, and then I will imitate the fantastic ways of whimsical ladies to their lovers, till I make you ashamed of your love; and this is the way I propose to cure you.' Orlando had no great faith in the remedy, yet he agreed to come every day to Ganymede's cottage, and feign a playful courtship; and every day Orlando visited Ganymede and Aliena, and Orlando called the shepherd Ganymede his Rosalind, and every day talked over all the fine words and flattering compliments which young men delight to use when they court their mistresses. It does not appear, however, that Ganymede made any progress in curing Orlando of his love for Rosalind.

Though Orlando thought all this was but a sportive play (not dreaming that Ganymede was his very Rosalind), yet the opportunity it gave him of saying all the fond things he had in his heart, pleased his fancy almost as well as it did Ganymede's, who enjoyed the secret jest in knowing these fine love-speeches were all addressed to the right person.

In this manner many days passed pleasantly on with these young people; and the good-natured Aliena, seeing it made Ganymede happy, let him have his own way, and was diverted at the mock-courtship, and did not care to remind Ganymede that the Lady Rosalind had not yet made herself known to the duke her father, whose place of resort in the forest they had learnt from Orlando. Ganymede met the duke one day, and had some talk with him, and the duke asked of what parentage he came. Ganymede answered that he came of as good parentage as he did, which made the duke smile, for he did not suspect the pretty shepherd-boy came of royal lineage. Then seeing the duke look well and happy,

*Ganymede assumed the forward manners often seen in youths
when they are between boys and men*

Ganymede was content to put off all further explanation for a few days longer.

One morning, as Orlando was going to visit Ganymede, he saw a man lying asleep on the ground, and a large green snake had twisted itself about his neck. The snake, seeing Orlando approach, glided away among the bushes. Orlando went nearer, and then he discovered a lioness lie crouching, with her head on the ground, with a cat-like watch, waiting until the sleeping man awaked (for it is said that lions will prey on nothing that is dead or sleeping). It seemed as if Orlando was sent by Providence to free the man from the danger of the snake and lioness; but when Orlando looked in the man's face, he perceived that the sleeper who was exposed to this double peril, was his own brother Oliver, who had so cruelly used him, and had threatened to destroy him by fire; and he was almost tempted to leave him a prey to the hungry lioness; but brotherly affection and the gentleness of his nature soon overcame his first anger against his brother; and he drew his sword, and attacked the lioness, and slew her, and thus preserved his brother's life both from the venomous snake and from the furious lioness; but before Orlando could conquer the lioness, she had torn one of his arms with her sharp claws.

While Orlando was engaged with the lioness, Oliver awaked, and perceiving that his brother Orlando, whom he had so cruelly treated, was saving him from the fury of a wild beast at the risk of his own life, shame and remorse at once seized him, and he repented of his unworthy conduct, and besought with many tears his brother's pardon for the injuries he had done him. Orlando rejoiced to see him so penitent, and readily forgave him: they embraced each other; and from that hour Oliver loved Orlando with a true brotherly affection, though he had come to the forest bent on his destruction.

The wound in Orlando's arm having bled very much, he found himself too weak to go to visit Ganymede, and therefore he desired his brother to go and tell Ganymede, 'whom,' said Orlando, 'I in sport do call my Rosalind,' the accident which had befallen him.

Thither then Oliver went, and told to Ganymede and Aliena how Orlando had saved his life: and when he had finished the story of Orlando's bravery, and his own providential escape, he owned to them that he was Orlando's brother, who had so cruelly used him; and then he told them of their reconciliation.

The sincere sorrow that Oliver expressed for his offences made such a lively impression on the kind heart of Aliena, that she instantly fell in love with him; and Oliver observing how much she pitied the distress he told her he felt for his fault, he as suddenly fell in love with her. But while love was thus stealing into the hearts of Aliena and Oliver, he was no less busy with Ganymede, who hearing of the danger Orlando had been in, and that he was wounded by the lioness, fainted; and when he recovered, he pretended that he had counterfeited the swoon in the imaginary character of Rosalind, and Ganymede said to Oliver: 'Tell your brother Orlando how well I counterfeited a swoon.' But Oliver saw by the paleness of his complexion that he did really faint, and much wondering at the weakness of the young man, he said: 'Well, if you did counterfeit, take a good heart, and counterfeit to be a man.' 'So I do,' replied Ganymede, truly, 'but I should have been a woman by right.'

Oliver made this visit a very long one, and when at last he returned back to his brother, he had much news to tell him; for besides the account of Ganymede's fainting at the hearing that Orlando was wounded, Oliver told him how he had fallen in love with the fair shepherdess Aliena, and that she had lent a favourable ear to his suit, even in this their first interview; and he talked to his brother, as of a thing almost settled, that he should marry Aliena, saying, that he so well loved her, that he would live here as a shepherd, and settle his estate and house at home upon Orlando.

'You have my consent,' said Orlando. 'Let your wedding be to-morrow, and I will invite the duke and his friends. Go and persuade your shepherdess to this: she is now alone; for look, here comes her brother.' Oliver went to Aliena; and Ganymede, whom Orlando had perceived approaching, came to inquire after the health of his wounded friend.

When Orlando and Ganymede began to talk over the sudden love which had taken place between Oliver and Aliena, Orlando said he had advised his brother to persuade his fair shepherdess to be married on the morrow, and then he added how much he could wish to be married on the same day to his Rosalind.

Ganymede, who well approved of this arrangement said that if Orlando really loved Rosalind as well as he professed to do, he should have his wish; for on the morrow he would engage to make Rosalind appear in her own person, and also that Rosalind should be willing to marry Orlando.

This seemingly wonderful event, which, as Ganymede was the lady Rosalind, he could so easily perform, he pretended he would bring to pass by the aid of magic, which he said he had learnt of an uncle who was a famous magician.

The fond lover Orlando, half believing and half doubting what he heard, asked Ganymede if he spoke in sober meaning. 'By my life I do,' said Ganymede; 'therefore put on your best clothes, and bid the duke and your friends to your wedding; for if you desire to be married to-morrow to Rosalind, she shall be here.'

The next morning, Oliver having obtained the consent of Aliena, they came into the presence of the duke, and with them also came Orlando.

They being all assembled to celebrate this double marriage, and as yet only one of the brides appearing, there was much of wondering and conjecture, but they mostly thought that Ganymede was making a jest of Orlando.

The duke, hearing that it was his own daughter that was to be brought in this strange way, asked Orlando if he believed the shepherd-boy could really do what he had promised; and while Orlando was answering that he knew not what to think, Ganymede entered, and asked the duke, if he brought his daughter, whether he would consent to her marriage with Orlando. 'That I would,' said the duke, 'if I had kingdoms to give with her.' Ganymede then said to Orlando: 'And you say you will marry her if I bring her here.' 'That I would,' said Orlando, 'if I were king of many kingdoms.'

Ganymede and Aliena then went out together, and Ganymede throwing off his male attire, and being once more dressed in woman's apparel, quickly became Rosalind without the power of magic; and Aliena changing her country garb for her own rich clothes, was with as little trouble transformed into the lady Celia.

While they were gone, the duke said to Orlando, that he thought the shepherd Ganymede very like his daughter Rosalind; and Orlando said, he also had observed the resemblance.

They had no time to wonder how all this would end, for Rosalind and Celia in their own clothes entered; and no longer pretending that it was by the power of magic that she came there, Rosalind threw herself on her knees before her father, and begged his blessing. It seemed so wonderful to all present that she should so suddenly appear, that it might well have passed for magic; but Rosalind would no longer trifle with her father, and told him the story of her banishment, and of her dwelling in the forest as a shepherd-boy, her cousin Celia passing as her sister.

The duke ratified the consent he had already given to the marriage; and Orlando and Rosalind, Oliver and Celia, were married at the same time. And though their wedding could not be celebrated in this wild forest with any of the parade or splendour usual on such occasions, yet a happier wedding-day was never passed: and while they were eating their venison under the cool shade of the pleasant trees, as if nothing should be wanting to complete the felicity of this good duke and the true lovers, an unexpected messenger arrived to tell the duke the joyful news, that his dukedom was restored to him.

The usurper, enraged at the flight of his daughter Celia, and hearing that every day men of great worth resorted to the forest of Arden to join the lawful duke in his exile, much envying that his brother should be so highly respected in his adversity, put himself at the head of a large force, and advanced towards the forest, intending to seize his brother, and put him with all his faithful followers to the sword; but, by a wonderful interposition of Providence, this bad brother was converted from his evil intention; for just as he entered the skirts of the wild forest, he was met by an old religious man, a hermit, with whom he had much talk, and who in the end completely turned his heart from his wicked design. Thenceforward he became a true penitent, and resolved, relinquishing his unjust dominion, to spend the remainder of his days in a religious house. The first act of his newly-conceived penitence was to send a messenger to his brother (as has been related) to offer to restore to him his dukedom, which he had usurped so long, and with it the lands and revenues of his friends, the faithful followers of his adversity.

This joyful news, as unexpected as it was welcome, came opportunely to heighten the festivity and rejoicings at the wedding of the princesses. Celia complimented her cousin on this good fortune which had happened to the duke, Rosalind's father, and wished her joy very sincerely, though she herself was no longer heir to the dukedom, but by this restoration which her father had made, Rosalind was now the heir: so completely was the love of these two cousins unmixed with anything of jealousy or of envy.

The duke had now an opportunity of rewarding those true friends who had stayed with him in his banishment; and these worthy followers, though they had patiently shared his adverse fortune, were very well pleased to return in peace and prosperity to the palace of their lawful duke.

THE TWO GENTLEMEN OF VERONA

THERE lived in the city of Verona two young gentlemen, whose names were Valentine and Proteus, between whom a firm and uninterrupted friendship had long subsisted. They pursued their studies together, and their hours of leisure were always passed in each other's company, except when Proteus visited a lady he was in love with; and these visits to his mistress, and this passion of Proteus for the fair Julia, were the only topics on which these two friends disagreed; for Valentine, not being himself a lover, was sometimes a little weary of hearing his friend for ever talking of his Julia, and then he would laugh at Proteus, and in pleasant terms ridicule the passion of love, and declare that no such idle fancies should ever enter his head, greatly preferring (as he said) the free and happy life he led, to the anxious hopes and fears of the lover Proteus.

One morning Valentine came to Proteus to tell him that they must for a time be separated, for that he was going to Milan. Proteus, unwilling to part with his friend, used many arguments to prevail upon Valentine not to leave him: but Valentine said: 'Cease to persuade me, my loving Proteus. I will not, like a sluggard, wear out my youth in idleness at home. Home-keeping youths have ever homely wits. If your affection were not chained to the sweet glances of your honoured Julia, I would entreat you to accompany me, to see the wonders of the world abroad; but since you are a lover, love on still, and may your love be prosperous!'

They parted with mutual expressions of unalterable friendship. 'Sweet Valentine, adieu!' said Proteus; 'think on me, when you see some rare object worthy of notice in your travels, and wish me partaker of your happiness.'

Valentine began his journey that same day towards Milan; and when his friend had left him, Proteus sat down to write a letter to Julia, which he gave to her maid Lucetta to deliver to her mistress.

Julia loved Proteus as well as he did her, but she was a lady of a noble spirit, and she thought it did not become her maiden dignity too easily to be won; therefore she affected to be insensible of his passion, and gave him much uneasiness in the prosecution of his suit.

And when Lucetta offered the letter to Julia, she would not receive it, and chid her maid for taking letters from Proteus, and ordered her to leave the room. But she so much wished to see what was written in the letter, that she soon called in her maid again; and when Lucetta returned, she said: 'What o'clock is it?' Lucetta, who knew her mistress more desired to see the letter than to know the time of day, without answering her question, again offered the rejected letter. Julia, angry that her maid should thus take the liberty of seeming to know what she really wanted, tore the letter in pieces, and threw it on the floor, ordering her maid once more out of the room. As Lucetta was retiring, she stopped to pick up the fragments of the torn letter; but Julia, who meant not so to part with them, said, in pretended anger: 'Go, get you gone, and let the papers lie; you would be fingering them to anger me.'

Julia then began to piece together as well as she could the torn fragments. She first made out these words: 'Love-wounded Proteus'; and lamenting over these and such like loving words, which she made out though they were all torn asunder, or, she said *wounded* (the expression 'Love-wounded Proteus' giving her that idea), she talked to these kind words, telling them she would lodge them in her bosom as in a bed, till their wounds were healed, and that she would kiss each several piece, to make amends.

In this manner she went on talking with a pretty

ladylike childishness, till finding herself unable to make out the whole, and vexed at her own ingratitude in destroying such sweet and loving words, as she called them, she wrote a much kinder letter to Proteus than she had ever done before.

Proteus was greatly delighted at receiving this favourable answer to his letter; and while he was reading it, he exclaimed: 'Sweet love, sweet lines, sweet life!' In the midst of his raptures he was interrupted by his father. 'How now!' said the old gentleman; 'what letter are you reading there?'

'My lord,' replied Proteus, 'it is a letter from my friend Valentine, at Milan.'

'Lend me the letter,' said his father: 'let me see what news.'

'There are no news, my lord,' said Proteus, greatly alarmed, 'but that he writes how well beloved he is of the duke of Milan, who daily graces him with favours; and how he wishes me with him, the partner of his fortune.'

'And how stand you affected to his wish?' asked the father.

'As one relying on your lordship's will, and not depending on his friendly wish,' said Proteus.

Now it had happened that Proteus' father had just been talking with a friend on this very subject: his friend had said, he wondered his lordship suffered his son to spend his youth at home, while most men were sending their sons to seek preferment abroad; 'some,' said he, 'to the wars, to try their fortunes there, and some to discover islands far away, and some to study in foreign universities; and there is his companion Valentine, he is gone to the duke of Milan's court. Your son is fit for any of these things, and it will be a great disadvantage to him in his riper age not to have travelled in his youth.'

Proteus' father thought the advice of his friend was very good, and upon Proteus telling him that Valentine 'wished him with him, the partner of his fortune,' he at once determined to send his son to Milan; and without giving Proteus any reason for this sudden resolution, it being the usual habit of this positive old gentleman to command his son, not reason with him, he said: 'My will is the same as Valentine's wish'; and seeing his son look astonished, he added: 'Look not amazed, that I so suddenly resolve you shall spend some time in the duke of Milan's court; for what I will I will, and there is an end. To-morrow be in readiness to go. Make no excuses; for I am peremptory.'

Proteus knew it was of no use to make objections to his father, who never suffered him to dispute his will; and he blamed himself for telling his father an untruth about Julia's letter, which had brought upon him the sad necessity of leaving her.

Now that Julia found she was going to lose Proteus for so long a time, she no longer pretended indifference; and they bade each other a mournful farewell, with many vows of love and constancy. Proteus and Julia exchanged rings, which they both promised to keep for ever in remembrance of each other; and thus, taking a sorrowful leave, Proteus set out on his journey to Milan, the abode of his friend Valentine.

Valentine was in reality what Proteus had feigned to his father, in high favour with the duke of Milan; and another event had happened to him, of which Proteus did not even dream, for Valentine had given up the freedom of which he used so much to boast, and was become as passionate a lover as Proteus.

She who had wrought this wondrous change in Valentine was the lady Silvia, daughter of the duke of Milan, and she also loved him; but they concealed their love from the duke, because although he showed much kindness for Valentine, and invited him every day to his palace, yet he designed to marry his daughter to a young courtier whose name was Thurio. Silvia despised this Thurio, for he had none of the fine sense and excellent qualities of Valentine.

These two rivals, Thurio and Valentine, were one day on a visit to Silvia, and Valentine was entertaining Silvia with turning everything Thurio said into ridicule, when the duke himself entered the room, and told Valentine the welcome news of his friend Proteus' arrival. Valentine said: 'If I had wished a thing, it would have been to have seen him here!' And then he highly praised Proteus to the duke, saying: 'My lord, though I have been a truant of my time, yet hath my friend made use and fair advantage of his days, and is complete in person and in mind, in all good grace to grace a gentleman.'

'Welcome him then according to his worth,' said the duke. 'Silvia, I speak to you, and you, Sir Thurio; for Valentine, I need not bid him do so.' They were here interrupted by the entrance of Proteus, and Valentine introduced him to Silvia, saying: 'Sweet lady, entertain him to be my fellow-servant to your ladyship.'

When Valentine and Proteus had ended their visit, and were alone together, Valentine said: 'Now tell me how all does from whence you came? How does your lady, and how thrives your love?' Proteus replied: 'My tales of love used to weary you. I know you joy not in a love discourse.'

'Ay, Proteus,' returned Valentine, 'but that life is altered now. I have done penance for condemning love. For in revenge of my contempt of love, love has chased sleep from my enthralled eyes. O gentle Proteus, Love is a mighty lord, and hath so humbled me, that I confess there is no woe like his correction, nor so such joy on earth as in his service. I now like no discourse except it be of love. Now I can break my fast, dine, sup, and sleep, upon the very name of love.'

This acknowledgment of the change which love had made in the disposition of Valentine was a great triumph to his friend Proteus. But 'friend' Proteus must be called no longer, for the same all-powerful deity Love, of whom they were speaking (yea, even while they were talking of the change he had made in Valentine), was working in the heart of Proteus; and he, who had till this time been a pattern of true love and perfect friendship, was now, in one short interview with Silvia, become a false friend and a faithless lover; for at the first sight of Silvia all his love for Julia vanished away like a dream, nor did his long friendship for Valentine deter him from endeavouring to supplant him in her affections; and although, as it will always be, when people of dispositions naturally good become unjust, he had many scruples before he determined to forsake Julia, and become the rival of Valentine; yet he at length overcame his sense of duty, and yielded himself up, almost without remorse, to his new unhappy passion.

Valentine imparted to him in confidence the whole history of his love, and how carefully they had concealed it from the duke her father, and told him, that, despairing of ever being able to obtain his consent, he had prevailed upon Silvia to leave her father's palace that night, and go with him to Mantua; then he showed Proteus a ladder of ropes, by help of which he meant to assist Silvia to get out of one of the windows of the palace after it was dark.

Upon hearing this faithful recital of his friend's dearest secrets, it is hardly possible to be believed, but so it was, that Proteus resolved to go to the duke, and disclose the whole to him.

This false friend began his tale with many artful speeches to the duke, such as that by the laws of friendship he ought to conceal what he was going to reveal, but that the gracious favour the duke had shown him, and the duty he owed his grace, urged him to tell that which else no worldly good should draw from him. He then told all he had heard from Valentine, not omitting the ladder of ropes, and the manner in which Valentine meant to conceal them under a long cloak.

The duke thought Proteus quite a miracle of integrity, in that he preferred telling his friend's intention rather than he would conceal an unjust action, highly commended him, and promised him not to let Valentine know from whom he had learnt this intelligence, but by some artifice to make Valentine betray the secret himself. For this purpose the duke awaited the coming of Valentine in the evening, whom he soon saw hurrying towards the palace, and he perceived somewhat was wrapped within his cloak, which he concluded was the rope-ladder.

The duke upon this stopped him, saying: 'Whither away so fast, Valentine?' 'May it please your grace,' said Valentine, 'there is a messenger that stays to bear my letters to my friends, and I am going to deliver them.' Now this falsehood of Valentine's had no better success in the event than the untruth Proteus told his father.

'Be they of much import?' said the duke.

'No more, my lord,' said Valentine, 'than to tell my father I am well and happy at your grace's court.'

'Nay then,' said the duke, 'no matter; stay with me a while. I wish your counsel about some affairs that concern me nearly.' He then told Valentine an artful story, as a prelude to draw his secret from him, saying that Valentine knew he wished to match his daughter with Thurio, but that she was stubborn and disobedient to his commands, 'neither regarding,' said he, 'that she is my child, nor fearing me as if I were her father. And I may say to thee, this pride of hers has drawn my love from her. I had thought my age should have been cherished by her childlike duty. I now am resolved to take a wife, and turn her out to whosoever will take her in. Let her beauty be her wedding dower, for me and my possessions she esteems not.'

Valentine, wondering where all this would end, made answer: 'And what would your grace have me do in all this?'

'Why,' said the duke, 'the lady I would wish to marry is nice and coy, and does not much esteem my aged eloquence. Besides, the fashion of courtship is much changed since I was young; now I would willingly have you to be my tutor to instruct me how I am to woo.'

Valentine gave him a general idea of the modes of courtship then practised by young men, when they wished to win a fair lady's love, such as presents, frequent visits; and the like.

The duke replied to this, that the lady did refuse a present which he sent her, and that she was so strictly kept by her father, that no man might have access to her by day.

'Why then,' said Valentine, 'you must visit her by night.'

'But at night,' said the artful duke, who was now coming to the drift of his discourse, 'her doors are fast locked.'

Valentine then unfortunately proposed that the duke should go into the lady's chamber at night by means of a ladder of ropes, saying he would procure him one fitting for that purpose; and in conclusion advised him to conceal this ladder of ropes under such a cloak as that which he now wore. 'Lend me your cloak,' said the duke, who had feigned this long story on purpose to have a pretence to get off the cloak; so upon saying these words, he caught hold of Valentine's cloak, and throwing it back, he discovered not only the ladder of ropes, but also a letter of Silvia's, which he instantly opened and read; and this letter contained a full account of their intended elopement. The duke, after upbraiding Valentine for his ingratitude in thus returning the favour he had shown him, by endeavouring to steal away his daughter, banished him from the court and city of Milan for ever; and Valentine was forced to depart that night, without even seeing Silvia.

While Proteus at Milan was thus injuring Valentine, Julia at Verona was regretting the absence of Proteus; and her regard for him at last so far overcame her sense of propriety, that she resolved to leave Verona, and seek her lover at Milan; and to secure herself from danger on the road, she dressed her maiden Lucetta and herself in men's clothes, and they set out in this disguise, and arrived at Milan soon after Valentine was banished from that city through the treachery of Proteus.

Julia entered Milan about noon, and she took up her abode at an inn; and her thoughts being all on her dear Proteus, she entered into conversation with the inn-keeper, or host, as he was called, thinking by that means to learn some news of Proteus.

The host was greatly pleased that this handsome young gentleman (as he took her to be), who from his appearance he concluded was of high rank, spoke so familiarly to him; and being a good-natured man, he was sorry to see him look so melancholy; and to amuse his young guest, he offered to take him to hear some fine music, with which, he said, a gentleman that evening was going to serenade his mistress.

The reason Julia looked so very melancholy was, that she did not well know what Proteus would think of the imprudent step she had taken; for she knew he had loved her for her noble maiden pride and dignity of character, and she feared she should lower herself in his esteem: and this it was that made her wear a sad and thoughtful countenance.

She gladly accepted the offer of the host to go with him, and hear the music; for she secretly hoped she might meet Proteus by the way.

But when she came to the palace whither the host conducted her, a very different effect was produced to what the kind host intended; for there, to her heart's sorrow, she beheld her lover, the inconstant Proteus, serenading the lady Silvia with music, and addressing discourse of love and admiration to her. And Julia overheard Silvia from a window talk with Proteus, and reproach him for forsaking his own true lady, and for his ingratitude to his friend Valentine; and then Silvia left the window, not choosing to listen to his music and his fine speeches; for she was a faithful lady to her banished Valentine, and abhorred the ungenerous conduct of his false friend Proteus.

Though Julia was in despair at what she had just witnessed, yet did she still love the truant Proteus; and hearing that he had lately parted with a servant, she contrived with the assistance of her host, the friendly innkeeper, to hire herself to Proteus as a page; and Proteus knew not she was Julia, and he sent her with letters and presents to her rival Silvia, and he even sent by her the very ring she gave him as a parting gift at Verona.

When she went to that lady with the ring, she was most glad to find that Silvia utterly rejected the suit of Proteus; and Julia, or the page Sebastian as she was called, entered into conversation with Silvia about Proteus' first love, the forsaken lady Julia. She putting in (as one may say) a good word for herself, said she knew Julia; as well she might, being herself the Julia of whom she spoke; telling how fondly Julia loved her master Proteus, and how his unkind neglect would grieve her: and then she with a pretty equivocation went on: 'Julia is about my height, and of my complexion, the colour of her eyes and hair the same as mine': and indeed Julia looked a most beautiful youth in her boy's attire. Silvia was moved to pity this lovely lady, who was so sadly forsaken by the man she loved; and when Julia offered the ring which Proteus had sent, refused it, saying: 'The more shame for him that he sends me that ring; I will not take it; for I have often heard him say his Julia gave it to him. I love thee, gentle youth, for pitying her, poor lady! Here is a purse; I give it you for Julia's sake.' These comfortable words coming from her kind rival's tongue cheered the drooping heart of the disguised lady.

But to return to the banished Valentine; who scarce knew which way to bend his course, being unwilling to return home to his father a disgraced and banished man: as he was wandering over a lonely forest, not far distant from Milan, where he had left his heart's dear treasure, the lady Silvia, he was set upon by robbers, who demanded his money.

Valentine told them that he was a man crossed by adversity, that he was going into banishment, and that he had no money, the clothes he had on being all his riches.

The robbers, hearing that he was a distressed man, and being struck with his noble air and manly behaviour, told him if he would live with them, and be their chief, or captain, they would put themselves under his command; but that if he refused to accept their offer, they would kill him.

Valentine, who cared little what became of himself, said he would consent to live with them and be their captain, provided they did no outrage on women or poor passengers.

Thus the noble Valentine became, like Robin Hood, of whom we read in ballads, a captain of robbers and outlawed banditti; and in this situation he was found by Silvia, and in this manner it came to pass.

Silvia, to avoid a marriage with Thurio, whom her father insisted upon her no longer refusing, came at last to the resolution of following Valentine to Mantua, at which place she had heard her lover had taken refuge; but in this account she was misinformed, for he still lived in the forest among the robbers, bearing the name of their captain, but taking no part in their depredations, and using the authority which they had imposed upon him in no other way than to compel them to show compassion to the travellers they robbed.

Silvia contrived to effect her escape from her father's palace in company with a worthy old gentleman, whose name was Eglamour, whom she took along with her for protection on the road. She had to pass through the forest where Valentine and the banditti dwelt; and one of these robbers seized on Silvia, and would also have taken Eglamour, but he escaped.

The robber who had taken Silvia, seeing the terror she was in, bid her not be alarmed, for that he was only going to carry her to a cave where his captain lived, and that she need not be afraid, for their captain had an honourable mind, and always showed humanity to women. Silvia found little comfort in hearing she was going to be carried as a prisoner before the captain of a lawless banditti. 'O Valentine,' she cried, 'this I endure for thee!'

But as the robber was conveying her to the cave of his captain, he was stopped by Proteus, who, still attended by Julia in the disguise of a page, having heard of the flight of Silvia, had traced her steps to this forest. Proteus now rescued her from the hands of the robber; but scarce had she time to thank him for the service he had done her, before he began to distress her afresh with his love suit; and while he was rudely pressing her to consent to marry him, and his page (the forlorn Julia) was standing beside him in great anxiety of mind, fearing lest the great service which Proteus had just done to Silvia should win her to show him some favour, they were all strangely surprised with the sudden appearance of Valentine, who, having heard his robbers had taken a lady prisoner, came to console and relieve her.

Proteus was courting Silvia, and he was so much ashamed of being caught by his friend, that he was all at once seized with penitence and remorse; and he expressed such a lively sorrow for the injuries he had done to Valentine, that Valentine, whose nature was noble and generous, even to a romantic degree, not only forgave and restored him to his former place in his friendship, but in a sudden flight of heroism he said: 'I freely do forgive you; and all the interest I have in Silvia, I give it up to you.' Julia, who was standing beside her master as a page, hearing this strange offer, and fearing Proteus would not be able with this new-found virtue to refuse Silvia, fainted, and they were all employed in recovering her: else would Silvia have been offended at being thus made over to Proteus, though she could scarcely think that Valentine would long persevere in this overstrained and too generous act of friendship. When Julia recovered from the fainting fit, she said: 'I had forgot, my master ordered me to deliver this ring to Silvia.' Proteus, looking upon the ring, saw that it was the one he gave to Julia, in return for that which he received from her, and which he had sent by the supposed page to Silvia. 'How is this?' said he, 'this is Julia's ring: how came you by it, boy?' Julia answered: 'Julia herself did give it me, and Julia herself hath brought it hither.'

Proteus, now looking earnestly upon her, plainly perceived that the page Sebastian was no other than the lady Julia herself; and the proof she had given of her constancy and true love so wrought in him, that his love for her returned into his heart, and he took again his own dear lady, and joyfully resigned all pretensions to the lady Silvia to Valentine, who had so well deserved her.

Proteus and Valentine were expressing their happiness in their reconciliation, and in the love of their faithful ladies when they were surprised with the sight of the duke of Milan and Thurio, who came there in pursuit of Silvia.

Thurio first approached, and attempted to seize Silvia, saying: 'Silvia is mine.' Upon this Valentine said to him in a very spirited manner: 'Thurio, keep back: if once again you say that Silvia is yours, you shall embrace your death. Here she stands, take but possession of her with a torch! I dare you but to breathe upon my love.' Hearing this threat, Thurio, who was a great coward, drew back, and said he cared not for her, and that none but a fool would fight for a girl who loved him not.

The duke, who was a very brave man himself, said now in great anger: 'The more base and degenerate in you to take such means for her as you have done, and leave her on such slight conditions.' Then turning to Valentine, he said: 'I do applaud your spirit, Valentine, and think you worthy of an empress's love. You shall have Silvia, for you have well deserved her.' Valentine then with great humility kissed the duke's hand, and accepted the noble present which he had made him of his daughter with becoming thankfulness: taking occasion of this joyful minute to entreat the good-humoured duke to pardon the thieves with whom he had associated in the forest, assuring him, that when reformed and restored to society, there would be found among them many good, and fit for great employment; for the most of them had been banished, like Valentine, for state offences, rather than for any black crimes they had been guilty of. To this the ready duke consented: and now nothing remained but that Proteus, the false friend, was ordained, by way of penance for his love-prompted faults, to be present at the recital of the whole story of his loves and falsehoods before the duke; and the shame of the recital to his awakened conscience was judged sufficient punishment: which being done, the lovers, all four, returned back to Milan, and their nuptials were solemnized in the presence of the duke, with high triumphs and feasting.

THE MERCHANT OF VENICE

SHYLOCK, the Jew, lived at Venice: he was an usurer, who had amassed an immense fortune by lending money at great interest to Christian merchants. Shylock, being a hard-hearted man, exacted the payment of the money he lent with such severity that he was much disliked by all good men, and particularly by Antonio, a young merchant of Venice; and Shylock as much hated Antonio, because he used to lend money to people in distress, and would never take any interest for the money he lent; therefore there was great enmity between this covetous Jew and the generous merchant Antonio. Whenever Antonio met Shylock on the Rialto (or Exchange), he used to reproach him with his usuries and hard dealings, which the Jew would bear with seeming patience, while he secretly meditated revenge.

Antonio was the kindest man that lived, the best conditioned, and had the most unwearied spirit in doing courtesies; indeed, he was one in whom the ancient Roman honour more appeared than in any that drew breath in Italy. He was greatly beloved by all his fellow-citizens; but the friend who was nearest and dearest to his heart was Bassanio, a noble Venetian, who, having but a small patrimony, had nearly exhausted his little fortune by living in too expensive a manner for his slender means, as young men of high rank with small fortunes are too apt to do. Whenever Bassanio wanted money, Antonio assisted him; and it seemed as if they had but one heart and one purse between them.

One day Bassanio came to Antonio, and told him that he wished to repair his fortune by a wealthy marriage with a lady whom he dearly loved, whose father, that was lately dead, had left her sole heiress to a large estate;

and that in her father's lifetime he used to visit at her house, when he thought he had observed this lady had sometimes from her eyes sent speechless messages, that seemed to say he would be no unwelcome suitor; but not having money to furnish himself with an appearance befitting the lover of so rich an heiress, he besought Antonio to add to the many favours he had shown him, by lending him three thousand ducats.

Antonio had no money by him at that time to lend his friend; but expecting soon to have some ships come home laden with merchandise, he said he would go to Shylock, the rich money-lender, and borrow the money upon the credit of those ships.

Antonio and Bassanio went together to Shylock, and Antonio asked the Jew to lend him three thousand ducats upon any interest he should require, to be paid out of the merchandise contained in his ships at sea. On this, Shylock thought within himself: 'If I can once catch him on the hip, I will feed fat the ancient grudge I bear him; he hates our Jewish nation; he lends out money gratis, and among merchants he rails at me and my well-earned bargains, which he calls interest. Cursed be my tribe if I forgive him!' Antonio finding he was musing within himself and did not answer, and being impatient for the money, said: 'Shylock, do you hear? will you lend the money?' To this question the Jew replied: 'Signior Antonio, on the Rialto many a time and often you have railed at me about my monies and my usuries, and I have borne it with a patient shrug, for sufferance is the badge of all our tribe; and then you have called me unbeliever, cut-throat dog, and spit upon my Jewish garments, and spurned at me with your foot, as if I was a cur. Well then, it now appears you need my help; and you come to me, and say, *Shylock, lend me monies.* Has a dog money? Is it possible a cur should lend three thousand ducats? Shall I bend low and say, Fair sir, you spit upon me on Wednesday last, another

time you called me dog, and for these courtesies I am
to lend you monies.' Antonio replied: 'I am as like to
call you so again, to spit on you again, and spurn you
too. If you will lend me this money, lend it not to me
as to a friend, but rather lend it to me as to an enemy,
that, if I break, you may with better face exact the
penalty.' 'Why, look you,' said Shylock, 'how you
storm! I would be friends with you, and have your
love. I will forget the shames you have put upon me.
I will supply your wants, and take no interest for my
money.' This seemingly kind offer greatly surprised
Antonio; and then Shylock, still pretending kindness,
and that all he did was to gain Antonio's love, again
said he would lend him the three thousand ducats, and
take no interest for his money; only Antonio should
go with him to a lawyer, and there sign in merry sport
a bond, that if he did not repay the money by a certain
day, he would forfeit a pound of flesh, to be cut off from
any part of his body that Shylock pleased.

'Content,' said Antonio: 'I will sign to this bond,
and say there is much kindness in the Jew.'

Bassanio said Antonio should not sign to such a bond
for him; but still Antonio insisted that he would sign it,
for that before the day of payment came, his ships would
return laden with many times the value of the money.

Shylock, hearing this debate, exclaimed: 'O, father
Abraham, what suspicious people these Christians are!
Their own hard dealings teach them to suspect the
thoughts of others. I pray you tell me this, Bassanio:
if he should break this day, what should I gain by the
exaction of the forfeiture? A pound of man's flesh,
taken from a man, is not so estimable, nor profitable
neither, as the flesh of mutton or beef. I say, to buy
his favour I offer this friendship: if he will take it, so;
if not, adieu.'

At last, against the advice of Bassanio, who, notwithstanding all the Jew had said of his kind intentions, did

not like his friend should run the hazard of this shocking penalty for his sake, Antonio signed the bond, thinking it really was (as the Jew said) merely in sport.

The rich heiress that Bassanio wished to marry lived near Venice, at a place called Belmont: her name was Portia, and in the graces of her person and her mind she was nothing inferior to that Portia, of whom we read, who was Cato's daughter, and the wife of Brutus.

Bassanio being so kindly supplied with money by his friend Antonio, at the hazard of his life, set out for Belmont with a splendid train, and attended by a gentleman of the name of Gratiano.

Bassanio proving successful in his suit, Portia in a short time consented to accept of him for a husband.

Bassanio confessed to Portia that he had no fortune, and that his high birth and noble ancestry was all that he could boast of; she, who loved him for his worthy qualities, and had riches enough not to regard wealth in a husband, answered with a graceful modesty, that she would wish herself a thousand times more fair, and ten thousand times more rich, to be more worthy of him; and then the accomplished Portia prettily dispraised herself, and said she was an unlessoned girl, unschooled, unpractised, yet not so old but that she could learn, and that she would commit her gentle spirit to be directed and governed by him in all things; and she said: 'Myself and what is mine, to you and yours is now converted. But yesterday, Bassanio, I was the lady of this fair mansion, queen of myself, and mistress over these servants; and now this house, these servants, and myself, are yours, my lord; I give them with this ring'; presenting a ring to Bassanio.

Bassanio was so overpowered with gratitude and wonder at the gracious manner in which the rich and noble Portia accepted of a man of his humble fortunes, that he could not express his joy and reverence to the dear lady who so honoured him, by anything but broken words of love and thankfulness; and taking the ring, he vowed never to part with it.

Gratiano and Nerissa, Portia's waiting-maid, were in attendance upon their lord and lady, when Portia so gracefully promised to become the obedient wife of Bassanio; and Gratiano, wishing Bassanio and the generous lady joy, desired permission to be married at the same time.

'With all my heart, Gratiano,' said Bassanio, 'if you can get a wife.'

Gratiano then said that he loved the lady Portia's fair waiting gentlewoman Nerissa, and that she had promised to be his wife, if her lady married Bassanio. Portia asked Nerissa if this was true. Nerissa replied: 'Madam, it is so, if you approve of it.' Portia willingly consenting, Bassanio pleasantly said: 'Then our wedding-feast shall be much honoured by your marriage, Gratiano.'

The happiness of these lovers was sadly crossed at this moment by the entrance of a messenger, who brought a letter from Antonio containing fearful tidings. When Bassanio read Antonio's letter, Portia feared it was to tell him of the death of some dear friend, he looked so pale; and inquiring what was the news which had so distressed him, he said: 'O sweet Portia, here are a few of the unpleasantest words that ever blotted paper; gentle lady, when I first imparted my love to you, I freely told you all the wealth I had ran in my veins; but I should have told you that I had less than nothing, being in debt.' Bassanio then told Portia what has been here related, of his borrowing the money of Antonio, and of Antonio's procuring it of Shylock the Jew, and of the bond by which Antonio had engaged to forfeit a pound of flesh, if it was not repaid by a certain day: and then Bassanio read Antonio's letter: the words of which were: '*Sweet Bassanio, my ships are all lost, my bond to the Jew is forfeited, and since in paying it is impossible I should live, I could wish to see you at my death; notwithstanding use your pleasure;*

if your love for me do not persuade you to come, let not my letter.'
'O, my dear love,' said Portia, 'despatch all business,
and begone; you shall have gold to pay the money
twenty times over, before this kind friend shall lose a
hair by my Bassanio's fault; and as you are so dearly
bought, I will dearly love you.' Portia then said she
would be married to Bassanio before he set out, to give
him a legal right to her money; and that same day they
were married, and Gratiano was also married to Nerissa;
and Bassanio and Gratiano, the instant they were married,
set out in great haste for Venice, where Bassanio found
Antonio in prison.

The day of payment being past, the cruel Jew would
not accept of the money which Bassanio offered him,
but insisted upon having a pound of Antonio's flesh.
A day was appointed to try this shocking cause before
the duke of Venice, and Bassanio awaited in dreadful
suspense the event of the trial.

When Portia parted with her husband, she spoke cheer-
ingly to him, and bade him bring his dear friend along
with him when he returned; yet she feared it would go
hard with Antonio, and when she was left alone, she
began to think and consider within herself, if she could
by any means be instrumental in saving the life of her
dear Bassanio's friend; and notwithstanding when she
wished to honour her Bassanio, she had said to him with
such a meek and wifelike grace, that she would submit
in all things to be governed by his superior wisdom,
yet being now called forth into action by the peril of
her honoured husband's friend, she did nothing doubt
her own powers, and by the sole guidance of her own
true and perfect judgment, at once resolved to go herself
to Venice, and speak in Antonio's defence.

Portia had a relation who was a counsellor in the law;
to this gentleman, whose name was Bellario, she wrote,
and stating the case to him, desired his opinion, and
that with his advice he would also send her the dress

worn by a counsellor. When the messenger returned, he brought letters from Bellario of advice how to proceed, and also everything necessary for her equipment.

Portia dressed herself and her maid Nerissa in men's apparel, and putting on the robes of a counsellor, she took Nerissa along with her as her clerk; and setting out immediately, they arrived at Venice on the very day of the trial. The cause was just going to be heard before the duke and senators of Venice in the senate-house, when Portia entered this high court of justice, and presented a letter from Bellario, in which that learned counsellor wrote to the duke, saying, he would have come himself to plead for Antonio, but that he was prevented by sickness, and he requested that the learned young doctor Balthasar (so he called Portia) might be permitted to plead in his stead. This the duke granted, much wondering at the youthful appearance of the stranger, who was prettily disguised by her counsellor's robes and her large wig.

And now began this important trial. Portia looked around her, and she knew the merciless Jew; and she saw Bassanio, but he knew her not in her disguise. He was standing beside Antonio, in an agony of distress and fear for his friend.

The importance of the arduous task Portia had engaged in gave this tender lady courage, and she boldly proceeded in the duty she had undertaken to perform: and first of all she addressed herself to Shylock; and allowing that he had a right by the Venetian law to have the forfeit expressed in the bond, she spoke so sweetly of the noble quality of *mercy*, as would have softened any heart but the unfeeling Shylock's; saying, that it dropped as the gentle rain from heaven upon the place beneath; and how mercy was a double blessing, it blessed him that gave, and him that received it; and how it became monarchs better than their crowns, being an attribute of God Himself; and that earthly power came nearest to God's, in proportion as mercy tempered justice; and she bid Shylock remember that as we all pray for mercy, that same prayer should teach us to show mercy. Shylock only answered her by desiring to have the penalty forfeited in the bond. 'Is he not able to pay the money?' asked Portia. Bassanio then offered the Jew the payment of the three thousand ducats as many times over as he should desire; which Shylock refusing, and still insisting upon having a pound of Antonio's flesh, Bassanio begged the learned young counsellor would endeavour to wrest the law a little, to save Antonio's life. But Portia gravely answered, that laws once established must never be altered. Shylock hearing Portia say that the law might not be altered, it seemed to him that she was pleading in his favour, and he said: 'A Daniel is come to judgment! O wise young judge, how I do honour you! How much elder are you than your looks!'

Portia now desired Shylock to let her look at the bond; and when she had read it, she said: 'This bond is forfeited, and by this the Jew may lawfully claim a pound of flesh, to be by him cut off nearest Antonio's heart.' Then she said to Shylock: 'Be merciful: take the money, and bid me tear the bond.' But no mercy would the cruel Shylock show; and he said: 'By my soul I swear, there is no power in the tongue of men to alter me.' 'Why then, Antonio,' said Portia, 'you must prepare your bosom for the knife': and while Shylock was sharpening a long knife with great eagerness to cut off the pound of flesh, Portia said to Antonio: 'Have you anything to say?' Antonio with a calm resignation replied, that he had but little to say, for that he had prepared his mind for death. Then he said to Bassanio: 'Give me your hand, Bassanio! Fare you well! Grieve not that I am fallen into this misfortune for you. Commend me to your honourable wife, and tell her how I have loved you!' Bassanio in the deepest affliction

Shylock was sharpening a long knife

replied: 'Antonio, I am married to a wife, who is as dear to me as life itself; but life itself, my wife, and all the world, are not esteemed with me above your life; I would lose all, I would sacrifice all to this devil here, to deliver you.'

Portia hearing this, though the kind-hearted lady was not at all offended with her husband for expressing the love he owed to so true a friend as Antonio in these strong terms, yet could not help answering: 'Your wife would give you little thanks, if she were present, to hear you make this offer.' And then Gratiano, who loved to copy what his lord did, thought he must make a speech like Bassanio's, and he said, in Nerissa's hearing, who was writing in her clerk's dress by the side of Portia: 'I have a wife, whom I protest I love; I wish she were in heaven, if she could but entreat some power there to change the cruel temper of this currish Jew.' 'It is well you wish this behind her back, else you would have but an unquiet house,' said Nerissa.

Shylock now cried out impatiently: 'We trifle time; I pray pronounce the sentence.' And now all was awful expectation in the court, and every heart was full of grief for Antonio.

Portia asked if the scales were ready to weigh the flesh; and she said to the Jew: 'Shylock, you must have some surgeon by, lest he bleed to death.' Shylock, whose whole intent was that Antonio should bleed to death, said: 'It is not so named in the bond.' Portia replied: 'It is not so named in the bond, but what of that? It were good you did so much for charity.' To this all the answer Shylock would make was: 'I cannot find it; it is not in the bond.' 'Then,' said Portia, 'a pound of Antonio's flesh is thine. The law allows it, and the court awards it. And you may cut this flesh from off his breast. The law allows it and the court awards it.' Again Shylock exclaimed: 'O wise and upright judge! A Daniel is come to judgment!' And then he sharpened his long knife again, and looking eagerly on Antonio, he said: 'Come, prepare!'

'Tarry a little, Jew,' said Portia; 'there is something else. This bond here gives you no drop of blood; the words expressly are "a pound of flesh." If in the cutting off the pound of flesh you shed one drop of Christian blood, your lands and goods are by the law to be confiscated to the state of Venice.' Now as it was utterly impossible for Shylock to cut off the pound of flesh without shedding some of Antonio's blood, this wise discovery of Portia's, that it was flesh and not blood that was named in the bond, saved the life of Antonio; and all admiring the wonderful sagacity of the young counsellor, who had so happily thought of this expedient, plaudits resounded from every part of the senate-house; and Gratiano exclaimed, in the words which Shylock had used: 'O wise and upright judge! mark, Jew, a Daniel is come to judgment!'

Shylock, finding himself defeated in his cruel intent, said with a disappointed look, that he would take the money; and Bassanio, rejoiced beyond measure at Antonio's unexpected deliverance, cried out: 'Here is the money!' But Portia stopped him, saying: 'Softly; there is no haste; the Jew shall have nothing but the penalty: therefore prepare, Shylock, to cut off the flesh; but mind you shed no blood: nor do not cut off more nor less than just a pound; be it more or less by one poor scruple, nay if the scale turn but by the weight of a single hair, you are condemned by the laws of Venice to die, and all your wealth is forfeited to the senate.' 'Give me my money, and let me go,' said Shylock. 'I have it ready,' said Bassanio: 'here it is.'

Shylock was going to take the money, when Portia again stopped him, saying: 'Tarry, Jew; I have yet another hold upon you. By the laws of Venice, your wealth is forfeited to the state, for having conspired against the life of one of its citizens, and your life lies at the mercy of the duke; therefore, down on your knees, and ask him to pardon you.'

The duke then said to Shylock: 'That you may see the difference of our Christian spirit, I pardon you your life before you ask it; half your wealth belongs to Antonio, the other half comes to the state.'

The generous Antonio then said that he would give up his share of Shylock's wealth, if Shylock would sign a deed to make it over at his death to his daughter and her husband; for Antonio knew that the Jew had an only daughter who had lately married against his consent to a young Christian, named Lorenzo, a friend of Antonio's, which had so offended Shylock, that he had disinherited her.

The Jew agreed to this: and being thus disappointed in his revenge, and despoiled of his riches, he said: 'I am ill. Let me go home; send the deed after me, and I will sign over half my riches to my daughter.' 'Get thee gone, then,' said the Duke, 'and sign it; and if you repent your cruelty and turn Christian, the state will forgive you the fine of the other half of your riches.'

The duke now released Antonio, and dismissed the court. He then highly praised the wisdom and ingenuity of the young counsellor, and invited him home to dinner. Portia, who meant to return to Belmont before her husband, replied: 'I humbly thank your grace, but I must away directly.' The duke said he was sorry he had not leisure to stay and dine with him; and turning to Antonio, he added: 'Reward this gentleman; for in my mind you are much indebted to him.'

The duke and his senators left the court; and then Bassanio said to Portia: 'Most worthy gentleman, I and my friend Antonio have by your wisdom been this day acquitted of grievous penalties, and I beg you will accept of the three thousand ducats due unto the Jew.' 'And we shall stand indebted to you over and above,' said Antonio, 'in love and service evermore.'

Portia could not be prevailed upon to accept the money; but upon Bassanio still pressing her to accept of some reward, she said: 'Give me your gloves; I will wear them for your sake'; and then Bassanio taking off his gloves, she espied the ring which she had given him upon his finger: now it was the ring the wily lady wanted to get from him to make a merry jest when she saw her Bassanio again, that made her ask him for his gloves; and she said, when she saw the ring, 'and for your love I will take this ring from you.' Bassanio was sadly distressed that the counsellor should ask him for the only thing he could not part with, and he replied in great confusion, that he could not give him that ring, because it was his wife's gift, and he had vowed never to part with it; but that he would give him the most valuable ring in Venice, and find it out by proclamation. On this Portia affected to be affronted, and left the court, saying: 'You teach me, sir, how a beggar should be answered.'

'Dear Bassanio,' said Antonio, 'let him have the ring; let my love and the great service he has done for me be valued against your wife's displeasure,' Bassanio, ashamed to appear so ungrateful, yielded, and sent Gratiano after Portia with the ring; and then the *clerk* Nerissa, who had also given Gratiano a ring, she begged his ring, and Gratiano (not choosing to be outdone in generosity by his lord) gave it to her. And there was laughing among these ladies to think, when they got home, how they would tax their husbands with giving away their rings, and swear that they had given them as a present to some woman.

Portia, when she returned, was in that happy temper of mind which never fails to attend the consciousness of having performed a good action; her cheerful spirits enjoyed everything she saw: the moon never seemed to shine so bright before; and when that pleasant moon was hid behind a cloud, then a light which she saw from her house at Belmont as well pleased her charmed fancy, and she said to Nerissa: 'That light we see is burning in my hall; how far that little candle throws its beams, so shines a good deed in a naughty world'; and hearing the sound of music from her house, she said: 'Methinks that music sounds much sweeter than by day.'

And now Portia and Nerissa entered the house, and dressing themselves in their own apparel, they awaited the arrival of their husbands, who soon followed them with Antonio; and Bassanio presenting his dear friend to the lady Portia, the congratulations and welcomings of that lady were hardly over, when they perceived Nerissa and her husband quarrelling in a corner of the room. 'A quarrel already?' said Portia. 'What is the matter?' Gratiano replied: 'Lady, it is about a paltry gilt ring that Nerissa gave me, with words upon it like the poetry on a cutler's knife; *Love me, and leave me not.*'

'What does the poetry or the value of the ring signify?' said Nerissa. 'You swore to me when I gave it to you, that you would keep it till the hour of death; and now you say you gave it to the lawyer's clerk. I know you gave it to a woman.' 'By this hand,' replied Gratiano, 'I gave it to a youth, a kind of boy, a little scrubbed boy, no higher than yourself; he was clerk to the young counsellor that by his wise pleading saved Antonio's life: this prating boy begged it for a fee, and I could not for my life deny him.' Portia said: 'You were to blame, Gratiano, to part with your wife's first gift. I gave my lord Bassanio a ring, and I am sure he would not part with it for all the world.' Gratiano, in excuse for his fault, now said: 'My lord Bassanio gave his ring away to the counsellor, and then the boy, his clerk, that took some pains in writing, he begged my ring.'

Portia, hearing this, seemed very angry, and reproached Bassanio for giving away her ring; and she said, Nerissa had taught her what to believe, and that she knew some woman had the ring. Bassanio was very unhappy to have so offended his dear lady, and he said with great earnestness: 'No, by my honour, no woman had it, but a civil doctor, who refused three thousand ducats of me, and begged the ring, which when I denied him, he went displeased away. What could I do, sweet Portia? I was so beset with shame for my seeming ingratitude, that I was forced to send the ring after him. Pardon me, good lady; had you been there, I think you would have begged the ring of me to give the worthy doctor.'

'Ah!' said Antonio, 'I am the unhappy cause of these quarrels.'

Portia bid Antonio not to grieve at that, for that he was welcome notwithstanding; and then Antonio said: 'I once did lend my body for Bassanio's sake; and but for him to whom your husband gave the ring, I should have now been dead. I dare be bound again, my soul upon the forfeit, your lord will never more break his faith with you.' 'Then you shall be his surety,' said Portia; 'give him this ring, and bid him keep it better than the other.'

When Bassanio looked at this ring, he was strangely surprised to find it was the same he gave away; and then Portia told him how she was the young counsellor, and Nerissa was her clerk; and Bassanio found, to his unspeakable wonder and delight, that it was by the noble courage and wisdom of his wife that Antonio's life was saved.

And Portia again welcomed Antonio, and gave him letters which by some chance had fallen into her hands, which contained an account of Antonio's ships, that were supposed lost, being safely arrived in the harbour. So these tragical beginnings of this rich merchant's story were all forgotten in the unexpected good fortune which ensued; and there was leisure to laugh at the comical adventure of the rings, and the husbands that did not know their own wives: Gratiano merrily swearing, in a sort of rhyming speech, that

> . . . while he lived, he'd fear no other thing
> So sore, as keeping safe Nerissa's ring.

CYMBELINE

DURING the time of Augustus Caesar, emperor of Rome, there reigned in England (which was then called Britain) a king whose name was Cymbeline.

Cymbeline's first wife died when his three children (two sons and a daughter) were very young. Imogen, the eldest of these children, was brought up in her father's court; but by a strange chance the two sons of Cymbeline were stolen out of their nursery, when the eldest was but three years of age, and the youngest quite an infant; and Cymbeline could never discover what was become of them, or by whom they were conveyed away.

Cymbeline was twice married: his second wife was a wicked, plotting woman, and a cruel stepmother to Imogen, Cymbeline's daughter by his first wife.

The queen, though she hated Imogen, yet wished her to marry a son of her own by a former husband (she also having been twice married): for by this means she hoped upon the death of Cymbeline to place the crown of Britain upon the head of her son Cloten; for she knew that, if the king's sons were not found, the princess Imogen must be the king's heir. But this design was prevented by Imogen herself, who married without the consent or even knowledge of her father or the queen.

Posthumus (for that was the name of Imogen's husband) was the best scholar and most accomplished gentleman of that age. His father died fighting in the wars for Cymbeline, and soon after his birth his mother died also for grief at the loss of her husband.

Cymbeline, pitying the helpless state of this orphan, took Posthumus (Cymbeline having given him that name, because he was born after his father's death), and educated him in his own court.

Imogen and Posthumus were both taught by the same masters, and were playfellows from their infancy; they loved each other tenderly when they were children, and their affection continuing to increase with their years, when they grew up they privately married.

The disappointed queen soon learnt this secret, for she kept spies constantly in watch upon the actions of her daughter-in-law, and she immediately told the king of the marriage of Imogen with Posthumus.

Nothing could exceed the wrath of Cymbeline, when he heard that his daughter had been so forgetful of her high dignity as to marry a subject. He commanded Posthumus to leave Britain, and banished him from his native country for ever.

The queen, who pretended to pity Imogen for the grief she suffered at losing her husband, offered to procure them a private meeting before Posthumus set out on his journey to Rome, which place he had chosen for his residence in his banishment: this seeming kindness she showed, the better to succeed in her future designs in regard to her son Cloten; for she meant to persuade Imogen, when her husband was gone, that her marriage was not lawful, being contracted without the consent of the king.

Imogen and Posthumus took a most affectionate leave of each other. Imogen gave her husband a diamond ring, which had been her mother's, and Posthumus promised never to part with the ring; and he fastened a bracelet on the arm of his wife, which he begged she would preserve with great care, as a token of his love; they then bid each other farewell, with many vows of everlasting love and fidelity.

Imogen remained a solitary and dejected lady in her father's court, and Posthumus arrived at Rome, the place he had chosen for his banishment.

Posthumus fell into company at Rome with some gay young men of different nations, who were talking freely of ladies: each one praising the ladies of his own country, and his own mistress. Posthumus, who had ever his own dear lady in his mind, affirmed that his wife, the fair Imogen, was the most virtuous, wise, and constant lady in the world.

One of those gentlemen, whose name was Iachimo, being offended that a lady of Britain should be so praised above the Roman ladies, his country-women, provoked Posthumus by seeming to doubt the constancy of his so highly-praised wife; and at length, after much altercation, Posthumus consented to a proposal of Iachimo's, that he (Iachimo) should go to Britain, and endeavour to gain the love of the married Imogen. They then laid a wager, that if Iachimo did not succeed in this wicked design, he was to forfeit a large sum of money; but if he could win Imogen's favour, and prevail upon her to give him the bracelet which Posthumus had so earnestly desired she would keep as a token of his love, then the wager was to terminate with Posthumus giving to Iachimo the ring, which was Imogen's love present when she parted with her husband. Such firm faith had Posthumus in the fidelity of Imogen, that he thought he ran no hazard in this trial of her honour.

Iachimo, on his arrival in Britain, gained admittance, and a courteous welcome from Imogen, as a friend of her husband; but when he began to make professions of love to her, she repulsed him with disdain, and he soon found that he could have no hope of succeeding in his dishonourable design.

The desire Iachimo had to win the wager made him now have recourse to a stratagem to impose upon Posthumus, and for this purpose he bribed some of Imogen's attendants, and was by them conveyed into her bedchamber, concealed in a large trunk, where he remained shut up till Imogen was retired to rest, and had fallen asleep; and then getting out of the trunk, he examined the chamber with great attention, and wrote down everything he saw there, and particularly noticed a mole which he observed upon Imogen's neck, and then softly unloosing the bracelet from her arm, which Posthumus had given to her, he retired into the chest again; and the next day he set off for Rome with great expedition, and boasted to Posthumus that Imogen had given him the bracelet, and likewise permitted him to pass a night in her chamber: and in this manner Iachimo told his false tale: 'Her bedchamber,' said he, 'was hung with tapestry of silk and silver, the story was *the proud Cleopatra when she met her Anthony*, a piece of work most bravely wrought.'

'This is true,' said Posthumus; 'but this you might have heard spoken of without seeing.'

'Then the chimney,' said Iachimo, 'is south of the chamber, and the chimney-piece is *Diana bathing*; never saw I figures livelier expressed.'

'This is a thing you might have likewise heard,' said Posthumus, 'for it is much talked of.'

Iachimo as accurately described the roof of the chamber; and added: 'I had almost forgot her andirons; they were *two winking Cupids* made of silver, each on one foot standing.' He then took out the bracelet, and said: 'Know you this jewel, sir? She gave me this. She took it from her arm. I see her yet; her pretty action did outsell her gift, and yet enriched it too. She gave it me, and said, *she prized it once*.' He last of all described the mole he had observed upon her neck.

Posthumus, who had heard the whole of this artful recital in an agony of doubt, now broke out into the most passionate exclamations against Imogen. He delivered up the diamond ring to Iachimo, which he had agreed to forfeit to him, if he obtained the bracelet from Imogen.

Posthumus then in a jealous rage wrote to Pisanio, a gentleman of Britain, who was one of Imogen's attendants, and had long been a faithful friend to Posthumus;

and after telling him what proof he had of his wife's disloyalty, he desired Pisanio would take Imogen to Milford-Haven, a seaport of Wales, and there kill her. And at the same time he wrote a deceitful letter to Imogen desiring her to go with Pisanio, for that finding he could live no longer without seeing her, though he was forbidden upon pain of death to return to Britain, he would come to Milford-Haven, at which place he begged she would meet him. She, good unsuspecting lady, who loved her husband above all things, and desired more than her life to see him, hastened her departure with Pisanio, and the same night she received the letter she set out.

When their journey was nearly at an end, Pisanio, who, though faithful to Posthumus, was not faithful to serve him in an evil deed, disclosed to Imogen the cruel order he had received.

Imogen, who, instead of meeting a loving and beloved husband, found herself doomed by that husband to suffer death, was afflicted beyond measure.

Pisanio persuaded her to take comfort, and wait with patient fortitude for the time when Posthumus should see and repent his injustice: in the meantime, as she refused in her distress to return to her father's court, he advised her to dress herself in boy's clothes for more security in travelling; to which device she agreed, and thought in that disguise she would go over to Rome, and see her husband, whom, though he had used her so barbarously, she could not forget to love.

When Pisanio had provided her with her new apparel, he left her to her uncertain fortune, being obliged to return to court; but before he departed he gave her a phial of cordial, which he said the queen had given him as a sovereign remedy in all disorders.

The queen, who hated Pisanio because he was a friend to Imogen and Posthumus, gave him this phial, which she supposed contained poison, she having ordered her physician to give her some poison, to try its effects (as she said) upon animals; but the physician, knowing her malicious disposition, would not trust her with real poison, but gave her a drug which would do no other mischief than causing a person to sleep with every appearance of death for a few hours. This mixture, which Pisanio thought a choice cordial, he gave to Imogen, desiring her, if she found herself ill upon the road, to take it; and so, with blessings and prayers for her safety and happy deliverance from her undeserved troubles, he left her.

Providence strangely directed Imogen's steps to the dwelling of her two brothers, who had been stolen away in their infancy. Bellarius, who stole them away, was a lord in the court of Cymbeline, and having been falsely accused to the king of treason, and banished from the court, in revenge he stole away the two sons of Cymbeline, and brought them up in a forest, where he lived concealed in a cave. He stole them through revenge, but he soon loved them as tenderly as if they had been his own children, educated them carefully, and they grew up fine youths, their princely spirits leading them to bold and daring actions; and as they subsisted by hunting, they were active and hardy, and were always pressing their supposed father to let them seek their fortune in the wars.

At the cave where these youths dwelt it was Imogen's fortune to arrive. She had lost her way in a large forest, through which her road lay to Milford-Haven (from which she meant to embark for Rome); and being unable to find any place where she could purchase food, she was with weariness and hunger almost dying; for it is not merely putting on a man's apparel that will enable a young lady, tenderly brought up, to bear the fatigue of wandering about lonely forests like a man. Seeing this cave, she entered, hoping to find someone within of whom she could procure food. She found the cave empty, but looking about she discovered some cold meat, and her hunger was so pressing, that she could not wait for an invitation, but sat down and began to eat. 'Ah,' said she, talking to herself, 'I see a man's life is a tedious one; how tired am I! for two nights together I have made the ground my bed: my resolution helps me, or I should be sick. When Pisanio showed me Milford-Haven from the mountain top, how near it seemed!' Then the thoughts of her husband and his cruel mandate came across her, and she said: 'My dear Posthumus, thou art a false one!'

The two brothers of Imogen, who had been hunting with their reputed father, Bellarius, were by this time returned home. Bellarius had given them the names of Polydore and Cadwal, and they knew no better, but supposed that Bellarius was their father; but the real names of these princes were Guiderius and Arviragus.

Bellarius entered the cave first, and seeing Imogen, stopped them, saying: 'Come not in yet; it eats our victuals, or I should think it was a fairy.'

'What is the matter, sir?' said the young men. 'By Jupiter,' said Bellarius again, 'there is an angel in the cave, or if not, an earthly paragon.' So beautiful did Imogen look in her boy's apparel.

She, hearing the sound of voices, came forth from the cave, and addressed them in these words: 'Good masters, do not harm me; before I entered your cave, I had thought to have begged or bought what I have eaten. Indeed I have stolen nothing, nor would I, though I had found gold strewed on the floor. Here is money for my meat, which I would have left on the board when I had made my meal, and parted with prayers for the provider.' They refused her money with great earnestness. 'I see you are angry with me,' said the timid Imogen; 'but, sirs, if you kill me for my fault, know that I should have died if I had not made it.'

'Whither are you bound?' asked Bellarius, 'and what is your name?'

'Fidele is my name,' answered Imogen. 'I have a kinsman, who is bound for Italy; he embarked at Milford-Haven, to whom being going, almost spent with hunger, I am fallen into this offence.'

'Prithee, fair youth,' said old Bellarius, 'do not think us churls, nor measure our good minds by this rude place we live in. You are well encountered; it is almost night. You shall have better cheer before you depart, and thanks to stay and eat it. Boys, bid him welcome.'

The gentle youths, her brothers, then welcomed Imogen to their cave with many kind expressions, saying they would love her (or, as they said, *him*) as a brother; and they entered the cave, where (they having killed venison when they were hunting) Imogen delighted them with her neat housewifery, assisting them in preparing their supper; for though it is not the custom now for young women of high birth to understand cookery, it was then, and Imogen excelled in this useful art; and, as her brothers prettily expressed it, Fidele cut their roots in characters, and sauced their broth, as if Juno had been sick, and Fidele were her dieter. 'And then,' said Polydore to his brother, 'how angel-like he sings!'

They also remarked to each other, that though Fidele smiled so sweetly, yet so sad a melancholy did overcloud his lovely face, as if grief and patience had together taken possession of him.

For these her gentle qualities (or perhaps it was their near relationship, though they knew it not) Imogen (or, as the boys called her, *Fidele*) became the doting-piece of her brothers, and she scarcely less loved them, thinking that but for the memory of her dear Posthumus, she could live and die in the cave with these wild forest youths; and she gladly consented to stay with them, till she was enough rested from the fatigue of travelling to pursue her way to Milford-Haven.

When the venison they had taken was all eaten and they were going out to hunt for more. Fidele could not accompany them because she was unwell. Sorrow, no doubt, for her husband's cruel usage, as well as the fatigue of wandering in the forest, was the cause of her illness.

They then bid her farewell, and went to their hunt, praising all the way the noble parts and graceful demeanour of the youth Fidele.

Imogen was no sooner left alone then she recollected the cordial Pisanio had given her, and drank it off, and presently fell into a sound and deathlike sleep.

When Bellarius and her brothers returned from hunting, Polydore went first into the cave, and supposing her asleep, pulled off his heavy shoes, that he might tread softly and not awake her; so did true gentleness spring up in the minds of these princely foresters; but he soon discovered that she could not be awakened by any noise, and concluded her to be dead, and Polydore lamented over her with dear and brotherly regret, as if they had never from their infancy been parted.

Bellarius also proposed to carry her out into the forest, and there celebrate her funeral with songs and solemn dirges, as was then the custom.

Imogen's two brothers then carried her to a shady covert, and there laying her gently on the grass, they sang repose to her departed spirit, and covering her over with leaves and flowers, Polydore said: 'While summer lasts and I live here, Fidele, I will daily strew thy grave. The pale primrose, that flower most like thy face; the blue-bell, like thy clear veins; and the leaf of eglantine, which is not sweeter than was thy breath; all these will I strew over thee. Yea, and the furred moss in winter, when there are no flowers to cover thy sweet corse.'

Imogen's two brothers then carried her to a shady covert

When they had finished her funeral obsequies they departed very sorrowful.

Imogen had not been long left alone, when, the effect of the sleepy drug going off, she awaked, and easily shaking off the slight covering of leaves and flowers they had thrown over her, she arose, and imagining she had been dreaming, she said: 'I thought I was a cave-keeper, and cook to honest creatures; how came I here covered with flowers?' Not being able to find her way back to the cave, and seeing nothing of her new companions, she concluded it was certainly all a dream; and once more Imogen set out on her weary pilgrimage, hoping at last she should find her way to Milford-Haven, and thence get a passage in some ship bound for Italy; for all her thoughts were still with her husband Posthumus, whom she intended to seek in the disguise of a page.

But great events were happening at this time, of which Imogen knew nothing; for a war had suddenly broken out between the Roman emperor Augustus Caesar and Cymbeline, the king of Britain; and a Roman army had landed to invade Britain, and was advanced into the very forest over which Imogen was journeying. With this army came Posthumus.

Though Posthumus came over to Britain with the Roman army, he did not mean to fight on their side against his own countrymen, but intended to join the army of Britain, and fight in the cause of his king who had banished him.

He still believed Imogen false to him; yet the death of her he had so fondly loved, and by his own orders too (Pisanio having written him a letter to say he had obeyed his command, and that Imogen was dead), sat heavy on his heart, and therefore he returned to Britain, desiring either to be slain in battle, or to be put to death by Cymbeline for returning home from banishment.

Imogen, before she reached Milford-Haven, fell into the hands of the Roman army; and her presence and deportment recommending her, she was made a page to Lucius, the Roman general.

Cymbeline's army now advanced to meet the enemy, and when they entered this forest, Polydore and Cadwal joined the king's army. The young men were eager to engage in acts of valour, though they little thought they were going to fight for their own royal father: and old Bellarius went with them to the battle. He had long since repented of the injury he had done to Cymbeline in carrying away his sons; and having been a warrior in his youth, he gladly joined the army to fight for the king he had so injured.

And now a great battle commenced between the two armies, and the Britons would have been defeated, and Cymbeline himself killed, but for the extraordinary valour of Posthumus and Ballarius and the two sons of Cymbeline. They rescued the king, and saved his life, and so entirely turned the fortune of the day, that the Britons gained the victory.

When the battle was over, Posthumus, who had not found the death he sought for, surrendered himself up to one of the officers of Cymbeline, willing to suffer the death which was to be his punishment if he returned from banishment.

Imogen and the master she served were taken prisoners, and brought before Cymbeline, as was also her old enemy Iachimo, who was an officer in the Roman army; and when these prisoners were before the king, Posthumus was brought in to receive his sentence of death; and at this strange juncture of time, Bellarius with Polydore and Cadwal were also brought before Cymbeline, to receive the rewards due to the great services they had by their valour done for the king. Pisanio, being one of the king's attendants, was likewise present.

Therefore there were now standing in the king's

presence (but with very different hopes and fears) Posthumus and Imogen, with her new master the Roman general; the faithful servant Pisanio, and the false friend Iachimo; and likewise the two lost sons of Cymbeline, with Bellarius, who had stolen them away.

The Roman general was the first who spoke; the rest stood silent before the king, though there was many a beating heart among them.

Imogen saw Posthumus, and knew him, though he was in the disguise of a peasant; but he did not know her in her male attire; and she knew Iachimo, and she saw a ring on his finger which she perceived to be her own, but she did not know him as yet to have been the author of all her troubles: and she stood before her own father a prisoner of war.

Pisanio knew Imogen, for it was he who had dressed her in the garb of a boy. 'It is my mistress,' thought he; 'since she is living, let the time run on to good or bad.' Bellarius knew her too, and softly said to Cadwal: 'Is not this boy revived from death?' 'One sand,' replied Cadwal, 'does not more resemble another than that sweet rosy lad is like the dead Fidele.' 'The same dead thing alive,' said Polydore. 'Peace, peace,' said Bellarius; 'if it were he, I am sure he would have spoken to us.' 'But we saw him dead,' again whispered Polydore. 'Be silent,' replied Bellarius.

Posthumus waited in silence to hear the welcome sentence of his own death; and he resolved not to disclose to the king that he had saved his life in the battle, lest that should move Cymbeline to pardon him.

Lucius, the Roman general, who had taken Imogen under his protection as his page, was the first (as has been before said) who spoke to the king. He was a man of high courage and noble dignity, and this was his speech to the king:

'I hear you take no ransom for your prisoners, but doom them all to death: I am a Roman, and with a

Roman heart will suffer death. But there is one thing for which I would entreat.' Then bringing Imogen before the king, he said: 'This boy is a Briton born. Let him be ransomed. He is my page. Never master had a page so kind, so duteous, so diligent on all occasions, so true, so nurse-like. He hath done no Briton wrong, though he hath served a Roman. Save him, if you spare no one beside.'

Cymbeline looked earnestly on his daughter Imogen. He knew her not in that disguise; but it seemed that all-powerful Nature spake in his heart, for he said: 'I have surely seen him, his face appears familiar to me. I know not why or wherefore I say, Live, boy; but I give you your life, and ask of me what boon you will, and I will grant it you. Yea, even though it be the life of the noblest prisoner I have.'

'I humbly thank your highness,' said Imogen.

What was then called granting a boon was the same as a promise to give any one thing, whatever it might be, that the person on whom that favour was conferred chose to ask for. They all were attentive to hear what thing the page would ask for; and Lucius her master said to her: 'I do not beg my life, good lad, but I know that is what you will ask for.' 'No, no, alas!' said Imogen, 'I have other work in hand, good master; your life I cannot ask for.'

This seeming want of gratitude in the boy astonished the Roman general.

Imogen then, fixing her eye on Iachimo, demanded no other boon than this: that Iachimo should be made to confess whence he had the ring he wore on his finger.

Cymbeline granted her this boon, and threatened Iachimo with the torture if he did not confess how he came by the diamond ring on his finger.

Iachimo then made a full acknowledgment of all his villany, telling, as has been before related, the whole story of his wager with Posthumus, and how he had succeeded in imposing upon his credulity.

What Posthumus felt at hearing this proof of the innocence of his lady cannot be expressed. He instantly came forward, and confessed to Cymbeline the cruel sentence which he had enjoined Pisanio to execute upon the princess; exlaiming wildly: 'O Imogen, my queen, my life, my wife! O Imogen, Imogen, Imogen!'

Imogen could not see her beloved husband in this distress without discovering herself, to the unutterable joy of Posthumus, who was thus relieved from a weight of guilt and woe, and restored to the good graces of the dear lady he had so cruelly treated.

Cymbeline, almost as much overwhelmed as he with joy, at finding his lost daughter so strangely recovered, received her to her former place in his fatherly affection, and not only gave her husband Posthumus his life, but consented to acknowledge him for his son-in-law.

Bellarius chose this time of joy and reconciliation to make his confession. He presented Polydore and Cadwal to the king, telling him they were his two lost sons, Guiderius and Arviragus.

Cybeline forgave old Bellarius; for who could think of punishments at a season of such universal happiness? To find his daughter living, and his lost sons in the persons of his young deliverers, that he had seen so bravely fight in his defence, was unlooked-for joy indeed!

Imogen was now at leisure to perform good services for her late master, the Roman general Lucius, whose life the king her father readily granted at her request; and by the mediation of the same Lucius a peace was concluded between the Romans and the Britons, which was kept inviolate many years.

How Cymbeline's wicked queen, through despair of bringing her projects to pass, and touched with remorse of conscience, sickened and died, having first lived to see her foolish son Cloten slain in a quarrel which he had provoked, are events too tragical to interrupt this happy conclusion by more than merely touching upon. It is sufficient that all were made happy who were deserving; and even the treacherous Iachimo, in consideration of his villainy having missed its final aim, was dismissed without punishment.

KING LEAR

LEAR, king of Britain, had three daughters; Goneril, wife to the duke of Albany; Regan, wife to the duke of Cornwall; and Cordelia, a young maid, for whose love the king of France and duke of Burgundy were joint suitors, and were at this time making stay for that purpose in the court of Lear.

The old king, worn out with age and the fatigues of government, he being more than fourscore years old, determined to take no further part in state affairs, but to leave the management to younger strengths, that he might have time to prepare for death, which must at no long period ensue. With this intent he called his three daughters to him, to know from their own lips which of them loved him best, that he might part his kingdom among them in such proportions as their affection for him should seem to deserve.

Goneril, the eldest, declared that she loved her father more than words could give out, that he was dearer to her than the light of her own eyes, dearer than life and liberty, with a deal of such professing stuff, which is easy to counterfeit where there is no real love, only a few fine words delivered with confidence being wanted in that case. The king, delighted to hear from her own mouth this assurance of her love, and thinking truly that her heart went with it, in a fit of fatherly fondness bestowed upon her and her husband one-third of his ample kingdom.

Then calling to him his second daughter, he demanded what she had to say. Regan, who was made of the same hollow metal as her sister, was not a whit behind in her profession, but rather declared that what her sister had spoken came short of the love which she professed to bear for his highness; insomuch that she found all other joys dead, in comparison with the pleasure which she took in the love of her dear king and father.

Lear blessed himself in having such loving children, as he thought; and could do no less, after the handsome assurances which Regan had made, than bestow a third of his kingdom upon her and her husband, equal in size to that which he had already given away to Goneril.

Then turning to his youngest daughter Cordelia, whom he called his joy, he asked what she had to say, thinking no doubt that she would glad his ears with the same loving speeches which her sisters had uttered, or rather that her expressions would be so much stronger than theirs, as she had always been his darling, and favoured by him above either of them. But Cordelia, disgusted with the flattery of her sisters, whose hearts she knew were far from their lips, and seeing that all their coaxing speeches were only intended to wheedle the old king out of his dominions, that they and their husbands might reign in his lifetime, made no other reply but this,—that she loved his majesty according to her duty, neither more nor less.

The king, shocked with this appearance of ingratitude in his favourite child, desired her to consider her words, and to mend her speech, lest it should mar her fortunes.

Cordelia then told her father, that he was her father, that he had given her breeding, and loved her; that she returned those duties back as was most fit, and did obey him, love him, and most honour him. But that she could not frame her mouth to such large speeches as her sisters had done, or promise to love nothing else in the world. Why had her sisters husbands, if (as they said) they had no love for anything but their father? If she should ever wed, she was sure the lord to whom she gave her hand would want half her love, half of her care and duty; she should never marry like her sisters, to love her father all.

Cordelia, who in earnest loved her old father even

almost as extravagantly as her sisters pretended to do, would have plainly told him so at any other time, in more daughter-like and loving terms, and without these qualifications, which did indeed sound a little ungracious; but after the crafty flattering speeches of her sisters, which she had seen drawn such extravagant rewards, she thought the handsomest thing she could do was to love and be silent. This put her affection out of suspicion of mercenary ends, and showed that she loved, but not for gain; and that her professions, the less ostentatious they were, had so much the more of truth and sincerity than her sisters'.

This plainness of speech, which Lear called pride, so enraged the old monarch—who in his best of times always showed much of spleen and rashness, and in whom the dotage incident to old age had so clouded over his reason, that he could not discern truth from flattery, nor a gay painted speech from words that came from the heart—that in a fury of resentment he retracted the third part of his kingdom, which yet remained, and which he had reserved for Cordelia, and gave it away from her, sharing it equally between her two sisters and their husbands, the dukes of Albany and Cornwall; whom he now called to him, and in presence of all his courtiers bestowing a coronet between them, invested them jointly with all the power, revenue, and execution of government, only retaining to himself the name of king; all the rest of royalty he resigned; with this reservation, that himself, with a hundred knights for his attendants, was to be maintained by monthly course in each of his daughters' palaces in turn.

So preposterous a disposal of his kingdom, so little guided by reason, and so much by passion, filled all his courtiers with astonishment and sorrow; but none of them had the courage to interpose between this incensed king and his wrath, except the earl of Kent, who was beginning to speak a good word for Cordelia, when the passionate Lear on pain of death commanded him to desist; but the good Kent was not so to be repelled. He had been ever loyal to Lear, whom he had honoured as a king, loved as a father, followed as a master; and he had never esteemed his life further than as a pawn to wage against his royal master's enemies, nor feared to lose it when Lear's safety was the motive; nor now that Lear was most his own enemy, did this faithful servant of the king forget his old principles, but manfully opposed Lear, to do Lear good; and was unmannerly only because Lear was mad. He had been a most faithful counsellor in times past to the king, and he besought him now, that he would see with his eyes (as he had done in many weighty matters), and go by his advice still; and in his best consideration recall this hideous rashness: for he would answer with his life, his judgment that Lear's youngest daughter did not love him least, nor were those empty-hearted whose low sound gave no token of hollowness. When power bowed to flattery, honour was bound to plainness. For Lear's threats, what could he do to him, whose life was already at his service? That should not hinder duty from speaking.

The honest freedom of this good earl of Kent only stirred up the king's wrath the more, and like a frantic patient who kills his physician, and loves his mortal disease, he banished this true servant, and allotted him but five days to make his preparations for departure; but if on the sixth his hated person was found within the realm of Britain, that moment was to be his death. And Kent bade farewell to the king, and said, that since he chose to show himself in such fashion, it was but banishment to stay there; and before he went, he recommended Cordelia to the protection of the gods, the maid who had so rightly thought, and so discreetly spoken; and only wished that her sisters' large speeches might be answered with deeds of love; and then he went, as he said, to shape his old course to a new country.

The king of France and duke of Burgundy were now called in to hear the determination of Lear about his youngest daughter, and to know whether they would persist in their courtship to Cordelia, now that she was under her father's displeasure, and had no fortune but her own person to recommend her: and the duke of Burgundy declined the match, and would not take her to wife upon such conditions; but the king of France, understanding what the nature of the fault had been which had lost her the love of her father, that it was only a tardiness of speech, and the not being able to frame her tongue to flattery like her sisters, took this young maid by the hand, and saying that her virtues were a dowry above a kingdom, bade Cordelia to take farewell of her sisters and of her father, though he had been unkind, and she should go with him, and be queen of him and of fair France, and reign over fairer possessions than her sisters: and he called the duke of Burgundy in contempt a waterish duke, because his love for this young maid had in a moment run all away like water.

Then Cordelia with weeping eyes took leave of her sisters, and besought them to love their father well, and make good their professions: and they sullenly told her not to prescribe to them, for they knew their duty; but to strive to content her husband, who had taken her (as they tauntingly expressed it) as Fortune's alms. And Cordelia with a heavy heart departed, for she knew the cunning of her sisters, and she wished her father in better hands than she was about to leave him in.

Cordelia was no sooner gone, than the devilish dispositions of her sisters began to show themselves in their true colours. Even before the expiration of the first month, which Lear was to spend by agreement with his eldest daughter Goneril, the old king began to find out the difference between promises and performances. This wretch having got from her father all that he had to bestow, even to the giving away of the crown from off his head, began to grudge even those small remnants of royalty which the old man had reserved to himself, to please his fancy with the idea of being still a king. She could not bear to see him and his hundred knights. Every time she met her father, she put on a frowning countenance; and when the old man wanted to speak with her, she would feign sickness, or anything to get rid of the sight of him; for it was plain that she esteemed his old age a useless burden, and his attendants an unnecessary expense: not only she herself slackened in her expressions of duty to the king, but by her example, and (it is to be feared) not without her private instructions, her very servants affected to treat him with neglect, and would either refuse to obey his orders, or still more contemptuously pretend not to hear them. Lear could not but perceive this alteration in the behaviour of his daughter, but he shut his eyes against it as long as he could, as people commonly are unwilling to believe the unpleasant consequences which their own mistakes and obstinacy have brought upon them.

True love and fidelity are no more to be estranged by *ill*, than falsehood and hollow-heartedness can be conciliated by *good, usage*. This eminently appears in the instance of the good earl of Kent, who, though banished by Lear, and his life made forfeit if he were found in Britain, chose to stay and abide all consequences, as long as there was a chance of his being useful to the king his master. See to what mean shifts and disguises poor loyalty is forced to submit sometimes; yet it counts nothing base or unworthy, so as it can but do service where it owes an obligation! In the disguise of a serving man, all his greatness and pomp laid aside, this good earl proffered his services to the king, who, not knowing him to be Kent in that disguise, but pleased with a certain plainness, or rather bluntness in his answers, which the earl put on (so different from that smooth oily flattery which he had so much reason to be sick of, having found the effects not answerable in his daughter), a bargain was quickly struck, and Lear took Kent into his service by the name of Caius, as he called himself, never suspecting him to be his once great favourite, the high and mighty earl of Kent.

This Caius quickly found means to show his fidelity and love to his royal master: for Goneril's steward that same day behaving in a disrespectful manner to Lear, and giving him saucy looks and language, as no doubt he was secretly encouraged to do by his mistress, Caius, not enduring to hear so open an affront put upon his majesty, made no more ado but presently tripped up his heels, and laid the unmannerly slave in the kennel; for which friendly service Lear became more and more attached to him.

Nor was Kent the only friend Lear had. In his degree, and as far as so insignificant a personage could show his love, the poor fool, or jester, that had been of his palace while Lear had a palace, as it was the custom of kings and great personages at that time to keep a fool (as he was called) to make them sport after serious business: this poor fool clung to Lear after he had given away his crown, and by his witty sayings would keep up his good humour, though he could not refrain sometimes from jeering at his master for his imprudence in uncrowning himself, and giving all away to his daughters; at which time, as he rhymingly expressed it, these daughters

> For sudden joy did weep
> And he for sorrow sung,
> That such a king should play bo-peep
> And go the fools among.

And in such wild sayings, and scraps of songs, of which he had plenty, this pleasant honest fool poured out his heart even in the presence of Goneril herself, in many a bitter taunt and jest which cut to the quick: such as comparing the king to the hedge-sparrow, who feeds the young of the cuckoo till they grow old enough, and then has its head bit off for its pains; and saying, that an ass may know when the cart draws the horse (meaning that Lear's daughters, that ought to go behind, now ranked before their father); and that Lear was no longer Lear, but the shadow of Lear: for which free speeches he was once or twice threatened to be whipped.

The coolness and falling off of respect which Lear had begun to perceive, were not all which this foolish fond father was to suffer from his unworthy daughter: she now plainly told him that his staying in her palace was inconvenient so long as he insisted upon keeping up an establishment of a hundred knights; that this establishment was useless and expensive, and only served to fill her court with riot and feasting; and she prayed him that he would lessen their number, and keep none but old men about him, such as himself, and fitting his age.

Lear at first could not believe his eyes or ears, nor that it was his daughter who spoke so unkindly. He could not believe that she who had received a crown from him could seek to cut off his train, and grudge him the respect due to his old age. But she persisting in her undutiful demand, the old man's rage was so excited, that he called her a detested kite, and said that she spoke an untruth; and so indeed she did, for the hundred knights were all men of choice behaviour and sobriety of manners, skilled in all particulars of duty, and not given to rioting or feasting, as she said. And he bid his horses to be prepared, for he would go to his other daughter, Regan, he and his hundred knights; and he spoke of ingratitude, and said it was a marble-hearted devil, and showed more hideous in a child than the sea-monster. And he cursed his eldest daughter Goneril so as was terrible to hear; praying that she might never have a child, or if she had, that it might live to return that scorn and contempt upon her which she had shown to him: that she might feel how sharper than a serpent's tooth it was to have a thankless child. And Goneril's husband, the duke of Albany, beginning to excuse himself for any share which Lear might suppose he had in the unkindness, Lear would not hear him out, but in a rage ordered his horses to be saddled, and set out with his followers for the abode of Regan, his other daughter. And Lear thought to himself how small the fault of Cordelia (if it was a fault) now appeared, in comparison with her sister's, and he wept; and then he was ashamed that such a creature as Goneril should have so much power over his manhood as to make him weep.

Regan and her husband were keeping their court in great pomp and state at their palace; and Lear despatched his servant Caius with letters to his daughter, that she might be prepared for his reception, while he and his train followed after. But it seems that Goneril had been beforehand with him, sending letters also to Regan, accusing her father of waywardness and ill humours, and advising her not to receive so great a train as he was bringing with him. This messenger arrived at the same time with Caius, and Caius and he met: and who should it be but Caius's old enemy the steward, whom he had formerly tripped up by the heels for his saucy behaviour to Lear. Caius not liking the fellow's look, and suspecting what he came for, began to revile him, and challenged him to fight, which the fellow refusing, Caius, in a fit of honest passion, beat him soundly, as such a mischief-maker and carrier of wicked messages deserved; which coming to the ears of Regan and her husband, they ordered Caius to be put in the stocks, though he was a messenger from the king her father, and in that character demanded the highest respect: so that the first thing the king saw when he entered the castle, was his faithful servant Caius sitting in that disgraceful situation.

This was but a bad omen of the reception which he was to expect; but a worse followed, when, upon inquiry for his daughter and her husband, he was told they were weary with travelling all night, and could not see him; and when lastly, upon his insisting in a positive and angry manner to see them, they came to greet him, whom should he see in their company but the hated Goneril, who had come to tell her own story, and set her sister against the king her father!

This sight much moved the old man, and still more to see Regan take her by the hand; and he asked Goneril if she was not ashamed to look upon his old white beard. And Regan advised him to go home again with Goneril, and live with her peaceably, dismissing half of his attendants, and to ask her forgiveness; for he was old and wanted discretion, and must be ruled and led by persons that had more discretion than himself. And Lear showed how preposterous that would sound, if he were to go down on his knees, and beg of his own daughter for food and raiment, and he argued against such an unnatural dependence, declaring his resolution never to return with her, but to stay where he was with Regan, he and his hundred knights; for he said that she had not forgot the half of the kingdom which he had endowed her with, and that her eyes were not fierce like Goneril's, but mild and kind. And he said that rather than return to Goneril, with half his train cut off, he would go over to France, and beg a wretched pension of the king there, who had married his youngest daughter without a portion.

But he was mistaken in expecting kinder treatment of Regan than he had experienced from her sister Goneril. As if willing to outdo her sister in unfilial behaviour, she declared that she thought fifty knights too many to wait upon him: that five-and-twenty were enough. Then Lear, nigh heart-broken, turned to Goneril and said that he would go back with her, for her fifty doubled five-and-twenty, and so her love was twice as much as Regan's. But Goneril excused herself, and said, what need of so many as five-and-twenty? or even ten? or five? when he might be waited upon by her servants, or her sister's servants? So these two wicked daughters, as if they strove to exceed each other in cruelty to their old father, who had been so good to them, by little and little would have abated him of all his train, all respect (little enough for him that once commanded a kingdom), which was left him to show that he had once been a king! Not that a splendid train is essential to happiness, but from a king to a beggar is a hard change, from commanding millions to be without one attendant; and it was the ingratitude in his daughters' denying it, more than what he would suffer by the want of it, which pierced this poor king to the heart; insomuch, that with this double ill-usage, a vexation for having so foolishly given away a kingdom, his wits began to be unsettled, and while he said he knew not what, he vowed revenge against those unnatural hags, and to make examples of them that should be a terror to the earth!

While he was thus idly threatening what his weak arm could never execute, night came on, and a loud storm of thunder and lightning with rain; and his daughters still persisting in their resolution not to admit his followers, he called for his horses, and chose rather to encounter the utmost fury of the storm abroad, than stay under the same roof with these ungrateful daughters: and they, saying that the injuries which wilful men procure to themselves are their just punishment, suffered him to go in that condition and shut their doors upon him.

The wind were high, and the rain and storm increased, when the old man sallied forth to combat with the elements, less sharp than his daughters' unkindness. For many miles about there was scarce a bush; and there upon a heath, exposed to the fury of the storm in a dark night, did king Lear wander out, and defy the winds and the thunder; and he bid the winds to blow the earth into the sea, or swell the waves of the sea till they drowned the earth, that no token might remain of any

There upon a heath, exposed to the fury of the storm on a dark night, did King Lear wander out

such ungrateful animal as man.   The old king was now left with no other companion than the poor fool, who still abided with him, with his merry conceits striving to outjest misfortune, saying it was but a naughty night to swim in, and truly the king had better go in and ask his daughter's blessing:

> But he that has a little tiny wit,
>   With heigh ho, the wind and the rain!
> Must make content with his fortunes fit,
>   Though the rain it raineth every day:

and swearing it was a brave night to cool a lady's pride.

Thus poorly accompanied, this once great monarch was found by his ever-faithful servant the good earl of Kent, now transformed to Caius, who ever followed close at his side, though the king did not know him to be the earl; and he said: 'Alas! sir, are you here? creatures that love night, love not such nights as these.   This dreadful storm has driven the beasts to their hiding places.   Man's nature cannot endure the affliction or the fear.'   And Lear rebuked him and said, these lesser evils were not felt, where a greater malady was fixed.   When the mind is at ease, the body has leisure to be delicate, but the temper in his mind did take all feeling else from his senses, but of that which beat at his heart.   And he spoke of filial ingratitude, and said it was all one as if the mouth should tear the hand for lifting food to it; for parents were hands and food and everything to children.

But the good Caius still persisting in his entreaties that the king would not stay out in the open air, at last persuaded him to enter a little wretched hovel which stood upon the heath, where the fool first entering, suddenly ran back terrified, saying that he had seen a spirit.   But upon examination this spirit proved to be nothing more than a poor Bedlam beggar, who had crept into this deserted hovel for shelter, and with his talk about devils frighted the fool, one of those poor lunatics who are either mad, or feign to be so, the better to extort charity from the compassionate country people, who go about the country, calling themselves poor Tom and poor Turlygood, saying: 'Who gives anything to poor Tom?' sticking pins and nails and sprigs of rosemary into their arms to make them bleed; and with such horrible actions, partly by prayers, and partly with lunatic curses, they move or terrify the ignorant country-folks into giving them alms. This poor fellow was such a one; and the king seeing him in so wertched a plight, wi⁺h nothing but a blanket about his loins to cover his nakedness, could not be persuaded but that the fellow was some father who had given all away to his daughters, and brought himself to that pass: for nothing he thought could bring a man to such wretchedness but the having unkind daughters.

And from this and many such wild speeches which he uttered, the good Caius plainly perceived that he was not in his perfect mind, but that his daughters' ill usage had really made him go mad. And now the loyalty of this worthy earl of Kent showed itself in more essential services than he had hitherto found opportunity to perform. For with the assistance of some of the king's attendants who remained loyal, he had the person of his royal master removed at daybreak to the castle of Dover, where his own friends and influence, as earl of Kent, chiefly lay; and himself embarking for France, hastened to the court of Cordelia, and did there in such moving terms represent the pitiful condition of her royal father, and set out in such lively colours the inhumanity of her sisters, that this good and loving child with many tears besought the king her husband that he would give her leave to embark for England, with a sufficient power to subdue these cruel daughters and their husbands, and restore the old king her father to his throne; which being granted, she set forth, and with a royal army landed at Dover.

Lear having by some chance escaped from the guardians which the good earl of Kent had put over him to take care of him in his lunacy, was found by some of Cordelia's train, wandering about the fields near Dover, in a pitiable condition, stark mad, and singing aloud to himself with a crown upon his head which he had made of straw, and nettles, and other wild weeds that he had picked up in the corn-fields. By the advice of the physicians, Cordelia, though earnestly desirous of seeing her father, was prevailed upon to put off the meeting, till by sleep and the operation of herbs which they gave him, he should be restored to greater composure. By the aid of these skilful physicians, to whom Cordelia promised all her gold and jewels for the recovery of the old king, Lear was soon in a condition to see his daughter.

A tender sight it was to see the meeting between this father and daughter; to see the struggles between the joy of this poor old king at beholding again his once darling child, and the shame at receiving such filial kindness from her whom he had cast off for so small a fault in his displeasure; both these passions struggling with the remains of his malady, which in his half-crazed brain sometimes made him that he scarce remembered where he was, or who it was that so kindly kissed him and spoke to him; and then he would beg the standers-by not to laugh at him, if he were mistaken in thinking this lady to be his daughter Cordelia! And then to see him fall on his knees to beg pardon of his child; and she, good lady, kneeling all the while to ask a blessing of him, and telling him that it did not become him to kneel, but it was her duty, for she was his child, his true and very child Cordelia! and she kissed him (as she said) to kiss away all her sisters' unkindness, and said that they might be ashamed of themselves, to turn their old kind father with his white beard out into the cold air, when her enemy's dog, though it had bit her (as she prettily expressed it), should have stayed by her fire such a night as that, and warmed himself. And she told her father how she had come from France with purpose to bring him assistance; and he said that she must forget and forgive, for he was old and foolish, and did not know what he did; but that to be sure she had great cause not to love him, but her sisters had none. And Cordelia said that she had no cause, no more than they had.

So we will leave this old king in the protection of his dutiful and loving child, where, by the help of sleep and medicine, she and her physicians at length succeeded in winding up the untuned and jarring senses which the cruelty of his other daughters had so violently shaken. Let us return to say a word or two about those cruel daughters.

These monsters of ingratitude, who had been so false to their old father, could not be expected to prove more faithful to their own husbands. They soon grew tired of paying even the appearance of duty and affection, and in an open way showed they had fixed their loves upon another. It happened that the object of their guilty loves was the same. It was Edmund, a natural son of the late earl of Gloucester, who by his treacheries had succeeded in disinheriting his brother Edgar, the lawful heir, from his earldom, and by his wicked practices was now earl himself; a wicked man, and a fit object for the love of such wicked creatures as Goneril and Regan. It falling out about this time that the duke of Cornwall, Regan's husband, died, Regan immediately declared her intention of wedding this earl of Gloucester, which rousing the jealousy of her sister, to whom as well as to Regan this wicked earl had at sundry times professed love, Goneril found means to make away with her sister by poison; but being detected in her practices, and imprisoned by her husband, the duke of Albany, for this deed, and for her guilty passion for the earl which had come to his ears, she, in a fit of disappointed love and rage, shortly put an end to her own life. Thus the justice of Heaven at last overtook these wicked daughters.

While the eyes of all men were upon this event, admiring the justice displayed in their deserved deaths, the same eyes were suddenly taken off from this sight to admire at the mysterious ways of the same power in the melancholy fate of the young and virtuous daughter, the lady Cordelia, whose good deeds did seem to deserve a more fortunate conclusion: but it is an awful truth, that innocence and piety are not always successful in this world. The forces which Goneril and Regan had sent out under the command of the bad earl of Gloucester were victorious, and Cordelia, by the practices of this wicked earl, who did not like that any should stand between him and the throne, ended her life in prison. Thus, Heaven took this innocent lady to itself in her young years, after showing her to the world an illustrious example of filial duty. Lear did not long survive this kind child.

Before he died, the good earl of Kent, who had still attended his old master's steps from the first of his daughters' ill usage to this sad period of his decay, tried to make him understand that it was he who had followed him under the name of Caius; but Lear's care-crazed brain at that time could not comprehend how that could be, or how Kent and Caius could be the same person: so Kent thought it needless to trouble him with explanations at such a time; and Lear soon after expiring, this faithful servant to the king, between age and grief for his old master's vexations, soon followed him to the grave.

How the judgment of Heaven overtook the bad earl of Gloucester, whose treasons were discovered, and himself slain in single combat with his brother, the lawful earl; and how Goneril's husband, the duke of

Albany, who was innocent of the death of Cordelia, and had never encouraged his lady in her wicked proceedings against her father, ascended the throne of Britain after the death of Lear, is needless here to narrate; Lear and his Three Daughters being dead, whose adventures alone concern our story.

MACBETH

WHEN Duncan the Meek reigned king of Scotland, there lived a great thane, or lord, called Macbeth. This Macbeth was a near kinsman to the king, and in great esteem at court for his valour and conduct in the wars; an example of which he had lately given, in defeating a rebel army assisted by the troops of Norway in terrible numbers.

The two Scottish generals, Macbeth and Banquo, returning victorious from this great battle, their way lay over a blasted heath, where they were stopped by the strange appearance of three figures like women, except that they had beards, and their withered skins and wild attire made them look not like any earthly creatures. Macbeth first addressed them, when they, seemingly offended, laid each one her choppy finger upon her skinny lips, in token of silence; and the first of them saluted Macbeth with the title of thane of Glamis. The general was not a little startled to find himself known by such creatures; but how much more, when the second of them followed up that salute by giving him the title of thane of Cawdor, to which honour he had no pretensions; and again the third bid him 'All hail! king that shalt be hereafter!' Such a prophetic greeting might well amaze him, who knew that while the king's sons lived he could not hope to succeed to the throne. Then turning to Banquo, they pronounced him, in a sort of riddling terms, to be *lesser than Macbeth and greater! not so happy, but much happier!* and prophesied that though he should never reign, yet his sons after him should be kings in Scotland. They then turned into air, and vanished: by which the generals knew them to be the weird sisters, or witches.

While they stood pondering on the the strangeness of

They were stopped by the strange appearance of three figures

this adventure, there arrived certain messengers from the king, who were empowered by him to confer upon Macbeth the dignity of thane of Cawdor: an event so miraculously corresponding with the prediction of the witches astonished Macbeth, and he stood wrapped in amazement, unable to make reply to the messengers; and in that point of time swelling hopes arose in his mind that the prediction of the third witch might in like manner have its accomplishment, and that he should one day reign king in Scotland.

Turning to Banquo, he said: 'Do you not hope that your children shall be kings, when what the witches promised to me has so wonderfully come to pass?' 'That hope,' answered the general, 'might enkindle you to aim at the throne; but oftentimes these ministers of darkness tell us truths in little things, to betray us into deeds of greatest consequence.'

But the wicked suggestions of the witches had sunk too deep into the mind of Macbeth to allow him to attend to the warnings of the good Banquo. From that time he bent all his thoughts how to compass the throne of Scotland.

Macbeth had a wife, to whom he communicated the strange prediction of the weird sisters, and its partial accomplishment. She was a bad, ambitious woman, and so as her husband and herself could arrive at greatness, she cared not much by what means. She spurred on the reluctant purpose of Macbeth, who felt compunction at the thoughts of blood, and did not cease to represent the murder of the king as a step absolutely necessary to the fulfilment of the flattering prophecy.

It happened at this time that the king, who out of his royal condescension would oftentimes visit his principal nobility upon gracious terms, came to Macbeth's house, attended by his two sons, Malcolm and Donalbain, and a numerous train of thanes and attendants, the more to honour Macbeth for the triumphal success of his wars.

The castle of Macbeth was pleasantly situated, and the air about it was sweet and wholesome, which appeared by the nests which the martlet, or swallow, had built under all the jutting friezes and buttresses of the building, wherever it found a place of advantage; for where those birds most breed and haunt, the air is observed to be delicate. The king entered well-pleased with the place, and not less so with the attentions and respect of his honoured hostess, lady Macbeth, who had the art of covering treacherous purposes with smiles; and could look like the innocent flower, while she was indeed the serpent under it.

The king being tired with his journey, went early to bed, and in his state-room two grooms of his chamber (as was the custom) slept beside him. He had been unusually pleased with his reception, and had made presents before he retired to his principal officers; and among the rest, had sent a rich diamond to lady Macbeth, greeting her by the name of his most kind hostess.

Now was the middle of night, when over half the world nature seems dead, and wicked dreams abuse men's minds asleep, and none but the wolf and the murderer is abroad. This was the time when lady Macbeth waked to plot the murder of the king. She would not have undertaken a deed so abhorrent to her sex, but that she feared her husband's nature, that it was too full of the milk of human kindness, to do a contrived murder. She knew him to be ambitious, but withal to be scrupulous, and not yet prepared for that height of crime which commonly in the end accompanies inordinate ambition. She had won him to consent to the murder, but she doubted his resolution; and she feared that the natural tenderness of his disposition (more humane than her own) would come between, and defeat the purpose. So with her own hands armed with a dagger, she approached the king's bed; having taken care to ply the grooms of his chamber so with wine, that they slept intoxicated, and careless of their charge. There lay Duncan in a sound sleep after the fatigues of his journey, and as she viewed him earnestly, there was something in his face, as he slept, which resembled her own father; and she had not the courage to proceed.

She returned to confer with her husband. His resolution had begun to stagger. He considered that there were strong reasons against the deed. In the first place, he was not only a subject, but a near kinsman to the king; and he had been his host and entertainer that day, whose duty, by the laws of hospitality, it was to shut the door against his murderers, not bear the knife himself. Then he considered how just and merciful a king this Duncan had been, how clear of offence to his subjects, how loving to his nobility, and in particular to him; that such kings are the peculiar care of Heaven, and their subjects doubly bound to revenge their deaths. Besides, by the favours of the king, Macbeth stood high in the opinion of all sorts of men, and how would those honours be stained by the reputation of so foul a murder!

In these conflicts of the mind lady Macbeth found her husband inclining to the better part, and resolving to proceed no further. But she being a woman not easily shaken from her evil purpose, began to pour in at his ears words which infused a portion of her own spirit into his mind, assigning reason upon reason why he should not shrink from what he had undertaken; how easy the deed was; how soon it would be over; and how the action of one short night would give to all their nights and days to come sovereign sway and royalty! Then she threw contempt on his change of purpose, and accused him of fickleness and cowardice; and declared that she had given suck, and knew how tender it was to love the babe that milked her; but she would, while it was smiling in her face, have plucked it from her breast, and dashed its brains out, if she had so sworn to do it, as he had sworn to perform that murder. Then she added, how practicable it was to lay the guilt of the deed upon the drunken sleepy grooms. And with the valour of her tongue she so chastised his sluggish resolutions, that he once more summoned up courage to the bloody business.

So, taking the dagger in his hand, he softly stole in the dark to the room where Duncan lay; and as he went, he thought he saw another dagger in the air, with the handle towards him, and on the blade and at the point of it drops of blood; but when he tried to grasp at it, it was nothing but air, a mere phantasm proceeding from his own hot and oppressed brain and the business he had in hand.

Getting rid of this fear, he entered the king's room, whom he despatched with one stroke of his dagger. Just as he had done the murder, one of the grooms, who slept in the chamber, laughed in his sleep, and the other cried: 'Murder,' which woke them both; but they said a short prayer; one of them said: 'God bless us!' and the other answered 'Amen'; and addressed themselves to sleep again. Macbeth, who stood listening to them, tried to say 'Amen,' when the fellow said 'God bless us!' but, though he had most need of a blessing, the word stuck in his throat, and he could not pronounce it.

Again he thought he heard a voice which cried: 'Sleep no more: Macbeth doth murder sleep, the innocent sleep, that nourishes life.' Still it cried: 'Sleep no more,' to all the house. 'Glamis hath murdered sleep, and therefore Cawdor shall sleep no more. Macbeth shall sleep no more.'

With such horrible imaginations Macbeth returned to his listening wife, who began to think he had failed of his purpose, and that the deed was somehow frustrated. He came in so distracted a state, that she reproached him with his want of firmness, and sent him to wash his hands of the blood which stained them, while she took his dagger, with purpose to stain the cheeks of the grooms with blood, to make it seem their guilt.

Morning came, and with it the discovery of the murder, which could not be concealed; and though Macbeth and his lady made great show of grief, and the proofs against the grooms (the dagger being produced against them and their faces smeared with blood) were sufficiently strong, yet the entire suspicion fell upon Macbeth, whose inducements to such a deed were so much more forcible than such poor silly grooms could be supposed to have; and Duncan's two sons fled. Malcolm, the eldest, sought for refuge in the English court; and the youngest, Donalbain, made his escape to Ireland.

The king's sons, who should have succeeded him, having thus vacated the throne, Macbeth as next heir was crowned king, and thus the prediction of the weird sisters was literally accomplished.

Though placed so high, Macbeth and his queen could not forget the prophecy of the weird sisters, that, though Macbeth should be king, yet not his children, but the children of Banquo, should be kings after him. The thought of this, and that they had defiled their hands with blood, and done so great crimes, only to place the posterity of Banquo upon the throne, so rankled within them, that they determined to put to death both Banquo and his son, to make void the predictions of the weird sisters, which in their own case had been so remarkably brought to pass.

For this purpose they made a great supper, to which they invited all the chief thanes; and, among the rest, with marks of particular respect, Banquo and his son Fleance were invited. The way by which Banquo was to pass to the palace at night was beset by murderers appointed by Macbeth, who stabbed Banquo; but in the scuffle Fleance escaped. From that Fleance descended a race of monarchs who afterwards filled the

Scottish throne, ending with James the Sixth of Scotland and the First of England, under whom the two crowns of England and Scotland were united.

At supper, the queen, whose manners were in the highest degree affable and royal, played the hostess with a gracefulness and attention which conciliated every one present, and Macbeth discoursed freely with his thanes and nobles, saying, that all that was honourable in the country was under his roof, if he had but his good friend Banquo present, whom yet he hoped he should rather have to chide for neglect, than to lament for any mischance.   Just at these words the ghost of Banquo, whom he had caused to be murdered, entered the room and placed himself on the chair which Macbeth was about to occupy.   Though Macbeth was a bold man, and one that could have faced the devil without trembling, at this horrible sight his cheeks turned white with fear, and he stood quite unmanned with his eyes fixed upon the ghost.   His queen and all the nobles, who saw nothing, but perceived him gazing (as they thought) upon an empty chair, took it for a fit of distraction; and she reproached him, whispering that it was but the same fancy which made him see the dagger in the air, when he was about to kill Duncan.   But Macbeth continued to see the ghost, and gave no heed to all they could say, while he addressed it with distracted words, yet so significant, that his queen, fearing the dreadful secret would be disclosed, in great haste dismissed the guests, excusing the infirmity of Macbeth as a disorder he was often troubled with.

To such dreadful fancies Macbeth was subject.   His queen and he had their sleeps afflicted with terrible dreams, and the blood of Banquo troubled them not more than the escape of Fleance, whom now they looked upon as father to a line of kings who should keep their posterity out of the throne.   With these miserable thoughts they found no peace, and Macbeth determined once more to seek out the weird sisters, and know from them the worst.

He sought them in a cave upon the heath, where they, who knew by foresight of his coming, were engaged in preparing their dreadful charms, by which they conjured up infernal spirits to reveal to them futurity. Their horrid ingredients were toads, bats, and serpents, the eye of a newt, and the tongue of a dog, the leg of a lizard, and the wing of the night-owl, the scale of a dragon, the tooth of a wolf, the maw of the ravenous salt-sea shark, the mummy of a witch, the root of the poisonous hemlock (this to have effect must be digged in the dark), the gall of a goat, and the liver of a Jew, with slips of the yew tree that roots itself in graves, and the finger of a dead child: all these were set on to boil in a great kettle, or cauldron, which, as fast as it grew too hot, was cooled with a baboon's blood: to these they poured in the blood of a sow that had eaten her young, and they threw into the flame the grease that had sweaten from a murderer's gibbet. By these charms they bound the infernal spirits to answer their questions.

It was demanded of Macbeth, whether he would have his doubts resolved by them, or by their masters, the spirits. He, nothing daunted by the dreadful ceremonies which he saw, boldly answered: 'Where are they? let me see them.' And they called the spirits, which were three. And the first arose in the likeness of an armed head, and he called Macbeth by name, and bid him beware of the thane of Fife; for which caution Macbeth thanked him; for Macbeth had entertained a jealousy of Macduff, the thane of Fife.

And the second spirit arose in the likeness of a bloody child, and he called Macbeth by name, and bid him have no fear, but laugh to scorn the power of man, for none of woman born should have power to hurt him; and he advised him to be bloody, bold, and resolute. 'Then live, Macduff!' cried the king; 'what need I fear of thee?

but yet I will make assurance doubly sure. Thou shalt not live; that I may tell pale-hearted Fear it lies, and sleep in spite of thunder.'

That spirit being dismissed, a third arose in the form of a child crowned, with a tree in his hand. He called Macbeth by name, and comforted him against conspiracies, saying, that he should never be vanquished, until the wood of Birnam to Dunsinane Hill should come against him. 'Sweet bodements! good!' cried Macbeth; 'who can unfix the forest, and move it from its earth-bound roots? I see I shall live the usual period of man's life, and not be cut off by a violent death. But my heart throbs to know one thing. Tell me, if your art can tell so much, if Banquo's issue shall ever reign in this kingdom?' Here the cauldron sank into the ground, and a noise of music was heard, and eight shadows, like kings, passed by Macbeth, and Banquo last, who bore a glass which showed the figures of many more, and Banquo all bloody smiled upon Macbeth, and pointed to them; by which Macbeth knew that these were the posterity of Banquo, who should reign after him in Scotland; and the witches, with a sound of soft music, and with dancing, making a show of duty and welcome to Macbeth, vanished. And from this time the thoughts of Macbeth were all bloody and dreadful.

The first thing he heard when he got out of the witches' cave, was that Macduff, thane of Fife, had fled to England, to join the army which was forming against him under Malcolm, the eldest son of the late king, with intent to displace Macbeth, and set Malcolm, the right heir, upon the throne. Macbeth, stung with rage, set upon the castle of Macduff, and put his wife and children, whom the thane had left behind, to the sword, and extended the slaughter to all who claimed the least relationship to Macduff.

These and such-like deeds alienated the minds of all his chief nobility from him. Such as could, fled to join

with Malcolm and Macduff, who were now approaching
with a powerful army, which they had raised in England;
and the rest secretly wished success to their arms,
though for fear of Macbeth they could take no active
part. His recruits went on slowly. Everybody hated
the tyrant; nobody loved or honoured him; but all
suspected him, and he began to envy the condition of
Duncan, whom he had murdered, who slept soundly in
his grave, against whom treason had done its worst:
steel nor poison, domestic malice nor foreign levies,
could hurt him any longer.

While these things were acting, the queen, who had
been the sole partner in his wickedness, in whose bosom
he could sometimes seek a momentary repose from those
terrible dreams which afflicted them both nightly, died,
it is supposed, by her own hands, unable to bear the
remorse of guilt, and public hate; by which event he
was left alone, without a soul to love or care for him, or
a friend to whom he could confide his wicked purposes.

He grew careless of life, and wished for death; but
the near approach of Malcolm's army roused in him
what remained of his ancient courage, and he determined
to die (as he expressed it) 'with armour on his back.'
Besides this, the hollow promises of the witches had
filled him with a false confidence, and he remembered
the sayings of the spirits, that none of woman born was
to hurt him, and that he was never to be vanquished till
Birnam wood should come to Dunisnane, which he
thought could never be. So he shut himself up in his
castle, whose impregnable strength was such as defied
a siege: here he sullenly waited the approach of Malcom.
When, upon a day, there came a messenger to him, pale
and shaking with fear, almost unable to report that
which he had seen; for he averred, that as he stood upon
his watch on the hill, he looked towards Birnam, and
to his thinking the wood began to move! 'Liar and
slave!' cried Macbeth: 'if thou speakest false, thou shalt

hang alive upon the next tree, till famine end thee. If thy tale be true, I care not if thou dost as much by me': for Macbeth now began to faint in resolution, and to doubt the equivocal speeches of the spirits. He was not to fear till Birnam wood should come to Dunsinane; and now a wood did move! 'However,' said he, 'if this which he avouches be true, let us arm and out. There is no flying hence, nor staying here. I begin to be weary of the sun, and wish my life at an end.' With these desperate speeches he sallied forth upon the besiegers, who had now come up to the castle.

The strange appearance which had given the messenger an idea of a wood moving is easily solved. When the besieging army marched through the wood of Birnam, Malcolm, like a skilful general, instructed his soldiers to hew down every one a bough and bear it before him, by way of concealing the true numbers of his host. This marching of the soldiers with boughs had at a distance the appearance which had frightened the messenger. Thus were the words of the spirit brought to pass, in a sense different from that in which Macbeth had understood them, and one great hold of his confidence was gone.

And now a severe skirmishing took place, in which Macbeth, though feebly supported by those who called themselves his friends, but in reality hated the tyrant and inclined to the party of Malcolm and Macduff, yet fought with the extreme of rage and valour, cutting to pieces all who were opposed to him, till he came to where Macduff was fighting. Seeing Macduff, and remembering the caution of the spirit who had counselled him to avoid Macduff, above all men, he would have turned, but Macduff, who had been seeking him through the whole fight, opposed his turning, and a fierce contest ensued; Macduff giving him many foul reproaches for the murder of his wife and children. Macbeth, whose soul was charged enough with blood of that family already, would still have declined the combat; but

Macduff still urged him to it, calling him tyrant, murderer, hell-hound, and villain.

Then Macbeth remembered the words of the spirit, how none of woman born should hurt him; and smiling confidently he said to Macduff: 'Thou losest thy labour, Macduff. As easily thou mayest impress the air with thy sword, as make me vulnerable. I bear a charmed life, which must not yield to one of woman born.'

'Despair thy charm,' said Macduff, 'and let that lying spirit whom thou hast served, tell thee, that Macduff was never born of woman, never as the ordinary manner of men is to be born, but was untimely taken from his mother.'

'Accursed be the tongue which tells me so,' said the trembling Macbeth, who felt his last hold of confidence give way; 'and let never man in future believe the lying equivocations of witches and juggling spirits, who deceive us in words which have double senses, and while they keep their promise literally, disappoint our hopes with a different meaning. I will not fight with thee.'

'Then live!' said the scornful Macduff; 'we will have a show of thee, as men show monsters, and a painted board, on which shall be written: "Here men may see the tyrant!"'

'Never,' said Macbeth, whose courage returned with despair; 'I will not live to kiss the ground before young Malcolm's feet, and to be baited with the curses of the rabble. Though Birnam wood be come to Dunsinane, and thou opposed to me, who wast never born of woman, yet will I try the last.' With these frantic words he threw himself upon Macduff, who, after a severe struggle, in the end overcame him, and cutting off his head, made a present of it to the young and lawful king, Malcolm; who took upon him the government which, by the machinations of the usurper, he had so long been deprived of, and ascended the throne of Duncan the Meek, amid the acclamations of the nobles and the people.

ALL'S WELL THAT ENDS WELL

BERTRAM, count of Rousillon, had newly come to his title and estate, by the death of his father. The king of France loved the father of Bertram, and when he heard of his death, he sent for his son to come immediately to his royal court in Paris, intending, for the friendship he bore the late count, to grace young Bertram with his especial favour and protection.

Bertram was living with his mother, the widowed countess, when Lafeu, an old lord of the French court, came to conduct him to the king. The king of France was an absolute monarch, and the invitation to court was in the form of a royal mandate, or positive command, which no subject, of what high dignity soever, might disobey; therefore though the countess, in parting with this dear son, seemed a second time to bury her husband, whose loss she had so lately mourned, yet she dared not to keep him a single day, but gave instant orders for his departure. Lafeu, who came to fetch him, tried to comfort the countess for the loss of her late lord, and her son's sudden absence; and he said, in a courtier's flattering manner, that the king was so kind a prince, she would find in his majesty a husband, and that he would be a father to her son; meaning only, that the good king would befriend the fortunes of Bertram. Lafeu told the countess that the king had fallen into a sad malady, which was pronounced by his physicians to be incurable. The lady expressed great sorrow on hearing this account of the king's ill health, and said, she wished the father of Helena (a young gentlewoman who was present in attendance upon her) were living, for that she doubted not he could have cured his majesty of his disease. And she told Lafeu something of the history of Helena, saying she was the only daughter of the famous physician Gerard de Narbon, and that he had recommended his daughter to her care when he was dying, so that since his death she had taken Helena under her protection; then the countess praised the virtuous disposition and excellent qualities of Helena, saying she inherited these virtues from her worthy father. While she was speaking, Helena wept in sad and mournful silence, which made the countess gently reprove her for too much grieving for her father's death.

Bertram now bade his mother farewell. The countess parted with this dear son with tears and many blessings, and commended him to the care of Lafeu, saying: 'Good my lord, advise him, for he is an unseasoned courtier.'

Bertram's last words were spoken to Helena, but they were words of mere civility, wishing her happiness; and he concluded his short farewell to her with saying: 'Be comfortable to my mother, your mistress, and make much of her.'

Helena had long loved Bertram, and when she wept in sad mournful silence, the tears she shed were not for Gerard de Narbon. Helena loved her father, but in the present feeling of a deeper love, the object of which she was about to lose, she had forgotten the very form and features of her dead father, her imagination presenting no image to her mind but Bertram's.

Helena had long loved Bertram, yet she always remembered that he was the count of Rousillon, descended from the most ancient family in France. She of humble birth. Her parents of no note at all. His ancestors all noble. And therefore she looked up to the high-born Bertram as to her master and to her dear lord, and dared not form any wish but to live his servant, and so living to die his vassal. So great the distance seemed to her between his height of dignity and her lowly fortunes, that she would day: 'It were all one that I should love a bright particular star, and think to wed it, Bertram is so far above me.'

Bertram's absence filled her eyes with tears and her heart with sorrow; for though she loved without hope, yet it was a pretty comfort to her to see him every hour, and Helena would sit and look upon his dark eye, his arched brow, and the curls of his fine hair, till she seemed to draw his portrait on the tablet of her heart, that heart too capable of retaining the memory of every line in the features of that loved face.

Gerard de Narbon, when he died, left her no other portion than some prescriptions of rare and well-proved virtue, which by deep study and long experience in medicine he had collected as sovereign and almost infallible remedies. Among the rest, there was one set down as an approved medicine for the disease under which Lafeu said the king at that time languished: and when Helena heard of the king's complaint, she, who till now had been so humble and so hopeless, formed an ambitious project in her mind to go herself to Paris, and undertake the cure of the king. But though Helena was the possessor of this choice prescription, it was unlikely, as the king as well as his physicians was of opinion that his disease was incurable, that they would give credit to a poor unlearned virgin, if she should offer to perform a cure. The firm hopes that Helena had of succeeding, if she might be permitted to make the trial, seemed more than even her father's skill warranted, though he was the most famous physician of his time; for she felt a strong faith that this good medicine was sanctified by all the luckiest stars in heaven to be the legacy that should advance her fortune, even to the high dignity of being count Rousillon's wife.

Bertram had not been long gone, when the countess was informed by her steward, that he had overheard Helena talking to herself, and that he understood from some words she uttered, she was in love with Bertram, and thought of following him to Paris. The countess dismissed the steward with thanks, and desired him to tell Helena she wished to speak with her. What she had just heard of Helena brought the remembrance of days long past into the mind of the countess; those days probably when her love for Bertram's father first began; and she said to herself: 'Even so it was with me when I was young. Love is a thorn that belongs to the rose of youth; for in the season of youth, if ever we are nature's children, these faults are ours, though then we think not they are faults.' While the countess was thus meditating on the loving errors of her own youth, Helena entered, and she said to her: 'Helena, you know I am a mother to you.' Helena replied: 'You are my honourable mistress.' 'You are my daughter,' said the countess again: 'I say I am your mother. Why do you start and look pale at my words?' With looks of alarm and confused thoughts, fearing the countess suspected her love, Helena still replied: 'Pardon me, madam, you are not my mother; the count Rousillon cannot be my brother, nor I your daughter.' 'Yet, Helena,' said the countess, 'you might be my daughter-in-law; and I am afraid that is what you mean to be, the words *mother* and *daughter* so disturb you. Helena, do you love my son?' 'Good madam, pardon me,' said the affrighted Helena. Again the countess repeated her question. 'Do you love my son?' 'Do not you love him, madam?' said Helena. The countess replied: 'Give me not this evasive answer, Helena. Come, come, disclose the state of your affections, for your love has to the full appeared.' Helena on her knees now owned her love, and with shame and terror implored the pardon of her noble mistress; and with words expressive of the sense she had of the inequality between their fortunes, she protested Bertram did not know she loved him, comparing her humble unaspiring love to a poor Indian, who adores the sun that looks upon his worshipper, but knows of him no more. The countess asked Helena if she had not lately an intent to go to Paris? Helena owned the design she had formed in her mind, when she heard Lafeu speak of the king's illness. 'This was your motive for wishing to go to Paris,' said the countess, 'was it? Speak truly.' Helena honestly answered: 'My lord your son made me to think of this; else Paris, and the medicine, and the king, had from the conversation of my thoughts been absent then.' The countess heard the whole of this confession without saying a word either of approval or of blame, but she strictly questioned Helena as to the probability of the medicine being useful to the king. She found that it was the most prized by Gerard de Narbon of all he possessed, and that he had given it to his daughter on his deathbed; and remembering the solemn promise she had made at that awful hour in regard to this young maid, whose destiny, and the life of the king himself, seemed to depend on the execution of a project (which though conceived by the fond suggestions of a loving maiden's thoughts, the countess knew not but it might be the unseen workings of Providence to bring to pass the recovery of the king, and to lay the foundation of the future fortunes of Gerard de Narbon's daughter), free leave she gave to Helena to pursue her own way, and generously furnished her with ample means and suitable attendants; and Helena set out for Paris with the blessings of the countess, and her kindest wishes for her success.

Helena arrived at Paris, and by the assistance of her friend the old lord Lafeu, she obtained an audience of the king. She had still many difficulties to encounter, for the king was not easily prevailed on to try the medicine offered him by this fair young doctor. But she told him she was Gerard de Narbon's daughter (with whose fame the king was well acquainted), and she offered the precious medicine as the darling treasure which contained the essence of all her father's long experience and skill, and she boldly engaged to forfeit her life, if it failed to restore his majesty to perfect health in the space of two days. The king at length consented to try it, and in two days' time Helena was to lose her life if the king did not recover; but if she succeeded, he promised to give her the choice of any man throughout all France (the princes only excepted) whom she could like for a husband; the choice of a husband being the fee Helena demanded if she cured the king of his disease.

Helena did not deceive herself in the hope she conceived of the efficacy of her father's medicine. Before two days were at an end, the king was restored to perfect health, and he assembled all the young noblemen of his court together, in order to confer the promised reward of a husband upou his fair physician; and he desired Helena to look round on this youthful parcel of noble bachelors, and choose her husband. Helena was not slow to make her choice, for among these young lords she saw the count Rousillon, and turning to Bertram, she said: 'This is the man. I dare not say, my lord, I take you, but I give me and my service ever whilst I live into your guiding power.' 'Why, then,' said the king 'young Bertram, take her; she is your wife.' Bertram did not hesitate to declare his dislike to this present of the king's of the self-offered Helena, who, he said, was a poor physician's daughter, bred at his father's charge, and now living a dependent on his mother's bounty. Helena heard him speak these words of rejection and of scorn, and she said to the king: 'That you are well, my lord, I am glad. Let the rest go.' But the king would not suffer his royal command to be so slighted; for the power of bestowing their nobles in marriage was one of the many privileges of the kings of France; and that same day Bertram was married to Helena, a forced and uneasy marriage to Bertram, and of no promising hope to the poor lady, who, though she gained the noble husband she had hazarded her life to obtain, seemed to have won but a splendid blank, her husband's love not being a gift in the power of the king of France to bestow.

Helena was no sooner married than she was desired

by Bertram to apply to the king for him for leave of absence from court; and when she brought him the king's permission for his departure, Bertram told her that he was not prepared for this sudden marriage, it had much unsettled him, and therefore she must not wonder at the course he should pursue. If Helena wondered not, she grieved when she found it was his intention to leave her. He ordered her to go home to his mother. When Helena heard this unkind command, she replied: 'Sir, I can nothing say to this, but that I am your most obedient servant, and shall ever with true observance seek to eke out that desert, wherein my homely stars have failed to equal my great fortunes.' But this humble speech of Helena's did not at all move the haughty Bertram to pity his gentle wife, and he parted from her without even the common civility of a kind farewell.

Back to the countess then Helena returned. She had accomplished the purport of her journey, she had preserved the life of the king, and she had wedded her heart's dear lord, the count Rousillon; but she returned back a dejected lady to her noble mother-in-law, and as soon as she entered the house she received a letter from Bertram which almost broke her heart.

The good countess received her with a cordial welcome, as if she had been her son's own choice, and a lady of a high degree, and she spoke kind words to comfort her for the unkind neglect of Bertram in sending his wife home on her bridal day alone. But this gracious reception failed to cheer the sad mind of Helena, and she said: 'Madam my lord is gone, for ever gone.' She then read these words out of Bertram's letter: *When you can get the ring from my finger, which never shall come off, then call me husband, but in such a Then I write a Never.* 'This is a dreadful sentence!' said Helena. The countess begged her to have patience, and said, now Bertram was gone, she should be her child, and that she deserved a lord that twenty such rude boys as Bertram might tend upon, and hourly call her mistress. But in vain by respectful condescension and kind flattery this matchless mother tried to soothe the sorrows of her daughter in-law.

Helena still kept her eyes fixed upon the letter, and cried out in an agony of grief: *Till I have no wife, I have nothing in France.* The countess asked her if she found those words in the letter? 'Yes, madam,' was all poor Helena could answer.

The next morning Helena was missing. She left a letter to be delivered to the countess after she was gone, to acquaint her with the reason of her sudden absence: in this letter she informed her that she was so much grieved at having driven Bertram from his native country and his home, that to atone for her offence, she had undertaken a pilgrimage to the shrine of St. Jaques le Grand, and concluded with requesting the countess to inform her son that the wife he so hated had left his house for ever.

Bertram, when he left Paris, went to Florence, and there became an officer in the duke of Florence's army, and after a successful war, in which he distinguished himself by many brave actions, Bertram received letters from his mother, containing the acceptable tidings that Helena would no more disturb him; and he was preparing to return home, when Helena herself, clad in her pilgrim's weeds, arrived at the city of Florence.

Florence was a city through which the pilgrims used to pass on their way to St. Jaques le Grand; and when Helena arrived at this city, she heard that a hospitable widow dwelt there, who used to receive into her house the female pilgrims that were going to visit the shrine of that saint, giving them lodging and kind entertainment. To this good lady, therefore, Helena went, and the widow gave her a courteous welcome, and invited her to see whatever was curious in that famous city, and told her that if she would like to see the duke's army,

she would take her where she might have a full view of it.
'And you will see a countryman of yours,' said the
widow; 'his name is count Rousillon, who has done
worthy service in the duke's wars.'   Helena wanted no
second invitation, when she found Bertram was to make
part of the show.   She accompanied her hostess; and a
sad and mournful pleasure it was to her to look once
more upon her dear husband's face.   'Is he not a handsome man?' said the widow.   'I like him well,' replied
Helena, with great truth.   All the way they walked, the
talkative widow's discourse was all of Bertram: she told
Helena the story of Bertram's marriage, and how he had
deserted the poor lady his wife, and entered into the
duke's army to avoid living with her.   To this account
of her own misfortunes Helena patiently listened, and
when it was ended, the history of Bertram was not yet
done, for then the widow began another tale, every word
of which sank deep into the mind of Helena; for the story
she now told was of Bertram's love for her daughter.

Though Bertram did not like the marriage forced on
him by the king, it seems he was not insensible to love,
for since he had been stationed with the army at Florence,
he had fallen in love with Diana, a fair young gentlewoman, the daughter of this widow who was Helena's
hostess; and every night, with music of all sorts, and
songs composed in praise of Diana's beauty, he would
come under her window, and solicit her love; and all his
suit to her was, that she would permit him to visit her
by stealth after the family were retired to rest; but Diana
would by no means be persuaded to grant this improper
request, nor give any encouragement to his suit, knowing
him to be a married man; for Diana had been brought
up under the counsels of a prudent mother, who, though
she was now in reduced circumstances, was well born,
and descended from the noble family of the Capulets.

All this the good lady related to Helena, highly
praising the virtuous principles of her discreet daughter,

which she said were entirely owing to the excellent education and good advice she had given her; and she further said, that Bertram had been particularly importunate with Diana to admit him to the visit he so much desired that night, because he was going to leave Florence early the next morning.

Though it grieved Helena to hear of Bertram's love for the widow's daughter, yet from the story the ardent mind of Helena conceived a project (nothing discouraged at the ill success of her former one) to recover her truant lord. She disclosed to the widow that she was Helena, the deserted wife of Bertram, and requested that her kind hostess and her daughter would suffer this visit from Bertram to take place, and allow her to pass herself upon Bertram for Diana; telling them, her chief motive for desiring to have this secret meeting with her husband, was to get a ring from him, which he had said, if ever she was in possession of he would acknowledge her as his wife.

The widow and her daughter promised to assist her in this affair, partly moved by pity for this unhappy forsaken wife, and partly won over to her interest by the promises of reward which Helena made them, giving them a purse of money in earnest of her future favour. In the course of that day Helena caused information to be sent to Bertram that she was dead; hoping that when he thought himself free to make a second choice by the news of her death, he would offer marriage to her in her feigned character of Diana. And if she could obtain the ring and this promise too, she doubted not she should make some future good come of it.

In the evening, after it was dark, Bertram was admitted into Diana's chamber, and Helena was there ready to receive him. The flattering compliments and love discourse he addressed to Helena were precious sounds to her, though she knew they were meant for Diana; and Bertram was so well pleased with her, that he made her a solemn promise to be her husband, and to love her for ever; which she hoped would be prophetic of a real affection, when he should know it was his own wife, the despised Helena, whose conversation had so delighted him.

Bertram never knew how sensible a lady Helena was, else perhaps he would not have been so regardless of her; and seeing her every day, he had entirely overlooked her beauty; a face we are accustomed to see constantly, losing the effect which is caused by the first sight either of beauty or of plainness; and of her understanding it was impossible he should judge, because she felt such reverence, mixed with her love for him, that she was always silent in his presence: but now that her future fate, and the happy ending of all her love-projects, seemed to depend on her leaving a favourable impression on the mind of Bertram from this night's interview, she exerted all her wit to please him; and the simple graces of her lively conversation and the endearing sweetness of her manners so charmed Bertram, that he vowed she should be his wife.   Helena begged the ring from off his finger as a token of his regard, and he gave it to her; and in return for this ring, which it was of such importance to her to possess, she gave him another ring, which was one the king had made her a present of.   Before it was light in the morning, she sent Bertram away; and he immediately set out on his journey towards his mother's house.

Helena prevailed on the widow and Diana to accompany her to Paris, their further assistance being necessary to the full accomplishment of the plan she had formed. When they arrived there, they found the king was gone upon a visit to the countess of Rousillon, and Helena followed the king with all the speed she could make.

The king was still in perfect health, and his gratitude to her who had been the means of his recovery was so lively in his mind, that the moment he saw the countess of Rousillon, he began to talk of Helena, calling her a precious jewel that was lost by the folly of her son; but seeing the subject distressed the countess, who sincerely lamented the death of Helena, he said: 'My good lady, I have forgiven and forgotten all.'   But the good-natured old Lafeu, who was present, and could not bear that the memory of his favourite Helena should be so lightly passed over, said: 'This I must say, the young lord did great offence to his majesty, his mother, and his lady; but to himself he did the greatest wrong of all, for he has lost a wife whose beauty astonished all eyes, whose words took all ears captive, whose deep perfection made all hearts wish to serve her.'   The king said: 'Praising what is lost makes the remembrance dear.   Well—call him hither'; meaning Bertram, who now presented himself before the king: and, on his expressing deep sorrow for the injuries he had done to Helena, the king, for his dead father's and his admirable mother's sake, pardoned him and restored him once more to his favour. But the gracious countenance of the king was soon changed towards him, for he perceived that Bertram wore the very ring upon his finger which he had given to Helena: and he well remembered that Helena had called all the saints in heaven to witness she would never part with that ring, unless she sent it to the king himself upon some great disaster befalling her; and Bertram, on the king's questioning him how he came by the ring, told an improabable story of a lady throwing it to him out of a window, and denied ever having seen Helena since the day of their marriage.   The king, knowing Bertram's dislike to his wife, feared he had destroyed her: and he ordered his guards to seize Bertram, saying: 'I am wrapt in dismal thinking, for I fear the life of Helena was foully snatched.'   At this moment Diana and her mother entered, and presented a petition to the king, wherein they begged his majesty to exert his royal power to compel Bertram to marry Diana, he having made her a solemn promise of marriage. Bertram, fearing the king's anger, denied he had made any such promise; and then Diana produced the ring (which Helena had put into her hands) to confirm the truth of her words; and she said that she had given Bertram the ring he then wore, in exchange for that, at the time he vowed to marry her. On hearing this, the king ordered the guards to seize her also; and her account of the ring differing from Bertram's, the king's suspicions were confirmed: and he said, if they did not confess how they came by this ring of Helena's, they should be both put to death. Diana requested her mother might be permitted to fetch the jeweller of whom she bought the ring, which being granted, the widow went out, and presently returned leading in Helena herself.

The good countess, who in silent grief had beheld her son's danger, and had even dreaded that the suspicion of his having destroyed his wife might possibly be true, finding her dear Helena, whom she loved with even a maternal affection, was still living, felt a delight she was hardly able to support; and the king, scarce believing for joy that it was Helena, said: 'Is this indeed the wife of Bertram that I see?' Helena, feeling herself yet an unacknowledged wife, replied: 'No, my good lord, it is but the shadow of a wife you see, the name and not the thing.' Bertram cried out: 'Both, both! O pardon!' 'O my lord,' said Helena, 'when I personated this fair maid, I found you wondrous kind; and look, here is your letter!' reading to him in a joyful tone those words which she had once repeated so sorrowfully: *When from my finger you can get this ring*—'This is done; it was to me you gave the ring. Will you be mine, now you are doubly won?' Bertram replied: 'If you can make it plain that you were the lady I talked with that night, I will love you dearly ever, ever dearly.' This was no difficult task, for the widow and Diana came with Helena to prove this fact; and the king was so well pleased with

Diana, for the friendly assistance she had rendered the dear lady he so truly valued for the service she had done him, that he promised her also a noble husband: Helena's history giving him a hint, that it was a suitable reward for kings to bestow upon fair ladies when they perform notable services.

Thus Helena at last found that her father's legacy was indeed sanctified by the luckiest stars in heaven; for she was now the beloved wife of her dear Bertram, the daughter-in-law of her noble mistress, and herself the countess of Rousillon.

THE TAMING OF THE SHREW

KATHARINE, the Shrew, was the eldest daughter of Baptista, a rich gentleman of Padua. She was a lady of such an ungovernable spirit and fiery temper, such a loud-tongued scold, that she was known in Padua by no other name than Katharine the Shrew. It seemed very unlikely, indeed impossible, that any gentleman would ever be found who would venture to marry this lady, and therefore Baptista was much blamed for deferring his consent to many excellent offers that were made to her gentle sister Bianca, putting off all Bianca's suitors with this excuse, that when the eldest sister was fairly off his hands, they should have free leave to address young Bianca.

It happened, however, that a gentleman, named Petruchio, came to Padua, purposely to look out for a wife, who, nothing discouraged by these reports of Katharine's temper, and hearing she was rich and handsome, resolved upon marrying this famous termagant, and taming her into a meek and manageable wife. And truly none was so fit to set about this herculean labour as Petruchio, whose spirit was as high as Katharine's, and he was a witty and most happy-tempered humourist, and withal so wise, and of such a true judgment, that he well knew how to feign a passionate and furious deportment, when his spirits were so calm that himself could have laughed merrily at his own angry feigning, for his natural temper was careless and easy; the boisterous airs he assumed when he became the husband of Katharine being but in sport, or more properly speaking, affected by his excellent discernment, as the only means to overcome, in her own way, the passionate ways of the furious Katharine.

A courting then Petruchio went to Katharine the

Shrew; and first of all he applied to Baptista her father, for leave to woo his *gentle daughter* Katharine, as Petruchio called her, saying archly, that having heard of her bashful modesty and mild behaviour, he had come from Verona to solicit her love. Her father, though he wished her married, was forced to confess Katharine would ill answer this character, it being soon apparent of what manner of gentleness she was composed, for her music-master rushed into the room to complain that the gentle Katharine, his pupil, had broken his head with her lute, for presuming to find fault with her performance; which, when Petruchio heard, he said: 'It is a brave wench; I love her more than ever, and long to have some chat with her'; and hurrying the old gentleman for a positive answer, he said: 'My business is in haste, signior Baptista, I cannot come every day to woo. You knew my father: he is dead, and has left me heir to all his lands and goods. Then tell me, if I get your daughter's love, what dowry you will give with her.' Baptista thought his manner was somewhat blunt for a lover; but being glad to get Katharine married, he answered that he would give her twenty thousand crowns for her dowry, and half his estate at his death: so this odd match was quickly agreed on, and Baptista went to apprise his shrewish daughter of her lover's addresses, and sent her in to Petruchio to listen to his suit.

In the meantime Petruchio was settling with himself the mode of courtship he should pursue; and he said: 'I will woo her with some spirit when she comes. If she rails at me, why then I will tell her she sings as sweetly as a nightingale; and if she frowns. I will say she looks as clear as roses newly washed with dew. If she will not speak a word, I will praise the eloquence of her language; and if she bids me leave her. I will give her thanks as if she bid me stay with her a week.' Now the stately Katharine entered, and Petruchio first addressed her with 'Good morrow, Kate, for that is your name, I hear.' Katharine, not liking this plain salutation, said disdainfully: 'They call me Katharine who do speak to me.' 'You lie,' replied the lover; 'for you are called plain Kate, and bonny Kate, and sometimes Kate the Shrew: but, Kate, you are the prettiest Kate in Christendom, and therefore, Kate, hearing your mildness praised in every town, I am come to woo you for my wife.'

A strange courtship they made of it. She in loud and angry terms showing him how justly she had gained the name of Shrew, while he still praised her sweet and courteous words, till at length, hearing her father coming, he said (intending to make as quick a wooing as possible): 'Sweet Katharine, let us set this idle chat aside, for your father has consented that you shall be my wife, your dowry is agreed on, and whether you will or no, I will marry you.'

And now Baptista entering, Petruchio told him his daughter had received him kindly, and that she had promised to be married the next Sunday. This Katharine denied, saying she would rather see him hanged on Sunday, and reproached her father for wishing to wed her to such a mad-cap ruffian as Petruchio. Petruchio desired her father not to regard her angry words, for they had agreed she should seem reluctant before him, but that when they were alone he had found her very fond and loving; and he said to her: 'Give me your hand, Kate; I will go to Venice to buy you fine apparel against our wedding day. Provide the feast, father, and bid the wedding guests. I will be sure to bring rings, fine array, and rich clothes, that my Katharine may be fine; and kiss me, Kate, for we will be married on Sunday.'

On the Sunday all the wedding guests were assembled, but they waited long before Petruchio came, and Katharine wept for vexation to think that Petruchio had only been making a jest of her. At last, however, he appeared; but he brought none of the bridal finery he had promised Katharine, nor was he dressed himself like a bridegroom, but in strange disordered attire, as if he meant to make a sport of the serious business he came about; and his servant and the very horses on which they rode were in like manner in mean and fantastic fashion habited.

Petruchio could not be persuaded to change his dress; he said Katharine was to be married to him, and not to his clothes; and finding it was in vain to argue with him, to the church they went, he still behaving in the same mad way, for when the priest asked Petruchio if Katharine should be his wife, he swore so loud that she should, that, all amazed, the priest let fall his book, and as he stooped to take it up, this mad-brained bridegroom gave him such a cuff, that down fell the priest and his book again.   And all the while they were being married he stamped and swore so, that the high-spirited Katharine trembled and shook with fear.   After the ceremony was over, while they were yet in the church, he called for wine, and drank a loud health to the company, and threw a sop which was at the bottom of the glass full in the sexton's face, giving no other reason for this strange act, than that the sexton's beard grew thin and hungerly, and seemed to ask the sop as he was drinking.   Never sure was there such a mad marriage; but Petruchio did but put this wildness on, the better to succeed in the plot he had formed to tame his shrewish wife.

Baptista had provided a sumptuous marriage feast, but when they returned from church, Petruchio, taking hold of Katharine, declared his intention of carrying his wife home instantly: and no remonstrance of his father-in-law, or angry words of the enraged Katharine, could make him change his purpose. He claimed a husband's right to dispose of his wife as he pleased, and away he hurried Katharine off: he seeming so daring and resolute that no one dared attempt to stop him.

Petruchio mounted his wife upon a miserable horse, lean and lank, which he had picked out for the purpose, and himself and his servant no better mounted; they journeyed on through rough and miry ways, and ever when this horse of Katharine's stumbled, he would storm and swear at the poor jaded beast, who could scarce crawl under his burthen, as if he had been the most passionate man alive.

At length, after a weary journey, during which Katharine had heard nothing but the wild ravings of Petruchio at the servant and the horses, they arrived at his house. Petruchio welcomed her kindly to her home, but he resolved she should have neither rest nor food that night. The tables were spread, and supper soon served; but Petruchio, pretending to find fault with every dish, threw the meat about the floor, and ordered the servants to remove it away; and all this he did, as he said, in love for his Katharine, that she might not eat meat that was not well dressed. And when Katharine, weary and supperless, retired to rest, he found the same fault with the bed, throwing the pillows and bedclothes about the room, so that she was forced to sit down in a chair, where if she chanced to drop asleep, she was presently awakened by the loud voice of her husband, storming at the servants for the ill-making of his wife's bridal-bed.

The next day Petruchio pursued the same course, still speaking kind words to Katharine, but when she attempted to eat, finding fault with everything that was set before her throwing the breakfast on the floor as he had done the supper; and Katharine, the haughty Katherine, was fain to beg the servants would bring her secretly a morsel of food; but they being instructed by Petruchio, replied, they dared not give her anything unknown to their master. 'Ah,' said she, 'did he marry me to famish me? Beggars that come to my father's door have food given them. But I, who never knew what it was to entreat for anything, am starved for want of food, giddy for want of sleep, with oaths kept waking,

Petruchio, pretending to find fault with every dish, threw the meat about the floor

and with brawling fed; and that which vexes me more than all, he does it under the name of perfect love, pretending that if I sleep or eat, it were present death to me.' Here the soliloquy was interrupted by the entrance of Petruchio: he, not meaning she should be quite starved, had brought her a small portion of meat, and he said to her: 'How fares my sweet Kate? Here, love, you see how diligent I am, I have dressed your meat myself. I am sure this kindness merits thanks. What, not a word? Nay, then you love not the meat, and all the pains I have taken is to no purpose.' He then ordered the servant to take the dish away. Extreme hunger, which had abated the pride of Katharine, made her say, though angered to the heart: 'I pray you let it stand.' But this was not all Petruchio intended to bring her to, and he replied: 'The poorest service is repaid with thanks, and so shall mine before you touch the meat.' On this Katharine brought out a reluctant 'I thank you, sir.' And now he suffered her to make a slender meal, saying: 'Much good may it do your gentle heart, Kate; eat apace! And now, my honey love, we will return to your father's house, and revel it as bravely as the best, with silken coats and caps and golden rings, with ruffs and scarfs and fans and double change of finery'; and to make her believe he really intended to give her these gay things, he called in a tailor and a haberdasher, who brought some new clothes he had ordered for her, and then giving her plate to the servant to take away, before she had half satisfied her hunger, he said: 'What, have you dined?' The haberdasher presented a cap, saying: 'Here is the cap your worship bespoke'; on which Petruchio began to storm afresh, saying the cap was moulded in a porringer, and that it was no bigger than a cockle or walnut shell, desiring the haberdasher to take it away and make it bigger. Katharine said: 'I will have this; all gentlewomen wear such caps as these.' 'When you are gentle,' replied

Petruchio, 'you shall have one too, and not till then.'
The meat Katharine had eaten had a little revived her
fallen spirits, and she said: 'Why, sir, I trust I may have
leave to speak, and speak I will: I am no child, no babe;
your betters have endured to hear me say my mind; and
if you cannot, you had better stop your ears.' Petruchio
would not hear these angry words, for he had happily
discovered a better way of managing his wife than
keeping up a jangling argument with her; therefore his
answer was: 'Why, you say true; it is a paltry cap, and
I love you for not liking it.' 'Love me, or love me not,'
said Katharine, 'I like the cap, and I will have this cap
or none.' 'You say you wish to see the gown,' said
Petruchio, still affecting to misunderstand her. The
tailor then came forward and showed her a fine gown he
had made for her. Petruchio, whose intent was that
she should have neither cap nor gown, found as much
fault with that. 'O mercy, Heaven!' said he, 'what
stuff is here! What, do you call this a sleeve? it is like
a demi-cannon, carved up and down like an apple tart.'
The tailor said: 'You bid me make it according to the
fashion of the times'; and Katharine said, she never saw
a better fashioned gown. This was enough for Petruchio, and privately desiring these people might be paid
for their goods, and excuses made to them for the
seemingly strange treatment he bestowed upon them, he
with fierce words and furious gestures drove the tailor
and the haberdasher out of the room; and then, turning
to Katharine, he said: 'Well, come, my Kate, we will
go to your father's even in these mean garments we now
wear.' And then he ordered his horses, affirming they
should reach Baptista's house by dinner-time, for that
it was but seven o'clock. Now it was not early morning,
but the very middle of the day, when he spoke this;
therefore Katharine ventured to say, though modestly,
being almost overcome by the vehemence of his manner:
'I dare assure you, sir, it is two o'clock, and will be

supper-time before we get there.' But Petruchio meant that she should be so completely subdued, that she should assent to everything he said, before he carried her to her father; and therefore, as if he were lord even of the sun, and could command the hours, he said it should be what time he pleased to have it, before he set forward; 'For,' he said, 'whatever I say or do, you still are crossing it. I will not go to-day, and when I go, it shall be what o'clock I say it is.' Another day Katherine was forced to practise her newly found obedience, and not till he had brought her proud spirit to such a perfect subjection, that she dared not remember there was such a word as contradiction, would Petruchio allow her to go to her father's house; and even while they were upon their journey thither, she was in danger of being turned back again, only because she happened to hint it was the sun, when he affirmed the moon shone brightly at noonday. 'Now, by my mother's son,' said he, 'and that is myself, it shall be the moon, or stars, or what I list, before I journey to your father's house.' He then made as if he were going back again; but Katherine, no longer Katherine the Shrew, but the obedient wife, said: 'Let us go forward, I pray, now we have come so far, and it shall be the sun, or moon, or what you please, and if you please to call it a rush candle henceforth, I vowed it shall be so for me.' This he was resolved to prove, therefore he said again: 'I say, it is the moon.' 'I know it is the moon,' replied Katherine. 'You lie, it is the blessed sun,' said Petruchio. 'Then it is the blessed sun,' replied Katherine; 'but sun it is not, when you say it is not. What you will have it named, even so it is, and so it ever shall be for Katherine.' Now then he suffered her to proceed on her journey; but further to try if this yielding humour would last, he addressed an old gentleman they met on the road as if he had been a young woman, saying to him: 'Good morrow, gentle mistress'; and asked Katherine if she had ever beheld a fairer

gentlewoman, praising the red and white of the old
man's cheeks, and comparing his eyes to two bright
stars; and again he addressed him, saying: 'Fair lovely
maid, once more good day to you!' and said to his wife:
'Sweet Kate, embrace her for her beauty's sake.' The
now completely vanquished Katharine quickly adopted
her husband's opinion, and made her speech in like sort
to the old gentleman, saying to him: 'Young budding
virgin, you are fair, and fresh, and sweet: whither are
you going, and where is your dwelling? Happy are
the parents of so fair a child.' 'Why, how now, Kate,'
said Petruchio; 'I hope you are not mad. This is a
man, old and wrinkled, faded and withered, and not a
maiden, as you say he is.' On this Katharine said:
'Pardon me, old gentleman; the sun has so dazzled my
eyes, that everything I look on seemeth green. Now I
perceive you are a reverend father: I hope you will
pardon me for my sad mistake.' 'Do, good old grand-
sire,' said Petruchio, 'and tell us which way you are
travelling. We shall be glad of your good company, if
you are going our way.' The old gentleman replied:
'Fair sir, and you my merry mistress, your strange encounter has much amazed me. My name is Vincentio,
and I am going to visit a son of mine who lives at Padua.'
Then Petruchio knew the old gentleman to be the father
of Lucentio, a young gentleman who was to be married
to Baptista's younger daughter, Bianca, and he made
Vincentio very happy, by telling him the rich marriage
his son was about to make: and they all journeyed on
plesaantly together till they came to Baptista's house,
where there was a large company assembled to celebrate
the wedding of Bianca and Lucentio, Baptista having
willingly consented to the marriage of Bianca when he
had got Katharine off his hands.

When they entered, Baptista welcomed them to the
wedding feast, and there was present also another newly
married pair.

Lucentio, Bianca's husband, and Hortensio, the other new married man, could not forbear sly jests, which seemed to hint at the shrewish disposition of Petruchio's wife, and these fond bridegrooms seemed high pleased with the mild tempers of the ladies they had chosen, laughing at Petruchio for his less fortunate choice. Petruchio took little notice of their jokes till the ladies were retired after dinner, and then he perceived Baptista himself joined in the laugh against him: for when Petruchio affirmed that his wife would prove more obedient than theirs, the father of Katharine said: 'Now, in good sadness, son Petruchio, I fear you have got the veriest shrew of all.' 'Well,' said Petruchio, 'I say no, and therefore for assurance that I speak the truth, let us each one send for his wife, and he whose wife is most obedient to come at first when she is sent for, shall win a wager which we will propose.' To this the other two husbands willingly consented, for they were quite confident that their gentle wives would prove more obedient than the headstrong Katharine; and they proposed a wager of twenty crowns, but Petruchio merrily said, he would lay as much as that upon his hawk or hound, but twenty times as much upon his wife. Lucentio and Hortensio raised the wager to a hundred crowns, and Lucentio first sent his servant to desire Bianca would come to him. But the servant returned, and said: 'Sir, my mistress sends you word she is busy and cannot come.' 'How,' said Petruchio, 'does she say she is busy and cannot come? Is that an answer for a wife?' Then they laughed at him, and said, it would be well if Katharine did not send him a worse answer. And now it was Hortensio's turn to send for his wife; and he said to his servant: 'Go, and entreat my wife to come to me.' 'Oh ho! entreat her!' said Petruchio. 'Nay, then, she needs must come.' 'I am afraid, sir,' said Hortensio, 'your wife will not be entreated.' But presently this civil husband looked a little blank, when the servant returned without his mistress; and he said to him: 'How now! Where is my wife?' 'Sir,' said the servant, 'my mistress says, you have some goodly jest in hand, and therefore she will not come. She bids you come to her.' 'Worse and worse!' said Petruchio; and then he sent his servant, saying: 'Sirrah, go to your mistress, and tell her I command her to come to me.' The company had scarcely time to think she would not obey this summons, when Baptista, all in amaze, exclaimed: 'Now, by my *holidame*, here comes Katharine!' and she entered, saying meekly to Petruchio: 'What is your will, sir, that you send for me?' 'Where is your sister and Hortensio's wife?' said he. Katharine replied: 'They sit conferring by the parlour fire.' 'Go, fetch them hither!' said Petruchio. Away went Katharine without reply to perform her husband's command. 'Here is a wonder,' said Lucentio, 'if you talk of a wonder.' 'And so it is,' said Hortensio; 'I marvel what it bodes.' 'Marry, peace it bodes,' said Petruchio, 'and love, and quiet life, and right supremacy; and, to be short, everything that is sweet and happy.' Katharine's father, overjoyed to see this reformation in his daughter, said: 'Now, fair befall thee, son Petruchio! you have won the wager, and I will add another twenty thousand crowns to her dowry, as if she were another daughter, for she is changed as if she had never been.' 'Nay,' said Petruchio, 'I will win the wager better yet, and show more signs of her new-built virtue and obedience.' Katharine now entering with the two ladies, he continued: 'See where she comes, and brings your froward wives as prisoners to her womanly persuasion. Katharine, that cap of yours does not become you; off with that bauble, and throw it under foot.' Katharine instantly took off her cap, and threw it down. 'Lord!' said Hortensio's wife, 'may I never have a cause to sigh till I am brought to such a silly pass!' And Bianca, she too said: 'Fie, what foolish duty call you this?' On this

Bianca's husband said to her: 'I wish your duty were as foolish too! The wisdom of your duty, fair Bianca, has cost me a hundred crowns since dinner-time.' 'The more fool you,' said Bianca, 'for laying on my duty.' 'Katharine,' said Petruchio, 'I charge you tell these headstrong women what duty they owe their lords and husbands.' And to the wonder of all present, the reformed shrewish lady spoke as eloquently in praise of the wifelike duty of obedience, as she had practised it implicitly in a ready submission to Petruchio's will. And Katharine once more became famous in Padua, not as heretofore, as Katharine the Shrew, but as Katharine the most obedient and duteous wife in Padua.

THE COMEDY OF ERRORS

THE states of Syracuse and Ephesus being at variance, there was a cruel law made at Ephesus, ordaining that if any merchant of Syracuse was seen in the city of Ephesus, he was to be put to death, unless he could pay a thousand marks for the ransom of his life.

Aegeon, an old merchant of Syracuse, was discovered in the streets of Ephesus, and brought before the duke, either to pay this heavy fine, or to receive sentence of death.

Aegeon had no money to pay the fine, and the duke, before he pronounced the sentence of death upon him, desired him to relate the history of his life, and to tell for what cause he had ventured to come to the city of Ephesus, which it was death for any Syracusan merchant to enter.

Aegeon said, that he did not fear to die, for sorrow had made him weary of his life, but that a heavier task could not have been imposed upon him than to relate the events of his unfortunate life. He then began his own history, in the following words:

'I was born at Syracuse, and brought up to the profession of a merchant. I married a lady, with whom I lived very happily, but being obliged to go to Epidamnum, I was detained there by my business six months, and then, finding I should be obliged to stay some time longer, I sent for my wife, who, as soon as she arrived, was brought to bed of two sons, and what was very strange, they were both so exactly alike, that it was impossible to distinguish the one from the other. At the same time that my wife was brought to bed of these twin boys, a poor woman in the inn where my wife lodged was brought to bed of two sons, and these twins were as much like each other as my two sons were. The parents of these children being exceeding poor, I bought the two boys, and brought them up to attend upon my sons.

'My sons were very fine children, and my wife was not a little proud of two such boys: and she daily wishing to return home, I unwillingly agreed, and in an evil hour we got on shipboard; for we had not sailed above a league from Epidamnum before a dreadful storm arose, which continued with such violence, that the sailors seeing no chance of saving the ship, crowded into the boat to save their own lives, leaving us alone in the ship, which we every moment expected would be destroyed by the fury of the storm.

'The incessant weeping of my wife, and the piteous complaints of the pretty babes, who, not knowing what to fear, wept for fashion, because they saw their mother weep, filled me with terror for them, though I did not for myself fear deaih; and all my thoughts were bent to contrive means for their safety. I tied my youngest son to the end of a small spare mast, such as seafaring men provide against storms; at the other end I bound the youngest of the twin slaves, and at the same time I directed my wife how to fasten the other children in like manner to another mast. She thus having the care of the two eldest children, and I of the two younger, we bound ourselves separately to these masts with the children; and but for this contrivance we had all been lost, for the ship split on a mighty rock, and was dashed in pieces; and we, clinging to these slender masts, were supported above the water, where I, having the care of two children, was unable to assist my wife, who with the other children was soon separated from me; but while they were yet in my sight, they were taken up by a boat of fishermen, from Corinth (as I supposed), and seeing them in safety, I had no care but to struggle with the wild sea-waves, to preserve my dear son and the youngest slave. At length we, in our turn, were taken up by a ship, and the sailors, knowing me, gave us kind welcome and assistance, and landed us in safety at Syracuse; but from that sad hour I have never known what became of my wife and eldest child.

'My youngest son, and now my only care, when he was eighteen years of age, began to be inquisitive after his mother and his brother, and often importuned me that he might take his attendant, the young slave, who had also lost his brother, and go in search of them: at length I unwillingly gave consent, for though I anxiously desired to hear tidings of my wife and eldest son, yet in sending my younger one to find them, I hazarded the loss of them also. It is now seven years since my son left me; five years have I passed in travelling through the world in search of him: I have been in farthest Greece, and through the bounds of Asia, and coasting homewards, I landed here in Ephesus, being unwilling to leave any place unsought that harbours men; but this day must end the story of my life, and happy should I think myself in my death, if I were assured my wife and sons were living.'

Here the hapless Aegeon ended the account of his misfortunes; and the duke, pitying this unfortunate father, who had brought upon himself this great peril by his love for his lost son, said, if it were not against the laws, which his oath and dignity did not permit him to alter, he would freely pardon him; yet, instead of dooming him to instant death, as the strict letter of the law required, he would give him that day to try if he could beg or borrow the money to pay the fine.

This day of grace did seem no great favour to Aegeon, for not knowing any man in Ephesus, there seemed to him but little chance that any stranger would lend or give him a thousand marks to pay the fine; and helpless and hopeless of any relief, he retired from the presence of the duke in the custody of a jailor.

Aegeon supposed he knew no person in Ephesus; but at the very time he was in danger of losing his life through the careful search he was making after his youngest son, that son and his eldest son also were both in the city of Ephesus.

Aegeon's sons, besides being exactly alike in face and person, were both named alike, being both called Antipholus, and the two twin slaves were also both named Dromio. Aegeon's youngest son, Antipholus of Syracuse, he whom the old man had come to Ephesus to seek, happened to arrive at Ephesus with his slave Dromio that very same day that Aegeon did; and he being also a merchant of Syracuse, he would have been in the same danger that his father was, but by good fortune he met a friend who told him the peril an old merchant of Syracuse was in, and advised him to pass for a merchant of Epidamnum; this Antipholus agreed to do, and he was sorry to hear one of his own countrymen was in this danger, but he little thought this old merchant was his own father.

The eldest son of Aegeon (who must be called Antipholus of Ephesus, to distinguish him from his brother Antipholus of Syracuse) had lived at Ephesus twenty years, and, being a rich man, was well able to have paid the money for the ransom of his father's life; but Antipholus knew nothing of his father, being so young when he was taken out of the sea with his mother by the fishermen that he only remembered he had been so preserved, but he had no recollection of either his father or his mother; the fishermen who took up this Antipholus and his mother and the young slave Dromio, having carried the two children away from her (to the great grief of that unhappy lady), intending to sell them.

Antipholus and Dromio were sold by them to duke Menaphon, a famous warrior, who was uncle to the duke of Ephesus, and he carried the boys to Ephesus when he went to visit the duke his nephew.

The duke of Ephesus taking a liking to young Antipholus, when he grew up, made him an officer in his army, in which he distinguished himself by his great bravery in the wars, where he saved the life of his patron the duke, who rewarded his merit by marrying him to Adriana, a rich lady of Ephesus; with whom he was living (his slave Dromio still attending him) at the time his father came there.

Antipholus of Syracuse, when he parted with his friend, who advised him to say he came from Epidamnum, gave his slave Dromio some money to carry to the inn where he intended to dine, and in the mean time he said he would walk about and view the city, and observe the manners of the people.

Dromio was a pleasant fellow, and when Antipholus was dull and melancholy he used to divert himself with the odd humours and merry jests of his slave, so that the freedoms of speech he allowed in Dromio were greater than is usual between masters and their servants.

When Antipholus of Syracuse had sent Dromio away, he stood awhile thinking over his solitary wanderings in search of his mother and his brother, of whom in no place where he landed could he hear the least tidings; and he said sorrowfully to himself: 'I am like a drop of water in the ocean, which seeking to find its fellow drop, loses itself in the wide sea. So I unhappily, to find a mother and a brother, do lose myself.'

While he was thus meditating on his weary travels, which had hitherto been so useless, Dromio (as he thought) returned. Antipholus, wondering that he came back so soon, asked him where he had left the money. Now it was not his own Dromio, but the twin-brother that lived with Antipholus of Ephesus, that he spoke to. The two Dromios and the two Antipholuses were still as much alike as Aegeon had said they were in their infancy; therefore no wonder Antipholus thought it was his own slave returned, and asked him why he came back so soon. Dromio replied: 'My mistress sent me to bid you come to dinner. The capon burns, and the pig falls from the spit, and the meat will be all cold if you do not come home.' 'These jests are out of season,' said Antipholus: 'where did you leave the money?' Dromio still answering, that his mistress had sent him to fetch Antipholus to dinner: 'What mistress?' said Antipholus. 'Why, your worship's wife, sir,' replied Dromio. Antipholus having no wife, he was very angry with Dromio, and said: 'Because I familiarly sometimes chat with you, you presume to jest with me in this free manner. I am not in a sportive humour now: where is the money? we being strangers here, how dare you trust so great a charge from your own custody?' Dromio hearing his master, as he thought him, talk of their being strangers, supposing Antipholus was jesting, replied merrily: 'I pray you, sir, jest as you sit at dinner. I had no charge but to fetch you home, to dine with my mistress and her sister.' Now Antipholus lost all patience, and beat Dromio, who ran home, and told his mistress that his master had refused to come to dinner, and said that he had no wife.

Adriana, the wife of Antipholus of Ephesus, was very angry when she heard that her husband said he had no wife; for she was of a jealous temper, and she said her husband meant that he loved another lady better than herself; and she began to fret, and say unkind words of jealousy and reproach of her husband; and her sister Luciana, who lived with her, tried in vain to persuade her out of her groundless suspicions.

Antipholus of Syracuse went to the inn, and found Dromio with the money in safety there, and seeing his own Dromio, he was going again to chide him for his free jests, when Adriana came up to him, and not doubting but it was her husband she saw, she began to reproach him for looking strange upon her (as well he might, never having seen this angry lady before); and then she told him how well he loved her before they were married, and that now he loved some other lady instead of her.

'How comes it now, my husband,' said she, 'O how comes it that I have lost your love?' 'Plead you to me, fair dame?' said the astonished Antipholus. It was in vain he told her he was not her husband, and that he had been in Ephesus but two hours; she insisted on his going home with her, and Antipholus as last, being unable to get away, went with her to his brother's house, and dined with Adriana and her sister, the one calling him husband, and the other brother, he, all amazed, thinking he must have been married to her in his sleep, or that he was sleeping now. And Dromio, who followed them, was no less surprised, for the cook-maid, who was his brother's wife, also claimed him for her husband.

While Antipholus of Syracuse was dining with his brother's wife, his brother, the real husband, returned home to dinner with his slave Dromio; but the servants would not open the door, because their mistress had ordered them not to admit any company; and when they repeatedly knocked, and said they were Antipholus and Dromio, the maids laughed at them, and said that Antipholus was at dinner with their mistress, and Dromio was in the kitchen; and though they almost knocked the door down, they could not gain admittance, and at last Antipholus went away very angry, and strangely surprised at hearing a gentleman was dining with his wife.

When Antipholus of Syracuse had finished his dinner, he was so perplexed at the lady's still persisting in calling him husband, and at hearing that Dromio had also been claimed by the cook-maid, that he left the house, as soon as he could find any pretence to get away; for though he was very much pleased with Luciana, the sister, yet the jealous-tempered Adriana he disliked very much, nor was Dromio at all better satisfied with his fair wife in the kitchen; therefore both master and man were glad to get away from their new wives as fast as they could.

The moment Antipholus of Syracuse had left the house, he was met by a goldsmith, who mistaking him, as Adriana had done, for Antipholus of Ephesus, gave him a gold chain, calling him by his name; and when Antipholus would have refused the chain, saying it did not belong to him, the goldsmith replied he made it by his own orders; and went away, leaving the chain in the hands of Antipholus, who ordered his man Dromio to get his things on board a ship, not choosing to stay in a place any longer, where he met with such strange adventures that he surely thought himself bewitched.

The goldsmith who had given the chain to the wrong Antipholus, was arrested immediately after for a sum of money he owed; and Antipholus, the married brother, to whom the goldsmith thought he had given the chain, happened to come to the place where the officer was arresting the goldsmith, who, when he saw Antipholus, asked him to pay for the gold chain he had just delivered to him, the price amounting to nearly the same sum as that for which he had been arrested. Antipholus denying the having received the chain, and the goldsmith persisting to declare that he had but a few minutes before given it to him, they disputed this matter a long time, both thinking they were right: for Antipholus knew the goldsmith never gave him the chain, and so like were the two brothers, the goldsmith was as certain he had delivered the chain into his hands, till at last the officer took the goldsmith away to prison for the debt he owed, and at the same time the goldsmith made the officer arrest Antipholus for the price of the chain; so that at the conclusion of their dispute, Antipholus and the merchant were both taken away to prison together.

As Antipholus was going to prison, he met Dromio of Syracuse, his brother's slave, and mistaking him for his own, he ordered him to go to Adriana his wife, and tell her to send the money for which he was arrested. Dromio wondering that his master should send him back to the strange house where he dined, and from which he had just before been in such haste to depart, did not dare to reply, though he came to tell his master the ship was ready to sail: for he saw Antipholus was in no humour to be jested with. Therefore he went away, grumbling within himself, that he must return to Adriana's house, 'Where,' said he, 'Dowsabel claims me for a husband: but I must go, for servants must obey their masters' commands.'

Adriana gave him the money, and as Dromio was returning, he met Antipholus of Syracuse, who was still in amaze at the surprising adventures he met with; for his brother being well known in Ephesus, there was hardly a man he met in the streets but saluted him as an old acquaintance: some offered him money which they said was owing to him, some invited him to come and see them, and some gave thanks for kindnesses they said he had done them, all mistaking him for his brother. A tailor showed him some silks he had bought for him, and insisted upon taking measure of him for some clothes.

Antipholus began to think he was among a nation of sorcerers and witches, and Dromio did not at all relieve his master from his bewildered thoughts, by asking him how he got free from the officer who was carrying him to prison, and giving him the purse of gold which Adriana had sent to pay the debt with. This talk of Dromio's of the arrest and of a prison, and of the money he had brought from Adriana, perfectly confounded Antipholus, and he said: 'This fellow Dromio is certainly distracted, and we wander here in illusions'; and quite terrified at his own confused thoughts, he cried out: 'Some blessed power deliver us from this strange place!'

And now another stranger came up to him, and she was a lady, and she too called him Antipholus, and told him he had dined with her that day, and asked him for a gold chain which she said he had promised to give her. Antipholus now lost all patience, and calling her a sorceress, he denied that he had ever promised her a chain, or dined with her, or had ever seen her face before that moment. The lady persisted in affirming he had dined with her, and had promised her a chain, which Antipholus still denying, she further said, that she had given him a valuable ring, and if he would not give her the gold chain, she insisted upon having her own ring again. On this Antipholus became quite frantic, and again calling her sorceress and witch, and denying all knowledge of her or her ring, ran away from her, leaving her astonished at his words and his wild looks, for nothing to her appeared more certain than that he had dined with her, and that she had given him a ring, in consequence of his promising to make her a present of a gold chain. But this lady had fallen into the same mistake the others had done, for she had taken him for his brother: the married Antipholus had done all the things she taxed this Antipholus with.

When the married Antipholus was denied entrance into his own house (those within supposing him to be already there), he had gone away very angry, believing it to be one of his wife's jealous freaks, to which she was very subject, and remembering that she had often falsely accused him of visiting other ladies, he, to be revenged on her for shutting him out of his own house, determined to go and dine with this lady, and she receiving him with great civility, and his wife having so highly offended him, Antipholus promised to give her a gold chain, which he had intended as a present for his wife; it was the same chain which the goldsmith by mistake had given to his brother. The lady liked so well the thoughts of having a fine gold chain, that she gave the married Antipholus a ring; which when, as she supposed (taking his brother for him), he denied, and said he did not know her, and left her in such a wild passion, she began to think he was certainly out of his senses; and presently she resolved to go and tell Adriana that her husband was mad. And while she was telling it to Adriana, he came, attended by the jailor (who allowed him to come home to get the money to pay the debt), for the purse of money, which Adriana had sent by Dromio, and he had delivered to the other Antipholus.

Adriana believed the story the lady told her of her husband's madness must be true, when he reproached her for shutting him out of his own house; and remembering how he had protested all dinner-time that he was not her husband, and had never been in Ephesus till that day, she had no doubt that he was mad; she therefore paid the jailor the money, and having discharged him, she ordered her servants to bind her husband with ropes, and had him conveyed into a dark room, and sent for a doctor to come and cure him of his madness: Antipholus all the while hotly exclaiming against this false accusation, which the exact likeness he bore to his brother had brought upon him. But his rage only the more confirmed them in the belief that he was mad; and Dromio persisting in the same story, they bound him also, and took him away along with his master.

Soon after Adriana had put her husband into confinement, a servant came to tell her that Antipholus and Dromio must have broken loose from their keepers, for that they were both walking at liberty in the next street. On hearing this, Adriana ran out to fetch him home, taking some people with her to secure her husband again; and her sister went along with her. When they came to the gates of a convent in their neighbourhood, there they saw Antipholus and Dromio, as they thought being again deceived by the likeness of the twin-brothers.

Antipholus of Syracuse was still beset with the perplexities this likeness had brought upon him. The chain which the goldsmith had given him was about his neck, and the goldsmith was reproaching him for denying that he had it, and refusing to pay for it, and Antipholus was protesting that the goldsmith freely gave him the chain in the morning, and that from that hour he had never seen the goldsmith again.

And now Adriana came up to him and claimed him as her lunatic husband, who had escaped from his keepers; and the men she brought with her were going to lay violent hands on Antipholus and Dromio; but they ran into the convent, and Antipholus begged the abbess to give him shelter in her house.

And now came out the lady abbess herself to inquire into the cause of this disturbance. She was a grave and venerable lady, and wise to judge of what she saw, and she would not too hastily give up the man who had sought protection in her house; so she strictly questioned the wife about the story she told of her husband's madness, and she said: 'What is the cause of this sudden distemper of your husband's? Has he lost his wealth at sea? Or is it the death of some dear friend that has disturbed his mind?' Adriana replied, that no such things as these had been the cause. 'Perhaps,' said the abbess, 'he has fixed his affections on some other lady than you his wife; and that has driven him to this state.' Adriana said she had long thought the love of some other lady was the cause of his frequent absences from home. Now it was not his love for another, but the teasing jealousy of his wife's temper, that often obliged Antipholus to leave his home; and (the abbess suspecting this from the vehemence of Adriana's manner) to learn the truth, she said: 'You should have reprehended him for this.' 'Why, so I did,' replied Adriana. 'Ay,' said the abbess, 'but perhaps not enough.' Adriana, willing to convince the abbess that she had said enough to Antipholus on this subject, replied: 'It was the constant subject of our conversation: in bed I would not let him sleep for speaking of it. At table I would not let him eat for speaking of it. When I was alone with him, I talked of nothing else; and in company I gave him frequent hints of it. Still all my talk was how vile and bad it was in him to love any lady better than me.'

The lady abbess, having drawn this full confession

from the jealous Adriana, now said: 'And therefore comes it that your husband is mad. The venomous clamour of a jealous woman is a more deadly poison than a mad dog's tooth. It seems his sleep was hindered by your railing; no wonder that his head is light: and his meat was sauced with your upbraidings; unquiet meals make ill digestions, and that has thrown him into this fever. You say his sports were disturbed by your brawls; being debarred from the enjoyment of society and recreation, what could ensue but dull melancholy and comfortless despair? The consequence is then, that your jealous fits have made your husband mad.'

Luciana would have excused her sister, saying, she always reprehended her husband mildly; and she said to her sister: 'Why do you hear these rebukes without answering them?' But the abbess had made her so plainly perceive her fault, that she could only answer: 'She has betrayed me to my own reproof.'

Adriana, though ashamed of her own conduct, still insisted on having her husband delivered up to her; but the abbess would suffer no person to enter her house, nor would she deliver up this unhappy man to the care of the jealous wife, determining herself to use gentle means for his recovery, and she retired into her house again, and ordered her gates to be shut against them.

During the course of this eventful day, in which so many errors had happened from the likeness the twin brothers bore to each other, old Aegeon's day of grace was passing away, it being now near sunset; and at sunset he was doomed to die, if he could not pay the money.

The place of his execution was near this convent, and here he arrived just as the abbess retired into the convent; the duke attending in person, that if any offered to pay the money, he might be present to pardon him.

Adriana stopped this melancholy procession, and cried out to the duke for justice, telling him that the abbess had refused to deliver up her lunatic husband to her care. While she was speaking, her real husband and his servant Dromio, who had got loose, came before the duke to demand justice, complaining that his wife had confined him on a false charge of lunacy; and telling in what manner he had broken his bands, and eluded the vigilance of his keepers. Adriana was strangely surprised to see her husband, when she thought he had been within the convent.

Aegeon, seeing his son, concluded this was the son who had left him to go in search of his mother and his brother; and he felt secure that his dear son would readily pay the money demanded for his ransom. He therefore spoke to Antipholus in words of fatherly affection, with joyful hope that he should now be released. But to the utter astonishment of Aegeon, his son denied all knowledge of him, as well he might, for this Antipholus had never seen his father since they were separated in the storm in his infancy; but while the poor old Aegeon was in vain endeavouring to make his son acknowledge him, thinking surely that either his griefs and the anxieties he had suffered had so strangely altered him that his son did not know him, or else that he was ashamed to acknowledge his father in his misery; in the midst of this perplexity, the lady abess and the other Antipholus and Dromio came out and the wondering Adriana saw two husbands and two Dromios standing before her.

And now these riddling errors, which had so perplexed them all, were clearly made out. When the duke saw the two Antipholuses and the two Dromios both so exactly alike, he at once conjectured aright of these seeming mysteries, for he remembered the story Aegeon had told him in the morning; and he said, these men must be the two sons of Aegeon and their twin slaves.

But now an unlooked-for joy indeed completed the history of Aegeon; and the tale he had in the morning told in sorrow, and under sentence of death, before the setting sun went down was brought to a happy conclusion, for the venerable lady abbess made herself known to be the long-lost wife of Aegeon, and the fond mother of the two Antipholuses.

When the fishermen took the eldest Antipholus and Dromio away from her, she entered a nunnery, and by her wise and virtuous conduct, she was at length made lady abbess of this convent, and in discharging the rites of hospitality to an unhappy stranger she had unknowingly protected her own son.

Joyful congratulations and affectionate greetings between these long separated parents and their children made them for a while forget that Aegeon was yet under sentence of death; but when they were become a little calm, Antipholus of Ephesus offered the duke the ransom money for his father's life; but the duke freely pardoned Aegeon, and would not take the money.   And the duke went with the abbess and her newly found husband and children into the convent, to hear this happy family discourse at leisure of the blessed ending of their adverse fortunes.   And the two Dromios' humble joy must not be forgotten; they had their congratulations and greetings too, and each Dromio pleasantly complimented his brother on his good looks, being well pleased to see his own person (as in a glass) show so handsome in his brother.

Adriana had so well profited by the good counsel of her mother-in-law, that she never after cherished unjust suspicions, or was jealous of her husband.

Antipholus of Syracuse married the fair Luciana, the sister of his brother's wife; and the good old Aegeon, with his wife and sons, lived at Ephesus many years. Nor did the unravelling of these perplexities so entirely remove every ground of mistake for the future, but that sometimes, to remind them of adventures past, comical blunders would happen, and the one Antipholus, and the one Dromio, be mistaken for the other, making altogether a pleasant and diverting Comedy of Errors.

MEASURE FOR MEASURE

IN the city of Vienna there once reigned a duke of such a mild and gentle temper, that he suffered his subjects to neglect the laws with impunity; and there was in particular one law, the existence of which was almost forgotten, the duke never having put it in force during his whole reign. This was a law dooming any man to the punishment of death, who should live with a woman that was not his wife; and this law, through the lenity of the duke, being utterly disregarded, the holy institution of marriage became neglected, and complaints were every day made to the duke by the parents of the young ladies in Vienna, that their daughters had been seduced from their protection, and were living as the companions of single men.

The good duke perceived with sorrow this growing evil among his subjects; but he thought that a sudden change in himself from the indulgence he had hitherto shown, to the strict severity requisite to check this abuse, would make his people (who had hitherto loved him) consider him as a tyrant; therefore he determined to absent himself a while from his dukedom, and depute another to the full exercise of his power, that the law against these dishonourable lovers might be put in effect, without giving offence by an unusual severity in his own person.

Angelo, a man who bore the reputation of a saint in Vienna for his strict and rigid life, was chosen by the duke as a fit person to undertake this important change; and when the duke imparted his design to lord Escalus, his chief counsellor, Escalus said: 'If any man in Vienna be of worth to undergo such ample grace and honour, it is lord Angelo.' And now the duke departed from Vienna under pretence of making a journey into Poland,

leaving Angelo to act as the lord deputy in his absence;
but the duke's absence was only a feigned one, for he
privately returned to Vienna, habited like a friar, with
the intent to watch unseen the conduct of the saintly-
seeming Angelo.

It happened just about the time that Angelo was invested with his new dignity, that a gentleman, whose
name was Claudio, had seduced a young lady from her
parents; and for this offence, by command of the new
lord deputy, Claudio was taken up and committed to
prison, and by virtue of the old law which had been so
long neglected, Angelo sentenced Claudio to be beheaded. Great interest was made for the pardon of
young Claudio, and the good old lord Escalus himself
interceded for him. 'Alas,' said he, 'this gentleman
whom I would save had an honourable father, for whose
sake I pray you pardon the young man's transgression.'
But Angelo replied: 'We must not make a scare-crow
of the law, setting it up to frighten birds of prey, till
custom, finding it harmless, makes it their perch, and
not their terror. Sir, he must die.'

Lucio, the friend of Claudio, visited him in the prison,
and Claudio said to him: 'I pray you, Lucio, do me this
kind service. Go to my sister Isabel, who this day
proposes to enter the convent of Saint Clare; acquaint
her with the danger of my state; implore her that she
make friends with the strict deputy; bid her go herself
to Angelo. I have great hopes in that; for she can discourse with prosperous art, and well she can persuade;
besides, there is a speechless dialect in youthful sorrow,
such as moves men.'

Isabel, the sister of Claudio, had, as he said, that day
entered her noviciate in the convent, and it was her
intent, after passing through her probation as a novice,
to take the veil, and she was inquiring of a nun concerning the rules of the convent, when they heard the voice
of Lucio, who, as he entered that religious house, said:

'Peace be in this place!' 'Who is it that speaks?' said Isabel. 'It is a man's voice,' replied the nun: 'Gentle Isabel, go to him, and learn his business; you may, I may not. When you have taken the veil, you must not speak with men but in the presence of the prioress; then if you speak you must not show your face, or if you show your face, you must not speak.' 'And have you nuns no further privileges?' said Isabel. 'Are not these large enough?' replied the nun. 'Yes, truly,' said Isabel: 'I speak not as desiring more, but rather wishing a more strict restraint upon the sisterhood, the votarists of Saint Clare.' Again they heard the voice of Lucio, and the nun said: 'He calls again. I pray you answer him.' Isabel then went out to Lucio, and in answer to his salutation, said: 'Peace and Prosperity! Who is it that calls?' Then Lucio, approaching her with reverence, said: 'Hail, virgin, if such you be, as the roses on your cheeks proclaim you are no less! can you bring me to the sight of Isabel, a novice of this place, and the fair sister to her unhappy brother Claudio?' 'Why her unhappy brother?' said Isabel, 'let me ask! for I am that Isabel, and his sister.' 'Fair and gentle lady,' he replied, 'your brother kindly greets you by me; he is in prison.' 'Woe is me! for what?' said Isabel. Lucio then told her, Claudio was imprisoned for seducing a young maiden. 'Ah,' said she, 'I fear it is my cousin Juliet.' Juliet and Isabel were not related, but they called each other cousin in remembrance of their school days' friendship; and as Isabel knew that Juliet loved Claudio, she feared she had been led by her affection for him into this transgression. 'She it is,' replied Lucio. 'Why then, let my brother marry Juliet,' said Isabel. Lucio replied that Claudio would gladly marry Juliet, but that the lord deputy had sentenced him to die for his offence; 'Unless,' said he, 'you have the grace by your fair prayer to soften Angelo, and that is my business between you and your poor brother.' 'Alas!' said Isabel, 'what poor ability is there in me to do him good? I doubt I have no power to move Angelo.' 'Our doubts are traitors,' said Lucio, 'and make us lose the good we might often win, by fearing to attempt it. Go to lord Angelo! When maidens sue, and kneel, and weep, men give like gods.' 'I will see what I can do,' said Isabel: 'I will but stay to give the prioress notice of the affair, and then I will go to Angelo. Command me to my brother: soon at night I will send him word of my success.'

Isabel hastened to the palace, and threw herself on her knees before Angelo, saying: 'I am a woful suitor to your honour, if it will please your honour to hear me.' 'Well, what is your suit?' said Angelo. She then made her petition in the most moving terms for her brother's life. But Angelo said: 'Maiden, there is no remedy; your brother is sentenced, and he must die.' 'O just, but severe law,' said Isabel: 'I had a brother then— Heaven keep your honour!' and she was about to depart. But Lucio, who had accompanied her, said: 'Give it not over so; return to him again, entreat him, kneel down before him, hang upon his gown. You are too cold; if you should need a pin, you could not with a more tame tongue desire it.' Then again Isabel on her knees implored for mercy. 'He is sentenced,' said Angelo: 'it is too late.' 'Too late!' said Isabel: 'Why, no: I that do speak a word may call it back again. Believe this, my lord, no ceremony that to great ones belongs, not the king's crown, nor the deputed sword, the marshal's truncheon, nor the judge's robe, becomes them with one half so good a grace as mercy does.' 'Pray you begone,' said Angelo. But still Isabel entreated; and she said: 'If my brother had been as you, and you as he, you might have slipped like him, but he, like you, would not have been so stern. I would to heaven I had your power, and you were Isabel. Should it then be thus? No, I would tell you what it were to be a judge, and what a prisoner.' 'Be content, fair maid!' said Angelo: 'it is the law, not I, condemns your brother. Were he my kinsman, my brother, or my son, it should be thus with him. He must die to-morrow.' 'To-morrow?' said Isabel; 'Oh, that is sudden: spare him, spare him; he is not prepared for death. Even for our kitchens we kill the fowl in season; shall we serve Heaven with less respect than we minister to our gross selves? Good, good, my lord, bethink you, none have died for my brother's offence, though many have committed it. So you would be the first that gives this sentence, and he the first that suffers it. Go to your own bosom, my lord; knock there, and ask your heart what it does know that is like my brother's fault; if it confess a natural guiltiness such as his is, let it not sound a thought against my brother's life!' Her last words more moved Angelo than all she had before said, for the beauty of Isabel had raised a guilty passion in his heart, and he began to form thoughts of dishonourable love, such as Claudio's crime had been; and the conflict in his mind made him to turn away from Isabel; but she called him back, saying: 'Gentle my lord, turn back; hark, how I will bribe you. Good my lord, turn back!' 'How, bribe me!' said Angelo, astonished that she should think of offering him a bribe. 'Ay,' said Isabel, 'with such gifts that Heaven itself shall share with you; not with golden treasures, or those glittering stones, whose price is either rich or poor as fancy values them, but with true prayers that shall be up to Heaven before sunrise,—prayers from preserved souls, from fasting maids whose minds are dedicated to nothing temporal.' 'Well, come to me to-morrow,' said Angelo. And for this short respite of her brother's life, and for this permission that she might be heard again, she left him with the joyful hope that she should at last prevail over his stern nature: and as she went away she said: 'Heaven keep your honour safe! Heaven save your honour!' Which when Angelo heard, he said within his heart: 'Amen, I would be saved from thee and from thy virtues': and then, affrighted at his own evil thoughts, he said: 'What is this? What is this? Do I love her, that I desire to hear her speak again, and feast upon her eyes? What is it I dream on? The cunning enemy of mankind, to catch a saint, with saints does bait the hook. Never could an immodest woman once stir my temper, but this virtuous woman subdues me quite. Even till now, when men were fond, I smiled and wondered at them.'

In the guilty conflict in his mind Angelo suffered more that night than the prisoner he had so severely sentenced; for in the prison Claudio was visited by the good duke, who, in his friar's habit, taught the young man the way to heaven, preaching to him the words of penitence and peace. But Angelo felt all the pangs of irresolute guilt: now wishing to seduce Isabel from the paths of innocence and honour, and now suffering remorse and horror for a crime as yet but intentional. But in the end his evil thoughts prevailed; and he who had so lately started at the offer of a bribe, resolved to tempt this maiden with so high a bribe, as she might not be able to resist, even with the precious gift of her dear brother's life.

When Isabel came in the morning, Angelo desired she might be admitted alone to his presence: and being there, he said to her, if she would yield to him her virgin honour and transgress even as Juliet had done with Claudio, he would give her her brother's life; 'For,' said he, 'I love you, Isabel.' 'My brother,' said Isabel, 'did so love Juliet, and yet you tell me he shall die for it.' 'But,' said Angelo, 'Claudio shall not die, if you will consent to visit me by stealth at night, even as Juliet left her father's house at night to come to Claudio.' Isabel, in amazement at his words, that he should tempt her to the same fault for which he passed sentence upon her brother, said: 'I would do as much for my poor brother as for myself; that is, were I under sentence of death, the impression of keen whips I would wear as rubies, and go to my death as to a bed that longing I had been sick for, ere I would yield myself up to this shame.' And then she told him, she hoped he only spoke these words to try her virtue. But he said: 'Believe me, on my honour, my words express my purpose.' Isabel, angered to the heart to hear him use the word Honour to express such dishonourable purposes, said: 'Ha! little honour to be much believed; and most pernicious purpose. I will proclaim thee, Angelo, look for it! Sign me a present pardon for my brother, or I will tell the world aloud what man thou art!' 'Who will believe you, Isabel?' said Angelo; 'my unsoiled name, the austereness of my life, my word vouched against yours, will outweigh your accusation. Redeem your brother by yielding to my will, or he shall die to-morrow. As for you, say what you can, my false will overweigh your true story. Answer me to-morrow.'

'To whom should I complain? Did I tell this, who would believe me?' said Isabel, as she went towards the dreary prison where her brother was confined. When she arrived there, her brother was in pious conversation with the duke, who in his friar's habit had also visited Juliet, and brought both these guilty lovers to a proper sense of their fault; and unhappy Juliet with tears and a true remorse confessed that she was more to blame than Claudio, in that she willingly consented to his dishonourable solicitations.

As Isabel entered the room where Claudio was confined, she said: 'Peace be here, grace, and good company!' 'Who is there?' said the disguised duke; 'come in; the wish deserves a welcome.' 'My business as a word or two with Claudio,' said Isabel. Then the duke left them together, and desired the provost, who had the charge of the prisoners, to place him where he might overhear their conversation.

'Now, sister, what is the comfort?' said Claudio.

Isabel told him he must prepare for death on the morrow. 'Is there no remedy?' said Claudio. 'Yes, brother,' replied Isabel, 'there is, but such a one, as if you consented to it would strip your honour from you, and leave you naked.' 'Let me know the point,' said Claudio. 'O, I do fear you, Claudio!' replied his sister; 'and I quake, lest you should wish to live, and more respect the trifling term of six or seven winters added to your life, then your perpetual honour! Do you dare to die? The sense of death is most in apprehension, and the poor beetle that we tread upon, feels a pang as great as when a giant dies.' 'Why do you give me this shame?' said Claudio. 'Think you I can fetch a resolution from flowery tenderness? If I must die, I will encounter darkness as a bride, and hug it in my arms.' 'There spoke my brother,' said Isabel; 'there my father's grave did utter forth a voice. Yes, you must die; yet would you think it, Claudio! this outward sainted deputy, if I would yield to him my virgin honour, would grant your life. O, were it but my life, I would lay it down for your deliverance as frankly as a pin!' 'Thanks, dear Isabel,' said Claudio. 'Be ready to die to-morrow,' said Isabel. 'Death is a fearful thing,' said Claudio. 'And shamed life a hateful,' replied his sister. But the thoughts of death now overcame the constancy of Claudio's temper, and terrors, such as the guilty only at their deaths do know, assailing him, he cried out: 'Sweet sister, let me live! The sin you do to save a brother's life, nature dispenses with the deed so far, that it becomes a virtue.' 'O faithless coward! O dishonest wretch!' said Isabel; 'would you preserve your life by your sister's shame? O fie, fie, fie! I thought, my brother, you had in you such a mind of honour, that had you twenty heads to render up on twenty blocks, you would have yielded them up all, before your sister should stoop to such dishonour.' 'Nay, hear me, Isabel!' said Claudio. But what he would have said in defence of his weakness, in desiring to live by the dishonour of his virtuous sister, was interrupted by the entrance of the duke; who said: 'Claudio, I have overheard what has passed between you and your sister. Angelo had never the purpose to corrupt her; what he said, has only been to make trial of her virtue. She having the truth of honour in her, has given him that gracious denial which he is most glad to receive. There is no hope that he will pardon you; therefore pass your hours in prayer, and make ready for death.' Then Claudio repented of his weakness, and said: 'Let me ask my sister's pardon! I am so out of love with life, that I will sue to be rid of it.' And Claudio retired, overwhelmed with shame and sorrow for his fault.

The duke being now alone with Isabel, commended her virtuous resolution, saying: 'The hand that made you fair, has made you good.' 'O,' said Isabel, 'how much is the good duke deceived in Angelo! if ever he return, and I can speak to him, I will discover his government.' Isabel knew not that she was even now making the discovery she threatened. The duke replied: 'That shall not be much amiss; yet as the matter now stands, Angelo will repel your accusation; therefore lend an attentive ear to my advisings. I believe that you may most righteously do a poor wronged lady a merited benefit, redeem your brother from the angry law, do no stain to your own most gracious person, and much please the absent duke, if peradventure he shall ever return to have notice of this business. Isabel said, she had a spirit to do anything he desired, provided it was nothing wrong. 'Virtue is bold, and never fearful,' said the duke: and then he asked her, if she had ever heard of Mariana, the sister of Frederick, the great soldier who was drowned at sea. 'I have heard of the lady,' said Isabel, 'and good words went with her name.' 'This lady,' said the duke, 'is the wife of Angelo; but her marriage dowry was on board the vessel in which her

brother perished, and mark how heavily this befell to
the poor gentlewoman! for, beside the loss of a most
noble and renowned brother, who in his love towards
her was ever most kind and natural, in the wreck of her
fortune she lost the affections of her husband, the well-
seeming Angelo; who pretending to discover some dishonour in this honourable lady (though the true cause
was the loss of her dowry) left her in tears, and dried
not one of them with his comfort. His unjust unkindness, that in all reason should have quenched her love,
has, like an impediment in the current, made it more
unruly, and Mariana loves her cruel husband with the
full continuance of her first affection.' The duke then
more plainly unfolded his plan. It was, that Isabel
should go to lord Angelo, and seemingly consent to
come to him as he desired at midnight; that by this means
she would obtain the promised pardon; and that Mariana
should go in her stead to the appointment, and pass
herself upon Angelo in the dark for Isabel. 'Nor,
gentle daughter,' said the feigned friar, 'fear you to do
this thing; Angelo is her husband, and to bring them
thus together is no sin.' Isabel being pleased with this
project, departed to do as he directed her; and he went
to apprise Mariana of their intention. He had before
this time visited this unhappy lady in his assumed character, giving her religious instruction and friendly consolation, at which times he had learned her sad story
from her own lips; and now she, looking upon him as a
holy man, readily consented to be directed by him in
this undertaking.

When Isabel returned from her interview with Angelo,
to the house of Mariana, where the duke had appointed
her to meet him, he said: 'Well met, and in good time;
what is the news from this good deputy?' Isabel
related the manner in which she had settled the affair.
'Angelo,' said she, 'has a garden surrounded with a
brick wall, on the western side of which is a vineyard,

and to that vineyard is a gate.' And then she showed
to the duke and Mariana two keys that Angelo had given
her; and she said: 'This bigger key opens the vineyard
gate; this other a little door which leads from the vineyard to the garden. There I have made my promise
at the dead of the night to call upon him, and have got
from him his word of assurance for my brother's life.
I have taken a due and wary note of the place; and with
whispering and most guilty diligence he showed me the
way twice over.' 'Are there no other tokens agreed
upon between you, that Mariana must observe?' said
the duke. 'No, none,' said Isabel, 'only to go when it
is dark. I have told him my time can be but short; for
I have made him think a servant comes along with me,
and that this servant is persuaded I come about my
brother.' The duke commended her discreet management, and she, turning to Mariana, said: 'Little have you
to say to Angelo, when you depart from him, but soft
and low: *Remember now my brother!*'

Mariana was that night conducted to the appointed
place by Isabel, who rejoiced that she had, as she supposed, by this device preserved both her brother's life
and her own honour. But that her brother's life was
safe the duke was not well satisfied, and therefore at
midnight he again repaired to the prison, and it was well
for Claudio that he did so, else would Claudio have that
night been beheaded; for soon after the duke entered
the prison, an order came from the cruel deputy, commanding that Claudio should be beheaded, and his head
sent to him by five o'clock in the morning. But the
duke persuaded the provost to put off the execution of
Claudio, and to deceive Angelo, by sending him the
head of a man who died that morning in the prison.
And to prevail upon the provost to agree to this, the
duke, whom still the provost suspected not to be anything more or greater than he seemed, showed the provost
a letter written with the duke's hand, and sealed with

his seal, which when the provost saw, he concluded this friar must have some secret order from the absent duke, and therefore he consented to spare Claudio; and he cut off the dead man's head, and carried it to Angelo.

Then the duke in his own name, wrote to Angelo a letter, saying, that certain accidents had put a stop to his journey, and that he should be in Vienna by the following morning, requiring Angelo to meet him at the entrance of the city, there to deliver up his authority; and the duke also commanded it to be proclaimed, that if any of his subjects craved redress for injustice, they should exhibit their petitions in the street on his first entrance into the city.

Early in the morning Isabel came to the prison, and the duke, who there awaited her coming, for secret reasons thought it good to tell her that Claudio was beheaded; therefore when Isabel inquired if Angelo had sent the pardon for her brother, he said: 'Angelo has released Claudio from this world. His head is off, and sent to the deputy.' The much-grieved sister cried out: 'O unhappy Claudio, wretched Isabel, injurious world, most wicked Angelo!' The seeming friar bid her take comfort, and when she was become a little calm, he acquainted her with the near prospect of the duke's return, and told her in what manner she should proceed in preferring her complaint against Angelo; and he bade her not fear if the cause should seem to go against her for a while. Leaving Isabel sufficiently instructed, he next went to Mariana, and gave her counsel in what manner she also should act.

Then the duke laid aside his friar's habit, and in his own royal robes, amidst a joyful crowd of his faithful subjects, assembled to greet his arrival, entered the city of Vienna, where he was met by Angelo, who delivered up his authority in the proper form. And there came Isabel, in the manner of a petitioner for redress, and said: 'Justice, most royal duke! I am the sister of one

Claudio, who, for the seducing a young maid, was
condemned to lose his head. I made my suit to lord
Angelo for my brother's pardon. It were needless to
tell your grace how I prayed and kneeled, how he repelled me, and how I replied; for this was of much
length. The vile conclusion I now begin with grief
and shame to utter. Angelo would not but by my
yielding to his dishonourable love release my brother;
and after much debate within myself, my sisterly remorse
overcame my virtue, and I did yield to him. But the
next morning betimes, Angelo, forfeiting his promise,
sent a warrant for my poor brother's head!' The duke
affected to disbelieve her story; and Angelo said that
grief for her brother's death, who had suffered by the
due course of the law, had disordered her senses. And
now another suitor approached, which was Mariana;
and Mariana said: 'Noble prince, as there comes light
from heaven, and truth from breath, as there is sense in
truth and truth in virtue, I am this man's wife, and my
good lord, the words of Isabel are false; for the night
she says was with Angelo, I passed that night with
him in the garden-house. As this is true, let me in
safety rise, or else for ever be fixed here a marble monument.' Then did Isabel appeal for the truth of what
she had said to friar Lodowick, that being the name the
duke had assumed in his disguise. Isabel and Mariana
had both obeyed his instructions in what they said, the
duke intending that the innocence of Isabel should be
plainly proved in that public manner before the whole
city of Vienna; but Angelo little thought that it was
from such a cause that they thus differed in their story,
and he hoped from their contradictory evidence to be
able to clear himself from the accusation of Isabel; and
he said, assuming the look of offended innocence: 'I
did but smile till now; but, good my lord, my patience
here is touched, and I perceive these poor distracted
women are but the instruments of some greater one,

who sets them on. Let me have way, my lord, to find
this practice out.' 'Ay, with all my heart,' said the
duke, 'and punish them to the height of your pleasure.
You, lord Escalus, sit with lord Angelo, lend him your
pains to discover this abuse; the friar is sent for that set
them on, and when he comes, do with your injuries as
may seem best in any chastisement. I for a while will
leave you, but stir not you, lord Angelo, till you have
well determined upon this slander.' The duke then
went away, leaving Angelo well pleased to be deputed
judge and umpire in his own cause. But the duke was
absent only while he threw off his royal robes and put
on his friar's habit; and in that disguise again he presented himself before Angelo and Escalus: and the
good old Escalus, who thought Angelo had been falsely
accused, said to the supposed friar: 'Come, sir, did
you set these women on to slander lord Angelo?' He
replied: 'Where is the duke? It is he who should hear
me speak.' Escalus said: 'The duke is in us, and we will
hear you. Speak justly.' 'Boldly at least,' retorted the
friar; and then he blamed the duke for leaving the cause
of Isabel in the hands of him she had accused, and spoke
so freely of many corrupt practices he had observed,
while, as he said, he had been a looker-on in Vienna,
that Escalus threatened him with the torture for speaking
words against the state, and for censuring the conduct
of the duke, and ordered him to be taken away to prison.
Then, to the amazement of all present, and to the utter
confusion of Angelo, the supposed friar threw off his
disguise, and they saw it was the duke himself.

The duke first addressed Isabel. He said to her:
'Come hither, Isabel. Your friar is now your prince,
but with my habit I have not changed my heart. I am
still devoted to your service.' 'O give me pardon,' said
Isabel, 'that I, your vassal, have employed and troubled
your unknown sovereignty.' He answered that he had
most need of forgiveness from her, for not having

prevented the death of her brother—for not yet would he tell her that Claudio was living; meaning first to make a further trial of her goodness. Angelo now knew the duke had been a secret witness of his bad deeds, and he said: 'O my dread lord, I should be guiltier than my guiltiness, to think I can be undiscernible, when I perceive your grace, like power divine, has looked upon my actions. Then, good prince, no longer prolong my shame, but let my trial be my own confession. Immediate sentence and death is all the grace I beg.' The duke replied: 'Angelo, thy faults are manifest. We do condemn thee to the very block where Claudio stooped to death; and with like haste away with him; and for his possessions, Mariana, we do instate and widow you withal, to buy a better husband.' 'O my dear lord,' said Mariana, 'I crave no other, nor no better man': and then on her knees, even as Isabel had begged the life of Claudio, did this kind wife of an ungrateful husband beg the life of Angelo; and she said: 'Gentle my liege, O good my lord! Sweet Isabel, take my part! Lend me your knees, and all my life to come I will lend you all my life, to do you service!' The duke said: 'Against all sense you importune her. Should Isabel kneel down to beg for mercy, her brother's ghost would break his paved bed, and take her hence in horror.' Still Mariana said: 'Isabel, sweet Isabel, do but kneel by me, hold up your hand, say nothing! I will speak all. They say, best men are moulded out of faults, and for the most part become much the better for being a little bad. So may my husband. Oh Isabel, will you not lend a knee?' The duke then said: 'He dies for Claudio.' But much pleased was the good duke, when his own Isabel, from whom he expected all gracious and honourable acts, kneeled down before him, and said: 'Most bounteous sir, look, if it please you, on this man condemned, as if my brother lived. I partly think a due sincerity governed his deeds, till he did look on me. Since it is so, let him not die! My brother had but justice, in that he did the thing for which he died.'

The duke, as the best reply he could make to this noble petitioner for her enemy's life, sending for Claudio from his prison-house, where he lay doubtful of his destiny, presented to her this lamented bother living; and he said to Isabel: 'Give me your hand, Isabel; for your lovely sake I pardon Claudio. Say you will be mine, and he shall be my brother too.' By this time lord Angelo perceived he was safe; and the duke, observing his eye to brighten up a little, said: 'Well, Angelo, look that you love your wife; her worth has obtained your pardon: joy to you, Mariana! Love her, Angelo! I have confessed her, and know her virtue.' Angelo remembered, when dressed in a little brief authority, how hard his heart had been, and felt how sweet is mercy.

The duke commanded Claudio to marry Juliet, and offered himself again to the acceptance of Isabel, whose virtuous and noble conduct had won her prince's heart. Isabel, not having taken the veil, was free to marry; and the friendly offices, while hid under the disguise of a humble friar, which the noble duke had done for her, made her with grateful joy accept the honour he offered her; and when she became duchess of Vienna, the excellent example of the virtuous Isabel worked such a complete reformation among the young ladies of that city, that from that time none ever fell into the transgression of Juliet, the repentant wife of the reformed Claudio. And the mercy-loving duke long reigned with his beloved Isabel, the happiest of husbands and of princes.

TWELFTH NIGHT; OR, WHAT YOU WILL

SEBASTIAN and his sister Viola, a young gentleman and lady of Messaline, were twins, and (which was accounted a great wonder) from their birth they so much resembled each other, that, but for the difference in their dress, they could not be known apart. They were both born in one hour, and in one hour they were both in danger of perishing, for they were shipwrecked on the coast of Illyria, as they were making a sea-voyage together. The ship, on board of which they were, split on a rock in a violent storm, and a very small number of the ship's company escaped with their lives. The captain of the vessel, with a few of the sailors that were saved, got to land in a small boat, and with them they brought Viola safe on shore, where she, poor lady, instead of rejoicing at her own deliverance, began to lament her brother's loss; but the captain comforted her with the assurance that he had seen her brother, when the ship split, fasten himself to a strong mast, on which, as long as he could see anything of him for the distance, he perceived him borne up above the waves. Viola was much consoled by the hope this account gave her, and now considered how she was to dispose of herself in a strange country, so far from home; and she asked the captain if he knew anything of Illyria. 'Ay, very well, madam,' replied the captain, 'for I was born not three hours' travel from this place.' 'Who governs here?' said Viola. The captain told her, Illyria was governed by Orsino, a duke noble in nature as well as dignity. Viola said, she had heard her father speak of Orsino, and that he was unmarried then. 'And he is so now,' said the captain; 'or was so very lately, for, but a month ago, I went from here, and then it was the general talk (as you know what great ones do, the people will prattle of) that Orsino sought the love of fair Olivia, a virtuous maid, the daughter of a count who died twelve months ago, leaving Olivia to the protection of her brother, who shortly after died also; and for the love of this dear brother, they say, she has abjured the sight and company of men.' Viola, who was herself in such a sad affliction for her brother's loss, wished she could live with this lady, who so tenderly mourned a brother's death. She asked the captain if he could introduce her to Olivia, saying she would willingly serve this lady. But he replied, this would be a hard thing to accomplish, because the lady Olivia would admit no person into her house since her brother's death, not even the duke himself. Then Viola formed another project in her mind, which was, in a man's habit, to serve the duke Orsino as a page. It was a strange fancy in a young lady to put on male attire, and pass for a boy; but the forlorn and unprotected state of Viola, who was young and of uncommon beauty, alone, and in a foreign land, must plead her excuse.

She having observed a fair behaviour in the captain, and that he showed a friendly concern for her welfare, entrusted him with her design, and he readily engaged to assist her. Viola gave him money, and directed him to furnish her with suitable apparel, ordering her clothes to be made of the same colour and in the same fashion her brother Sebastian used to wear, and when she was dressed in her manly garb, she looked so exactly like her brother that some strange errors happened by means of their being mistaken for each other; for, as will afterwards appear, Sebastian was also saved.

Viola's good friend, the captain, when he had transformed this pretty lady into a gentleman, having some interest at court, got her presented to Orsino under the feigned name of Cesario. The duke was wonderfully pleased with the address and graceful deportment of this handsome youth, and made Cesario one of his pages that being the office Viola wished to obtain: and she so well fulfilled the duties of her new station, and showed such a ready observance and faithful attachment to her lord, that she soon became his most favoured attendant. To Cesario Orsino confided the whole history of his love for the lady Olivia. To Cesario he told the long and unsuccessful suit he had made to one who, rejecting his long services, and despising his person, refused to admit him to her presence; and for the love of this lady who had so unkindly treated him, the noble Orsino, forsaking the sports of the field and all manly exercises in which he used to delight, passed his hours in ignoble sloth, listening to the effeminate sounds of soft music, gentle airs, and passionate love-songs; and neglecting the company of the wise and learned lords with whom he used to associate, he was now all day long conversing with young Cesario. Unmeet companion no doubt his grave courtiers thought Cesario was for their once noble master, the great duke Orsino.

It is a dangerous matter for young maidens to be the confidants of handsome young dukes; which Viola too soon found to her sorrow, for all that Orsino told her he endured for Olivia, she presently perceived she suffered for the love of him; and much it moved her wonder, that Olivia could be so regardless of this her peerless lord and master, whom she thought no one could behold without the deepest admiration, and she ventured gently to hint to Orsino, that it was a pity he should affect a lady who was so blind to his worthy qualities; and she said: 'If a lady were to love you, my lord, as you love Olivia (and perhaps there may be one who does), if you could not love her in return, would you not tell her that you could not love, and must she not be content with this answer?' But Orsino would not admit of this reasoning, for he denied that it was possible for any woman to love as he did. He said, no woman's heart was big enough to hold so much love, and therefore it was unfair to compare the love of any lady for him, to his love for Olivia. Now, though Viola had the utmost deference for the duke's opinions, she could not help thinking this was not quite true, for she thought her heart had full as much love in it as Orsino's had; and she said: 'Ah, but I know, my lord.' 'What do you know, Cesario?' said Orsino. 'Too well I know,' replied Viola, 'what love women may owe to men. They are as true of heart as we are. My father had a daughter loved a man, as I perhaps, were I a woman, should love your lordship.' 'And what is her history?' said Orsino. 'A blank, my lord,' replied Viola: 'she never told her love, but let concealment, like a worm in the bud, feed on her damask cheek. She pined in thought, and with a green and yellow melancholy, she sat like Patience on a monument, smiling at Grief.' The duke inquired if this lady died of her love, but to this question Viola returned an evasive answer; as probably she had feigned the story, to speak words expressive of the secret love and silent grief she suffered for Orsino.

While they were talking, a gentleman entered whom the duke had sent to Olivia, and he said: 'So please you, my lord, I might not be admitted to the lady, but by her handmaid she returned you this answer: Until seven years hence, the element itself shall not behold her face; but like a cloistress she will walk veiled, watering her chamber with her tears for the sad remembrance of her dead brother.' On hearing this, the duke exclaimed: 'O she that has a heart of this fine frame, to pay this debt of love to a dead brother, how will she love, when the rich golden shaft has touched her heart!' And then he said to Viola: 'You know, Cesario, I have told you all the secrets of my heart; therefore, good youth, go to Olivia's house. Be not denied access; stand at her doors, and tell her, there your fixed foot shall grow till you have audience.' 'And if I do speak to her, my lord, what then?' said Viola. 'O then,' replied Orsino, 'unfold to her the passion of my love. Make a long discourse to her of my dear faith. It will well become you to act my woes, for she will attend more to you than to one of graver aspect.'

Away then went Viola; but not willingly did she undertake this courtship, for she was to woo a lady to become a wife to him she wished to marry: but having undertaken the affair, she performed it with fidelity; and Olivia soon heard that a youth was at her door who insisted upon being admitted to her presence. 'I told him,' said the servant, 'that you were sick: he said he knew you were, and therefore he came to speak with you. I told him that you were asleep: he seemed to have a foreknowledge of that too, and said, that therefore he must speak with you. What is to be said to him, lady? for he seems fortified against all denial, and will speak with you, whether you will or no.' Olivia, curious to see who this peremptory messenger might be, desired he might be admitted; and throwing her veil over her face, she said she would once more hear Orsino's embassy, not doubting but that he came from the duke, by his importunity. Viola, entering, put on the most manly air she could assume, and affecting the fine courtier language of great men's pages, she said to the veiled lady: 'Most radiant, exquisite, and matchless beauty, I pray you tell me if you are the lady of the house; for I should be sorry to cast away my speech upon another; for besides that it is excellently well penned, I have taken great pains to learn it.' 'Whence come you, sir?' said Olivia. 'I can say little more than I have studied,' replied Viola; 'and that question is out of my part.' 'Are you a comedian?' said Olivia. 'No,' replied Viola; 'and yet I am not that which I play'; meaning that she, being a woman, feigned herself to be a man. And again she asked Olivia if she were the lady of the house. Olivia said she was; and then Viola, having more curiosity to see her rival's features, than haste to deliver her master's message, said: 'Good madam, let me see your face.' With this bold request Olivia was not averse to comply; for this haughty beauty, whom the duke Orsino had loved so long in vain, at first sight conceived a passion for the supposed page, the humble Cesario.

When Viola asked to see her face, Olivia said: 'Have you any commission from your lord and master to negotiate with my face?' And then, forgetting her determination to go veiled for seven long years, she drew aside her veil, saying: 'But I will draw the curtain and show the picture. Is it not well done?' Viola replied: 'It is beauty truly mixed; the red and white upon your cheeks is by Nature's own cunning hand laid on. You are the most cruel lady living, if you will lead these graces to the grave, and leave the world no copy.' 'O, sir,' replied Olivia, 'I will not be so cruel. The world may have an inventory of my beauty. As, *item*, two lips, indifferent red; *item*, two grey eyes, with lids to them; one neck; one chin; and so forth. Were you sent here to praise me?' Viola replied: 'I see what you are: you are too proud, but you are fair. My lord and master loves you. O such a love could but be recompensed, though you were crowned the queen of beauty: for Orsino loves you with adoration and with tears, with groans that thunder love, and sighs of fire.' 'Your lord,' said Olivia, 'knows well my mind. I cannot love him; yet I doubt not he is virtuous; I know him to be noble and of high estate, of fresh and spotless youth. All voices proclaim him learned, courteous, and valiant; yet I cannot love him, he might have taken his answer long ago.' 'If I did love you as my master does,' said Viola, 'I would make me a willow cabin at your gates, and call upon your name, I would write complaining sonnets on Olivia, and sing them in the dead of the night; your name should sound among the hills, and I would make Echo, the babbling gossip of the air, cry out *Olivia*. O you should not rest between the elements of earth and air, but you should pity me.' 'You might do much,' said Olivia: 'what is your parentage?' Viola replied: 'Above my fortunes, yet my state is well. I am a gentleman.' Olivia now reluctantly dismissed Viola, saying: 'Go to your master, and tell him, I cannot love him. Let him send no more, unless perchance you come again to tell me how he takes it.' And Viola departed, bidding the lady farewell by the name of Fair Cruelty. When she was gone, Olivia repeated the words, *Above my fortunes, yet my state is well. I am a gentleman.* And she said aloud: 'I will be sworn he is; his tongue, his face, his limbs, action, and spirit, plainly show he is a gentleman.' And then she wished Cesario was the duke; and perceiving the fast hold he had taken on her affections, she blamed herself for her sudden love: but the gentle blame which people lay upon their own faults has no deep root; and presently the noble lady Olivia so far forgot the inequality between her fortunes and those of this seeming page, as well as the maidenly reserve which is the chief ornament of a lady's character, that she resolved to court the love of young Cesario, and sent a servant after him with a diamond ring, under the pretence that he had left it with her as a present from Orsino. She hoped by thus artfully making Cesario a present of the ring, she should give him some intimation of her design; and truly it did make Viola suspect; for knowing that Orsino had sent no ring by her, she began to recollect that Olivia's looks and manner were expressive of admiration, and she presently guessed her master's mistress had fallen in love with her. 'Alas,' said she, 'the poor lady might as well love a dream. Disguise I see is wicked, for it has caused Olivia to breathe as fruitless sighs for me as I do for Orsino.'

Viola returned to Orsino's palace, and related to her lord the ill success of the negotiation, repeating the command of Olivia, that the duke should trouble her no more.   Yet still the duke persisted in hoping that the gentle Cesario would in time be able to persuade her to show some pity, and therefore he bade him he should go to her again the next day.   In the meantime, to pass away the tedious interval, he commanded a song which he loved to be sung; and he said: 'My good Cesario, when I heard that song last night, methought it did relieve my passion much.   Mark it, Cesario, it is old and plain.   The spinsters and the knitters when they sit in the sun, and the young maids that weave their thread with bone, chant this song.   It is silly, yet I love it, for it tells of the innocence of love in the old times.'

SONG

Come away, come away, Death,
    And in sad cypress let me be laid;
Fly away, fly away, breath,
    I am slain by a fair cruel maid.
My shroud of white stuck all with yew, O prepare it!
My part of death no one so true did share it.

    Not a flower, not a flower sweet,
        On my black coffin let there be strewn:
    Not a friend, not a friend greet
        My poor corpse, where my bones shall be thrown
A thousand thousand sighs to save, lay me O where
Sad true lover never find my grave, to weep there!

Viola did not fail to mark the words of the old song, which in such true simplicity described the pangs of unrequited love, and she bore testimony in her countenance of feeling what the song expressed.   Her sad looks were observed by Orsino, who said to her: 'My life upon it, Cesario, though you are so young, your eye has looked upon some face that it loves: has it not, boy?'
'A little, with your leave,' replied Viola.   'And what kind of woman, and of what age is she?' said Orsino.
'Of your age and of your complexion, my lord,' said Viola; which made the duke smile to hear this fair young boy loved a woman so much older than himself, and

of a man's dark complexion; but Viola secretly meant Orsino, and not a woman like him.

When Viola made her second visit to Olivia, she found no difficulty in gaining access to her. Servants soon discover when their ladies delight to converse with hand-some young messengers; and the instant Viola arrived, the gates were thrown wide open, and the duke's page was shown into Olivia's apartment with great respect; and when Viola told Olivia that she was come once more to plead in her lord's behalf, this lady said: 'I desired you never to speak of him again; but if you would undertake another suit, I had rather hear you solicit, than music from the spheres.' This was pretty plain speaking, but Olivia soon explained herself still more plainly, and openly confessed her love; and when she saw displeasure with perplexity expressed in Viola's face, she said: 'O what a deal of scorn looks beautiful in the contempt and anger of his lip! Cesario, by the roses of the spring, by maidhood, honour, and by truth, I love you so, that, in spite of your pride, I have neither wit nor reason to conceal my passion.' But in vain the lady wooed; Viola hastened from her presence, threaten-ing never more to come to plead Orsino's love; and all the reply she made to Olivia's fond solicitation was, a declaration of a resolution *Never to love any woman*.

No sooner had Viola left the lady than a claim was made upon her valour. A gentleman, a rejected suitor of Olivia, who had learned how that lady had favoured the duke's messenger, challenged him to fight a duel. What should poor Viola do, who, though she carried a manlike outside, had a true woman's heart, and feared to look on her own sword?

When she saw her formidable rival advancing towards her with his sword drawn, she began to think of con-fessing that she was a woman; but she was relieved at once from her terror, and the shame of such a discovery, by a stranger that was passing by, who made up to

She began to think of confessing that she was a woman

them, and as if he had been long known to her, and were
her dearest friend, said to her opponent: 'If this young
gentleman has done offence, I will take the fault on me;
and if you offend him, I will for his sake defy you.'
Before Viola had time to thank him for his protection,
or to inquire the reason of his kind interference, her
new friend met with an enemy where his bravery was
of no use to him; for the officers of justice coming up
in that instant, apprehended the stranger in the duke's
name, to answer for an offence he had committed some
years before: and he said to Viola: 'This comes with
seeking you': and then he asked her for a purse, saying:
'Now my necessity makes me ask for my purse, and it
grieves me much more for what I cannot do for you,
than for what befalls myself. You stand amazed, but
be of comfort.' His words did indeed amaze Viola,
and she protested she knew him not, nor had ever
received a purse from him; but for the kindness he had
just shown her, she offered him a small sum of money,
being nearly the whole she possessed. And now the
stranger spoke severe things, charging her with ingratitude and unkindness. He said: 'This youth, whom
you see here, I snatched from the jaws of death, and for
his sake alone I came to Illyria, and have fallen into this
danger.' But the officers cared little for hearkening
to the complaints of their prisoner, and they hurried
him off, saying: 'What is that to us?' And as he was
carried away, he called Viola by the name of Sebastian,
reproaching the supposed Sebastian for disowning his
friend, as long as he was within hearing. When Viola
heard herself called Sebastian, though the stranger was
taken away too hastily for her to ask an explanation, she
conjectured that this seeming mystery might arise from
her being mistaken for her brother; and she began to
cherish hopes that it was her brother whose life this
man said he had preserved. And so indeed it was.
The stranger, whose name was Antonio, was a

sea-captain. He had taken Sebastian up into his ship, when, almost exhausted with fatigue, he was floating on the mast to which he had fastened himself in the storm. Antonio conceived such a friendship for Sebastian, that he resolved to accompany him whithersoever he went; and when the youth expressed a curiosity to visit Orsino's court, Antonio, rather than part from him, came to Illyria, though he knew, if his person should be known there, his life would be in danger, because in a sea-fight he had once dangerously wounded the duke Orsino's nephew. This was the offence for which he was now made a prisoner.

Antonio and Sebastian had landed together but a few hours before Antonio met Viola. He had given his purse to Sebastian, desiring him to use it freely if he saw anything he wished to purchase, telling him he would wait at the inn, while Sebastian went to view the town; but Sebastian not returning at the time appointed, Antonio had ventured out to look for him, and Viola being dressed the same, and in face so exactly resembling her brother, Antonio drew his sword (as he thought) in defence of the youth he had saved, and when Sebastian (as he supposed) disowned him, and denied him his own purse, no wonder he accused him of ingratitude.

Viola, when Antonio was gone, fearing a second invitation to fight, slunk home as fast as she could. She had not been long gone, when her adversary thought he saw her return; but it was her brother Sebastian, who happened to arrive at this place, and he said: 'Now, sir, have I met with you again? There's for you'; and struck him a blow. Sebastian was no coward; he returned the blow with interest, and drew his sword.

A lady now put a stop to this duel, for Olivia came out of the house, and she too mistaking Sebastian for Cesario, invited him to come into her house, expressing much sorrow at the rude attack he had met with. Though Sebastian was as much surprised at the courtesy of this lady as at the rudeness of his unknown foe, yet he went very willingly into the house, and Olivia was delighted to find Cesario (as she thought him) become more sensible of her attentions; for though their features were exactly the same, there was none of the contempt and anger to be seen in his face, which she had complained of when she told her love to Cesario.

Sebastian did not at all object to the fondness the lady lavished on him. He seemed to take it in very good part, yet he wondered how it had come to pass, and he was rather inclined to think Olivia was not in her right senses; but perceiving that she was mistress of a fine house, and that she ordered her affairs and seemed to govern her family discreetly, and that in all but her sudden love for him she appeared in the full possession of her reason, he well approved of the courtship; and Olivia finding Cesario in this good humour, and fearing he might change his mind, proposed that, as she had a priest in the house, they should be instantly married. Sebastian assented to this proposal; and when the marriage ceremony was over, he left his lady for a short time, intending to go and tell his friend Antonio the good fortune that he had met with. In the meantime Orsino came to visit Olivia: and at the moment he arrived before Olivia's house, the officers of justice brought their prisoner, Antonio, before the duke. Viola was with Orsino, her master; and when Antonio saw Viola, whom he still imagined to be Sebastian, he told the duke in what manner he had rescued this youth from the perils of the sea; and after fully relating all the kindness he had really shown to Sebastian, he ended his complaint with saying, that for three months, both day and night, this ungrateful youth had been with him. But now the lady Olivia coming forth from her house, the duke could no longer attend to Antonio's story; and he said: 'Here comes the countess: now Heaven walks on earth! but for thee, fellow, thy words are madness. Three months has this youth attended on me': and then he ordered Antonio to be taken aside. But Orsino's heavenly countess soon gave the duke cause to accuse Cesario as much of ingratitude as Antonio had done, for all the words he could hear Olivia speak were words of kindness to Cesario: and when he found his page had obtained this high place in Olivia's favour, he threatened him with all the terrors of his just revenge; and as he was going to depart, he called Viola to follow him, saying: 'Come, boy, with me. My thoughts are ripe for mischief.' Though it seemed in his jealous rage he was going to doom Viola to instant death, yet her love made her no longer a coward, and she said she would most joyfully suffer death to give her master ease. But Olivia would not so lose her husband, and she cried: 'Where goes my Cesario?' Viola replied: 'After him I love more than my life.' Olivia, however, prevented their departure by loudly proclaiming that Cesario was her husband, and sent for the priest, who declared that not two hours had passed since he had married the lady Olivia to this young man. In vain Viola protested she was not married to Olivia; the evidence of that lady and the priest made Orsino believe that his page had robbed him of the treasure he prized above his life. But thinking that it was past recall, he was bidding farewell to his faithless mistress, and the *young dissembler*, her husband, as he called Viola, warning her never to come in his sight again, when (as it seemed to them) a miracle appeared! for another Cesario entered, and addressed Olivia as his wife. This new Cesario was Sebastian, the real husband of Olivia; and when their wonder had a little ceased at seeing two persons with the same face, the same voice, and the same habit, the brother and sister began to question each other; for Viola could scarce be persuaded that her brother was living, and Sebastian knew not how to account for the sister he supposed drowned being found in the habit of a young man.

But Viola presently acknowledged that she was indeed Viola, and his sister, under that disguise.

When all the errors were cleared up which the extreme likeness between this twin brother and sister had occasioned, they laughed at the lady Olivia for the pleasant mistake she had made in falling in love with a woman; and Olivia showed no dislike to her exchange, when she found she had wedded the brother instead of the sister.

The hopes of Orsino were for ever at an end by this marriage of Olivia, and with his hopes, all his fruitless love seemed to vanish away, and all his thoughts were fixed on the event of his favourite, young Cesario, being changed into a fair lady. He viewed Viola with great attention, and he remembered how very handsome he had always thought Cesario was, and he concluded she would look very beautiful in a woman's attire; and then he remembered how often she had said *she loved him*, which at the time seemed only the dutiful expressions of a faithful page; but now he guessed that something more was meant, for many of her pretty sayings, which were like riddles to him, came now into his mind, and he no sooner remembered all these things than he resolved to make Viola his wife; and he said to her (he still could not help calling her *Cesario* and *boy*): 'Boy, you have said to me a thousand times that you should never love a woman like to me, and for the faithful service you have done for me so much beneath your soft and tender breeding, and since you have called me master so long, you shall now be your master's mistress, and Orsino's true duchess.'

Olivia, perceiving Orsino was making over that heart, which she had so ungraciously rejected, to Viola, invited them to enter her house, and offered the assistance of the good priest, who had married her to Sebastian in the morning, to perform the same ceremony in the remaining part of the day for Orsino and Viola. Thus the twin brother and sister were both wedded on the same day: the storm and shipwreck, which had separated them, being the means of bringing to pass their high and mighty fortunes. Viola was the wife of Orsino, the duke of Illyria, and Sebastian the husband of the rich and noble countess, the lady Olivia.

TIMON OF ATHENS

TIMON, a lord of Athens, in the enjoyment of a princely fortune, affected a humour of liberality which knew no limits. His almost infinite wealth could not flow in so fast, but he poured it out faster upon all sorts and degrees of people. Not the poor only tasted of his bounty, but great lords did not disdain to rank themselves among his dependants and followers. His table was resorted to by all the luxurious feasters, and his house was open to all comers and goers at Athens. His large wealth combined with his free and prodigal nature to subdue all hearts to his love; men of all minds and dispositions tendered their services to lord Timon, from the glass-faced flatterer, whose face reflects as in a mirror the present humour of his patron, to the rough and unbending cynic, who affecting a contempt of men's persons, and an indifference to worldly things, yet could not stand out against the gracious manners and munificent soul of lord Timon, but would come (against his nature) to partake of his royal entertainments, and return most rich in his own estimation if he had received a nod or a salutation from Timon.

If a poet had composed a work which wanted a re-commendatory introduction to the world, he had no more to do but to dedicate it to lord Timon, and the poem was sure of sale, besides a present purse from the patron, and daily access to his house and table. If a painter had a picture to dispose of, he had only to take it to lord Timon, and pretend to consult his taste as to the merits of it; nothing more was wanting to persuade the liberal-hearted lord to buy it. If a jeweller had a stone of price, or a mercer rich costly stuffs, which for their costliness lay upon his hands, lord Timon's house was a ready mart always open, where they might get

off their wares or their jewellery at any price, and the
good-natured lord would thank them into the bargain,
as if they had done him a piece of courtesy in letting
him have the refusal of such precious commodities.
So that by this means his house was thronged with
superfluous purchases, of no use but to swell uneasy
and ostentatious pomp; and his person was still more
inconveniently beset with a crowd of these idle visitors,
lying poets, painters, sharking tradesmen, lords, ladies,
needy courtiers, and expectants, who continually filled
his lobbies, raining their fulsome flatteries in whispers
in his ears, sacrificing to him with adulation as to a
God, making sacred the very stirrup by which he mounted
his horse, and seeming as though they drank the free
air but through his permission and bounty.

Some of these daily dependants were young men of
birth, who (their means not answering to their extrava-
gance) had been put in prison by creditors, and redeemed
thence by lord Timon; these young prodigals thenceforward fastened upon his lordship, as if by common
sympathy he were necessarily endeared to all such spend-
thrifts and loose livers, who, not being able to follow
him in his wealth, found it easier to copy him in prodigality and copious spending of what was their own.
One of these flesh-flies was Ventidius, for whose debts,
unjustly contracted, Timon but lately had paid down
the sum of five talents.

But among this confluence, this great flood of visitors,
none were more conspicuous than the makers of presents
and givers of gifts. It was fortunate for these men if
Timon took a fancy to a dog or a horse, or any piece of
cheap furniture which was theirs. The thing so praised,
whatever it was, was sure to be sent the next morning
with the compliments of the giver for lord Timon's
acceptance, and apologies for the unworthiness of the
gift; and this dog or horse, or whatever it might be,
did not fail to produce from Timon's bounty, who would

not be outdone in gifts, perhaps twenty dogs or horses, certainly presents of far richer worth, as these pretended donors knew well enough, and that their false presents were but the putting out of so much money at large and speedy interest. In this way lord Lucius had lately sent to Timon a present of four milk-white horses, trapped in silver, which this cunning lord had observed Timon upon some occasion to commend; and another lord, Lucullus, had bestowed upon him in the same pretended way of free gift a brace of greyhounds, whose make and fleetness Timon had been heard to admire; these presents the easy-hearted lord accepted without suspicion of the dishonest views of the presenters; and the givers of course were rewarded with some rich return, a diamond or some jewel of twenty times the value of their false and mercenary donation.

Sometimes these creatures would go to work in a more direct way, and with gross and palpable artifice, which yet the credulous Timon was too blind to see, would affect to admire and praise something that Timon possessed, a bargain that he had bought, or some late purchase, which was sure to draw from this yielding and soft-hearted lord a gift of the thing commended, for no service in the world done for it but the easy expense of a little cheap and obvious flattery. In this way Timon but the other day had given to one of these mean lords the bay courser which he himself rode upon, because his lordship had been pleased to say that it was a handsome beast and went well; and Timon knew that no man ever justly praised what he did not wish to possess. For lord Timon weighed his friends' affection with his own, and so fond was he of bestowing, that he could have dealt kingdoms to these supposed friends, and never have been weary.

Not that Timon's wealth all went to enrich these wicked flatterers; he could do noble and praiseworthy actions; and when a servant of his once loved the daughter of a rich Athenian, but could not hope to obtain her by reason that in wealth and rank the maid was so far above him, lord Timon freely bestowed upon his servant three Athenian talents, to make his fortune equal with the dowry which the father of the young maid demanded of him who should be her husband. But for the most part, knaves and parasites had the command of his fortune, false friends whom he did not know to be such, but, because they flocked around his person, he thought they must needs love him; and because they smiled and flattered him, he thought surely that his conduct was approved by all the wise and good. And when he was feasting in the midst of all these flatterers and mock friends, when they were eating him up, and draining his fortunes dry with large draughts of richest wines drunk to his health and prosperity, he could not perceive the difference of a friend from a flatterer, but to his deluded eyes (made proud with the sight) it seemed a precious comfort to have so many like brothers commanding one another's fortunes (though it was his own fortune which paid all the costs), and with joy they would run over at the spectacle of such, as it appeared to him, truly festive and fraternal meeting.

But while he thus outwent the very heart of kindness, and poured out his bounty, as if Plutus, the god of gold, had been but his steward; while thus he proceeded without care or stop, so senseless of expense that he would neither inquire how he could maintain it, nor cease his wild flow of riot; his riches, which were not infinite, must needs melt away before a prodigality which knew no limits. But who should tell him so? his flatterers? they had no interest in shutting his eyes. In vain did his honest steward Flavius try to represent to him his condition, laying his accounts before him, begging of him, praying of him, with an importunity that on any other occasion would have been unmannerly in a servant, beseeching him with tears to look into the state of his affairs. Timon would still put him off, and turn the discourse to something else; for nothing is so deaf to remonstrance as riches turned to poverty, nothing is so unwilling to believe its situation, nothing so incredulous to its own true state, and hard to give credit to a reverse. Often had this good steward, this honest creature, when all the rooms of Timon's great house have been choked up with riotous feeders at his master's cost, when the floors have wept with drunken spilling of wine, and every apartment has blazed with lights and resounded with music and feasting, often had he retired by himself to some solitary spot, and wept faster than the wine ran from the wasteful casks within, to see the mad bounty of his lord, and to think, when the means were gone which brought him praises from all sorts of people, how quickly the breath would be gone of which the praise was made; praises won in feasting would be lost in feasting, and at one cloud of winter-showers these flies would disappear.

But now the time was come that Timon could shut his ears no longer to the representations of this faithful steward. Money must be had; and when he ordered Flavius to sell some of his land for that purpose, Flavius informed him, what he had in vain endeavoured at several times before to make him listen to, that most of his land was already sold or forfeited, and that all he possessed at present was not enough to pay the one half of what he owed. Struck with wonder at this presentation, Timon hastily replied: 'My lands extend from Athens to Lacedaemon.' 'O my good lord,' said Flavius, 'the world is but a world, and has bounds; were it all yours to give in a breath, how quickly were it gone!'

Timon consoled himself that no villanous bounty had yet come from him, that if he had given his wealth away unwisely, it had not been bestowed to feed his vices, but to cherish his friends; and he made the kind-hearted steward (who was weeping) to take comfort in the assurance that his master could never lack means, while he had so many noble friends; and this infatuated lord persuaded himself that he had nothing to do but to send and borrow, to use every man's fortune (that had ever tasted his bounty) in this extremity, as freely as his own. Then with a cheerful look, as if confident of the trial, he severally despatched messengers to lord Lucius, to lords Lucullus and Sempronius, men upon whom he had lavished his gifts in past times without measure or moderation; and to Ventidius, whom he had lately released out of prison by paying his debts, and who, by the death of his father, was now come into the possession of an ample fortune, and well enabled to requite Timon's courtesy: to request of Ventidius the return of those five talents which he had paid for him, and of each of those noble lords the loan of fifty talents; nothing doubting that their gratitude would supply his wants (if he needed it) to the amount of five hundred times fifty talents.

Lucullus was the first applied to. This mean lord had been dreaming overnight of a silver bason and cup, and when Timon's servant was announced, his sordid mind suggested to him that this was surely a making out of his dream, and that Timon had sent him such a present: but when he understood the truth of the matter, and that Timon wanted money, the quality of his faint and watery friendship showed itself, for with many protestations he vowed to the servant that he had long foreseen the ruin of his master's affairs, and many a time had he come to dinner to tell him of it, and had come again to supper to try to persuade him to spend less, but he would take no counsel nor warning by his coming: and true it was that he had been a constant attender (as he said) at Timon's feasts, as he had in greater things tasted his bounty; but that he ever came with that intent, or gave good counsel or reproof to Timon, was a base unworthy lie, which he suitably followed up with meanly offering the servant a bribe, to go home to his master and tell him that he had not found Lucullus at home.

As little success had the messenger who was sent to lord Lucius. This lying lord, who was full of Timon's meat, and enriched almost to bursting with Timon's costly presents, when he found the wind changed, and the fountain of so much bounty suddenly stopped, at first could hardly believe it; but on its being confirmed, he affected great regret that he should not have it in his power to serve lord Timon, for unfortunately (which was a base falsehood) he had made a great purchase the day before, which had quite disfurnished him of the means at present, the more beast he, he called himself, to put it out of his power to serve so good a friend; and he counted it one of his greatest afflictions that his ability should fail him to pleasure such an honourable gentleman.

Who can call any man friend that dips in the same dish with him? just of this metal is every flatterer. In the recollection of everybody Timon had been a father to this Lucius, had kept up his credit with his purse; Timon's money had gone to pay the wages of his servants, to pay the hire of the labourers who had sweat to build the fine houses which Lucius's pride had made necessary to him: yet, oh! the monster which man makes himself when he proves ungrateful! this Lucius now denied to Timon a sum, which, in respect of what Timon had bestowed on him, was less than charitable men afford to beggars.

Sempronius, and every one of these mercenary lords to whom Timon applied in their turn, returned the same evasive answer or direct denial; even Ventidius, the redeemed and now rich Ventidius, refused to assist him with the loan of those five talents which Timon had not lent but generously given him in his distress.

Now was Timon as much avoided in his poverty as he had been courted and resorted to in his riches. Now the same tongues which had been loudest in his praises, extolling him as bountiful, liberal, and open handed, were not ashamed to censure that very bounty as folly, that liberality as profuseness, though it had shown itself folly in nothing so truly as in the selection of such unworthy creatures as themselves for its objects. Now was Timon's princely mansion forsaken, and become a shunned and hated place, a place for men to pass by, not a place, as formerly, where every passenger must stop and taste of his wine and good cheer; now, instead of being thronged with feasting and tumultuous guests, it was beset with impatient and clamorous creditors, usurers, extortioners, fierce and intolerable in their demands, pleading bonds, interest, mortgages; iron-hearted men that would take no denial nor putting off, that Timon's house was now his jail, which he could not pass, nor go in nor out for them; one demanding his due of fifty talents, another bringing in a bill of five thousand crowns, which if he would tell out his blood by drops, and pay them so, he had not enough in his body to discharge, drop by drop.

In this desperate and irremediable state (as it seemed) of his affairs, the eyes of all men were suddenly surprised at a new and incredible lustre which this setting sun put forth. Once more lord Timon proclaimed a feast, to which he invited his accustomed guests, lords, ladies, all that was great or fashionable in Athens. Lord Lucius and Lucullus came, Ventidius, Sempronius, and the rest. Who more sorry now than these fawning wretches, when they found (as they thought) that Lord Timon's poverty was all pretence, and had been only to make trial of their loves, to think that they should not have seen through the artifice at the time, and have had the cheap credit of obliging his lordship? yet who more glad to find the fountain of that noble bounty, which they had thought dried up, still fresh and running? They came dissembling, protesting, expressing deepest sorrow and shame, that when his lordship sent to them, they should have been so unfortunate as to want the present means to oblige so honourable a friend. But Timon begged them not to give such trifles a thought, for he had altogether forgotten it. And these base fawning lords, though they had denied him money in his adversity, yet could not refuse their presence at this new blaze of his returning prosperity. For the swallow follows not summer more willingly than men of these dispositions follow the good fortunes of the great, nor more willingly leaves winter than these shrink from the first appearance of a reverse; such summer birds are men. But now with music and state the banquet of smoking dishes was served up; and when the guests had a little done admiring whence the bankrupt Timon could find means to furnish so costly a feast, some doubting whether the scene which they saw was real, as scarce trusting their own eyes; at a signal given, the dishes were uncovered, and Timon's drift appeared: instead of those varieties and far-fetched dainties which they expected, that Timon's epicurean table in past times had so liberally presented, now appeared under the covers of these dishes a preparation more suitable to Timon's poverty, nothing but a little smoke and lukewarm water, fit feast for this knot of mouth-friends, whose professions were indeed smoke, and their hearts lukewarm and slippery as the water with which Timon welcomed his astonished guests, bidding them, 'Uncover, dogs, and lap'; and before they could recover their surprise, sprinkling it in their faces, that they might have enough, and throwing dishes and all after them, who now ran huddling out, lords, ladies, with their caps snatched up in haste, a splendid confusion, Timon pursuing them, still calling them what they were, 'smooth smiling parasites, destroyers under the mask of courtesy, affable wolves, meek bears, fools of fortune, feast-friends, time-flies.' They, crowding out to avoid him, left the house more willingly than they had entered it; some losing their gowns and caps, and some their jewels in the hurry, all glad to escape out of the presence of such a mad lord, and from the ridicule of his mock banquet.

This was the last feast which ever Timon made, and in it he took farewell of Athens and the society of men; for, after that, he betook himself to the woods, turning his back upon the hated city and upon all mankind, wishing the walls of that detestable city might sink, and the houses fall upon their owners, wishing all plagues which infest humanity, war, outrage, poverty, diseases, might fasten upon its inhabitants, praying the just gods to confound all Athenians, both young and old, high and low; so wishing, he went to the woods, where he said he should find the unkindest beast much kinder than mankind. He stripped himself naked, that he might retain no fashion of a man, and dug a cave to live in, and lived solitary in the manner of a beast, eating the wild roots, and drinking water, flying from the face of his kind, and choosing rather to herd with wild beasts, as more harmless and friendly than man.

What a change from lord Timon the rich, lord Timon the delight of mankind, to Timon the naked, Timon the man-hater! Where were his flatterers now? Where were his attendants and retinue? Would the bleak air, that boisterous servitor, be his chamberlain, to put his shirt on warm? Would those stiff trees that had outlived the eagle, turn young and airy pages to him, to skip on his errands when he bade them? Would the cool brook, when it was iced with winter, administer to him his warm broths and caudles when sick of an overnight's surfeit? Or would the creatures that lived in those wild woods come and lick his hand and flatter him?

Here on a day, when he was digging for roots, his poor sustenance, his spade struck against something heavy, which proved to be gold, a great heap which some miser had probably buried in a time of alarm, thinking to have come again, and taken it from its prison, but died before the opportunity had arrived, without making any man privy to the concealment; so it lay, doing neither good nor harm, in the bowels of the earth, its mother, as if it had never come from thence, till the accidental striking of Timon's spade against it once more brought it to light.

Here was a mass of treasure which, if Timon had retained his old mind, was enough to have purchased him friends and flatterers again; but Timon was sick of the false world, and the sight of gold was poisonous to his eyes; and he would have restored it to the earth, but that, thinking of the infinite calamities which by means of gold happen to mankind, how the lucre of it causes robberies, oppression, injustice, briberies, violence, and murder, among men, he had a pleasure in imagining (such a rooted hatred did he bear to his species) that out of this heap, which in digging he had discovered, might arise some mischief to plague mankind. And some soldiers passing through the woods near to his cave at that instant, which proved to be a part of the troops of the Athenian captain Alcibiades, who upon some disgust taken against the senators of Athens (the Athenians were ever noted to be a thankless and ungrateful people, giving disgust to their generals and best friends), was marching at the head of the same triumphant army which he had formerly headed in their defence, to war against them; Timon, who liked their business well, bestowed upon their captain the gold to pay his soldiers, requiring no other service from him, than that he should with his conquering army lay Athens level with the ground, and burn, slay, kill all her inhabitants; not sparing the old men for their white beards, for (he said) they were usurers, nor the young children for their seeming innocent smiles, for those (he said) would live, if they grew up, to be traitors; but to steel his eyes and ears against any sights or sounds that might awaken compassion; and not to let the cries of virgins, babes, or mothers, hinder him from making one universal massacre of the city, but to confound them all in his conquest; and when he had conquered, he prayed that the gods would confound him also, the conqueror: so thoroughly did Timon hate Athens, Athenians, and all mankind.

While he lived in this forlorn state, leading a life more brutal than human, he was suddenly surprised one day with the appearance of a man standing in an admiring posture at the door of his cave. It was Flavius, the honest steward, whom love and zealous affection to his master had led to seek him out at his wretched dwelling, and to offer his services; and the first sight of his master, the once noble Timon, in that abject condition, naked as he was born, living in the manner of a beast among beasts, looking like his own sad ruins and a monument of decay, so affected this good servant, that he stood speechless, wrapped up in horror, and confounded. And when he found utterance at last to his words, they were so choked with tears, that Timon had much ado to know him again, or to make out who it was that had come (so contrary to the experience he had had of mankind) to offer him service in extremity. And being in the form and shape of a man, he suspected him for a traitor, and his tears for false; but the good servant by so many tokens confirmed the truth of his fidelity, and made it clear that nothing but love and zealous duty to his once dear master had brought him there, that Timon was forced to confess that the world contained one honest man; yet, being in the shape and form of a man, he could not look upon his man's face without abhorrence, or hear words uttered from his man's lips without loathing; and this singly honest man was forced to depart, because he was a man, and because, with a heart more gentle and compassionate than is usual to man, he bore man's detested form and outward feature.

But greater visitants than a poor steward were about to interrupt the savage quiet of Timon's solitude. For now the day was come when the ungrateful lords of Athens sorely repented the injustice which they had done to the noble Timon. For Alcibiades, like an incensed wild boar, was raging at the walls of their city, and with his hot siege threatened to lay fair Athens in the dust. And now the memory of lord Timon's former prowess and military conduct came fresh into their forgetful minds, for Timon had been their general in past times, and a valiant and expert soldier, who alone of all the Athenians was deemed able to cope with a besieging army such as then threatened them, or to drive back the furious approaches of Alcibiades.

A deputation of the senators was chosen in this emergency to wait upon Timon. To him they come in their extremity, to whom, when he was in extremity they had shown but small regard; as if they presumed upon his gratitude whom they had disobliged, and had derived a claim to his courtesy from their own most discourteous and unpiteous treatment.

Now they earnestly beseech him, implore him with tears, to return and save that city, from which their ingratitude had so lately driven him; now they offer him riches, power, dignities, satisfaction for past injuries, and public honours, and the public love; their persons, lives, and fortunes, to be at his disposal, if he will but come back and save them. But Timon the naked, Timon the man-hater, was no longer lord Timon, the lord of bounty, the flower of valour, their defence in war, their ornament in peace. If Alcibiades killed his countrymen, Timon cared not. If he sacked fair Athens, and slew her old men and her infants, Timon would rejoice. So he told them; and that there was not a knife in the unruly camp which he did not prize above the reverendest throat in Athens.

This was all the answer he vouchsafed to the weeping disappointed senators; only at parting he bade them commend him to his countrymen, and tell them, that to ease them of their griefs and anxieties, and to prevent the consequences of fierce Alcibiades' wrath, there was yet a way left, which he would teach them, for he had yet so much affection left for his dear countrymen as to be willing to do them a kindness before his death. These words a little revived the senators, who hoped that his kindness for their city was returning. Then Timon told them that he had a tree, which grew near his cave, which he should shortly have occasion to cut down, and he invited all his friends in Athens, high or low, of what degree soever, who wished to shun affliction, to come and take a taste of his tree before he cut it down; meaning, that they might come and hang themselves on it, and escape affliction that way.

And this was the last courtesy of all his noble bounties, which Timon showed to mankind, and this the last sight of him which his countrymen had: for not many days after, a poor soldier, passing by the sea-beach, which was at a little distance from the woods which Timon frequented, found a tomb on the verge of the sea, with an inscription upon it, purporting that it was the grave of Timon the man-hater, who 'While he lived, did hate all living men, and dying wished a plague might consume all caitiffs left!'

Whether he finished his life by violence, or whether mere distaste of life and the loathing he had for mankind brought Timon to his conclusion, was not clear, yet all men admired the fitness of his epitaph, and the consistency of his end; dying, as he had lived, a hater of mankind: and some there were who fancied a conceit in the very choice which he had made of the sea-beach for his place of burial, where the vast sea might weep for ever upon his grave, as in contempt of the transient and shallow tears of hypocritical and deceitful mankind.

ROMEO AND JULIET

THE two chief families in Verona were the rich Capulets and the Montagues. There had been an old quarrel between these families, which was grown to such a height, and so deadly was the enmity between them, that it extended to the remotest kindred, to the followers and retainers of both sides, insomuch that a servant of the house of Montague could not meet a servant of the house of Capulet, nor a Capulet encounter with a Montague by chance, but fierce words and sometimes bloodshed ensued; and frequent were the brawls from such accidental meetings, which disturbed the happy quiet of Verona's streets.

Old lord Capulet made a great supper, to which many fair ladies and many noble guests were invited. All the admired beauties of Verona were present, and all comers were made welcome if they were not of the house of Montague. At this feast of Capulets, Rosaline, beloved of Romeo, son to the old lord Montague, was present; and though it was dangerous for a Montague to be seen in this assembly, yet Benvolio, a friend of Romeo, persuaded the young lord to go to this assembly in the disguise of a mask, that he might see his Rosaline, and seeing her, compare her with some choice beauties of Verona, who (he said) would make him think his swan a crow. Romeo had small faith in Benvolio's words; nevertheless, for the love of Rosaline, he was persuaded to go. For Romeo was a sincere and passionate lover, and one that lost his sleep for love, and fled society to be alone, thinking on Rosaline, who disdained him, and never requited his love, with the least show of courtesy or affection; and Benvolio wished to cure his friend of this love by showing him diversity of ladies and company. To this feast of Capulets then young Romeo with Benvolio and their friend Mercutio went masked. Old Capulet bid them welcome, and told them that ladies who had their toes unplagued with corns would dance with them. And the old man was light hearted and merry, and said that he had worn a mask when he was young, and could have told a whispering tale in a fair lady's ear. And they fell to dancing, and Romeo was suddenly struck with the exceeding beauty of a lady who danced there, who seemed to him to teach the torches to burn bright, and her beauty to show by night like a rich jewel worn by a blackamoor; beauty too rich for use, too dear for earth! like a snowy dove trooping with crows (he said), so richly did her beauty and perfections shine above the ladies her companions. While he uttered these praises, he was overheard by Tybalt, a nephew of lord Capulet, who knew him by his voice to be Romeo. And this Tybalt, being of a fiery and passionate temper, could not endure that a Montague should come under cover of a mask, to fleer and scorn (as he said) at their solemnities. And he stormed and raged exceedingly, and would have struck young Romeo dead. But his uncle, the old lord Capulet, would not suffer him to do any injury at that time, both out of respect to his guests, and because Romeo had borne himself like a gentleman, and all tongues in Verona bragged of him to be a virtuous and well-governed youth. Tybalt, forced to be patient against his will, restrained himself, but swore that this vile Montague should at another time dearly pay for his intrusion.

The dancing being done, Romeo watched the place where the lady stood; and under favour of his masking habit, which might seem to excuse in part the liberty, he presumed in the gentlest manner to take her by the hand, calling it a shrine, which if he profaned by touching it, he was a blushing pilgrim, and would kiss it for atonement. 'Good pilgrim,' answered the lady, 'your devotion shows by far too mannerly and too courtly:

saints have hands, which pilgrims may touch, but kiss not.' 'Have not saints lips, and pilgrims too?' said Romeo. 'Ay,' said the lady, 'lips which they must use in prayer.' 'O then, my dear saint,' said Romeo, 'hear my prayer, and grant it, lest I despair.' In such like allusions and loving conceits they were engaged, when the lady was called away to her mother. And Romeo inquiring who her mother was, discovered that the lady whose peerless beauty he was so much struck with, was young Juliet, daughter and heir to the lord Capulet, the great enemy of the Montagues; and that he had unknowingly engaged his heart to his foe. This troubled him, but it could not dissuade him from loving. As little rest had Juliet, when she found that the gentleman that she had been talking with was Romeo and a Montague, for she had been suddenly smit with the same hasty and inconsiderate passion for Romeo, which he had conceived for her; and a prodigious birth of love it seemed to her, that she must love her enemy, and that her affections should settle there, where family considerations should induce her chiefly to hate.

It being midnight, Romeo with his companions departed; but they soon missed him, for, unable to stay away from the house where he had left his heart, he leaped the wall of an orchard which was at the back of Juliet's house. Here he had not been long, ruminating on his new love, when Juliet appeared above at a window, through which her exceeding beauty seemed to break like the light of the sun in the east; and the moon, which shone in the orchard with a faint light, appeared to Romeo as if sick and pale with grief at the superior lustre of this new sun. And she, leaning her cheek upon her hand, he passionately wished himself a glove upon that hand, that he might touch her cheek. She all this while thinking herself alone, fetched a deep sigh, and exclaimed: 'Ah me!' Romeo, enraptured to hear her speak, said softly, and unheard by her: 'O speak again, bright angel, for such you appear, being over my head, like a winged messenger from heaven whom mortals fall back to gaze upon.' She, unconscious of being overheard, and full of the new passion which that night's adventure had given birth to, called upon her lover by name (whom she supposed absent): 'O Romeo, Romeo!' said she, 'wherefore art thou Romeo? Deny thy father, and refuse thy name, for my sake; or if thou wilt not, be but my sworn love, and I no longer will be a Capulet.' Romeo, having this encouragement, would fain have spoken, but he was desirous of hearing more; and the lady continued her passionate discourse with herself (as she thought), still chiding Romeo for being Romeo and a Montague, and wishing him some other name, or that he would put away that hated name, and for that name which was no part of himself, he should take all herself. At this loving word Romeo could no longer refrain, but taking up the dialogue as if her words had been addressed to him personally, and not merely in fancy, he bade her call him Love, or by whatever other name she pleased, for he was no longer Romeo, if that name was displeasing to her. Juliet, alarmed to hear a man's voice in the garden, did not at first know who it was, that by favour of the night and darkness had thus stumbled upon the discovery of her secret; but when he spoke again, though her ears had not yet drunk a hundred words of that tongue's uttering, yet so nice is a lover's hearing, that she immediately knew him to be young Romeo, and she expostulated with him on the danger to which he had exposed himself by climbing the orchard walls, for if any of her kinsmen should find him there, it would be death to him, being a Montague. 'Alack,' said Romeo, 'there is more peril in your eye, than in twenty of their swords. Do you but look kind upon me, lady, and I am proof against their enmity. Better my life should be ended by their hate, than that hated life should be prolonged, to live without your love.' 'How came you into this place,' said Juliet, 'and by whose direction?' 'Love directed me,' answered Romeo: 'I am no pilot, yet wert thou as far apart from me, as that vast shore which is washed with the farthest sea, I should venture for such mechandise.' A crimson blush came over Juliet's face, yet unseen by Romeo by reason of the night, when she reflected upon the discovery which she had made, yet not meaning to make it, of her love to Romeo. She would fain have recalled her words, but that was impossible: fain would she have stood upon form, and have kept her lover at a distance, as the custom of discreet ladies is, to frown and be perverse, and give their suitors harsh denials at first; to stand off, and affect a coyness or indifference, where they most love, that their lovers may not think them too lightly or too easily won; for the difficulty of attainment increases the value of the object. But there was no room in her case for denials, or puttings off, or any of the customary arts of delay and protracted courtship. Romeo had heard from her own tongue, when she did not dream that he was near her, a confession of her love. So with an honest frankness, which the novelty of her situation excused, she confirmed the truth of what he had before heard, and addressing him by the name of *fair Montague* (love can sweeten a sour name), she begged him not to impute her easy yielding to levity or an unworthy mind, but that he must lay the fault of it (if it were a fault) upon the accident of the night which had so strangely discovered her thoughts. And she added, that though her behaviour to him might not be sufficiently prudent, measured by the custom of her sex, yet that she would prove more true than many whose prudence was dissembling, and their modesty artificial cunning.

Romeo was beginning to call the heavens to witness, that nothing was farther from his thoughts than to impute a shadow of dishonour to such an honoured lady, when she stopped him, begging him not to swear; for although she joyed in him, yet she had no joy of that night's contract: it was too rash, too unadvised, too sudden. But he being urgent with her to exchange a vow of love with him that night, she said that she already had given him hers before he requested it; meaning, when he overheard her confession; but she would retract what she then bestowed, for the pleasure of giving it again, for her bounty was as infinite as the sea, and her love as deep. From this loving conference she was called away by her nurse, who slept with her, and thought it time for her to be in bed, for it was near to daybreak; but hastily returning, she said three or four words more to Romeo, the purport of which was, that if his love was indeed honourable, and his purpose marriage, she would send a messenger to him to-morrow, to appoint a time for their marriage, when she would lay all her fortunes at his feet, and follow him as her lord through the world. While they were settling this point, Juliet was repeatedly called for by her nurse, and went in and returned, and went and returned again, for she seemed as jealous of Romeo going from her, as a young girl of her bird, which she will let hop a little from her hand, and pluck it back with a silken thread; and Romeo was as loath to part as she; for the sweetest music to lovers is the sound of each other's tongues at night. But at last they parted, wishing mutually sweet sleep and rest for that night.

The day was breaking when they parted, and Romeo, who was too full of thoughts of his mistress and that blessed meeting to allow him to sleep, instead of going home, bent his course to a monastery hard by, to find friar Lawrence. The good friar was already up at his devotions, but seeing young Romeo abroad so early, he conjectured rightly that he had not been abed that night, but that some distemper of youthful affection had kept him waking. He was right in imputing the cause of Romeo's wakefulness to love, but he made a wrong guess at the object, for he thought that his love for Rosaline had kept him waking. But when Romeo revealed his new passion for Juliet, and requested the assistance of the friar to marry them that day, the holy man lifted up his eyes and hands in a sort of wonder at the sudden change in Romeo's affections, for he had been privy to all Romeo's love for Rosaline, and his many complaints of her disdain: and he said, that young men's love lay not truly in their hearts, but in their eyes. But Romeo replying, that he himself had often chidden him for doting on Rosaline, who could not love him again, whereas Juliet both loved and was beloved by him, the friar assented in some measure to his reasons; and thinking that a matrimonial alliance between young Juliet and Romeo might happily be the means of making up the long breach between the Capulets and the Montagues; which no one more lamented than this good friar, who was a friend to both the families and had often interposed his mediation to make up the quarrel without effect; partly moved by policy, and partly by his fondness for young Romeo, to whom he could deny nothing, the old man consented to join their hands in marriage.

Now was Romeo blessed indeed, and Juliet, who knew his intent from a messenger which she had despatched according to promise, did not fail to be early at the cell of friar Lawrence, where their hands were joined in holy marriage; the good friar praying the heavens to smile upon that act, and in the union of this young Montague and young Capulet to bury the old strife and long dissensions of their families.

The ceremony being over, Juliet hastened home, where she stayed impatient for the coming of night, at which time Romeo promised to come and meet her in the orchard, where they had met the night before; and the time between seemed as tedious to her, as the night before some great festival seems to an impatient child, that has got new finery which it may not put on till the morning.

That same day, about noon, Romeo's friends, Benvolio and Mercutio, walking through the streets of Verona, were met by a party of the Capulets with the impetuous Tybalt at their head. This was the same angry Tybalt who would have fought with Romeo at old lord Capulet's feast. He, seeing Mercutio, accused him bluntly of associating with Romeo, a Montague. Mercutio, who had as much fire and youthful blood in him as Tybalt, replied to this accusation with some sharpness; and in spite of all Benvolio could say to moderate their wrath, a quarrel was beginning, when Romeo himself passing that way, the fierce Tybalt turned from Mercutio to Romeo, and gave him the disgraceful appellation of villain. Romeo wished to avoid a quarrel with Tybalt above all men, because he was the kinsman of Juliet, and much beloved by her; besides, this young Montague had never thoroughly entered into the family quarrel, being by nature wise and gentle, and the name of a Capulet, which was his dear lady's name, was now rather a charm to allay resentment, than a watchword to excite fury. So he tried to reason with Tybalt, whom he saluted mildly by the name of *good Capulet*, as if he, though a Montague, had some secret pleasure in uttering that name: but Tybalt, who hated all Montagues as he hated hell, would hear no reason, but drew his weapon; and Mercutio, who knew not of Romeo's secret motive for desiring peace with Tybalt, but looked upon his present forbearance as a sort of calm dishonourable submission, with many disdainful words provoked Tybalt to the prosecution of his first quarrel with him; and Tybalt and Mercutio fought, till Mercutio fell, receiving his death's wound while Romeo and Benvolio were vainly endeavouring to part the combatants. Mercutio being dead, Romeo kept his temper no longer, but returned the scornful appellation of villain which

Tybalt had given him; and they fought till Tybalt was slain by Romeo. This deadly broil falling out in the midst of Verona at noonday, the news of it quickly brought a crowd of citizens to the spot, and among them the old lords Capulet and Montague, with their wives; and soon after arrived the prince himself, who being related to Mercutio, whom Tybalt had slain, and having had the peace of his government often disturbed by these brawls of Montagues and Capulets, came determined to put the law in strictest force against those who should be found to be offenders. Benvolio, who had been eyewitness to the fray, was commanded by the prince to relate the origin of it; which he did, keeping as near the truth as he could without injury to Romeo, softening and excusing the part which his friends took in it. Lady Capulet, whose extreme grief for the loss of her kinsman Tybalt made her keep no bounds in her revenge, exhorted the prince to do strict justice upon his murderer, and to pay no attention to Benvolio's representation, who, being Romeo's friend and a Montague, spoke partially. Thus she pleaded against her new son-in-law, but she knew not yet that he was her son-in-law and Juliet's husband. On the other hand was to be seen Lady Montague pleading for her child's life, and arguing with some justice that Romeo had done nothing worthy of punishment in taking the life of Tybalt, which was already forfeited to the law by his having slain Mercutio. The prince, unmoved by the passionate exclamations of these women, on a careful examination of the facts, pronounced his sentence, and by that sentence Romeo was banished from Verona.

Heavy news to young Juliet, who had been but a few hours a bride, and now by this decree seemed everlastingly divorced! When the tidings reached her, she at first gave way to rage against Romeo, who had slain her dear cousin: she called him a beautiful tyrant, a fiend angelical, a ravenous dove, a lamb with a wolf's

At the cell of Friar Lawrence

nature, a serpent-heart hid with a flowering face, and
other like contradictory names, which denoted the
struggles in her mind between her love and her resentment: but in the end love got the mastery, and the tears
which she shed for grief that Romeo had slain her
cousin, turned to drops of joy that her husband lived
whom Tybalt would have slain. Then came fresh tears,
and they were altogether of grief for Romeo's banishment. That word was more terrible to her than the
death of many Tybalts.

Romeo, after the fray, had taken refuge in friar
Lawrence's cell, where he was first made acquainted
with the prince's sentence, which seemed to him far
more terrible than death. To him it appeared there was
no world out of Verona's walls, no living out of the sight
of Juliet. Heaven was there where Juliet lived, and
all beyond was purgatory, torture, hell. The good
friar would have applied the consolation of philosophy
to his griefs: but this frantic young man would hear of
none, but like a madman he tore his hair, and threw
himself all along upon the ground, as he said, to take
the measure of his grave. From this unseemly state
he was roused by a message from his dear lady, which a
little revived him; and then the friar took the advantage
to expostulate with him on the unmanly weakness which
he had shown. He had slain Tybalt, but would he also
slay himself, slay his dear lady, who lived but in his life?
The noble form of man, he said, was but a shape of wax,
when it wanted the courage which should keep it firm.
The law had been lenient to him, that instead of death,
which he had incurred, had pronounced by the prince's
mouth only banishment. He had slain Tybalt, but
Tybalt would have slain him: there was a sort of happiness in that. Juliet was alive, and (beyond all hope) had
become his dear wife; therein he was most happy. All
these blessings, as the friar made them out to be, did
Romeo put from him like a sullen misbehaved wench.

And the friar bade him beware, for such as despaired, (he said) died miserable. Then when Romeo was a little calmed, he counselled him that he should go that night and secretly take his leave of Juliet, and thence proceed straightways to Mantua, at which place he should sojourn, till the friar found fit occasion to publish his marriage, which might be a joyful means of reconciling their families; and then he did not doubt but the prince would be moved to pardon him, and he would return with twenty times more joy than he went forth with grief. Romeo was convinced by these wise counsels of the friar, and took his leave to go and seek his lady, proposing to stay with her that night, and by daybreak pursue his journey alone to Mantua; to which place the good friar promised to send him letters from time to time, acquainting him with the state of affairs at home.

That night Romeo passed with his dear wife, gaining secret admission to her chamber, from the orchard in which he had heard her confession of love the night before. That had been a night of unmixed joy and rapture; but the pleasures of this night, and the delight which these lovers took in each other's society, were sadly allayed with the prospect of parting, and the fatal adventures of the past day. The unwelcome daybreak seemed to come too soon, and when Juliet heard the morning song of the lark, she would have persuaded herself that it was the nightingale, which sings by night; but it was too truly the lark which sang, and a discordant and unpleasing note it seemed to her; and the streaks of day in the east too certainly pointed out that it was time for these lovers to part. Romeo took his leave of his dear wife with a heavy heart, promising to write to her from Mantua every hour in the day; and when he had descended from her chamber-window, as he stood below her on the ground, in that sad foreboding state of mind in which she was, he appeared to her eyes as one dead in the bottom of a tomb. Romeo's mind misgave him in like manner: but now he was forced hastily to depart, for it was death for him to be found within the walls of Verona after daybreak.

This was but the beginning of the tragedy of this pair of star-crossed lovers. Romeo had not been gone many days, before the old lord Capulet proposed a match for Juliet. The husband he had chosen for her, not dreaming that she was married already, was count Paris, a gallant, young, and noble gentleman, no unworthy suitor to the young Juliet, if she had never seen Romeo.

The terrified Juliet was in a sad perplexity at her father's offer. She pleaded her youth unsuitable to marriage, the recent death of Tybalt, which had left her spirits too weak to meet a husband with any face of joy, and how indecorous it would show for the family of the Capulets to be celebrating a nuptial feast, when his funeral solemnities were hardly over: she pleaded every reason against the match, but the true one, namely, that she was married already. But lord Capulet was deaf to all her excuses, and in a peremptory manner ordered her to get ready, for by the following Thursday she should be married to Paris: and having found her a husband, rich, young, and noble, such as the proudest maid in Verona might joyfully accept, he could not bear that out of an affected coyness, as he construed her denial, she should oppose obstacles to her own good fortune.

In this extremity Juliet applied to the friendly friar, always her counsellor in distress, and he asking her if she had resolution to undertake a desperate remedy, and she answering that she would go into the grave alive rather than marry Paris, her own dear husband living; he directed her to go home, and appear merry, and give her consent to marry Paris, according to her father's desire, and on the next night, which was the night before the marriage, to drink off the contents of a phial which he then gave her, the effect of which would be that for two-and-forty hours after drinking it she should appear cold and lifeless; and when the bridegroom came to fetch her in the morning, he would find her to appearance dead; that then she would be borne, as the manner in that country was, uncovered on a bier, to be buried in the family vault; that if she could put off womanish fear, and consent to this terrible trial, in forty-two hours after swallowing the liquid (such was its certain operation) she would be sure to awake, as from a dream; and before she should awake, he would let her husband know their drift, and he should come in the night, and bear her thence to Mantua. Love, and the dread of marrying Paris, gave young Juliet strength to undertake this horrible adventure; and she took the phial of the friar, promising to observe his directions.

Going from the monastery, she met the young count Paris, and modestly dissembling, promised to become his bride. This was joyful news to the lord Capulet and his wife. It seemed to put youth into the old man; and Juliet, who had displeased him exceedingly, by her refusal of the count, was his darling again, now she promised to be obedient. All things in the house were in a bustle against the appoaching nuptials. No cost was spared to prepare such festival rejoicings as Verona had never before witnessed.

On the Wednesday night Juliet drank off the potion. She had many misgivings lest the friar, to avoid the blame which might be imputed to him for marrying her to Romeo, had given her poison; but then he was always known for a holy man: then lest she should awake before the time that Romeo was to come for her; whether the terror of the place, a vault of dead Capulets' bones, and where Tybalt, all bloody, lay festering in his shroud, would not be enough to drive her distracted: again she thought of all the stories she had heard of spirits haunting the places where their bodies were bestowed. But then her love for Romeo, and her aversion for Paris returned, and she desperately swallowed the draught, and became insensible.

When young Paris came early in the morning with music to awaken his bride, instead of a living Juliet, her chamber presented the dreary spectacle of a lifeless corse. What death to his hopes! What confusion then reigned through the whole house! Poor Paris lamenting his bride, whom most detestable death had beguiled him of, had divorced from him even before their hands were joined. But still more piteous it was to hear the mournings of the old lord and lady Capulet, who having but this one, one poor loving child to rejoice and solace in, cruel death had snatched her from their sight, just as these careful parents were on the point of seeing her advanced (as they thought) by a promising and advantageous match. Now all things that were ordained for the festival were turned from their properties to do the office of a black funeral. The wedding cheer served for a sad burial feast, the bridal hymns were changed for sullen dirges, the sprightly instruments to melancholy bells, and the flowers that should have been strewed in the bride's path, now served but to strew her corse. Now, instead of a priest to marry her, a priest was needed to bury her; and she was borne to church indeed, not to augment the cheerful hopes of the living, but to swell the dreary numbers of the dead.

Bad news, which always travels faster than good, now brought the dismal story of his Juliet's death to Romeo, at Mantua, before the messenger could arrive, who was sent from friar Lawrence to apprise him that these were mock funerals only, and but the shadow and representation of death, and that his dear lady lay in the tomb but for a short while, expecting when Romeo would come to release her from that dreary mansion. Just before, Romeo had been unusually joyful and lighthearted. He had dreamed in the night that he was dead (a strange dream, that gave a dead man leave to think), and that his lady came and found him dead, and breathed such life with kisses in his lips, that he revived, and was an emperor! And now that a messenger came from Verona, he thought surely it was to confirm some good news which his dreams had presaged. But when the contrary to this flattering vision appeared, and that it was his lady who was dead in truth, whom he could not revive by any kisses, he ordered horses to be got ready, for he determined that night to visit Verona, and to see his lady in her tomb. And as mischief is swift to enter into the thoughts of desperate men, he called to mind a poor apothecary, whose shop in Mantua he had lately passed, and from the beggarly appearance of the man, who seemed famished, and the wretched show in his show of empty boxes ranged on dirty shelves, and other tokens of extreme wretchedness, he had said at the time (perhaps having some misgivings that his own disastrous life might haply meet with a conclusion so desperate), 'If a man were to need poison, which by the law of Mantua it is death to sell, here lives a poor wretch who would sell it him.' These words of his now came into his mind, and he sought out the apothecary, who after some pretended scruples, Romeo offering him gold, which his poverty could not resist, sold him a poison, which, if he swallowed, he told him, if he had the strength of twenty men, would quickly despatch him.

With this poison he set out for Verona, to have a sight of his dear lady in her tomb, meaning, when he had satisfied his sight, to swallow the poison, and be buried by her side. He reached Verona at midnight, and found the churchyard, in the midst of which was situated the ancient tomb of the Capulets. He had provided a light, and a spade, and wrenching iron, and was proceeding to break open the monument, when he was interrupted by a voice, which by the name of *vile Montague*, bade him desist from his unlawful business. It was the young count Paris, who had come to the tomb of Juliet at that unseasonable time of night, to strew flowers and to weep over the grave of her that should have been his bride. He knew not what an interest Romeo had in the dead, but knowing him to be a Montague, and (as he supposed) a sworn foe to all the Capulets, he judged that he was come by night to do some villanous shame to the dead bodies; therefore in an angry tone he bade him desist; and as a criminal, condemned by the laws of Verona to die if he were found within the walls of the city, he would have apprehended him. Romeo urged Paris to leave him, and warned him by the fate of Tybalt, who lay buried there, not to provoke his anger, or draw down another sin upon his head, by forcing him to kill him. But the count in scorn refused his warning, and laid hands on him as a felon, which Romeo resisting, they fought, and Paris fell. When Romeo, by the help of a light, came to see who it was that he had slain, that it was Paris, who (he learned in his way from Mantua) should have married Juliet, he took the dead youth by the hand, as one whom misfortune had made a companion, and said that he would bury him in a triumphal grave, meaning in Juliet's grave, which he now opened: and there lay his lady, as one whom death had no power upon to change a feature or complexion, in her matchless beauty; or as if Death were amorous, and the lean abhorred monster kept her there for his delight; for she lay yet fresh and blooming, as she had fallen to sleep when she swallowed that benumbing potion; and near her lay Tybalt in his bloody shroud, whom Romeo seeing, begged pardon of his lifeless corse, and for Juliet's sake called him *cousin*, and said that he was about to do him a favour by putting his enemy to death. Here Romeo took his last leave of his lady's lips, kissing them; and here he shook the burden of his cross stars from his weary body, swallowing that poison which the apothecary had sold him, whose operation was fatal and real, not like that dissembling potion which Juliet had swallowed, the effect of which was now nearly expiring, and she about to awake to complain that Romeo had not kept his time, or that he had come too soon.

For now the hour was arrived at which the friar had promised that she should awake; and he, having learned that his letters which he had sent to Mantua, by some unlucky detention of the messenger, had never reached Romeo, came himself, provided with the pickaxe and lantern, to deliver the lady from her confinement; but he was surprised to find a light already burning in the Capulets' monument, and to see swords and blood near it, and Romeo and Paris lying breathless by the monument.

Before he could entertain a conjecture, to imagine how these fatal accidents had fallen out, Juliet awoke out of her trance, and seeing the friar near her, she remembered the place where she was, and the occasion of her being there, and asked for Romeo, but the friar, hearing a noise, bade her come out of that place of death, and of unnatural sleep, for a greater power than they could contradict had thwarted their intents; and being frightened by the noise of people coming, he fled: but when Juliet saw the cup closed in her true love's hand, she guessed that poison had been the cause of his end, and she would have swallowed the dregs if any had been left, and she kissed his still warm lips to try if any poison yet did hang upon them; then hearing a nearer noise of people coming, she quickly unsheathed a dagger which she wore, and stabbing herself, died by her true Romeo's side.

The watch by this time had come up to the place. A page belonging to count Paris, who had witnessed the fight between his master and Romeo, had given the alarm, which had spread among the citizens, who went up and down the streets of Verona confusedly exclaiming, A Paris! a Romeo! a Juliet! as the rumour had imperfectly reached them, till the uproar brought lord

Montague and lord Capulet out of their beds, with the prince, to inquire into the causes of the disturbance. The friar had been apprehended by some of the watch, coming from the churchyard, trembling, sighing, and weeping, in a suspicious manner. A great multitude being assembled at the Capulets' monument, the friar was demanded by the prince to deliver what he knew of these strange and disastrous accidents.

And there, in the presence of the old lords Montague and Capulet, he faithfully related the story of their children's fatal love, the part he took in promoting their marriage, in the hope in that union to end the long quarrels between their families: how Romeo, there dead, was husband to Juliet; and Juliet, there dead, was Romeo's faithful wife; how before he could find a fit opportunity to divulge their marriage, another match was projected for Juliet, who, to avoid the crime of a second marriage, swallowed the sleeping draught (as he advised), and all thought her dead; how meantime he wrote to Romeo, to come and take her thence when the force of the potion should cease, and by what unfortunate miscarriage of the messenger the letters never reached Romeo: further than this the friar could not follow the story, nor knew more than that coming himself, to deliver Juliet from that place of death, he found the count Paris and Romeo slain. The remainder of the transactions was supplied by the narration of the page who had seen Paris and Romeo fight, and by the servant who came with Romeo from Verona, to whom this faithful lover had given letters to be delivered to his father in the event of his death, which made good the friar's words, confessing his marriage with Juliet, imploring the forgiveness of his parents, acknowledging the buying of the poison of the poor apothecary, and his intent in coming to the monument, to die, and lie with Juliet. All these circumstances agreed together to clear the friar from any hand he could be supposed to have in these complicated slaughters, further than as the unintended consequences of his own well meant, yet too artificial and subtle contrivances.

And the prince, turning to these old lords, Montague and Capulet, rebuked them for their brutal and irrational enmities, and showed them what a scourge Heaven had laid upon such offences, that it had found means even through the love of their children to punish their unnatural hate. And these old rivals, no longer enemies, agreed to bury their long strife in their children's graves; and lord Capulet requested lord Montague to give him his hand, calling him by the name of brother, as if in acknowledgment of the union of their families, by the marriage of the young Capulet and Montague; and saying that lord Montague's hand (in token of reconcilement) was all he demanded for his daughter's jointure: but lord Montague said he would give him more, for he would raise her a statue of pure gold, that while Verona kept its name, no figure should be so esteemed for its richness and workmanship as that of the true and faithful Juliet. And lord Capulet in return said that he would raise another statue to Romeo. So did these poor old lords, when it was too late, strive to outgo each other in mutual courtesies: while so deadly had been their rage and enmity in past times, that nothing but the fearful overthrow of their children (poor sacrifices to their quarrels and dissensions) could remove the rooted hates and jealousies of the noble families.

HAMLET, PRINCE OF DENMARK

GERTRUDE, queen of Denmark, becoming a widow by the sudden death of King Hamlet, in less than two months after his death married his brother Claudius, which was noted by all people at the time for a strange act of indiscretion, or unfeelingness, or worse: for this Claudius did no ways resemble her late husband in the qualities of his person or his mind, but was as contemptible in outward appearance, as he was base and unworthy in disposition; and suspicions did not fail to arise in the minds of some, that he had privately made away with his brother, the late king, with the view of marrying his widow, and ascending the throne of Denmark, to the exclusion of young Hamlet, the son of the buried king, and lawful successor to the throne.

But upon no one did this unadvised action of the queen make such impression as upon this young prince, who loved and venerated the memory of his dead father almost to idolatry, and being of a nice sense of honour, and a most exquisite practiser of propriety himself, did sorely take to heart this unworthy conduct of his mother Gertrude: insomuch that, between grief for his father's death and shame for his mother's marriage, this young prince was overclouded with a deep melancholy, and lost all his mirth and all his good looks; all his customary pleasure in books forsook him, his princely exercises and sports, proper to his youth, were no longer acceptable; he grew weary of the world, which seemed to him an unweeded garden, where all the wholesome flowers were choked up, and nothing but weeds could thrive. Not that the prospect of exclusion from the throne, his lawful inheritance, weighed so much upon his spirits, though that to a young and high-minded prince was a bitter wound and a sore indignity; but what so galled

him, and took away all his cheerful spirits, was, that his
mother had shown herself so forgetful to his father's
memory; and such a father! who had been to her so
loving and so gentle a husband! and then she always
appeared as loving and obedient a wife to him, and
would hang upon him as if her affection grew to him:
and now within two months, or as it seemed to young
Hamlet, less than two months, she had married again,
married his uncle, her dear husband's brother, in itself
a highly improper and unlawful marriage, from the
nearness of relationship, but made much more so by
the indecent haste with which it was concluded, and the
unkingly character of the man whom she had chosen
to be the partner of her throne and bed. This it was,
which more than the loss of ten kingdoms, dashed the
spirits and brought a cloud over the mind of this honourable young prince.

In vain was all that his mother Gertrude or the king
could do to contrive to divert him; he still appeared in
court in a suit of deep black, as mourning for the king
his father's death, which mode of dress he had never
laid aside, not even in compliment to his mother upon
the day she was married, nor could he be brought to
join in any of the festivities or rejoicings of that (as
appeared to him) disgraceful day.

What mostly troubled him was an uncertainty about
the manner of his father's death. It was given out by
Claudius that a serpent had stung him; but young Hamlet
had shrewd suspicions that Claudius himself was the
serpent; in plain English, that he had murdered him for
his crown, and that the serpent who stung his father did
now sit on the throne.

How far he was right in this conjecture, and what he
ought to think of his mother, how far she was privy to
this murder, and whether by her consent or knowledge,
or without, it came to pass, were the doubts which
continually harassed and distracted him.

A rumour had reached the ear of young Hamlet, that an apparition, exactly resembling the dead king his father, had been seen by the soldiers upon watch, on the platform before the palace at midnight, for two or three nights successively. The figure came constantly clad in the same suit of armour, from head to foot, which the dead king was known to have worn: and they who saw it (Hamlet's bosom friend Horatio was one) agreed in their testimony as to the time and manner of its appearance: that it came just as the clock struck twelve; that it looked pale, with a face more of sorrow than of anger; that its beard was grisly, and the colour a *sable silvered*, as they had seen it in his lifetime: that it made no answer when they spoke to it; yet once they thought it lifted up its head, and addressed itself to motion, as if it were about to speak; but in that moment the morning cock crew, and it shrunk in haste away, and vanished out of their sight.

The young prince, strangely amazed at their relation, which was too consistent and agreeing with itself to disbelieve, concluded that it was his father's ghost which they had seen, and determined to take his watch with the soldiers that night, that he might have a chance of seeing it; for he reasoned with himself, that such an appearance did not come for nothing, but that the ghost had something to impart, and though it had been silent hitherto, yet it would speak to him. And he waited with impatience for the coming of night.

When night came he took his stand with Horatio, and Marcellus, one of the guard, upon the platform, where this apparition was accustomed to walk: and it being a cold night, and the air unusually raw and nipping, Hamlet and Horatio and their companion fell into some talk about the coldness of the night, which was suddenly broken off by Horatio announcing that the ghost was coming.

At the sight of his father's spirit, Hamlet was struck with a sudden surprise and fear. He at first called upon the angels and heavenly ministers to defend them, for

he knew not whether it were a good spirit or bad;
whether it came for good or evil: but he gradually
assumed more courage; and his father (as it seemed to
him) looked upon him so piteously, and as it were
desiring to have conversation with him, and did in all
respects appear so like himself as he was when he lived,
that Hamlet could not help addressing him: he called
him by his name, Hamlet, King, Father! and conjured
him that he would tell the reason why he had left his
grave, where they had seen him quietly bestowed, to
come again and visit the earth and the moonlight: and
besought him that he would let them know if there was
anything which they could do to give peace to his spirit.
And the ghost beckoned to Hamlet, that he should go
with him to some more removed place, where they might
be alone; and Horatio and Marcellus would have dis-
suaded the young prince from following it, for they
feared lest it should be some evil spirit, who would
tempt him to the neighbouring sea, or to the top of some
dreadful cliff, and there put on some horrible shape which
might deprive the prince of his reason. But their counsels and entreaties could not alter Hamlet's determination, who cared too little about life to fear the losing of
it; and as to his soul, he said, what could the spirit do
to that, being a thing immortal as itself? And he felt
as hardy as a lion, and bursting from them, who did all
they could to hold him, he followed whithersoever the
spirit led him.

And when they were alone together, the spirit broke
silence, and told him that he was the ghost of Hamlet,
his father, who had been cruelly murdered, and he told
the manner of it; that it was done by his own brother
Claudius, Hamlet's uncle, as Hamlet had already but
too much suspected, for the hope of succeeding to his
bed and crown. That as he was sleeping in his garden,
his custom always in the afternoon, his treasonous
brother stole upon him in his sleep, and poured the juice

of poisonous henbane into his ears, which has such an antipathy to the life of man, that swift as quicksilver it courses through all the veins of the body, baking up the blood, and spreading a crustlike leprosy all over the skin: thus sleeping, by a brother's hand he was cut off at once from his crown, his queen, and his life: and he adjured Hamlet, if he did ever his dear father love, that he would revenge his foul murder. And the ghost lamented to his son, that his mother should so fall off from virtue, as to prove false to the wedded love of her first husband, and to marry his murderer; but he cautioned Hamlet, howsoever he proceeded in his revenge against his wicked uncle, by no means to act any violence against the person of his mother, but to leave her to heaven, and to the stings and thorns of conscience. And Hamlet promised to observe the ghost's direction in all things, and the ghost vanished.

And when Hamlet was left alone, he took up a solemn resolution, that all he had in his memory, all that he had ever learned by books or observation, should be instantly forgotten by him, and nothing live in his brain but the memory of what the ghost had told him, and enjoined him to do. And Hamlet related the particulars of the conversation which had passed to none but his dear friend Horatio; and he enjoined both to him and Marcellus the strictest secrecy as to what they had seen that night.

The terror which the sight of the ghost had left upon the senses of Hamlet, he being weak and dispirited before, almost unhinged his mind, and drove him beside his reason. And he, fearing that it would continue to have this effect, which might subject him to observation, and set his uncle upon his guard, if he suspected that he was meditating anything against him, or that Hamlet really knew more of his father's death than he professed, took up a strange resolution, from that time to counterfeit as if he were really and truly mad; thinking that he would be less an object of suspicion when his uncle should believe him incapable of any serious project, and that his real perturbation of mind would be best covered and pass concealed under a disguise of pretended lunacy.

From this time Hamlet affected a certain wildness and strangeness in his apparel, his speech, and behaviour, and did so excellently conterfeit the madman, that the king and queen were both deceived, and not thinking his grief for his father's death a sufficient cause to produce such a distemper, for they knew not of the appearance of the ghost, they concluded that his malady was love, and they thought they had found out the object.

Before Hamlet fell into the melancholy way which has been related, he had dearly loved a fair maid called Ophelia, the daughter of Polonius, the king's chief counsellor in affairs of state. He had sent her letters and rings, and made many tenders of his affection to her, and importuned her with love in honourable fashion: and she had given belief to his vows and importunities. But the melancholy which he fell into latterly had made him neglect her, and from the time he conceived the project of counterfeiting madness, he affected to treat her with unkindness, and a sort of rudeness: but she good lady, rather than reproach him with being false to her, persuaded herself that it was nothing but the disease in his mind, and no settled unkindness, which had made him less observant of her than formerly; and she compared the faculties of his once noble mind and excellent understanding, impaired as they were with the deep melancholy that oppressed him, to sweet bells which in themselves are capable of most exquisite music, but when jangled out of tune, or rudely handled, produce only a harsh and unpleasing sound.

Though the rough business which Hamlet had in hand, the revenging of his father's death upon his murderer, did not suit with the playful state of courtship, or admit of the society of so idle a passion as love now seemed to him, yet it could not hinder but that soft thoughts of his Ophelia would come between, and in one of these moments, when he thought that his treatment of this gentle lady had been unreasonably harsh, he wrote her a letter full of wild starts of passion, and in extravagant terms, such as agreed with his supposed madness, but mixed with some gentle touches of affection, which could not but show to this honoured lady that a deep love for her yet lay at the bottom of his heart. He bade her to doubt the stars were fire, and to doubt that the sun did move, to doubt truth to be a liar, but never to doubt that he loved; with more of such extravagant phrases. This letter Ophelia dutifully showed to her father, and the old man thought himself bound to communicate it to the king and queen, who from that time supposed that the true cause of Hamlet's madness was love. And the queen wished that the good beauties of Ophelia might be the happy cause of his wildness, for so she hoped that her virtues might happily restore him to his accustomed way again, to both their honours.

But Hamlet's malady lay deeper than she supposed, or than could be so cured. His father's ghost, which he had seen, still haunted his imagination, and the sacred injunction to revenge his murder gave him no rest till it was accomplished. Every hour of delay seemed to him a sin, and a violation of his father's commands. Yet how to compass the death of the king, surrounded as he constantly was with his guards, was no easy matter. Or if it had been, the presence of the queen, Hamlet's mother, who was generally with the king, was a restraint upon his purpose, which he could not break through. Besides, the very circumstance that the usurper was his mother's husband filled him with some remorse, and still blunted the edge of his purpose. The mere act of putting a fellow-creature to death was in itself odious and terrible to a disposition naturally so gentle as Hamlet's was. His very melancholy, and the dejection of spirits he had so long been in, produced an irresoluteness and wavering of purpose, which kept him from proceeding to extremities. Moreover, he could not help having some scruples upon his mind, whether the spirit which he had seen was indeed his father, or whether it might not be the devil, who he had heard has power to take any form he pleases, and who might have assumed his father's shape only to take advantage of his weakness and his melancholy, to drive him to the doing of so desperate an act as murder. And he determined that he would have more certain grounds to go upon than a vision, or apparition, which might be a delusion.

While he was in this irresolute mind there came to the court certain players, in whom Hamlet formerly used to take delight, and particularly to hear one of them speak a tragical speech, describing the death of old Priam, King of Troy, with the grief of Hecuba his queen. Hamlet welcomed his old friends, the players, and remembering how that speech had formerly given him pleasure, requested the player to repeat it; which he did in so lively a manner, setting forth the cruel murder of the feeble old king, with the destruction of his people and city by fire, and the mad grief of the old queen, running barefoot up and down the palace, with a poor clout upon that head where a crown had been, and with nothing but a blanket upon her loins, snatched up in haste, where she had worn a royal robe; that not only it drew tears from all that stood by, who thought they saw the real scene, so lively was it represented, but even the player himself delivered it with a broken voice and real tears. This put Hamlet upon thinking, if that player could so work himself up to passion by a mere fictitious speech, to weep for one that he had never seen, for Hecuba, that had been dead so many hundred years, how dull was he, who having a real motive and cue for passion, a real king and a dear father murdered, was yet so little moved, that his revenge all this while had seemed to have slept in dull and muddy forgetfulness! and while he meditated on actors and acting, and the powerful effects which a good play, represented to the life, has upon the spectator, he remembered the instance of some murderer, who seeing a murder on the stage, was by the mere force of the scene and resemblance of circumstances so affected, that on the spot he confessed the crime which he had committed. And he determined that these players should play something like the murder of his father before his uncle, and he would watch narrowly what effect it might have upon him, and from his looks he would be able to gather with more certainty if he were the murderer or not. To this effect he ordered a play to be prepared, to the representation of which he invited the king and queen.

The story of the play was of a murder done in Vienna upon a duke. The duke's name was Gonzago, his wife Baptista. The play showed how one Lucianus, a near relation to the duke, poisoned him in his garden for his estate, and how the murderer in a short time after got the love of Gonzago's wife.

At the representation of this play, the king, who did not know the trap which was laid for him, was present, with his queen and the whole court: Hamlet sitting attentively near him to observe his looks. The play began with a conversation between Gonzago and his wife, in which the lady made many protestations of love, and of never marrying a second husband, if she should outlive Gonzago; wishing she might be accursed if she ever took a second husband, and adding that no woman did so, but those wicked women who kill their first husbands. Hamlet observed the king his uncle change colour at this expression, and that it was as bad as wormwood both to him and to the queen. But when Lucianus, according to the story, came to poison

Gonzago sleeping in the garden, the strong resemblance which it bore to his own wicked act upon the late king, his brother, whom he had poisoned in his garden, so struck upon the conscience of this usurper, that he was unable to sit out the rest of the play, but on a sudden calling for lights to his chamber, and affecting or partly feeling a sudden sickness, he abruptly left the theatre. The king being departed, the play was given over. Now Hamlet had seen enough to be satisfied that the words of the ghost were true, and no illusion; and in a fit of gaiety, like that which comes over a man who suddenly has some great doubt or scruple resolved, he swore to Horatio, that he would take the ghost's word for a thousand pounds. But before he could make up his resolution as to what measures of revenge he should take, now he was certainly informed that his uncle was his father's murderer, he was sent for by the queen his mother, to a private conference in her closet.

It was by desire of the king that the queen sent for Hamlet, that she might signify to her son how much his late behaviour had displeased them both, and the king, wishing to know all that passed at that conference, and thinking that the too partial report of a mother might let slip some part of Hamlet's words, which it might much import the king to know, Polonius, the old counsellor of state, was ordered to plant himself behind the hangings in the queen's closet, where he might unseen hear all that passed. This artifice was particularly adapted to the disposition of Polonius, who was a man grown old in crooked maxims and policies of state, and delighted to get at the knowledge of matters in an indirect and cunning way.

Hamlet being come to his mother, she began to tax him in the roundest way with his actions and behaviour, and she told him that he had given great offence to *his father*, meaning the king, his uncle, whom, because he had married her, she called Hamlet's father. Hamlet.

sorely indignant that she should give so dear and
honoured a name as father seemed to him, to a wretch
who was indeed no better than the murderer of his true
father, with some sharpness replied: 'Mother, *you* have
much offended *my father*.'   The queen said that was but
an idle answer.   'As good as the question deserved,'
said Hamlet.   The queen asked him if he had forgotten
who it was he was speaking to?   'Alas!' replied Hamlet,
'I wish I could forget.   You are the queen, your husband's brother's wife; and you are my mother: I wish you
were not what you are.'   'Nay, then,' said the queen,
'if you show me so little respect, I will set those to you
that can speak,' and was going to send the king or
Polonius to him.   But Hamlet would not let her go,
now he had her alone, till he had tried if his words
could not bring her to some sense of her wicked life;
and, taking her by the wrist, he held her fast, and made
her sit down.   She, affrighted at his earnest manner,
and fearful lest in his lunacy he should do her a mischief,
cried out; and a voice was heard from behind the hangings: 'Help, help, the queen!' which Hamlet hearing,
and verily thinking that it was the king himself there
concealed, he drew his sword and stabbed at the place
where the voice came from, as he would have stabbed
a rat that ran there, till the voice ceasing, he concluded
the person to be dead.   But when he dragged for the
body, it was not the king, but Polonius, the old officious
counsellor, that had planted himself as a spy behind
the hangings.   'Oh me!' exclaimed the queen, 'what a
rash and bloody deed have you done!'   'A bloody deed,
mother,' replied Hamlet, 'but not so bad as yours, who
killed a king, and married his brother.'   Hamlet had
gone too far to leave off here.   He was now in the
humour to speak plainly to his mother, and he pursued
it.   And though the faults of parents are to be tenderly
treated by their children, yet in the case of great crimes
the son may have leave to speak even to his own mother

with some harshness, so as that harshness is meant for
her good, and to turn her from her wicked ways, and
not done for the purpose of upbraiding.   And now this
virtuous prince did in moving terms represent to the queen
the heinousness of her offence, in being so forgetful of the
dead king, his father, as in so short a space of time to
marry with his brother and reputed murderer: such an act
as, after the vows which she had sworn to her first husband, was enough to make all vows of women suspected,
and all virtue to be accounted hypocrisy, wedding contracts
to be less than gamesters' oaths, and religion to be a
mockery and a mere form of words.   He said she had
done such a deed, that the heavens blushed at it, and
the earth was sick of her because of it.   And he showed
her two pictures, the one of the late king, her first husband, and the other of the present king, her second husband, and he bade her mark the difference; what a grace
was on the brow of his father, how like a god he looked!
the curls of Apollo, the forehead of Jupiter, the eye of
Mars, and a posture like to Mercury newly alighted on
some heaven-kissing hill! this man, he said, *had been* her
husband.   And then he showed her whom she had got
in his stead: how like a blight or a mildew he looked,
for so he had blasted his wholesome brother.   And the
queen was sore ashamed that he should so turn her eyes
inward upon her soul, which she now saw so black and
deformed.   And he asked her how she could continue
to live with this man, and be a wife to him, who had
murdered her first husband, and got the crown by as
false means as a thief——and just as he spoke, the ghost
of his father, such as he was in his lifetime, and such
as he had lately seen it, entered the room, and Hamlet,
in great terror, asked what it would have; and the ghost
said that it came to remind him of the revenge he had
promised, which Hamlet seemed to have forgot; and
the ghost bade him speak to his mother, for the grief
and terror she was in would else kill her.   It then

vanished, and was seen by none but Hamlet, neither could he by pointing to where it stood, or by any description, make his mother perceive it; who was terribly frightened all this while to hear him conversing, as it seemed to her, with nothing; and she imputed it to the disorder of his mind. But Hamlet begged her not to flatter her wicked soul in such a manner as to think that it was his madness, and not her own offences, which had brought his father's spirit again on the earth. And he bade her feel his pulse, how temperately it beat, not like a madman's. And he begged of her with tears, to confess herself to heaven for what was past, and for the future to avoid the company of the king, and be no more as a wife to him: and when she should show herself a mother to him, by respecting his father's memory, he would ask a blessing of her as a son. And she promising to observe his directions, the conference ended.

And now Hamlet was at leisure to consider who it was that in his unfortunate rashness he had killed: and when he came to see that it was Polonius, the father of the lady Ophelia, whom he so dearly loved, he drew apart the dead body, and, his spirits being now a little quieter, he wept for what he had done.

The unfortunate death of Polonius gave the king a pretence for sending Hamlet out of the kingdom. He would willingly have put him to death, fearing him as dangerous; but he dreaded the people, who loved Hamlet, and the queen who, with all her faults, doted upon the prince, her son. So this subtle king, under pretence of providing for Hamlet's safety, that he might not be called to account for Polonius' death, caused him to be conveyed on board a ship bound for England, under the care of two courtiers, by whom he despatched letters to the English court, which in that time was in subjection and paid tribute to Denmark, requiring for special reasons there pretended, that Hamlet should be put to death as soon as he landed on English ground.

Hamlet, suspecting some treachery, in the night-time secretly got at the letters, and skilfully erasing his own name, he in the stead of it put in the names of those two courtiers, who had the charge of him, to be put to death: then sealing up the letters, he put them into their place again.   Soon after the ship was attacked by pirates, and a sea-fight commenced; in the course of which Hamlet, desirous to show his valour, with sword in hand singly boarded the enemy's vessel; while his own ship, in a cowardly manner, bore away, and leaving him to his fate, the two courtiers made the best of their way to England, charged with those letters the sense of which Hamlet had altered to their own deserved destruction.

The pirates, who had the prince in their power, showed themselves gentle enemies; and knowing whom they had got prisoner, in the hope that the prince might do them a good turn at court in recompense for any favour they might show him, they set Hamlet on shore at the nearest port in Denmark.   From that place Hamlet wrote to the king, acquainting him with the strange chance which had brought him back to his own country, and saying that on the next day he should present himself before his majesty.   When he got home, a sad spectacle offered itself the first thing to his eyes.

This was the funeral of the young and beautiful Ophelia, his once dear mistress.   The wits of this young lady had begun to turn ever since her poor father's death. That he should die a violent death, and by the hands of the prince whom she loved, so affected this tender young maid, that in a little time she grew perfectly distracted, and would go about giving flowers away to the ladies of the court, and saying that they were for her father's burial, singing songs about love and about death, and sometimes such as had no meaning at all, as if she had no memory of what happened to her.   There was a willow which grew slanting over a brook, and reflected its leaves on the stream.   To this brook she came one day when she was unwatched, with garlands she had been making, mixed up of daisies and nettles, flowers and weeds together, and clambering up to hang her garland upon the boughs of the willow, a bough broke, and precipitated this fair young maid, garland, and all that she had gathered, into the water, where her clothes bore her up for a while, during which she chanted scraps of old tunes, like one insensible to her own distress, or as if she were a creature natural to that element: but long it was not before her garments, heavy with the wet, pulled her in from her melodious singing to a muddy and miserable death. It was the funeral of this fair maid which her brother Laertes was celebrating, the king and queen and whole court being present, when Hamlet arrived. He knew not what all this show imported, but stood on one side, not inclining to interrupt the ceremony. He saw the flowers strewed upon her grave, as the custom was in maiden burials, which the queen herself threw in; and as she threw them she said: 'Sweets to the sweet! I thought to have decked thy bride-bed, sweet maid, not to have strewed thy grave. Thou shouldst have been my Hamlet's wife.' And he heard her brother wish that violets might spring from her grave: and he saw him leap into the grave all frantic with grief, and bid the attendants pile mountains of earth upon him, that he might be buried with her. And Hamlet's love for this fair maid came back to him, and he could not bear that a brother should show so much transport of grief, for he thought that he loved Ophelia better than forty thousand brothers. Then discovering himself, he leaped into the grave where Laertes was, all as frantic or more frantic than he, and Laertes knowing him to be Hamlet, who had been the cause of his father's and his sister's death, grappled him by the throat as an enemy, till the attendants parted them: and Hamlet, after the funeral, excused his hasty act in throwing himself into the grave as if to brave Laertes; but he said

To this brook Ophelia came one day when she was unwatched

he could not bear that any one should seem to outgo him in grief for the death of the fair Ophelia. And for the time these two noble youths seemed reconciled.

But out of the grief and anger of Laertes for the death of his father and Ophelia, the king, Hamlet's wicked uncle, contrived destruction for Hamlet. He set on Laertes, under cover of peace and reconciliation, to challenge Hamlet to a friendly trial of skill at fencing, which Hamlet accepting, a day was appointed to try the match. At this match all the court was present, and Laertes, by direction of the king, prepared a poisoned weapon. Upon this match great wagers were laid by the courtiers, as both Hamlet and Laertes were known to excel at this sword play; and Hamlet taking up the foils chose one, not at all suspecting the treachery of Laertes, or being careful to examine Laertes' weapon, who, instead of a foil or blunted sword, which the laws of fencing require, made use of one with a point, and poisoned. At first Laertes did but play with Hamlet, and suffered him to gain some advantages, which the dissembling king magnified and extolled beyond measure, drinking to Hamlet's success, and wagering rich bets upon the issue: but after a few passes, Laertes growing warm made a deadly thrust at Hamlet with his poisoned weapon, and gave him a mortal blow. Hamlet incensed, but not knowing the whole of the treachery, in the scuffle exchanged his own innocent weapon for Laertes' deadly one, and with a thrust of Laertes' own sword repaid Laertes home, who was thus justly caught in his own treachery. In this instant the queen shrieked out that she was poisoned. She had inadvertently drunk out of a bowl which the king had prepared for Hamlet, in case, that being warm in fencing, he should call for drink: into this the treacherous king had infused a deadly poison, to make sure of Hamlet, if Laertes had failed. He had forgotten to warn the queen of the bowl, which she drank of, and immediately died, exclaiming with her last breath that she was poisoned. Hamlet, suspecting some treachery, ordered the doors to be shut, while he sought it out.   Laertes told him to seek no farther, for he was the traitor; and feeling his life go away with the wound which Hamlet had given him, he made confession of the treachery he had used, and now he had fallen a victim to it: and he told Hamlet of the envenomed point, and said that Hamlet had not half an hour to live, for no medicine could cure him; and begging forgiveness of Hamlet, he died, with his last words accusing the king of being the contriver of the mischief.   When Hamlet saw his end draw near, there being yet some venom left upon the sword, he suddenly turned upon his false uncle, and thrust the point of it to his heart, fulfilling the promise which he had made to his father's spirit, whose injunction was now accomplished, and his foul murder revenged upon the murderer.   Then Hamlet, feeling his breath fail and life departing, turned to his dear friend Horatio, who had been spectator of this fatal tragedy; and with his dying breath requested him that he would live to tell his story to the world (for Horatio had made a motion as if he would slay himself to accompany the prince in death), and Horatio promised that he would make a true report, as one that was privy to all the circumstances.   And, thus satisfied, the noble heart of Hamlet cracked; and Horatio and the bystanders with many tears commended the spirit of this sweet prince to the guardianship of angels.   For Hamlet was a loving and a gentle prince, and greatly beloved for his many noble and princelike qualities; and if he had lived, would no doubt have proved a most royal and complete king to Denmark.

OTHELLO

BRABANTIO, the rich senator of Venice, had a fair daughter, the gentle Desdemona. She was sought to by divers suitors, both on account of her many virtuous qualities, and for her rich expectations. But among the suitors of her own clime and complexion, she saw none whom she could affect: for this noble lady, who regarded the mind more than the features of men, with a singularity rather to be admired than imitated, had chosen for the object of her affections, a Moor, a black, whom her father loved, and often invited to his house.

Neither is Desdemona to be altogether condemned for the unsuitableness of the person whom she selected for her lover. Bating that Othello was black, the noble Moor wanted nothing which might recommend him to the affections of the greatest lady. He was a soldier, and a brave one; and by his conduct in bloody wars against the Turks, had risen to the rank of general in the Venetian service, and was esteemed and trusted by the state.

He had been a traveller, and Desdemona (as is the manner of ladies) loved to hear him tell the story of his adventures, which he would run through from his earliest recollection; the battles, sieges, and encounters, which he had passed through; the perils he had been exposed to by land and by water; his hair-breadth escapes, when he had entered a breach, or marched up to the mouth of a cannon; and how he had been taken prisoner by the insolent enemy, and sold to slavery; how he demeaned himself in that state, and how he escaped: all these accounts, added to the narration of the strange things he had seen in foreign countries. the vast wilderness and romantic caverns, the quarries, the rocks and mountains, whose heads are in the clouds; of the savage nations, the cannibals who are man-eaters, and a race of people in Africa whose heads do grow beneath their shoulders: these travellers' stories would so enchain the attention of Desdemona, that if she were called off at any time by household affairs, she would despatch with all haste that business, and return, and with a greedy ear devour Othello's discourse. And once he took advantage of a pliant hour, and drew from her a prayer, that he would tell her the whole story of his life at large, of which she had heard so much, but only by parts: to which he consented, and beguiled her of many a tear, when he spoke of some distressful stroke which his youth had suffered.

His story being done, she gave him for his pains a world of sighs: she swore a pretty oath, that it was all passing strange, and pitiful, wondrous pitiful: she wished (she said) she had not heard it, yet she wished that heaven had made her such a man; and then she thanked him, and told him, if he had a friend who loved her, he had only to teach him how to tell his story, and that would woo her. Upon this hint, delivered not with more frankness than modesty, accompanied with certain bewitching prettiness, and blushes, which Othello could not but understand, he spoke more openly of his love, and in this golden opportunity gained the consent of the generous lady Desdemona privately to marry him.

Neither Othello's colour nor his fortune were such that it could be hoped Brabantio would accept him for a son-in-law. He had left his daughter free; but he did expect that, as the manner of noble Venetian ladies was, she would choose ere long a husband of senatorial rank or expectations; but in this he was deceived; Desdemona loved the Moor, though he was black, and devoted her heart and fortunes to his valiant parts and qualities; so was her heart subdued to an implicit devotion to the man she had selected for a husband, that his very colour, which to all but this discerning lady would have proved an insurmountable objection, was by her esteemed above all the white skins and clear complexions of the young Venetian nobility, her suitors.

Their marriage, which, though privately carried, could not long be kept a secret, came to the ears of the old man, Brabantio, who appeared in a solemn council of the senate, as an accuser of the Moor Othello, who by spells and witchcraft (he maintained) had seduced the affections of the fair Desdemona to marry him, without the consent of her father, and against the obligations of hospitality.

At this juncture of time it happened that the state of Venice had immediate need of the services of Othello, news having arrived that the Turks with mighty preparation had fitted out a fleet, which was bending its course to the island of Cyprus, with intent to regain that strong post from the Venetians, who then held it; in this emergency the state turned its eyes upon Othello, who alone was deemed adequate to conduct the defence of Cyprus against the Turks. So that Othello, now summoned before the senate, stood in their presence at once as a candidate for a great state employment, and as a culprit, charged with offences which by the laws of Venice were made capital.

The age and senatorial character of old Brabantio, commanded a most patient hearing from that grave assembly; but the incensed father conducted his accusation with so much intemperance, producing likelihoods and allegations for proofs, that, when Othello was called upon for his defence, he had only to relate a plain tale of the course of his love; which he did with such an artless eloquence, recounting the whole story of his wooing, as we have related it above, and delivered his speech with so noble a plainness (the evidence of truth), that the duke, who sat as chief judge, could not help confessing that a tale so told would have won his daughter too: and the spells and conjurations which Othello had used in his courtship, plainly appeared to have been no more than the honest arts of men in love; and the only witchcraft which he had used, the faculty of telling a soft tale to win a lady's ear.

This statement of Othello was confirmed by the testimony of the lady Desdemona herself, who appeared in court, and professing a duty to her father for life and education, challenged leave of him to profess a yet higher duty to her lord and husband, even so much as her mother had shown in preferring him (Brabantio) above *her* father.

The old senator, unable to maintain his plea, called the Moor to him with many expressions of sorrow, and, as an act of necessity, bestowed upon him his daughter, whom, if he had been free to withhold her (he told him), he would with all his heart have kept from him; adding, that he was glad at soul that he had no other child, for this behaviour of Desdemona would have taught him to be a tyrant, and hang clogs on them for her desertion.

This difficulty being got over. Othello, to whom custom had rendered the hardships of a military life as natural as food and rest are to other men, readily undertook the management of the wars in Cyprus: and Desdemona, preferring the honour of her lord (though with danger) before the indulgence of those idle delights in which new-married people usually waste their time, cheerfully consented to his going.

No sooner were Othello and his lady landed in Cyprus, than news arrived, that a desperate tempest had dispersed the Turkish fleet, and thus the island was secure from any immediate apprehension of an attack. But the war, which Othello was to suffer, was now beginning; and the enemies, which malice stirred up against his innocent lady, proved in their nature more deadly than strangers or infidels.

Among all the general's friends no one possessed

the confidence of Othello more entirely than Cassio. Michael Cassio was a young soldier, a Florentine, gay, amorous, and of pleasing address, favourite qualities with women; he was handsome and eloquent, and exactly such a person as might alarm the jealousy of a man advanced in years (as Othello in some measure was), who had married a young and beautiful wife; but Othello was as free from jealousy as he was noble, and as incapable of suspecting as of doing a base action. He had employed this Cassio in his love affair with Desdemona, and Cassio had been a sort of go-between in his suit: for Othello, fearing that himself had not those soft parts of conversation which please ladies, and finding these qualities in his friend, would often depute Cassio to go (as he phrased it) a courting for him: such innocent simplicity being rather an honour than a blemish to the character of the valiant Moor. So that no wonder, if next to Othello himself (but at far distance, as beseems a virtuous wife) the gentle Desdemona loved and trusted Cassio. Nor had the marriage of this couple made any difference in their behaviour to Michael Cassio. He frequented their house, and his free and rattling talk was no unpleasing variety to Othello, who was himself of a more serious temper: for such tempers are observed often to delight in their contraries, as a relief from the oppressive excess of their own: and Desdemona and Cassio would talk and laugh together, as in the days when he went a courting for his friend.

Othello had lately promoted Cassio to be the lieutenant, a place of trust, and nearest to the general's person. This promotion gave great offence to Iago, an older officer who thought he had a better claim than Cassio, and would often ridicule Cassio as a fellow fit only for the company of ladies, and one that knew no more of the art of war or how to set an army in array for battle, than a girl. Iago hated Cassio, and he hated Othello, as well for favouring Cassio, as for an unjust suspicion, which he had lightly taken up against Othello, that the Moor was too fond of Iago's wife Emilia. From these imaginary provocations, the plotting mind of Iago conceived a horrid scheme of revenge, which should involve both Cassio, the Moor, and Desdemona, in one common ruin.

Iago was artful, and had studied human nature deeply, and he knew that of all the torments which afflict the mind of man (and far beyond bodily torture), the pains of jealousy were the most intolerable, and had the sorest sting. If he could succeed in making Othello jealous of Cassio, he thought it would be an exquisite plot of revenge, and might end in the death of Cassio or Othello, or both; he cared not.

The arrival of the general and his lady, in Cyprus, meeting with the news of the dispersion of the enemy's fleet, made a sort of holiday in the island. Everybody gave themselves up to feasting and making merry. Wine flowed in abundance, and cups went round to the health of the black Othello, and his lady the fair Desdemona.

Cassio had the direction of the guard that night, with a charge from Othello to keep the soldiers from excess in drinking, that no brawl might arise, to fright the inhabitants, or disgust them with the new-landed forces. That night Iago began his deep-laid plans of mischief: under colour of loyalty and love to the general, he enticed Cassio to make rather too free with the bottle (a great fault in an officer upon guard). Cassio for a time resisted, but he could not long hold out against the honest freedom which Iago knew how to put on, but kept swallowing glass after glass (as Iago still plied him with drink and encouraging songs), and Cassio's tongue ran over in praise of the lady Desdemona, whom he again and again toasted, affirming that she was a most exquisite lady: until at last the enemy which he put into his mouth stole away his brains; and upon some provocation given him by a fellow whom Iago had set on, swords were drawn, and Montano, a worthy officer, who interfered to appease the dispute, was wounded in the scuffle. The riot now began to be general, and Iago, who had set on foot the mischief, was foremost in spreading the alarm, causing the castle-bell to be rung (as if some dangerous mutiny instead of a slight drunken quarrel had arisen): the alarm-bell ringing awakened Othello, who, dressing in a hurry, and coming to the scene of action, questioned Cassio of the cause. Cassio was now come to himself, the effect of the wine having a little gone off, but was too much ashamed to reply; and Iago, pretending a great reluctance to accuse Cassio, but, as it were, forced into it by Othello, who insisted to know the truth, gave an account of the whole matter (leaving out his own share in it, which Cassio was too far gone to remember) in such a manner, as while he seemed to màke Cassio's offence less, did indeed make it appear greater than it was. The result was, that Othello, who was a strict observer of discipline, was compelled to take away Cassio's place of lieutenant from him.

Thus did Iago's first artifice succeed completely; he had now undermined his hated rival, and thrust him out of his place: but a further use was hereafter to be made of the adventure of this disastrous night.

Cassio, whom this misfortune had entirely sobered, now lamented to his seeming friend Iago that he should have been such a fool as to transform himself into a beast. He was undone, for how could he ask the general for his place again? he would tell him he was a drunkard. He despised himself. Iago, affecting to make light of it, said, that he, or any man living, might be drunk upon occasion; it remained now to make the best of a bad bargain; the general's wife was now the general, and could do anything with Othello; that he were best to apply to the lady Desdemona to mediate for him with her lord; that she was of a frank, obliging disposition, and would readily undertake a good office of this sort, and set Cassio right again in the general's favour; and then this crack in their love would be made stronger than ever. A good advice of Iago, if it had not been given for wicked purposes, which will after appear.

Cassio did as Iago advised him, and made application to the lady Desdemona, who was easy to be won over in any honest suit; and she promised Cassio that she should be his solicitor with her lord, and rather die than give up his cause. This she immediately set about in so earnest and pretty a manner, that Othello, who was mortally offended with Cassio, could not put her off. When he pleaded delay, and that it was too soon to pardon such an offender, she would not be beat back, but insisted that it should be the next night, or the morning after, or the next morning to that at farthest. Then she showed how penitent and humbled poor Cassio was, and that his offence did not deserve so sharp a check. And when Othello still hung back: 'What! my lord,' said she, 'that I should have so much to do to plead for Cassio, Michael Cassio, that came a courting for you, and oftentimes, when I have spoken in dispraise of you, has taken your part! I count this but a little thing to ask of you. When I mean to try your love indeed, I shall ask a weighty matter.' Othello could deny nothing to such a pleader, and only requesting that Desdemona would leave the time to him, promised to receive Michael Cassio again in favour.

It happened that Othello and Iago had entered into the room where Desdemona was, just as Cassio, who had been imploring her intercession, was departing at the opposite door: and Iago, who was full of art, said in a low voice, as if to himself: 'I like not that.' Othello took no great notice of what he said; indeed, the conference which immediately took place with his lady put it out of his head; but he remembered it afterwards.

For when Desdemona was gone, Iago, as if for mere satisfaction of his thought, questioned Othello whether Michael Cassio, when Othello was courting his lady, knew of his love. To this the general answering in the affirmative, and adding, that he had gone between them very often during the courtship, Iago knitted his brow, as if he had got fresh light on some terrible matter, and cried: 'Indeed!' This brought into Othello's mind the words which Iago had let fall upon entering the room, and seeing Cassio with Desdemona; and he began to think there was some meaning in all this: for he deemed Iago to be a just man, and full of love and honesty, and what in a false knave would be tricks, in him seemed to be the natural workings of an honest mind, big with something too great for utterance: and Othello prayed Iago to speak what he knew, and to give his worst thoughts words. 'And what,' said Iago, 'if some thoughts very vile should have intruded into my breast, as where is the palace into which foul things do not enter?' Then Iago went on to say, what a pity it were, if any trouble should arise to Othello out of his imperfect observations; that it would not be for Othello's peace to know his thoughts; that people's good names were not to be taken away for slight suspicions; and when Othello's curiosity was raised almost to distraction with these hints and scattered words, Iago, as if in earnest care for Othello's peace of mind, besought him to beware of jealousy: with such art did this villain raise suspicions in the unguarded Othello, by the very caution which he pretended to give him against suspicion. 'I know,' said Othello, 'that my wife is fair, loves company and feasting, is free of speech, sings, plays, and dances well: but where virtue is, these qualities are virtuous. I must have proof before I think her dishonest.' Then Iago, as if glad that Othello was slow to believe ill of his lady, frankly declared that he had no proof, but begged Othello to observe her behaviour well, when Cassio was by; not to be jealous nor too secure neither, for that he (Iago) knew the dispositions of the Italian ladies, his countrywomen, better than Othello could do; and that in Venice the wives let heaven see many pranks they dared not show their husbands. Then he artfully insinuated that Desdemona deceived her father in marrying with Othello, and carried it so closely, that the poor old man thought that witch-craft had been used. Othello was much moved with this argument, which brought the matter home to him, for if she had decieved her father, why might she not deceive her husband?

Iago begged pardon for having moved him; but Othello, assuming an indifference, while he was really shaken with inward grief at Iago's words, begged him to go on, which Iago did with many apologies, as if unwilling to produce anything against Cassio, whom he called his friend: he then came strongly to the point, and reminded Othello how Desdemona had refused many suitable matches of her own clime and complexion, and had married him, a Moor, which showed unnatural in her, and proved her to have a headstrong will; and when her better judgment returned, how probable it was she should fall upon comparing Othello with the fine forms and clear white complexions of the young Italians her countrymen. He concluded with advising Othello to put off his reconcilement with Cassio a little longer, and in the meanwhile to note with what earnest-ness Desdemona should intercede in his behalf; for that much would be seen in that. So mischievously did this artful villain lay his plots to turn the gentle qualities of this innocent lady into her destruction, and make a net for her out of her own goodness to entrap her: first setting Cassio on to entreat her mediation, and then out of that very mediation contriving stratagems for her ruin.

The conference ended with Iago's begging Othello to account his wife innocent, until he had more decisive proof; and Othello promised to be patient; but from that moment the deceived Othello never tasted content of mind. Poppy, nor the juice of mandragora, nor all the sleeping potions in the world, could ever again restore to him that sweet rest, which he had enjoyed but yesterday. His occupation sickened upon him. He no longer took delight in arms. His heart, that used to be roused at the sight of troops, and banners, and battle-array, and would stir and leap at the sound of a drum, or a trumpet, or a neighing war-horse, seemed to have lost all that pride and ambition which are a soldier's virtue; and his military ardour and all his old joys forsook him. Sometimes he thought his wife honest, and at times he thought her not so; sometimes he thought Iago just, and at times he thought him not so; then he would wish that he had never known of it; he was not the worse for her loving Cassio, so long as he knew it not: torn to pieces with these distracting thoughts, he once laid hold on Iago's throat, and demanded proof of Desdemona's guilt, or threatened instant death for his having belied her. Iago, feigning indignation that his honesty should be taken for a vice, asked Othello, if he had not sometimes seen a handkerchief spotted with strawberries in his wife's hand. Othello answered, that he had given her such a one, and that it was his first gift. 'That same handkerchief,' said Iago, 'did I see Michael Cassio this day wipe his face with.' 'If it be as you say,' said Othello, 'I will not rest till a wide revenge swallow them up: and first, for a token of your fidelity, I expect that Cassio shall be put to death within three days; and for that fair devil (meaning his lady), I will withdraw and devise some swift means of death for her.'

Trifles light as air are to the jealous proofs as strong as holy writ. A handkerchief of his wife's seen in Cassio's hand, was motive enough to the deluded Othello to pass sentence of death upon them both, without once inquiring how Cassio came by it. Desdemona had never given such a present to Cassio, nor would this constant lady have wronged her lord with doing so naughty a thing as giving his presents to another man; both Cassio and Desdemona were innocent of any offence against Othello: but the wicked Iago, whose spirits never slept in contrivance of villany, had made his wife (a good, but a weak woman) steal this handkerchief from Desdomona, under pretence of getting the work copied, but in reality to drop it in Cassio's way, where he might find it, and give a handle to Iago's suggestion that it was Desdemona's present.

Othello, soon after meeting his wife, pretended that he had a headache (as he might indeed with truth), and desired her to lend him her handkerchief to hold to his temples. She did so. 'Not this,' said Othello, 'but that handkerchief I gave you.' Desdemona had it not about her (for indeed it was stolen, as we have related). 'How?' said Othello, 'this is a fault indeed. That handkerchief an Egyptian woman gave to my mother; the woman was a witch and could read people's thoughts: she told my mother, while she kept it, it would make her amiable, and my father would love her; but, if she lost it, or gave it away, my father's fancy would turn, and he would loathe her as much as he had loved her. She dying gave it to me, and bade me, if I ever married, to give it to my wife. I did so; take heed of it. Make it a darling as precious as your eye.' 'It is possible?' said the frighted lady. ''Tis true,' continued Othello; 'it is a magical handkerchief; a sibyl that had lived in the world two hundred years, in a fit of prophetic fury worked it; the silkworms that furnished the silk were hallowed, and it was dyed in a mummy of maidens' hearts conserved.' Desdemona, hearing the wondrous virtues of the handkerchief, was ready to die with fear, for she plainly perceived she had lost it, and with it, she feared, the affections of her husband. Then Othello started, and looked as if he were going to do some rash thing, and still he demanded the handkerchief, which when she could not produce, she tried to divert her husband from too serious thoughts, and cheerfully told him she saw all his talk about the handkerchief was only to put her off from her suit about Michael Cassio, whom she went on to praise (as Iago had foretold), till Othello in perfect distraction burst out of the room, and then Desdemona, though unwillingly, began to suspect that her lord was jealous.

What cause she could have ministered to him she knew not, and then she accused herself for accusing the noble Othello, and thought to be sure that some untoward news from Venice, or some state troubles had puddled his spirits, and made his temper not so sweet as formerly. And she said: 'Men are not gods, and we must not look for that observance from them when they are married, which they show us on the bridal day.' And she beshrewed herself for so unkindly judging of his unkindness.

Again Othello and Desdemona met, and he accused her more plainly of being unfaithful, and of loving another man, but he did not name whom: and Othello wept, and Desdemona said: 'Alas! the heavy day! why do you weep?' And Othello told her, he could have borne all sorts of evils with fortitude—poverty, and disease, and disgrace; but her infidelity had broken his heart: and he called her a weed, that looked so fair, and smelled so sweet, that the sense ached at it; and wished she had never been born. And when he had left her, this innocent lady was so stupefied with wonder at her lord's untrue suspicion of her, that a weight-like sleep came over her, and she only desired her attendant to make her bed, and to lay her wedding-sheets upon it, saying, that when people teach their babes, they do it by gentle means and easy tasks, and Othello might have chid her so; for in good faith she was but a child when she was chidden. And this was all the complaint which this gentle lady made.

Desdemona being retired to bed expecting her lord would follow her, soon fell into a slumber, the effect of her troubled spirits, when Othello entered the chamber, full of the black purpose which he had meditated of putting his lady to death. But when he saw her asleep, he thought he would not shed her blood, nor scar that white skin of hers, more white than alabaster. But he was resolved she should die; else (as he said) she would live to betray more men, as she had done him. Then he kissed her for the last time (as he said), and that kiss was so sweet, that he must needs kiss her again: and he wept, but he said they were cruel tears.

Desdemona was awakened with his kisses, and she looked upon Othello, and she saw him gnaw his under lip, and roll his eyes, and she knew he was always fatal when he looked so: and he bade her prepare for death, and to say her prayers, for he would not kill her soul. And this innocent wife, as she lay at his mercy, begged for compassion, and to know her fault, and then he named Cassio, and the handkerchief which (he said) she had given him; and as the guiltless lady was proceeding to clear herself he suddenly would hear no more, but covering her up in the bed-clothes, stifled her till she died.

In this instant of time was brought into the house Cassio, wounded and bleeding, whom Iago had set one of his creatures on to assassinate; but the fellow not succeeding in his attempt to kill Cassio (whom he wounded, but not mortally), and being himself killed by Iago to prevent discovery, in his pockets were found certain letters, which made the guilt of Iago, and the innocence of Cassio, clear beyond all doubt; and Cassio now came to beg pardon of Othello, and to ask wherein he had offended him, that he had employed Iago to murder him.

This discovery was as a thunderstroke to Othello,

who now plainly saw that he was no better than a murderer, and that his wife (poor innocent lady) had been ever faithful to him; the extreme anguish of which discovery making life insupportable, he fell upon his sword, and throwing himself upon the body of his dear injured lady, expired.

These rash acts raised much passion of horror and amazement in the bystanders, for Othello had borne a fair reputation, and till he was wrought upon by the arts of a villain, which his own noble nature never gave him leave to suspect, he was a loving and a doting husband. He had loved not wisely, but too well; and his manly eyes (when he learned his mistake), though not used to weep on every small occasion, dropped tears as fast as the Arabian trees their gum. And when he was dead all his former merits and his valiant acts were remembered. Nothing now remained for his successor but to put the utmost censure of the law in force against Iago, who was executed with strict tortures; and to send word to the state of Venice of the lamentable death of their renowned general.

PERICLES, PRINCE OF TYRE

PERICLES, prince of Tyre, became a voluntary exile from his dominions, to avert the dreadful calamities which Antiochus, the wicked emperor of Greece, threatened to bring upon his subjects and city of Tyre, in revenge for a discovery which the prince had made of a shocking deed which the emperor had done in secret; as commonly it proves dangerous to pry into the hidden crimes of great ones. Leaving the government of his people in the hands of his able and honest minister, Helicanus, Pericles set sail from Tyre, thinking to absent himself till the wrath of Antiochus, who was mighty, should be appeased.

The first place which the prince directed his course to was Tarsus, and hearing that the city of Tarsus was at that time suffering under a severe famine, he took with him store of provisions for its relief. On his arrival he found the city reduced to the utmost distress; and, he coming like a messenger from heaven with his unhoped-for succour, Cleon, the governor of Tarsus, welcomed him with boundless thanks. Pericles had not been here many days, before letters came from his faithful minister, warning him that it was not safe for him to stay at Tarsus, for Antiochus knew of his abode, and by secret emissaries despatched for that purpose sought his life. Upon receipt of these letters Pericles put out to sea again, amidst the blessings and prayers of a whole people who had been fed by his bounty.

He had not sailed far, when his ship was overtaken by a dreadful storm, and every man on board perished except Pericles, who was cast by the sea-waves naked on an unknown shore, where he had not wandered long before he met with some poor fishermen, who invited him to their homes, giving him clothes and provisions.

The fishermen told Pericles the name of their country was Pentapolis, and that their king was Simonides, commonly called the good Simonides, because of his peaceable reign and good government. From them he also learned that king Simonides had a fair young daughter, and that the following day was her birthday, when a grand tournament was to be held at court, many princes and knights being come from all parts to try their skill in arms for the love of Thaisa, this fair princess. While the prince was listening to this account, and secretly lamenting the loss of his good armour, which disabled him from making one among these valiant knights, another fisherman brought in a complete suit of armour that he had taken out of the sea with his fishing-net, which proved to be the very armour he had lost. When Pericles beheld his own armour, he said: 'Thanks, Fortune; after all my crosses you give me somewhat to repair myself. This armour was bequeathed to me by my dead father, for whose dear sake I have so loved it that whithersoever I went, I still have kept it by me, and the rough sea that parted it from me, having now become calm, hath given it back again, for which I thank it for, since I have my father's gift again, I think my shipwreck no misfortune.'

The next day Pericles clad in his brave father's armour, repaired to the royal court of Simonides, where he performed wonders at the tournament, vanquishing with ease all the brave knights and valiant princes who contended with him in arms for the honour of Thaisa's love. When brave warriors contended at court tournaments for the love of king's daughters, if one proved sole victor over all the rest, it was usual for the great lady for whose sake these deeds of valour were undertaken, to bestow all her respect upon the conqueror, and Thaisa did not depart from this custom, for she presently dismissed all the princes and knights whom Pericles had vanquished, and distinguished him by her especial favour and regard, crowning him with the wrath of victory, as king of that day's happiness; and Pericles became a most passionate lover of this beauteous princess from the first moment he beheld her.

The good Simonides so well approved of the valour and noble qualities of Pericles, who was indeed a most accomplished gentleman, and well learned in all excellent arts, that though he knew not the rank of this royal stranger (for Pericles for fear of Antiochus gave out that he was a private gentleman of Tyre), yet did not Simonides disdain to accept of the valiant unknown for a son-in-law, when he perceived his daughter's affections were firmly fixed upon him.

Pericles had not been many months married to Thaisa, before he received intelligence that his enemy Antiochus was dead; and that his subjects of Tyre, impatient of his long absence, threatened to revolt, and talked of placing Helicanus upon his vacant throne. This news came from Helicanus himself, who, being a loyal subject to his royal master, would not accept of the high dignity offered him, but sent to let Pericles know their intentions, that he might return home and resume his lawful right. It was matter of great surprise and joy to Simonides, to find that his son-in-law (the obscure knight) was the renowned prince of Tyre; yet again he regretted that he was not the private gentleman he supposed him to be, seeing that he must now part both with his admired son-in-law and his beloved daughter, whom he feared to trust to the perils of the sea, because Thaisa was with child; and Pericles himself wished her to remain with her father till after her confinemnet, but the poor lady so earnestly desired to go with her husband, that at last they consented, hoping she would reach Tyre before she was brought to bed.

The sea was no friendly element to unhappy Pericles, for long before they reached Tyre another dreadful tempest arose, which so terrified Thaisa that she was taken ill, and in a short space of time her nurse Lychorida came to Pericles with a little child in her arms, to tell the prince the sad tidings that his wife died the moment her little babe was born. She held the babe towards its father, saying: 'Here is a thing too young for such a place. This is the child of your dead queen.' No tongue can tell the dreadful sufferings of Pericles when he heard his wife was dead. As soon as he could speak, he said: 'O you gods, why do you make us love your goodly gifts, and then snatch those gifts away?' 'Patience, good sir,' said Lychorida, 'here is all that is left alive of our dead queen, a little daughter, and for your child's sake be more manly. Patience, good sir, even for the sake of this precious charge.' Pericles took the new-born infant in his arms, and he said to the little babe: 'Now may your life be mild, for a more blusterous birth had never babe! May your condition be mild and gentle, for you have had the rudest welcome that ever prince's child did meet with! May that which follows be happy, for you have had as chiding a nativity as fire, air, water, earth, and heaven could make to herald you from the womb! Even at the first, your loss,' meaning in the death of her mother, 'is more than all the joys, which you shall find upon this earth to which you are come a new visitor, shall be able to recompense.'

The storm still continuing to rage furiously, and the sailors having a superstition that while a dead body remained in the ship the storm would never cease, they came to Pericles to demand that his queen should be thrown overboard; and they said: 'What courage, sir? God save you!' 'Courage enough,' said the sorrowing prince: 'I do not fear the storm; it has done to me its worst; yet for the love of this poor infant, this fresh new seafarer, I wish the storm was over.' 'Sir,' said the sailors, 'your queen must overboard. The sea works high, the wind is loud, and the storm will not

abate till the ship be cleared of the dead.' Though
Pericles knew how weak and unfounded this superstition was, yet he patiently submitted, saying: 'As you
think meet.   Then she must overboard, most wretched
queen!'   And now this unhappy prince went to take a
last view of his dear wife, and as he looked on his Thaisa,
he said: 'A terrible childbed hast thou had, my dear; no
light, no fire; the unfriendly elements forget thee utterly,
nor have I time to bring thee hallowed to thy grave, but
must cast thee scarcely coffined into the sea, where for a
monument upon thy bones the humming waters must
overwhelm thy corpse, lying with simple shells.   O
Lychorida, bid Nestor bring me spices, ink, and paper,
my casket and my jewels, and bid Nicandor bring me
the satin coffin.   Lay the babe upon the pillow, and go
about this suddenly, Lychorida, while I say a priestly
farewell to my Thaisa.'

They brought Pericles a large chest, in which (wrapped
in a satin shroud) he placed his queen, and sweet-smelling
spices he strewed over her, and beside her he placed rich
jewels, and a written paper, telling who she was, and
praying if haply any one should find the chest which
contained the body of his wife, they would give her
burial: and then with his own hands he cast the chest
into the sea.   When the storm was over, Pericles ordered
the sailors to make for Tarsus.   'For,' said Pericles,
'the babe cannot hold out till we come to Tyre.   At
Tarsus I will leave it at careful nursing.'

After that tempestuous night when Thaisa was thrown
into the sea, and while it was yet early morning, as
Cerimon, a worthy gentleman of Ephesus, and a most
skilful physician, was standing by the sea-side, his
servants brought to him a chest, which they said the sea-
waves had thrown on the land.   'I never saw,' said one
of them, 'so huge a billow as cast it on our shore.'
Cerimon ordered the chest to be conveyed to his own
house, and when it was opened he beheld with wonder

the body of a young and lovely lady; and the sweet-smelling spices and rich casket of jewels made him conclude it was some great person who was thus strangely entombed: searching farther, he discovered a paper, from which he learned that the corpse which lay as dead before him had been a queen, and wife to Pericles, prince of Tyre; and much admiring at the strangeness of that accident, and more pitying the husband who had lost this sweet lady, he said: 'If you are living, Pericles, you have a heart that even cracks with woe.' Then observing attentively Thaisa's face, he saw how fresh and unlike death her looks were, and he said: 'They were too hasty that threw you into the sea': for he did not believe her to be dead. He ordered a fire to be made, and proper cordials to be brought, and soft music to be played, which might help to calm her amazed spirits if she should revive; and he said to those who crowded round her, wondering at what they saw: 'I pray you, gentlemen, give her air; this queen will live; she has not been entranced above five hours; and see, she begins to blow into life again; she is alive; behold, her eyelids move; this fair creature will live to make us weep to hear her fate.' Thaisa had never died, but after the birth of her little baby had fallen into a deep swoon, which made all that saw her conclude her to be dead; and now by the care of this kind gentleman she once more revived to light and life; and opening her eyes, she said: 'Where am I? Where is my lord? What world is this?' By gentle degrees Cerimon let her understand what had befallen her; and when he thought she was enough recovered to bear the sight, he showed her the paper written by her husband, and the jewels; and she looked on the paper, and said: 'It is my lord's writing. That I was shipped at sea, I well remember, but whether there delivered of my babe, by the holy gods I cannot rightly say; but since my wedded lord I never shall see again, I will put on a vestal livery, and never more have joy.' 'Madam,' said

Cerimon, 'if you purpose as you speak, the temple of
Diana is not far distant from hence; there you may
abide as a vestal.   Moreover, if you please, a niece of
mine shall there attend you.'   This proposal was accepted
with thanks by Thaisa; and when she was perfectly
recovered, Cerimon placed her in the temple of Diana,
where she became a vestal or priestess of that goddess,
and passed her days in sorrowing for her husband's
supposed loss, and in the most devout exercises of those
times.

Pericles carried his young daughter (whom he named
Marina, because she was born at sea) to Tarsus, intending
to leave her with Cleon, the governor of that city, and
his wife Dionysia, thinking, for the good he had done
to them at the time of their famine, they would be kind
to his little motherless daughter.   When Cleon saw prince
Pericles, and heard of the great loss which had befallen
him, he said: 'O your sweet queen, that it had pleased
Heaven you could have brought her hither to have
blessed my eyes with the sight of her!'   Pericles replied:
'We must obey the powers above us.   Should I rage
and roar as the sea does in which my Thaisa lies, yet the
end must be as it is.   My gentle babe, Marina here, I
must charge your charity with her.   I leave her the
infant of your care, beseeching you to give her princely
training.'   And then turning to Cleon's wife, Dionysia,
he said: 'Good madam, make me blessed in your care
in bringing up my child': and she answered: 'I have a
child myself who shall not be more dear to my respect
than yours, my lord'; and Cleon made the like promise,
saying: 'Your noble services, prince Pericles, in feeding
my whole people with your corn (for which in their
prayers they daily remember you) must in your child
be thought on.   If I should neglect your child, my whole
people that were by you relieved would force me to my
duty; but if to that I need a spur, the gods revenge it
on me and mine to the end of generation.'   Pericles,

being thus assured that his child would be carefully attended to, left her to the protection of Cleon and his wife Dionysia, and with her he left the nurse Lychorida. When he went away, the little Marina knew not her loss, but Lychorida wept sadly at parting with her royal master. 'O, no tears, Lychorida,' said Pericles: 'no tears; look to your little mistress, on whose grace you may depend hereafter.'

Pericles arrived in safety at Tyre, and was once more settled in the quiet possession of his throne, while his woeful queen, whom he thought dead, remained at Ephesus. Her little babe Marina, whom this hapless mother had never seen, was brought up by Cleon in a manner suitable to her high birth. He gave her the most careful education, so that by the time Marina attained the age of fourteen years, the most deeply-learned men were not more studied in the learning of those times than was Marina. She sang like one immortal, and danced as goddesslike, and with her needle she was so skilful that she seemed to compose nature's own shapes, in birds, fruits, or flowers, the natural roses being scarcely more like to each other than they were to Marina's silken flowers. But when she had gained from education all these graces, which made her the general wonder, Dionysia, the wife of Cleon, became her mortal enemy from jealousy, by reason that her own daughter, from the slowness of her mind, was not able to attain to that perfection wherein Marina excelled: and finding that all praise was bestowed on Marina, whilst her daughter, who was of the same age, and had been educated with the same care as Marina, though not with the same success, was in comparison disregarded, she formed a project to remove Marina out of the way, vainly imagining that her untoward daughter would be more respected when Marina was no more seen. To encompass this she employed a man to murder Marina, and she well timed her wicked design, when Lychorida, the faithful nurse, had just died. Dionysia was discoursing with the man she had commanded to commit this murder, when the young Marina was weeping over the dead Lychorida. Leonine, the man she employed to do this bad deed, though he was a very wicked man, could hardly be persuaded to undertake it, so had Marina won all hearts to love her. He said: 'She is a goodly creature!' 'The fitter then the gods should have her,' replied her merciless enemy: 'here she comes weeping for the death of her nurse Lychorida: are you resolved to obey me?' Leonine, fearing to disobey her, replied: 'I am resolved.' And so, in that one short sentence, was the matchless Marina doomed to an untimely death. She now approached, with a basket of flowers in her hand, which she said she would daily strew over the grave of good Lychorida. The purple violet and the marigold should as a carpet hang upon her grave, while summer days did last. 'Alas, for me!' she said, 'poor unhappy maid, born in a tempest, when my mother died. This world to me is like a lasting storm, hurrying me from my friends.' 'How now, Marina,' said the dissembling Dionysia, 'do you weep alone? How does it chance my daughter is not with you? Do not sorrow for Lychorida, you have a nurse in me. Your beauty is quite changed with this unprofitable woe. Come, give me your flowers, the sea-air will spoil them; and walk with Leonine: the air is fine, and will enliven you. Come, Leonine, take her by the arm, and walk with her.' 'No, madam,' said Marina, 'I pray you let me not deprive you of your servant': for Leonine was one of Dionysia's attendants. 'Come, come,' said this artful woman, who wished for a pretence to leave her alone with Leonine, 'I love the prince, your father, and I love you. We every day expect your father here; and when he comes, and finds you so changed by grief from the paragon of beauty we reported you, he will think we have taken no care of you. Go, I pray you, walk, and be cheerful once again. Be careful of that excellent complexion, which stole the hearts of old and young.' Marina, being thus importuned, said: 'Well, I will go, but yet I have no desire to it.' As Dionysia walked away, she said to Leonine: '*Remember what I have said!*'—shocking words, for their meaning was that he should remember to kill Marina.

Marina looked towards the sea, her birthplace, and said: 'Is the wind westerly that blows?' 'South-west,' replied Leonine. 'When I was born the wind was north,' said she: and then the storm and tempest, and all her father's sorrows, and her mother's death, came full into her mind; and she said: 'My father, as Lychorida told me, did never fear, but cried, *Courage, good seamen*, to the sailors, galling his princely hands with the ropes, and, clasping to the masts, he endured a sea that almost split the deck.' 'When was this?' said Leonine. 'When I was born,' replied Marina: 'never were wind and waves more violent'; and then she described the storm, the action of the sailors, the boatswain's whistle, and the loud call of the master, 'which,' said she, 'trebled the confusion of the ship.' Lychorida had so often recounted to Marina the story of her hapless birth that these things seemed ever present to her imagination. But here Leonine interrupted her with desiring her to say her prayers. 'What mean you?' said Marina, who began to fear, she knew not why. 'If you require a little space for prayer, I grant it,' said Leonine; 'but be not tedious, the gods are quick of ear, and I am sworn to do my work in haste.' 'Will you kill me?' said Marina: 'alas! why?' 'To satisfy my lady,' replied Leonine. 'Why would she have me killed?' said Marina: 'now, as I can remember, I never hurt her in all my life. I never spake bad word, nor did any ill turn to any living creature. Believe me now, I never killed a mouse, nor hurt a fly. I trod upon a worm once against my will, but I wept for it. How have I offended?'

The murderer replied: 'My commission is not to reason on the deed, but to do it.' And he was just going to kill her, when certain pirates happened to land at that very moment, who seeing Marina, bore her off as a prize to their ship.

The pirate who had made Marina his prize carried her to Mitylene, and sold her for a slave, where, though in that humble condition, Marina soon became known throughout the whole city of Mitylene for her beauty and her virtues; and the person to whom she was sold became rich by the money she earned for him. She taught music, dancing, and fine needleworks, and the money she got by her scholars she gave to her master and mistress; and the fame of her learning and her great industry came to the knowledge of Lysimachus, a young nobleman who was governor of Mitylene, and Lysimachus went himself to the house where Marina dwelt, to see this paragon of excellence, whom all the city praised so highly. Her conversation delighted Lysimachus beyond measure, for though he had heard much of this admired maiden, he did not expect to find her so sensible a lady, so virtuous, and so good, as he perceived Marina to be; and he left her, saying, he hoped she would persevere in her industrious and virtuous course, and that if ever she heard from him again it should be for her good. Lysimachus thought Marina such a miracle for sense, fine breeding, and excellent qualities, as well as for beauty and all outward graces, that he wished to marry her, and notwithstanding her humble situation, he hoped to find that her birth was noble; but ever when they asked her parentage she would sit still and weep.

Meantime, at Tarsus, Leonine, fearing the anger of Dionysia, told her he had killed Marina; and that wicked woman gave out that she was dead, and made a pretended funeral for her, and erected a stately monument; and shortly after Pericles, accompanied by his royal minister Helicanus, made a voyage from Tyre to Tarsus, on purpose to see his daughter, intending to take her home with him: and he never having beheld her since he left her an infant in the care of Cleon and his wife, how did this good prince rejoice at the thought of seeing this dear child of his buried queen! but when they told him Marina was dead, and showed the monument they had erected for her, great was the misery this most wretched father endured, and not being able to bear the sight of that country where his last hope and only memory of his dear Thaisa was entombed, he took ship, and hastily departed from Tarsus. From the day he entered the ship a dull and heavy melancholy seized him. He never spoke, and seemed totally insensible to everything around him.

Sailing from Tarsus to Tyre, the ship in its course passed by Mitylene, where Marina dwelt; the governor of which place, Lysimachus, observing this royal vessel from the shore, and desirous of knowing who was on board, went in a barge to the side of the ship, to satisfy his curiosity. Helicanus received him very courteously and told him that the ship came from Tyre, and that they were conducting thither Pericles, their prince; 'A man, sir,' said Helicanus, 'who has not spoken to any one these three months, nor taken any sustenance, but just to prolong his grief; it would be tedious to repeat the whole ground of his distemper, but the main springs from the loss of a beloved daughter and a wife.' Lysimachus begged to see this afflicted prince, and when he beheld Pericles, he saw he had been once a goodly person, and he said to him: 'Sir king, all hail, the gods preserve you, hail, royal sir!' But in vain Lysimachus spoke to him; Pericles made no answer, nor did he appear to perceive any stranger approached. And then Lysimachus bethought him of the peerless maid Marina, that haply with her sweet tongue she might win some answer from the silent prince: and with the consent of Helicanus he sent for Marina, and when she entered the ship in

which her own father sat motionless with grief, they
welcomed her on board as if they had known she was
their princess; and they cried: 'She is a gallant lady.'
Lysimachus was well pleased to hear their commenda-
tions, and he said: 'She is such a one, that were I well
assured she came of noble birth, I would wish no better
choice, and think me rarely blessed in a wife.' And
then he addressed her in courtly terms, as if the lowly-
seeming maid had been the high-born lady he wished
to find her, calling her *Fair and beautiful Marina*, telling
her a great prince on board that ship had fallen into a
sad and mournful silence; and, as if Marina had the power
of conferring health and felicity, he begged she would
undertake to cure the royal stranger of his melancholy.
'Sir,' said Marina, 'I will use my utmost skill in his
recovery, provided none but I and my maid be suffered
to come near him.'

She, who at Mitylene had so carefully concealed her
birth, ashamed to tell that one of royal ancestry was now
a slave, first began to speak to Pericles of the wayward
changes in her own fate, telling him from what a high
estate herself had fallen. As if she had known it was
her royal father she stood before, all the words she spoke
were of her own sorrows; but her reason for so doing
was, that she knew nothing more wins the attention of
the unfortunate than the recital of some sad calamity to
match their own. The sound of her sweet voice aroused
the drooping prince; he lifted up his eyes, which had
been so long fixed and motionless; and Marina, who was
the perfect image of her mother, presented to his amazed
sight the features of his dead queen. The long-silent
prince was once more heard to speak. 'My dearest wife,'
said the awakened Pericles, 'was like this maid, and such
a one might my daughter have been. My queen's square
brows, her stature to an inch, as wand-like straight, as
silver-voiced, her eyes as jewel-like. Where do you
live, young maid? Report your parentage. I think

you said you had been tossed from wrong to injury and that you thought your griefs would equal mine, if both were opened.' 'Some such thing I said,' replied Marina, 'and said no more than what my thoughts did warrant me as likely.' 'Tell me your story,' answered Pericles; 'if I find you have known the thousandth part of my endurance, you have borne your sorrows like a man, and I have suffered like a girl; yet you do look like Patience gazing on kings' graves, and smiling extremity out of act. How lost you your name, my most kind virgin? Recount your story I beseech you. Come, sit by me.' How was Pericles surprised when she said her name was *Marina*, for he knew it was no usual name, but had been invented by himself for his own child to signify *seaborn*: 'O, I am mocked,' said he, 'and you are sent hither by some incensed god to make the world laugh at me.' 'Patience, good sir,' said Marina, 'or I must cease here.' 'Nay,' said Pericles, 'I will be patient; you little know how you do startle me, to call yourself Marina.' 'The name,' she replied, 'was given me by one that had some power, my father, and a king.' 'How, a king's daughter!' said Pericles, 'and called Marina! But are you flesh and blood? Are you no fairy? Speak on; where were you born? and wherefore called Marina?' She replied: 'I was called Marina, because I was born at sea. My mother was the daughter of a king; she died the minute I was born, as my good nurse Lychorida has often told me weeping. The king, my father, left me at Tarsus, till the cruel wife of Cleon sought to murder me. A crew of pirates came and rescued me, and brought me here to Mitylene. But, good sir, why do you weep? It may be, you think me an impostor. But, indeed, sir, I am the daughter to king Pericles, if good king Pericles be living.' Then Pericles, terrified as he seemed at his own sudden joy, and doubtful if this could be real, loudly called for his attendants, who rejoiced at the sound of their beloved king's voice; and

he said to Helicanus: 'O Helicanus, strike me, give me
a gash, put me to present pain, lest this great sea of joys
rushing upon me, overbear the shores of my mortality.
O, come hither, thou that wast born at sea, buried at
Tarsus, and found at sea again. O Helicanus, down on
your knees, thank the holy gods! This is Marina. Now
blessings on thee, my child! Give me fresh garments,
mine own Helicanus! She is not dead at Tarsus as she
should have been by the savage Dionysia. She shall
tell you all, when you shall kneel to her and call her
your very princess. Who is this?' (observing Lysimachus for the first time). 'Sir,' said Helicanus, 'it is
the governor of Mitylene, who, hearing of your melancholy, came to see you.' 'I embrace you, sir,' said
Pericles. 'Give me my robes! I am wild with beholding——O heaven bless my girl! But hark, what
music is that?'—for now, either sent by some kind god,
or by his own delighted fancy deceived, he seemed to
hear soft music. 'My lord, I hear none,' replied Helicanus. 'None?' said Pericles; 'why it is the music of
the spheres.' As there was no music to be heard, Lysimachus concluded that the sudden joy had unsettled
the prince's understanding; and he said: 'It is not good
to cross him: let him have his way': and then they told
him they heard the music; and he now complaining of
a drowsy slumber coming over him, Lysimachus persuaded him to rest on a couch, and placing a pillow under
his head, he, quite overpowered with excess of joy,
sank into a sound sleep, and Marina watched in silence
by the couch of her sleeping parent.

While he slept, Pericles dreamed a dream which made
him resolve to go to Ephesus. His dream was, that
Diana, the goddess of the Ephesians, appeared to him,
and commanded him to go to her temple at Ephesus, and
there before her altar to declare the story of his life
and misfortunes; and by her silver bow she swore, that
if he performed her injunction, he should meet with

some rare felicity. When he awoke, being miraculously refreshed, he told his dream, and that his resolution was to obey the bidding of the goddess.

Then Lysimachus invited Pericles to come on shore, and refresh himself with such entertainment as he should find at Mitylene, which courteous offer Pericles accepting, agreed to tarry with him for the space of a day or two. During which time we may well suppose what feastings, what rejoicings, what costly shows and entertainments the governor made in Mitylene, to greet the royal father of his dear Marina, whom in her obscure fortunes he had so respected. Nor did Pericles frown upon Lysimachus's suit, when he understood how he had honoured his child in the days of her low estate, and that Marina showed herself not averse to his proposals; only he made it a condition, before he gave his consent, that they should visit with him the shrine of the Ephesian Diana: to whose temple they shortly after all three undertook a voyage; and, the goddess herself filling their sails with prosperous winds, after a few weeks they arrived in safety at Ephesus.

There was standing near the altar of the goddess, when Pericles with his train entered the temple, the good Cerimon (now grown very aged) who had restored Thaisa, the wife of Pericles, to life; and Thaisa, now a priestess of the temple, was standing before the altar; and though the many years he had passed in sorrow for her loss had much altered Pericles, Thaisa thought she knew her husband's features, and when he approached the altar and began to speak, she remembered his voice, and listened to his words with wonder and a joyful amazement. And these were the words that Pericles spoke before the altar: 'Hail, Diana! to perform thy just commands, I here confess myself the prince of Tyre, who, frighted from my country, at Pentapolis wedded the fair Thaisa: she died at sea in childbed, but brought forth a maid-child called Marina. She at

Tarsus was nursed with Dionysia, who at fourteen years thought to kill her, but her better stars brought her to Mitylene, by whose shores as I sailed, her good fortunes brought this maid on board, where by her most clear remembrance she made herself known to be my daughter.'

Thaisa, unable to bear the transports which his words had raised in her, cried out: 'You are, you are, O royal Pericles'——and fainted. 'What means this woman?' said Pericles: 'she dies! gentlemen, help.' 'Sir,' said Cerimon, 'if you have told Diana's altar true, this is your wife.' 'Reverend gentleman, no,' said Pericles: I threw her overboard with these very arms.' Cerimon then recounted how, early one tempestuous morning, this lady was thrown upon the Ephesian shore; how, opening the coffin, he found therein rich jewels, and a paper; how, happily, he recovered her, and placed her here in Diana's temple. And now, Thaisa being restored from her swoon said: 'O my lord, are you not Pericles? Like him you speak, like him you are. Did you not name a tempest, a birth, and death?' He astonished said: 'The voice of dead Thaisa!' 'That Thaisa am I,' she replied, 'supposed dead and drowned.' 'O true Diana!' exclaimed Pericles, in a passion of devout astonishment. 'And now,' said Thaisa, 'I know you better. Such a ring as I see on your finger did the king my father give you, when we with tears parted from him at Pentapolis.' 'Enough, you gods!' cried Pericles, 'your present kindness makes my past miseries sport. O come, Thaisa, be buried a second time within these arms.'

And Marina said: 'My heart leaps to be gone into my mother's bosom.' Then did Pericles show his daughter to her mother, saying: 'Look who kneels here, flesh of thy flesh, thy burthen at sea, and called Marina, because she was yielded there.' 'Blessed and my own!' said Thaisa: and while she hung in rapturous joy over her child, Pericles knelt before the altar, saying: 'Pure

Diana, bless thee for thy vision. For this, I will offer oblations nightly to thee.' And then and there did Pericles, with the consent of Thaisa, solemnly affiance their daughter, the virtuous Marina, to the well-deserving Lysimachus in marriage.

Thus have we seen in Pericles, his queen, and daughter, a famous example of virtue assailed by calamity (through the sufferance of Heaven, to teach patience and constancy to men), under the same guidance becoming finally successful, and triumphing over chance and change. In Helicanus we have beheld a notable pattern of truth, of faith, and loyalty, who, when he might have succeeded to a thone, chose rather to recall the rightful owner to his possession, than to become great by another's wrong. In the worthy Cerimon, who restored Thaisa to life, we are instructed how goodness directed by knowledge, in bestowing benefits upon mankind, approaches to the nature of the gods. It only remains to be told, that Dionysia, the wicked wife of Cleon, met with an end proportionable to her deserts; the inhabitants of Tarsus, when her cruel attempt upon Marina was known, rising in a body to revenge the daughter of their benefactor, and setting fire to the palace of Cleon, burnt both him and her, and their whole household: the gods seeming well pleased, that so foul a murder, though but intentional, and never carried into act, should be punished in a way befitting its enormity.